J.A. JANCE

"Jance knows how to grab our attention."
Washington Post

"Often, series writers' books seem to fade as the books pile up on the shelves. . . . Not so with Jance. Her books keep on sizzling, keep on fascinating, keep on getting better."
Asbury Park Press (NJ)

"She can move from an exciting, dangerous scene on one page to a sensitive, personal, touching moment on the next."

Chicago Tribune

"J.A. Jance is among the best—if not the best."
Chattanooga Times

"In the elite company of Sue Grafton and Patricia Cornwell."

Flint Journal

"Jance is one of those authors who makes readers feel as if they had lived all their lives in the setting of which she writes. . . . Joanna Brady is a real person."

Cleveland Plain Dealer

"Brady is a multidimensional character dealing with harsh reality in a harsh, if dramatically beautiful landscape. . . . Jance creates such a strong sense of place, you can feel the desert heat."

Colorado Springs Gazette

Books by J. A. Jance

SKELETON CANYON

J.A. JANCE

HARPER

An Imprint of HarperCollins*Publishers*

This is a work of fiction. Names, characters, places, and incidents are products of the author's imagination or are used fictitiously and are not to be construed as real. Any resemblance to actual events, locales, organizations, or persons, living or dead, is entirely coincidental.

HARPER

An Imprint of HarperCollins*Publishers*
195 Broadway
New York, NY 10007

Copyright © 1997 by J.A. Jance
Excerpt from *Betrayal of Trust* copyright © 2011 by J.A. Jance
ISBN 978-0-06-199895-9

First Harper premium printing: January 2011
First Avon Books paperback printing: August 1998
First Avon Books hardcover printing: August 1997

HarperCollins® and Harper® are registered trademarks of Harper-Collins Publishers.

Printed in the United States of America

Visit Harper paperbacks on the World Wide Web at
www.harpercollins.com

10 9 8 7 6

For Jim Hobbs,
the real mechanical wizard of Queen Anne Hill,
a friend from the bad old days
and from the new good days as well.

SKELETON CANYON

🌵 PROLOGUE

HANDS ON her hips, youthful breasts outthrust beneath the bulk of her red-and-gray sweater, seventeen-year-old Roxanne Brianna O'Brien, captain of the Bisbee High School pep squad, tossed her long blond hair and led her six-member team in a strutting parade around the end of the football field.

On a clear crisp late-November night, this was the end of halftime festivities and the beginning of the third quarter in a hard-fought football game between two teams whose long-term rivalry stretched all the way back to 1906. A ragtag marching band—comprised of mismatched players from both the Bisbee and Douglas music programs—had just delivered a faltering, musically challenged performance. Now it was time for the uniformed yell squads of both schools to travel to opposite sides of the field. There each would give an obligatory and good-sportsmanlike cheer in front of the opposing team's fans.

The Bisbee Pumas might have been two touchdowns behind at the half, but there was no sign of that in the proud carriage of their cheerleaders as they marched down the sidelines toward the part of the bleachers reserved for visiting Douglas supporters.

At the fifty-yard line, Brianna, who much preferred her middle name to the old-fashioned Roxanne, glanced toward the reserved-seat section where her parents usually sat. David O'Brien's wheelchair was parked in the bottom aisle. As the cheerleaders paraded past out on the field, Bree noticed that her father's silvery-maned head was inclined toward his program, studying it with frowning concentration. Brianna hoped he'd raise his eyes and at least glance in her direction. She longed for some acknowledgment from her father, for some sign of parental pride or approval. As usual, David was too preoccupied with something else to bother noticing her.

The same did not hold true for Bree's mother, Katherine. She smiled and nodded encouragement as her daughter went by. Katherine's beaming pride and unfailing enthusiasm were almost as hard for Bree to handle as her father's studied indifference. Under the harsh glare of the ballpark's newly installed field lights, Bree was careful not to let the hurt show through. After all, to those around her—fellow students who had elected her head cheerleader, homecoming queen, and the girl most likely to succeed—Brianna

O'Brien had it all—money, looks, and brains. Brianna alone knew the hurt and disappointment that lurked behind those outward trappings of youthful success.

Leading the girls down the field, Bree kept her smiling mask carefully in place. Once at the far end of the visitor section of the stands, she stopped and waited for the other girls to find their proper places. When the line was perfectly straight, she raised her arm like a conductor raising his baton to signal the beginning of a concert.

"Ready, girls?" Bree had to shout to be heard over the rising hubbub in the stands as the teams on the field began to form up in anticipation of the second-half kickoff. "Two bits, four bits, six bits, a peso. All for Douglas stand up and say so."

As the applauding Douglas fans surged to their feet, the Bisbee girls turned a series of handsprings up and down the sidelines. Then they resumed a parade stance and headed back toward their own side of the field via the end zone holding what were now Bisbee's goalposts. The cheerleaders' backs were turned to the players on the field when a referee blew his whistle, announcing the resumption of play.

The second-half kickoff flew high in the air, sending the ball tumbling toward the Bulldog offensive unit, stationed at the far end of the field. Fifteen yards from the goal line, the ball plummeted into the waiting hands of Douglas quarterback and team captain Ignacio Salazar Ybarra. He paused for a moment, searching the field for any sign of weakness among the Bisbee defenders. Seeing a hole, he clasped the ball firmly to his chest and started down the field, deftly dodging between other players—friend and foe alike—with all the grace and agility of a fleeing white-tailed deer.

As both teams rumbled down the field toward the marching cheerleaders, there was no hint on Roxanne Brianna O'Brien's shadowless face that in the next thirty seconds her young life would be inalterably changed.

Afterward, newspaper accounts of the game reported that throughout the first half of the game on that crisp fall evening, Bulldog Iggy Ybarra had played nothing short of inspired football with a confidence that came from knowing every yard gained carried him that much closer to winning a coveted football scholarship, one that would pay his way to college.

Pounding toward the goal line, Iggy angled across the field and then stayed just inside the sideline markers. He had outdistanced most of the Puma defenders and thought he was almost home free when, five yards short of the goal line, he heard someone gaining on him from behind. Dodging out of the way, he went one step farther than he meant to, crossing over the sideline marker in the process. He had just stepped out of bounds when someone smashed into him from behind. The two players crashed to the ground only a yard or so from the cheerleaders.

Bree was close enough to the action that, even over the raucous roar of enthusiastic fans, she heard the bone snap. Turning her head in horror, she saw a Douglas player crumple to the ground with Bisbee defender Frankie Lefthault on top of him. The awful groan that came as the Douglas boy fell seemed to have been wrenched from his very soul. Bree saw him lying there, writhing and helpless, moaning in agony while penalty flags blossomed and referee whistles sounded all over the field.

Long before anyone else reached the injured player, long before Frankie himself scrambled to his feet, Bree O'Brien was kneeling at the fallen boy's side, holding his hand. She responded out of instinct, out of an inborn compulsion to go to the aid of anything or anyone in need. It was only as she knelt there that she realized player number eleven on the Douglas Bulldog team was someone she actually knew.

The previous summer, Brianna had attended a two-week fine arts session at the University of Arizona in Tucson. There, she had met Nacio Ybarra, as he called himself. The two of them had wound up in the same drama workshop. In an honor bestowed by their peers, they had been paired to play the *Romeo and Juliet* balcony scene for the end-of-session grand finale.

In the process of working together, they had established an easy friendship. That last night, after the performance, they had taken a long walk, ending up at the fountain by Old Main. There they had exchanged several long unstaged kisses. The next morning, before going their separate ways, they had promised to keep in touch, but they had not done so. The hubbub of respective senior year activities and the twenty-three miles between them had proven insurmountable.

"Nacio," she whispered. "It's me, Bree. Hang on. Help is coming."

He looked up at her, but there was no sign of recognition in his pain-filled eyes. "Oh, God," he sobbed. "My leg. It's broken. I know it's broken."

"It's not my fault," Frankie wailed behind them. "I didn't do it on purpose. I didn't mean to hurt him."

By then coaches, trainers, managers, and referees were all converging on the scene. One of them brusquely thrust Bree out of the way. She retreated to a spot behind the goal line where, for the next few minutes, she and the other cheerleaders stood rooted to the ground. Around them, the entire ballpark went deathly still. The only sounds to be heard were the heart-wrenching, involuntary moans that periodically escaped Ignacio Ybarra's tightly clenched teeth.

One of the Douglas coaches popped out of the group huddled around Ignacio and gestured frantically toward a waiting ambulance that spent each home game parked just inside the ballpark gates at the far end of the field. Accompanied by the low growl of a siren, the ambulance picked its way down the visiting team's sidelines through clumps of stunned players from both teams. Two uniformed EMTs leaped from the ambulance. One brought out a stretcher while the other cut through the cluster of anxious onlookers.

All the while, that almost breathless silence

lingered over the stricken crowd. Except for mindlessly shifting out of the way to let the ambulance or stretcher pass, no one moved or spoke. Working quickly but expertly, the medics covered Ignacio Ybarra with blankets and then eased him onto the stretcher. They were trying to be gentle. They *were* being gentle. Even so, that little movement elicited another gasp of pain that was more shriek than groan. The desperate sound caused Brianna O'Brien's own knees to nearly buckle.

As the stretcher started toward the ambulance, the Douglas cheerleaders, still at the far end of the field, began leading a cheer to honor the injured player. Belatedly, the Bisbee squad joined in as fans from both towns stayed on their feet, offering encouragement.

"Well," Cynthia Jean Howell whispered in Bree's ear when the cheering ended, "with that damned quarterback out of the way, maybe we can finally do something about winning this game."

Stunned, Bree wheeled around to face her. When it came time to elect the captain of the cheerleading squad, C.J. Howell had come in second. Not on the best of terms before that, Bree and C.J. were even less friendly now.

"Shut up, C.J.!" Bree whispered back. "He might hear you."

C.J. shrugged. "So what?" she hissed. "Who cares if he does? Do you want to win this game or not?"

What happened next was strictly reflex. Bree's

right hand flashed out and connected with the other girl's cheek. The resulting slap knocked C.J.'s head sideways and left the plain imprint of an outspread palm on the carefully made-up contours of her narrow jaw.

As quickly as it happened, the other girls swooped in to separate them. "What's the matter with you?" C.J. sputtered. "Are you crazy or what?"

"Didn't you hear what happened?" Bree raged at the other girl. "That bone in his leg is shattered. What if he never walks again?"

"So?" C.J. returned, massaging the bright red skin of her cheek. "What business is it of yours? Besides, he's from Douglas, isn't he?"

"He may be from Douglas, but Ignacio Ybarra is a friend of mine. Don't you forget it!"

"That's your problem," C.J. returned.

At that point Bree might have gone after C.J. again had not one of the other girls restrained her. "Come on, Bree. Leave her alone."

In response, Roxanne Brianna O'Brien simply turned her back and walked, striding purposefully away from her own bleachers and back toward the Bulldog side of the field. Bree's best friend on the squad, sixteen-year-old Kim Young, hurried after her.

"Wait up, Bree. What are you doing?"

"I'm leaving."

"You can't just walk out like this. It's the middle of the game."

"I don't care."

"Ms. Barker will have a fit. She may even throw you off the squad."

"I don't care if she does," Bree replied grimly.

Kim stopped in her tracks and wavered back and forth as if undecided about whether she should follow Bree or go back to where the others stood waiting. Being elected cheerleader at the beginning of her junior year was Kimberly Young's sole claim to fame. She didn't want to do anything to jeopardize her shaky standing as one of the movers and shakers in the B.H.S. student body, not only for this year but for her senior year as well.

Forced to choose, Kim reluctantly opted for ambition and social standing over friendship. Shaking her head, she turned her back on Bree and raced across the field to catch up with the other cheerleaders while a resolute Bree watched her briefly and then continued her own solitary walk down the sidelines.

Barbara Barker, the cheerleading sponsor, headed Bree off before she made it as far as the fifty-yard line. "Where are you going, Bree?"

"The hospital," Bree answered.

"The hospital," Ms. Barker echoed. "What's the matter? Are you hurt?"

"I'm fine," Bree said. "A friend of mine's been hurt, and I'm going to check on him."

As the loaded ambulance made its way down the field, and while the referees pondered what to do about the unnecessary roughness penalty they had called against Frankie Lefthault, the cheerleading sponsor reached out as if to stop Brianna's headlong rush along the sidelines.

"Wait a minute, Bree. You know the rules. My

girls aren't allowed to walk off the field without permission in the middle of a game. If you go, I'll have to kick you off the squad."

"You can't kick me off," Brianna replied. "I already quit."

From her seat on the fifty-yard line, Katherine O'Brien had observed the unfolding drama both on the field and off it. At football games, regardless of what was happening to the team, Katherine's eyes seldom left her daughter. Watching the action through the fine pall of dust raised by hundreds of shuffling feet, Katherine hadn't heard a word of the heated exchange between Bree and C.J. Howell, but she had witnessed the assault. With a gasp of surprise, she had seen Bree's hand flash out and slap the other girl's cheek. As Bree stalked down the aisle, Katherine O'Brien, like Barbara Barker, rose to intercept her.

"Where are you going?" David demanded, reaching out to stop his wife.

"There's something the matter with Bree," Katherine said. "She needs me."

"Leave her be," David O'Brien admonished, taking Katherine by the hand. "She has to learn to sort these things out herself. You can't always go flying to her rescue, you know."

Fifty years of continuous self-effacement made it difficult for Katherine O'Brien to tolerate making a scene in public. In this case, however, the unmasked rage she had seen on her daughter's face somehow stiffened her spine.

"I've got to go to her," Katherine insisted, pulling her wrist free of her husband's grasp. "I'll be right back."

She reached Bree's side just in time to see her daughter pull away from Barbara Barker in much the same way Katherine herself had just broken free of David's restraining hand. "Bree," Katherine demanded, "what's going on?"

"A friend of mine is hurt," Bree replied. "As soon as I get out of this uniform, I'm going to the hospital to see if he's all right."

"You don't want to do that," Katherine said. "If you leave in the middle of the game, Ms. Barker may throw you off the squad."

"Don't worry about that," Bree returned. "She already has."

daughter pull away from Barbara Barkett in much
the same way Katherine herself had done. Looking

IT WAS five o'clock on a Friday afternoon in June
when Bree came into the kitchen. Even with the
air-conditioning going full blast, the kitchen was
hot compared to the rest of the house. Sweat rolled
down Mrs. Vorevkin's jowly cheeks as she stood
bent over the kitchen sink, cleaning and chop-
ping vegetables for the salad.

"I'm ready to go."

Olga turned and smiled at the young woman
whose tan, lithe, and cheerful presence never
failed to brighten any room she entered. "The
cool chest is in the pantry," Olga told her. "It's all
packed." She put down her knife and dried both
hands on her apron. "The soup is ready," she added.
"You should have some before you leave. Hot soup
on a hot day will cool you off. Besides, it's such a
long drive. You should eat something besides
sandwiches."

Bree sniffed the air. Over the years, the O'Briens

had gone through any number of cooks. Most of them hadn't lasted because they couldn't stand up to David O'Brien's stringent demands for quality and impeccable service. Olga, however, had been with the O'Briens a little over three years. She was an excellent cook who had come to them, by some circuitous path, from a job with the U.S. embassy in Moscow with an unexplained stop-off in New Orleans along the way. During her three years' tenure, she had developed a very loving friendship with this bright, golden-haired young woman who stood in her kitchen, waffling with indecision.

Bree glanced at her watch. Nacio, as she usually called him, would be off work in another hour. She wanted to be there in time to meet him when his shift ended, but there was just time for some of Mrs. V.'s delicious soup and a thick slab of the crusty white bread she made on a daily basis, summer and winter.

"All right," Bree agreed at last, slipping into her favorite place at the kitchen table. "But I'll have to hurry."

The soup was a clear broth with a few green slivers of scallion floating on the top. Five or six tiny homemade meat-filled dumplings sat on the bottom of the bowl. It was wonderful.

"What time will Mom and Dad be home?" Bree asked, glancing casually at her watch. She wanted to be through the security gates, off Purdy Lane, and on the highway headed for Douglas long before her parents returned. Not that it mattered that much whether or not they were home when

Bree left. She was going regardless. It was just always easier for her to leave without having to face them, without having to lie to them directly. Although, with practice, even that was easier now. Brianna was getting used to it.

Finishing the soup, Bree pushed her chair from the table, carried her dishes to the counter, and plucked a plump radish from the pile of clean ones Mrs. V. had stacked next to the sink. "Take two," Olga said with a smile. "They're not very filling."

Tossing her ponytail, Bree took a second radish and then hurried to the pantry. The cooler was right there, just as she had known it would be, packed with sandwiches, sodas, fruit, and, most likely, some little dessert surprise as well. Mrs. V. was a great believer in the Cajun tradition of *lagniappe*—something extra.

Bree lugged the cooler as far as the front door. As soon as she opened it, she almost choked on the raw stench of cigar smoke that lingered in a hazy cloud just outside. Alf Hastings, her father's director of operations, was sitting in the shade of the verandah next to the fountain. He hurried to his feet as Bree came through the door. "Let me help you with that," he offered.

Alf hadn't been on Green Brush Ranch long. Bree didn't know much about him other than he was one of those middle-aged men who gave her the creeps. She suspected there were times he made unnecessary security sweeps through the yard outside her bedroom window on the off chance he might catch her in the act of undressing.

"No, thanks," she said. "I can manage on my own."

Not one to take no for an answer, Hastings leered at her. "Looks pretty heavy to me," he said. "At least let me open the gate to the camper."

That was the last thing Brianna O'Brien wanted. If he opened the camper shell on the pickup, he was bound to see all the camping equipment she had smuggled out of the garage and stowed there without anyone—her parents especially—being the wiser.

"It goes in front," she told him, quickly putting the cooler down on the ground. "I'll have to go back inside to get the key."

He was still standing there puffing on what was left of his cigar when she came back out of the house with the key in hand.

"Off to Playas again?" he asked.

Bree gave him a sidelong look. Was he testing her? Had he seen her loading the stuff into the truck and figured out what was really going on? Or was he just making conversation?

"That's right," she said.

This time Alf made no offer to help, but she noticed that he had moved off to one side, no doubt hoping to look down her tank top when she bent down to pick up the cooler. *Give the dirty old man a thrill. If he's looking at my boobs, that means he probably isn't looking inside the camper.* Once the cooler was properly situated on the rider's side of the seat, she slammed the door shut.

"Hope you keep the doors locked when you

head off on your own like this," Alf said. "A young girl like you can't ever be too careful."

"I'm careful," she assured him, walking around to the driver's side and letting herself in. "Very careful."

As she turned the key in the ignition, she wondered if Alf would climb into the ATV parked under the portico, one of several used for routine security patrols around the ranch, and then follow her as far as the security gates. When she pulled out onto the road that led away from the house, he was still standing there, looking after her through a pall of cigar smoke.

"Asshole," Bree hissed between clenched teeth as she watched his reflection grow smaller in her rearview mirror.

AS THE sun went down in the west, Nacio Ybarra stood in the shade of the gas station's canopy and checked his watch. Bree should have been there by now. He was looking forward to seeing her, but he was dreading it, too. For a week now, Nacio's Aunt Yolanda had been doubled over with excruciating stomach cramps. Late that afternoon, her local doctor, unable to make a solid diagnosis, had finally managed to secure an appointment with a specialist in Tucson for the following morning. The problem was, the appointment and accompanying tests required an overnight stay in the hospital. Naturally, Nacio's

Uncle Frank, the owner of Frank's Union 76, was going to drive her there.

"I know you were planning on going camping with your friends," Uncle Frank had said apologetically. He had come into the bay where Nacio was fixing a flat to tell him about it. "But I need you to stay. Ronnie's way too new to be left to close up by himself. God knows what would happen if I did that. He can't even change a tire by himself. And as for Hector . . ." Frank rolled his eyes.

Ever since he was thirteen, Nacio Ybarra had worked as a gas jockey and mechanic at his Uncle Frank's Union 76, next door to the once-booming Kmart store on the outskirts of Douglas. There was no question about Frank's assessment of his other two employees. Ronnie Torres was an eager beaver, but he was only sixteen and had worked at the station for less than two weeks. Frank had hired Ron in hopes of grooming the younger boy to take his nephew's place when Nacio left for college in the fall.

As for Hector . . . Yolanda's younger brother was no doubt a skilled mechanic, but his penchant for Jose Cuervo made him a bad bet to be trusted with the day's receipts or to show up on a Saturday morning with the cash register change bag intact.

"Don't worry about it," Nacio said. "I'll stay long enough to close. What about opening in the morning?"

Frank nodded. "That too," he said. "I'll be here

by early afternoon, so once Hector gets workwise, you could probably take off later in the morning."

Frank Ybarra was the only father Ignacio Ybarra had ever known. Ignacio had never met his real one, whom he thought of only as a sperm donor. Nacio's mother, sixteen years old and eight and a half months pregnant at the time, had crossed the border west of Douglas and walked as far as the emergency entrance to the Cochise County Hospital. Her water had broken along the way. She had arrived in the hospital lobby with just time enough to be put on a gurney and wheeled into an emergency room before her son catapulted into the world. For years, Uncle Frank had teased his nephew that there was more than one way to be a wetback.

Having assured her son's U.S. citizenship, Imelda Ybarra had left him in the care of her older brother, Frank, and promptly returned to Mexico, resuming her designated role in a thriving business in Agua Prieta's red-light district. She had died a few years later of what her son now suspected was probably an early case of heterosexually transmitted AIDS. Frank and Yolanda had raised the boy as one of their own, watching in wonder and with no small pride as this towering foster son of theirs totally eclipsed the physical, academic, and athletic accomplishments of their four natural children.

For almost five years, Nacio had worked in Frank's gas station after school, on weekends, and during the summers. He was dependable and personable. The customers loved him, and most were aware that he was saving every penny toward college. Frank had always figured there would be plenty of scholarship help available to put someone as bright and talented as Nacio through school. That had seemed especially true when, at the beginning of his senior year in high school, he was as good as promised a full-ride football scholarship to Arizona State University in Tempe. Unfortunately, the football scholarship had disappeared the moment Nacio's leg had been broken during the Bisbee-Douglas game the previous fall. Doctors had managed to save the leg and pin it back together, but Ignacio Ybarra's football-playing days were gone forever.

The two academic scholarships Nacio had been granted instead of the athletic one were both to the University of Arizona in Tucson. Taken together, they didn't add up to nearly the same amount as the single sports scholarship would have been, and only one of them was renewable. That made Ignacio's job at Frank's Union 76 all the more important.

"Don't worry, Uncle Frank," Nacio had said. "You take care of Aunt Yoli. I'll handle the station."

A Tioga motor home with Kansas plates pulled in and swallowed up a huge tankful of fuel while Nacio washed the windshield and checked the oil. He was just finishing checking the air pressure in the last tire when Bree pulled up behind him. Naturally, Ronnie hurried out to wait on her before Nacio had a chance.

After running the motor home driver's credit

card through the machine, Nacio went over to the red Toyota Tacoma. "Hey, Ronnie," he called, without looking in Bree's direction but making sure his voice carried through her open window, "I'm going to grab a soda."

With that, Nacio limped off across the parking lot. The doctors kept telling him that eventually the leg would get better, but he doubted it. He went inside, bought himself a soda, and then came outside to sit on the picnic bench left behind by a short-lived and now departed latté stand. There he waited for Bree to join him.

Nacio hated having to meet her this way, having to sit stiffly on the bench as though they were nothing more than a pair of strangers passing the time of day. It was only when they were alone that they could be themselves—free to be young and in love.

He was struck by the irony of their living a real-life version of the Romeo and Juliet roles they had played all those months earlier. According to Bree, her father hated Mexicans, and Ignacio's Aunt Yolanda was forever pointing out the folly of mixed dating, which inevitably led to the far worse folly and inevitable heartbreak of mixed marriages. Such warnings had fallen on two sets of determinedly deaf ears.

Brianna O'Brien had returned to Nacio Ybarra's hazy line of vision while he was still so groggy from the anesthetic and painkillers that at first he had imagined her to be some kind of ethereal being—an angel perhaps—rather than the same flesh-and-blood, blond-haired beauty whose lips had breathed fire into his one hot June night in Tucson several months earlier. Even after the drugs wore off, he still expected she would simply disappear. But she didn't. Instead, she visited him every day of the three weeks he was stuck in the Copper Queen Hospital. Each time she came to his room, she brought with her a sense of joy and laughter and the hope that, although his leg was undeniably broken, his life was certainly not over.

Those visits had continued for a while even after Nacio was released from the hospital and allowed to return home to Douglas. They had ceased abruptly once Aunt Yolanda, alerted by a nosy neighbor, came home early one day and figured out that what was going on had slipped well beyond the sphere of ordinary friendship. Since then, the two young people had learned to be discretion itself, but that took work and a whole lot of creativity.

Bree would often come into the station in the late afternoons, pulling up to the full-service pumps about the time Uncle Frank went home for dinner. While Nacio pumped her gas and checked her tires, oil, water, and windshield fluid, while he cleaned all her windows and polished her rearview mirrors, they would hurriedly make arrangements for when and where they would meet again—often at a secluded spot halfway between Bisbee and Douglas on a long-deserted ranch road that ran alongside the railroad line near the Paul Spur Lime Plant.

They both lived for weekends like this one, though, when Bree would tell her parents she was going to New Mexico to visit her friend Crystal Phillips, and Nacio would tell Uncle Frank and Aunt Yolanda he was going camping with some of his friends from school. From Friday night until Sunday afternoon, it would just be the two of them. Usually they would rendezvous at a secret meeting place in the Peloncillo Mountains, east of Douglas, at a wild, deserted place called Hog Canyon. Once they met up, they'd spend the night there, sleeping on an air mattress in the back of Bree's truck. The next day, they'd leave Nacio's old Bronco parked out of sight somewhere in the canyon and head out for parts unknown. They loved wandering around in out-of-the way places in New Mexico, an area where they weren't likely to run into anyone they knew.

Bree always had plenty of money. They went where they wanted with the understanding that by three o'clock Sunday afternoon she would drop him off at his car and they would go their separate ways. That was how this weekend was supposed to work. Now, though, with Nacio unable to get away until sometime Saturday morning, he supposed they would have to scrap the whole thing.

"You look like you just lost your best friend," Bree said, sitting down on the same bench, but not so close that it looked as though they were actually sitting together.

"Aunt Yolanda's still sick. Uncle Frank's taking her up to Tucson to see an internist, and they won't be back until tomorrow afternoon," Nacio told her. "I'll have to close tonight and open tomorrow morning. I'm sorry, Bree. I don't know what to do."

Bree had spent every moment of that week longing for Friday, when the two of them could be together. Still, it never occurred to her to argue with him about it or try to change his mind. Ignacio had told her enough about his background—about how much his aunt and uncle had done for him—that she knew he owed them everything. Whatever they needed him to do, Nacio would do without question or else die in the attempt.

"Do you want to come over to the house?" Nacio asked after a pause. "Uncle Frank's up in Tucson. No one will know."

"Your neighbor will," Bree objected. "If she tells on us again like she did the last time, your aunt will have a fit."

Nacio nodded. "I guess we'll just have to forget it, then," he said reluctantly. "Unless you want to go back home and tell your parents you changed your mind and decided to leave tomorrow morning instead of tonight."

Bree considered. It had been hard enough to convince her parents that she needed to go back to Playas yet again. If she returned home, there was a chance Bree's father would put his foot down and not allow her to leave a second time.

"What if I went on out to the mountains tonight and waited for you to catch up with me tomorrow morning?" Bree asked.

Nacio swung around and stared at her in disbelief. "All by yourself? Wouldn't you be scared?"

Bree shrugged. "Not that scared. I'd be in the

truck. That would be safe enough." She looked at him and smiled. "Besides, if it means getting to see you later instead of not seeing you at all, I'd do it in a heartbeat."

Ignacio felt a sudden warm glow in his chest, a feeling that came over him whenever he realized how much Bree loved him, how much she cared. Aunt Yolanda was always saying that the only reason Anglo girls hung out with Hispanic boys was because they were sluts, not good enough to catch an Anglo boy of their own. Even so, she said, they always acted like they were better than everyone else and treated their Mexican boyfriends like shit. But Bree wasn't like that with Nacio Ybarra. Not at all.

"You shouldn't do that," he told her at once. "It could be dangerous. There are bears out there, to say nothing of mountain lions. . . ."

"Don't worry," Bree returned with a winning and confident smile. "I'll be fine. No mountain lion in its right mind would dare attack me. I'm a Puma, too, remember?"

Nacio was still laughing as Bree stood up and walked away with her hips swaying and her ponytail bouncing playfully back and forth in the warm summer sun.

TWO

JOANNA BRADY stopped at the door of her daughter's room and peered inside. Ten-year-old Jennifer Ann was sitting cross-legged in the midst of what looked like chaos. Frowning in concentration, she was going down a list checking off items as she went. The next day she was due to leave home for a two-week stay at Whispering Pines, a Girl Scout camp located in the Catalina Mountains north of Tucson.

"How's it going?" Joanna asked.

"Okay," Jenny replied. "I think I have everything. All I have to do now is get it into the duffel bag."

"Do you want some help?"

"No, Mom," Jenny replied. "The directions say I'm supposed to pack it myself."

"All right, then," Joanna said. "But don't stay up too late. Tomorrow's a big day."

Feeling slightly useless, Joanna backed away, went to her own room, and got ready for bed. The swamp cooler was running. She usually turned it off overnight, but the last few days had been so miserably hot that tonight she left it on.

"See there?" she said, addressing her husband Andy and counting on the drone of the cooler to cover her voice. After all, Andy had been dead since the previous fall, the victim of a Colombian drug lord's hired assassin, but Joanna Brady still talked to him sometimes, especially at night when she was all alone in what had once been their bedroom. "That's what happens. Kids grow up, and then they don't need their parents anymore. Not even to pack their bags."

She paused, as if to give Andy an opportunity to respond, but of course, being dead, he had nothing to say.

"What I can't figure out," she continued, "is if this is the way things are supposed to be, why do I feel so awful about it?"

Since Andy's death, his daughter, Jennifer, had gone through a dozen different guises and stages—from bossy to totally pliant and passive, from a whining clinging vine to this new stage of haughty independence. Faced with the prospect of Jenny's being gone for two whole weeks, her mother could have handled a bit of clinging right about then.

Closing her eyes, Joanna lay there and waited for sleep to come. *If Andy was still here and we were both handling this together,* she thought, *maybe it wouldn't be so hard.*

🌵 **FOR A** Friday evening it was still surprisingly quiet in the Blue Moon Saloon and Lounge in Old Bisbee's Brewery Gulch. So far this shift, Angie Kellogg, the bartender, had had little to do other than making sure her two regulars—the toothless Archie McBride and hard-of-hearing Willy Haskins—were supplied with beer and an occasional vodka chaser.

The two were both retired underground miners. They loved to regale Angie with tales of Bisbee's glory days, of how things used to be when payday weekends in Brewery Gulch had been nothing but boozing and brawling good times. In nine months of working at the Blue Moon, Angie had come to have a genuine affection for the two old men. Even half drunk, they always treated her with a degree of old-fashioned gentlemanly respect and never failed to apologize when one of them made an inadvertent slip and used what they considered a bad word in front of her. Even when they reached a point where she had to cut them off, they hardly ever gave her a hard time about it. Instead, they'd just get up and leave.

"No problem. We're eighty-sixed, old buddy. Little lady's jus' doin' her job," the more sober of the two would say to the other as they fell off their bar stools and headed for the door. "See you to-morrow."

Angie would nod and wave. "See you," she'd say. And after they left, she would stand there marveling at the fact that she liked them and they liked her. In her previous life as an East L.A. hooker, those kinds of easygoing relationships had never been possible. But here in Bisbee, Arizona, they were. Not only was she friends with those two harmless but kindhearted drunks, Angie also counted among her pals the local sheriff, Joanna Brady, and a Methodist minister by the name of Marianne Maculyea. In fact, on her days off, Angie sometimes baby-sat for Marianne and her husband, Jeff Daniels. She would take charge of their rough-and-tumble daughter Ruth while Jeff and Marianne took Ruth's twin sister, Esther, to one of her all-too-frequent visits to the cardiologist at University Medical Center in Tucson.

There were times on those days while Angie was pushing Ruth's dual but half-empty stroller up and down the sidewalks of Tombstone Canyon that she almost had to pinch herself to believe it was real. Day after day, month after month, she was beginning to learn that the lives most people lived were far different from the abusive one she had left behind three separate times now—first with her father in Michigan, next with her psychotic California pimp, and finally with her sinister and deadly boyfriend Tony Vargas. She had come to Bisbee convinced that the whole world was out to get her.

Joanna Brady and Marianne Maculyea had

been the first people to break through Angie's barriers of distrust. With men it was harder. All her life, Angie's good looks had made her a target for the unwanted attentions of almost every man she met. For years her body had been her only bartering chip. Men had preyed on that and she had hated them for it. Men were always the bad guys in the piece, from Daddy right on down the line.

Living in Bisbee, people like Marianne's husband, Jeff Daniels, and Angie's boss at the Blue Moon, Bobo Jenkins, were gradually causing Angie to wonder if it was time to rethink her position. Maybe all men *weren't* inherently bad. For one thing, neither Jeff nor Bobo had ever made a single pass at Angie, welcome or otherwise. Nor had there been any off-color remarks. Angie herself had told Bobo about her past, and she was sure Jeff knew about it as well. Nevertheless, both men treated her with a kind of brotherly respect that somehow made her feel both protected and appreciated. Still, being around them—especially alone—made her nervous. She couldn't shake her very real apprehension that at any moment one of them might turn on her and demand something she wasn't prepared to give.

The outside door swung open, and a tall, gangly man walked partway into the bar. He was still holding the door open and peering around uncertainly when a gust of dry wind blew in behind him. His straight, straw-colored hair stood on end. Self-consciously, he tried to smooth it with one hand, but it didn't work very well.

At the end of the bar, Archie and Willy stopped their constant bickering long enough to turn and examine the new arrival. The Blue Moon survived on a clientele of regulars. Only the most intrepid of tourists ventured this far up Brewery Gulch. Obviously the stranger wasn't a regular, but he didn't have the look of an ordinary tourist, either. Tanned and fit, he might have been in his early to mid-thirties. He was dressed in a set of camouflage shorts and shirt with a pair of well-worn hiking boots on his feet.

"So what have we got here?" Willy demanded loudly. "Some kind of Boy Scout?"

Angie shot Willy a withering look. "You hush, Willy, or you're out of here." She turned back to the newcomer with a welcoming smile. "What can I get you?"

"I'm looking for someone," the man said with what sounded like an English accent. "Her name's Angie. Is that you?"

Years of wariness asserted themselves. Angie's smile cooled. Tony Vargas was long dead, but that didn't mean one of his old associates wouldn't come looking for her someday. Still, this lanky, loose-jointed blond giant of a man didn't look like anyone the swarthy Tony Vargas would have counted among his acquaintances.

"That's me," Angie replied. "What do you want?"

Instead of moving forward, the man stood where he was and stared at her, saying nothing.

"Well?" Angie insisted.

"My name's Hacker," he said, taking another

tentative step or two into the bar. "Dennis Hacker, the Bird Man. Remember? You wrote and asked if you could come see my parrots."

Dennis Hacker had come to Angie's attention when his name appeared in the *Bisbee Bee* in conjunction with a homicide case. A dynamite explosion had destroyed a cabin in the Chiricahua Mountains near Pinery Canyon. Hacker, a witness to the explosion, was reported to be a naturalist on an Audubon Society-funded mission to reintroduce parrots into the southeastern Arizona mountains. Living in captivity, the parrots had somehow forgotten a few of the more important survival basics, including the vital ability to break open pinecones. Hacker had cast himself in the role of teacher and patiently instructed his pupils in pinecone-opening techniques before setting them loose in the wilderness.

Intrigued by this information and excited by her own fledgling interest in birding, Angie had written a note to Hacker, sent in care of the Audubon Society, asking if it would be possible for her to drive up to the Chiricahuas and try to catch a glimpse of his birds. The letter had been sent with high hopes, but after weeks and months passed with no answer, she had pretty much forgotten about it.

"Hey, Angie," Archie offered gallantly. "If this guy is botherin' you, just let us know. Me and Willy may be old, but the two of us can handle him if you need us to."

Ignoring him, Angie stared at Dennis Hacker.

"That was ages ago," she said. "When I didn't hear back from you, I thought you didn't like having visitors or maybe—"

"Sorry about that," Hacker interrupted. "I was gone for a while. Several months. My grandmother was taken ill. I had to fly back home. Fortunately, they were able to find a biology grad student from the U. of A. in Tucson to take care of my birds while I was gone."

"I hope she's all right, then," Angie returned.

"Grandmum?" Hacker nodded. "She's out of hospital now, but she's in her eighties. She isn't going to last forever."

Not knowing quite what to say next, Angie fell back into her role as barmaid. "Can I get you something?" she asked. "To drink, I mean?"

"You wouldn't happen to have any coffee, would you?"

A hoot of laughter from the far end of the bar caused Angie to send a second stifling glare in Archie and Willy's direction. "Sure," she said. "But it's not very fresh. It's early though, so if you don't mind waiting, I'll brew another pot."

Turning back to him after starting the coffee, Angie was puzzled. "How did you know I worked here?"

Hacker reached into his hip pocket and pulled out a thick leather wallet. From that he extracted a much-folded piece of paper that Angie recognized as her own letter.

"It says so right here," the Bird Man said. "That you work in a place called the Blue Moon, that you're interested in birds, and that on one of your days off you'd like to come see my parrots. I'd be happy to show them to you. If you still want to, that is."

The outside door opened again. A gang of middle-aged motorcycle enthusiasts tramped into the room. These weren't trendy yuppies out for a lark, but hard-core, tooth-missing, tattoo-wearing tough-guys—women included. For the next few minutes Angie was busy passing out pitchers of beer and margaritas. It wasn't until after the coffee finished brewing that she was able to return to Dennis Hacker.

"Are parrots the only kind of bird you're interested in?" he asked as she set a stout china mug in front of him.

"Oh, no. I like all kinds of birds. Why?"

"Hummingbirds?"

"I love hummingbirds."

"The problem is, I'm not in the Chiricahuas right now. I'm in the process of setting up camp over in the Peloncillos, farther east. Parrots should be able to make it there, too, eventually. But while I was looking around last week, I found a meadow in Skeleton Canyon, just off Starvation Canyon, where the whole place is teeming with hummingbirds—Anna's mostly, but other kinds, too. I thought, if you wanted to, I could pick you up on your next day off and we could hike up there so I could show them to you."

The mere mention of birds sent Angie Kellogg's carefully honed wariness flying right out the window. "Anna's?" she responded, her blue eyes sparkling. "Really?"

Hacker nodded. "Hundreds of them," he said. "When's your next day off?"

"Sunday," Angie answered. "I get off at two Sunday morning and don't have to be back until Monday at noon."

"What say I pick you up right about then?" Hacker asked.

"At two?" Angie asked, flustered.

Hacker nodded. "In order to see them at their best, we need to be in place no later than five-thirty or six in the morning. Skeleton Canyon is a good two-hour drive from here, and it'll take another hour or so to hike up to the meadow."

Angie hesitated, but only for a moment. "Sure," she said. "What should I wear?"

"Jeans. Hiking boots. Long-sleeved shirt."

"Hey, Angie," Willy Haskins called. "How does a man get some service around here?"

Shaking her head in annoyance, Angie started down the bar. By then some of the bikers' pitchers were empty. During the next few minutes, as she poured more beer and mixed more margaritas, she began having second thoughts. After all, this guy was a perfect stranger. It sounded as though the place they were going was somewhere out in the boondocks. The sensible thing would be to not go at all or else to not go with Hacker unless someone else went along as a chaperone—like Joanna Brady, for instance. But by the time Angie had a spare minute to tell him so, Dennis Hacker was gone. On the bar under his empty cup, Angie found six bucks—one for the coffee and a five-dollar tip.

Instead of making Angie feel better, the out-of-proportion tip only made things worse. She had spent too many years of her life in a world where money always required something in return.

She picked up the five and examined it for a moment, as if expecting to be able to read something of Dennis Hacker's motivation in the forbidding look on Abraham Lincoln's face. Finally, making up her mind, she folded up the crisp, new bill and stuffed it into her shirt pocket. She would call Joanna first thing in the morning, she decided, although Angie Kellogg's idea of morning was everyone else's afternoon. If Joanna Brady couldn't go along on this little adventure, neither would Angie Kellogg.

STOPPING ON the sidewalk outside the Blue Moon, Dennis Hacker paused long enough to wipe his glasses on his shirttail and to take a deep breath. He had carried the letter around with him for months, intrigued by the idea that there was a woman somewhere who sounded like she was almost as interested in birds as he was. What he hadn't anticipated was how beautiful she would be. Blond, blue-eyed, and beauty pageant beautiful. Movie star-type beautiful. And yet she had agreed to go with him on Sunday morning. Incredible. Unbelievable.

"Where'd you get this funny-looking outfit?"

Dennis Hacker turned around to see that the two old men from inside the bar had followed him out onto the sidewalk and were staring at his four-wheel-drive Hummer. They seemed harmless enough. "The dealer's up in Scottsdale," he told them.

One clapped the other on the shoulder. "Like hell," he said. "I'll bet you stole it right out from under the MPs' noses out there at Fort Huachuca."

Hacker was still too overcome by wonder to be offended. "Think whatever you like," he said. Then, replacing his glasses, he climbed into the Hummer. Dennis Hacker had come to town to replenish his supplies. On several other occasions, he had arrived intending to stop by the Blue Moon and introduce himself. Each time, he had lost his nerve at the last minute and hadn't gone inside. This time he had surprised himself.

Now, though, it was time to head for Safeway. For a change, Dennis actually found himself looking forward to the process of shopping. By nine at night, most of the housewives with their unruly little kids would have gone home, taking their offspring with them. He'd be able to lay in his supplies with a minimum of distractions. And this time, instead of just buying the basics, he was determined to pick up something special for that Sunday morning picnic breakfast.

BY THE light of a battery-operated lantern, Bree sat on one of two camp stools writing in her journal. With her shoulders hunched in concentration, she wrote quickly but carefully, pouring out the words that rushed through her heart and mind—her disappointment that Nacio wasn't with her right then, her anticipation of their being together the next morning.

Beyond that small halo of light, it was dark in the Peloncillos. Suddenly the silence was sliced open by a flap of wings and the cry of some night hunting bird. Putting the pen inside the book, Bree switched off the light, hoping to catch sight of the bird. For a moment, she could see nothing. Then, gradually, as her eyes adjusted to the darkness, bright stars began to appear in the sky above her head. The far-off call of a coyote was answered by another, followed by the yapping chorus of pups. There was something wild and wonderful in the sound—like infectious laughter. Bree smiled in response.

Overhead, the stars shone like glittering diamonds against a velvet sky. The starlight was so bright that the mountains, rocks, and trees around her emerged from the gloom. Sitting there in the half-lit dark, it was easy for Brianna to sense time falling away from her. This rugged almost-empty corner of the Arizona desert had changed so little that even now an occasional jaguar, roaming north from the mountains of Mexico, had been spotted by a solitary rancher. And if the wild canyons of the Peloncillos still played host to an assortment of wildlife, it wasn't so far off to imagine that human outlaws still ranged that same habitat as well.

Skeleton Canyon, a few miles from Bree's camping place in Hog Canyon, had been the place where Geronimo had finally surrendered to General Crook. It was also where members of Tombstone's marauding Clanton gang had ambushed and slaughtered a band of Mexican smugglers only to be ambushed and shot in turn. That story, more legend and lore than history, claimed that the smugglers' fortune in gold was still lost somewhere in the Peloncillos waiting to be found by some lucky hiker or hunter.

Bree and Nacio had talked about finding the gold one night and fantasized about what they would do with it. For Nacio, newfound wealth would have meant his being able to repay Aunt Yoli and Uncle Frank for their years of financial support. For Bree, having her own money would have meant independence. It would have allowed her freedom from the comfort and control of her father's checkbook.

For Bree and Nacio together, having money of their own would have meant an end to sneaking around. That was coming anyway, eventually. Once the two of them went away to school in Tucson in September, it would be easier to circumvent parental disapproval. They would be able to do the same things they did now—they just wouldn't have to lie about it.

Leaning back on the stool, Bree breathed deeply, thought about Nacio, and wished he were there with her to share the wonder of this beautiful night. She was still sitting that same way when she heard the sound of an approaching vehicle.

Nacio's coming, she thought joyfully. *Uncle Frank must have come home and let him off work after all.*

On other nights, lying together in the back of her truck, cuddling in the warmth of a double bedroll, Bree and Nacio had heard an occasional and virtually invisible vehicle pass by on the Forest Service road half a mile away. Now, though, staring off in the direction of the road, Bree was able to make out the glow of slow-moving headlights. Holding her breath, Bree waited to see if the vehicle would pass on by or if it really would turn left at the turnoff.

Long moments later, it did. The headlights that had been moving eastbound suddenly turned north. Clutching her journal to her, Brianna O'Brien leaped to her feet and hurried to meet her lover. She could hardly wait to see him. She wanted nothing more than to share the glories of this wonderful night with him. She wanted to lie in the bedroll with their bodies entwined and tell him how much she loved him.

The headlights were closer now, flickering through the darkness, when Bree decided what to do. She loved Nacio with all the devotion of newly awakened passion. She knew what pleasure he took in her body and she in his. And now, with the headlights flickering toward her, Bree knew there was a gift she could give Nacio—a gift only she could offer.

She had to hurry. In the process she put the journal down on a nearby rock and then failed to notice when it slipped off to one side. By the time the laboring engine of the approaching vehicle rounded the last outcropping of rock, she was ready and waiting.

Twin rays of light stabbed through the night and caught her there like a deer frozen and alert in the brilliant glow of a pair of high beams. Her arms were outstretched in greeting. A welcoming smile parted her lips.

The surprise for Nacio Ybarra—Bree's gift to him—had nothing to do with her arms or with her lips. It had to do with the rest of her, impaled on those piercing rays of light. She was smooth and pale and beautiful and as unashamedly naked as the day she was born.

THREE

DENNIS HACKER came home from his shopping trip and unloaded his supplies. At six-one, he had to be careful not to clip his head on the ceiling as he moved around the little two-wheeled caravan that Americans insisted on calling a trailer.

Once the groceries were put away, Dennis glanced at his cell phone before crawling into bed. It would be morning in England. If his grandmother, Emily Lockwood, was well enough, she would be downstairs, drinking her morning tea in her sunny kitchen and looking out at the beginnings of a lush summer garden.

He thought about calling her. That was why he had parked the trailer in this particular spot. It was the last usable place on Geronimo Trail where he could still send and receive a cell phone signal. He thought about telling her she might be right once again when it came to his contacting this young woman who had expressed such an

41

unusual interest in Dennis Hacker's beloved parrots.

Dennis considered calling his grandmother, but after some reflection, he didn't. It was too soon, way too soon. Besides, Sunday morning was when she usually called him. Leaving the phone alone, he clambered up into the upper bunk. He had to lie on a diagonal in order to fit his frame into the bed. He fell asleep almost instantly.

Hacker had lived alone in the wilderness for so long that he was comfortable with the animal-punctuated silence that surrounded him. He had just settled into a sound sleep when something startled him awake. The unusual noise was gone before he was fully conscious, but he could tell from the total silence around him that the animals had heard it as well. They, too, were hushed and listening.

Swinging down to the rag rug-covered linoleum floor, he opened the door and stepped out onto the wooden step. Under a star-studded sky, the Peloncillos were dead silent. After a minute or two, a coyote finally howled in the distance. The coyote's plaintive yelp seemed to settle Dennis Hacker's jangled nerves. Closing and locking both the metal door and the wooden screen door, he climbed back into bed and soon was fast asleep once more.

LONG AFTER Jenny's bedroom light went out, Joanna lay sleepless in her own room. Over the months since Andy's death she had learned to sleep in the dead middle of the bed. It blurred the lines between his side and hers, making the bed seem smaller and not quite so lonely.

For a change, Sheriff Brady wasn't worried about something at work. For the past two weeks all of Cochise County had been amazingly quiet. Other than rounding up the usual quota of undocumented aliens there had been no murders, no ugly domestic violence cases, no fatal traffic accidents, and only a few drunk drivers. The lack of new incidents had allowed her two detectives, Ernie Carpenter and Jaime Carbajal, to go back over a few old and still-unsolved cases to see if there was anything new that could be brought to bear.

For one thing, the county had recently installed an Automated Fingerprint Identification System. Usually the AFIS technician was so busy entering new prints into the system that there was no opportunity to do anything about cold cases. Already the extra effort was paying off. A perpetrator in a two-year-old Huachuca Mountains burglary case had been found in the Pima County jail in Tucson.

So, instead of worrying about work, Joanna was anticipating the next two weeks with a certain amount of dread. Jenny would be away at Camp Whispering Pines all that time. Although Joanna was confident Jenny would be fine, she wasn't so sure how she herself would fare. High Lonesome Ranch had seemed decidedly well-named in the months since Andy's death. With both Jenny and Andy gone, Joanna wasn't convinced she'd be able to handle it.

Turning over on her side, trying to find a more comfortable position, Joanna forced herself to think about something else—about the solo shopping trip she had planned for herself in Tucson after she dropped Jenny off up on Mount Lemmon.

It was summer, and the simmering heat required a change of wardrobe. She needed some lightweight work clothes, ones that would be reasonably cool, look professional, and also be built in a fashion that would accommodate the soft body armor she wore each day when she went to work. There were times when she looked at some of her female officers and felt almost envious of their uniforms. At least they didn't have to go to their closets every morning and decide what to wear.

Joanna wasn't wild about shopping. She didn't usually look forward to fighting her way in and out of malls jammed to the gills with mothers out shopping for early back-to-school bargains. Nonetheless, buying clothes was something that had to be done—a necessary evil. Then, when she came back from Tucson Saturday evening, she needed to see her mother.

Lately, both Joanna and her mother, Eleanor Lathrop, had been so busy they had barely seen each other. Not only that, there had been an alarming drop in the number of Eleanor's phone calls.

Time to do your daughterly duty, Joanna told herself. Besides, if she showed up to see her mother wearing one of the new outfits she had purchased earlier in the afternoon, she was bound to get an instant evaluation. There was comfort in knowing that, Joanna decided as she drifted off to sleep. Eleanor Lathrop had never been one to soft-pedal her opinions. She would take one look at whatever her daughter was wearing and say exactly what she thought.

Good, bad, or indifferent, at least I'll know what she thinks.

"I'M TOO hot," Jenny grumbled to her mother in an irritating whine. "Can't we stop and get something to drink?"

Joanna Brady was hot, too. Twenty miles earlier, just outside Tombstone, the air-conditioner in her Eagle had finally given up the ghost. For weeks now, she had heard an ominous howl in the AC's compressor, but she had hoped to nurse it along for a while longer—at least long enough to drive Jenny to camp. Naturally, it had quit working completely on the trip to Mount Lemmon and on what promised to be a record-breaking scorcher of a June day.

Still, none of that was sufficient reason for Jenny to dispense with the niceties.

"Is there a please hiding in there somewhere?" Joanna asked. "I didn't hear one."

"Pretty please," Jenny said.

Joanna nodded. "All right then," she agreed. "We'll stop in Benson for lunch."

"At Burger King?"

"I suppose."

As they drove down Benson's almost-deserted main drag, the thermometer on the bank read 105 degrees. Joanna shook her head, letting the hot wind from the open window blow over her face. If it was already this hot in Benson, what would it be like when they dropped farther down into the valley?

"Why couldn't we bring the other car?" Jenny had asked when the air-conditioning vents started blowing nothing but hot air.

Jenny was referring to the county-owned Crown Victoria Sheriff Joanna Brady now drove for work. The Blazer she would have preferred to use as an official vehicle was out of commission after being too near an unexpected blast of dynamite. Since the Cochise County Sheriff's Department was currently long on Crown Victorias and short on Blazers, Sheriff Joanna Brady was stuck with one of the former.

"Taking you to camp at Mount Lemmon on my day off hardly qualifies as county business," Joanna replied. "And since I'm trying to discourage unauthorized private use of official vehicles, that would be setting a pretty poor example."

"I know," Jenny said glumly. "But at least the air conditioner works."

"I'm sure I can get this one fixed."

"Before you come back to bring me home?"

"We'll see."

Fifteen minutes later, armed with the remains of two large Cokes and in somewhat better spirits, Joanna and Jenny headed north on I-10. The seventy-mile-an-hour speed limit on the interstate chewed up miles so fast that there was still some Coke left by the time they turned off the freeway onto Houghton Road. Using that and Old Spanish Trail, Joanna was able to make it to the Mount Lemmon Highway without ever having to endure central Tucson's heavier traffic.

Had Joanna been willing to get up at four A.M. and drive to Tucson, it would have been possible for Jenny to ride up to camp on a chartered bus that had left for Camp Whispering Pines from Tucson's Park Mall at six o'clock that morning. However, knowing that weekend nights often resulted in late-night calls, Joanna had opted instead to drive Jenny up to camp on her own. Joanna had used the too-early hour as a handy excuse. Although her rationale might have sounded reasonable enough to anyone else, Joanna herself knew that getting up at the crack of dawn was only part of her reluctance. The truth was that even today she was still having a hard time dealing with the idea of Jenny's going off to camp on her own for two whole weeks. After all, with Andy dead, Jennifer Ann Brady was all Joanna had left.

As soon as the General Hitchcock Highway began climbing up out of the desert floor into the

Catalina Mountains, the temperature began to fall. Halfway up the mountain, Jenny screeched with excitement when she spotted a multicolored Gila monster lumbering across the two-lane road. By the time they reached the turnoff to the camp, near Mount Lemmon's 9,100-foot summit, the breeze blowing in the windows felt pleasantly cool. Somewhere in the high eighties, Joanna estimated. But the improved comfort in the car did nothing to lessen her concern about saying goodbye to her daughter.

"You're sure you packed everything on the list?"

"Yes, Mom," Jenny said resignedly.

"Everything? Even the insect repellent?"

"Even that," Jenny replied with a scowl. "It was on the list, too. I checked everything off as I put it in the bag. You sound just like Grandma Lathrop, you know," she added.

Unfortunately, Joanna realized at once that Jenny's criticism was right on the money. Eleanor Matthews Lathrop was forever firing off barrages of blistering questions. To Joanna, who was usually on the receiving end, those questions always felt more like an attack than anything else. Now Joanna found herself wondering if her mother's unending grilling hadn't served to disguise what was really going on. Maybe Eleanor had been just as concerned about her daughter as Joanna was about hers. Maybe firing off all those questions had served as a substitute for the motherly concern Eleanor never seemed to know quite how to express.

Hoping to do better than that, Joanna sighed. "I'm going to miss you, sweetie," she said.

Jenny nodded. "I'll miss you, too," she replied seriously, sounding altogether too grown-up for Joanna's taste. "Will you be okay out on the ranch all alone?" Jenny continued.

Once again, Jenny's innocent remark was so impossibly dead-on that it took Joanna's breath away. She had to swallow the lump in her throat before she could answer. Joanna held herself back, refusing to blurt out the whole truth about her very real dread of being left alone.

In her heart of hearts, she knew this separation of mother and daughter was a necessary step for both of them. It offered them an opportunity to move beyond the tragedy of Andy's death and to find new ways of functioning in the world. That was something Eleanor Lathrop had resisted doing after the death of her husband, Joanna's father. When D. H. Lathrop died, Eleanor had tried too hard to keep Joanna cocooned with her, creating a kind of hypertogetherness that had done nothing but drive Joanna away. It had been a motherly mistake and probably perfectly understandable under the circumstances, but it was an error in judgment that Eleanor's daughter was trying desperately not to repeat.

"I won't be all alone," Joanna corrected, hoping to keep her answer light and accompanying the comment with what she trusted was a convincing enough smile. "Not with two dogs, one horse, and ten head of cattle to take care of," she added.

"You know what I mean," Jenny insisted with a frown.

"Yes," Joanna conceded. "I do know what you mean. I'll be fine."

"You'll write to me?"

"Every day."

By then they had threaded their way up the narrow road to the parking lot at Camp Whispering Pines. They stopped next to the sign that said NO MOTOR VEHICLES ALLOWED BEYOND THIS POINT. Off to the left ahead of them, nestled at the end of a small clearing and backed by a grove of towering pines, sat a low-slung dining hall. Tucked here and there among the trees were large wood-floored canvas tents, each of them large enough to hold eight cots. The place was at once familiar and foreign. Joanna had stayed there herself years earlier. What seemed inconceivable now was that Jenny was already a "Junior" Girl Scout and old enough to stay there on her own.

Joanna opened the trunk of the Eagle. By the time they had Jenny's bedroll and duffel bag unloaded, a smiling, shorts-clad, and deeply tanned camp counselor came hurrying down the path in their direction. "Hi," she said, smiling down at Jenny and holding out her hand. "I'm Lisa Christman. You must be Jenny Brady, and this must be your mother."

"How did you know?" Jenny asked, gravely shaking the proffered hand.

Lisa laughed. "For one thing, you're the only camper we were missing. For another, ten minutes ago we had a telephone call from someone looking for Sheriff Brady."

Joanna flushed with annoyance. She had deliberately left her pager at home, leaving word with Dispatch that this was to be a real day off. She had planned to spend the whole morning with Jenny. In the afternoon there was that much-needed wardrobe rehabilitation expedition. Both Joanna's chief deputies, Dick Voland and Frank Montoya, had known where she'd be, but she had given strict instructions that, if at all possible, she was to be left off call.

"There's a phone in the camp director's office," Lisa offered helpfully. "You're more than welcome to use that. In the meantime, I'll help Jenny pack her gear up to the cabin. Did you already have lunch?" she asked, addressing Jenny.

Struck suddenly both subdued and shy, Jenny nodded and backed away.

Lisa, clearly an old hand at bridging troublesome parental farewells, forged ahead. "You'll be in Badger," she continued. "That's just two cabins up the hill from the dining hall. There are some really great girls in there. If you can carry the bedroll, I'll take the bag. That way, I can help you find your bunk and be there to introduce you when the other girls come back from lunch. Is that all right?"

For a moment, Jennifer wavered, hovering between wanting to go with Lisa and wanting to climb back into her mother's wheezing Eagle. As directed, she reached down and picked up her bedroll, only to drop it again a moment later to throw her arms around Joanna's waist.

"I've changed my mind," she said tearfully. "I don't want to stay. I'd rather go back home with you."

Had the decision been left to Joanna, she would have simply loaded the bedroll and bag back into the car. Lisa, however, remained unmoved and unperturbed. "Hurry up now, Jenny," she insisted. "Tell your mother good-bye so she can go make her phone call. Then we'll need to hurry, or you'll miss this afternoon's nature hike."

To Joanna's amazement, that little bit of gentle prodding was all it took. With one more quick hug, Jenny let go of her mother, picked up her bedroll, and walked away without so much as a single backward glance. Joanna was the one who was left behind with a mist of tears covering her eyes. Grateful for the dark sunglasses that covered half her face, Joanna glanced at Lisa. If the counselor saw anything amiss, she pretended not to notice.

"You go ahead and make your phone call, Sheriff Brady," she said to Joanna.

"When I finish, I can come up . . ." Joanna began lamely.

Lisa shook her head. "No," she said. "It's probably better if you just go after that. Jenny will be fine. You'll see."

Sure I will, Joanna thought, looking after them. *Just wait until you're a mother. Then you'll know how it feels.*

IT WAS almost noon before Hector finally showed up at the station. He was sober by then, but he looked like hell.

"Where've you been?" Nacio demanded. "Uncle Frank just called looking for you. I was supposed to leave hours ago."

"I got held up," Hector said.

"Right," Nacio growled back at him. "You're just lucky Uncle Frank keeps you on. If it was up to me, you'd be out of here. Now, get to work. Mrs. Howard is due back in half an hour. Her Buick needs an oil change, and I haven't had a chance to get near it."

"What's the matter with you this morning, Pepito?" Hector asked with that slow, lazy smile of his. "Did that little blond *bruja* of yours cut you off?"

Nacio looked at him. He couldn't afford to make any denials. Half sick, he realized that if Hector knew about Bree, most likely so did Uncle Frank and Aunt Yoli.

"Shut up and get to work," he said. "We're too far behind this morning to stand around arguing."

Without another word, Hector headed for the Buick in the far bay and disappeared under the opened hood. An hour later, with things pretty much back under control, Nacio went in search of Ron Torres.

"Hector's here now. Uncle Frank should be in later on. Will you be all right until then?"

Ron grinned and gave him a thumbs-up. "No problem," he said, as a car pulled up to the full-service pumps. "We can handle it."

"Good, then," Nacio said, "because I'm going."

✿ FOUR

WITH A hard lump blocking her throat and almost cutting off her ability to breathe, Joanna watched Jenny walk away until she disappeared behind the dining hall with Lisa following twenty or thirty paces behind. It took every bit of effort Joanna could muster to restrain herself from jogging after them. Finally, sighing, she plucked her purse out of the Eagle and went off in search of the camp director's office. Joanna paused in the doorway of the dining hall.

Years before, when Joanna had attended this same camp, she had eaten meals at long narrow tables in this very room. The wood-and-stone building that had once seemed wonderfully spacious and comfortable now appeared cramped and surprisingly shabby. It was packed full of noisy, disheveled girls downing an uninspired-looking lunch. They sat on benches at drearily functional Formica-topped cafeteria tables. Seen through adult eyes, the place reminded Joanna of a few prison dining rooms she had seen. Still, the high-spirited girls who were wolfing down sandwiches at those tables seemed absolutely delighted by both the food and their surroundings.

"May I help you?" someone asked.

"I'm looking for the camp director," Joanna said.

"That's me. My name's Andrea Petty."

The smiling speaker was a young, nut-brown, shorts-clad African-American woman with a scatter of freckles sprinkled across an upturned nose. She wore a headful of shiny, beaded braids. She didn't look a day over sixteen.

"What can I do for you?" Andrea continued.

"My name's Joanna Brady. Lisa met my daughter and me at the car and said there was a message for me. She also said that if I needed to, I could use the phone in your office."

Andrea gave Joanna an appraising once-over. "All the message said was for you to call your office, but you don't look old enough to be a sheriff."

That makes us even, Joanna thought. *You don't look old enough to be a camp director, either.* "Thanks," she said. "If you don't mind, I'll take that as a compliment."

Andrea smiled back. "The phone's in here," she said, leading the way into a small Spartan office that opened off the south end of the dining hall. "It's behind the door. There's not much privacy. If you need me to leave . . ."

"No, that's all right," Joanna said. "I'm sure this will be fine."

Fumbling through her purse, she found her departmental telephone credit card and began punching numbers into the phone while a tearful girl about Jenny's age came edging her way past the partially opened door. With a badly scraped knee, she was in need of both sympathy and a little first aid.

"Sheriff Brady here," Joanna said when someone picked up the phone at the Cochise County Sheriff's Department, more than a hundred miles away. "I had a message to call in. What's happening?"

"Dick Voland said if you called to put you straight through to him," the desk clerk said. "Hang on."

With a severe budget crunch looming, Chief Deputy Richard Voland wasn't supposed to be in the office on Saturday. "What are you doing going to work on your day off, lobbying for comptime?" she asked as soon as Voland came on the phone. "You haven't moved out of your apartment and back into your office, have you?"

"I got called in," he said, ignoring the jibe. "We've got a problem."

"What *kind* of problem?"

"A missing person."

"A missing person?" Joanna echoed. "You've gone in to work on Saturday and you're calling all over God's creation looking for me on account of a missing person?"

"Wait until I tell you which one is missing," Voland replied. The seriousness in his tone was unmistakably convincing.

"Go ahead, then," Joanna said impatiently. "Who is it?"

"Roxanne O'Brien," Dick Voland answered. "David and Katherine O'Brien's daughter."

"Bree O'Brien? You're kidding."

Joanna's response was as reflexive as it was illogical. Of course, Dick Voland wasn't kidding. The possible disappearance of the only daughter of one of the county's most prominent couples was hardly a joking matter.

"When?" Joanna asked, not giving her chief deputy time to take offense. "And how? What happened?"

"She left home yesterday afternoon to drive to Playas, New Mexico. She was supposed to spend the weekend with a friend of hers, Crystal Phillips," Dick Voland said. "The problem is, she never made it. Katherine O'Brien called over there this morning to verify what time she'd be home tomorrow afternoon, but according to Ed Phillips, Crystal's daddy, Bree never showed up there. Not only that, she wasn't expected."

"Not expected? That sounds bad."

"Just wait," Voland continued. "You haven't heard anything yet. It gets worse. According to Katherine O'Brien, Bree has made three weekend trips to visit Crystal Phillips in the last three months—this one included. Crystal and Bree plan to be roommates at the University of Arizona this fall. As far as the O'Briens are concerned, the two girls have been getting together on weekends to make plans about that—about dorms and clothes and curtains and whatever else girls have to sort out before they can live together. But Ed Phillips and his wife, Lorraine, claim they've never laid eyes on her these last three months. They both say that the last time they saw Bree O'Brien was before they left Bisbee to move to Playas over a year ago."

As sheriff of Cochise County, Joanna Lathrop Brady had learned to make the necessarily swift and sometimes painful shifts from being a mother to being a law enforcement officer. At first those instant role changes had given her the mental equivalent of the bends. Now she was more accustomed to them.

"What are we doing about it, Dick? Have you been in touch with Randy Trotter over in New Mexico?"

"I tried," Voland returned. "Sheriff Trotter is on vacation. He's camping up in the White Mountains and isn't due back until a week from tomorrow. I have been in touch with the Hidalgo County Sheriff's Department, however. The undersheriff there has deputies looking for Bree O'Brien on his side of the state line. I've got cars looking for her on this side as well, ours and Department of Public Safety both."

"On Highway 80 and on Geronimo Trail?"

"Right," Dick Voland replied. "Deputy Hollicker took the initial call from the O'Briens. I sent Detective Carbajal out to see them, but that didn't work."

"What do you mean, it didn't work?"

"Old man O'Brien wouldn't talk to him. In fact, he ordered Jaime off the place and then called in here raising hell and asking what were we thinking of sending a kid out to investigate his daughter's disappearance. A kid and a Mexican to boot."

Joanna was stunned. "He actually said that?" she demanded. "The Mexican part?"

"Not in those exact words, but believe me, I caught his drift."

"Well," Joanna said, "if he's that down on Hispanics, it's not too smart of him to be living smack on the Mexican border."

Dick Voland chuckled. "That probably has more to do with where his granddaddy settled than it does with David O'Brien's personal preferences."

"In the meantime, what else is there to do?" Joanna asked.

"I told Mr. O'Brien that the only detective we have, other than Jaime Carbajal, is off duty today. According to Rose Carpenter, Ernie's out in Sierra Vista having some work done on his car. We paged him, but he's apparently in the middle of a brake job and can't get back here any sooner than another hour at the very earliest. O'Brien said that was fine. That the extra hour's wait would be worth it as long as he gets to talk to a real detective."

Had Joanna been on the scene herself, she might have insisted on Detective Carbajal's taking charge of the case and then been there to back him up. A little enforced respect might have been good for whatever unreasoning prejudices

ailed Mr. David O'Brien. But right then, Sheriff
Brady herself was more than a hundred miles
away from the problem. There was no point in
her causing trouble by countermanding Dick
Voland's orders.

"I guess that'll work. In the meantime, what's
your take on the situation, Dick?"

"I think the girl's a runaway," he answered at
once. "Her folks bought her a cute little bright-
red Toyota truck, one of those Tacoma four-by-
fours, for graduation. She's evidently got a purse
full of credit cards and probably a good deal of
cash as well. Once she starts using plastic for gas
or food, it won't take long to get a line on her."

Joanna was quiet for a moment, thinking about
what she knew about Brianna O'Brien, most of it
second- or thirdhand. Barely three weeks earlier,
the young woman's high school senior portrait
had graced the front page of the local paper, the
Bisbee Bee. During graduation ceremonies, she
had been honored as class valedictorian. In addition to that, Joanna knew she had also served as
a cheerleader and as student body vice president. Bree was popular, good-looking, and her
family had plenty of money. Why would someone like that—someone with brains and looks
and money—be a runaway?

Once again, Joanna kept that opinion to herself. Right then, standing in the director's office
at Camp Whispering Pines, was no time to discuss any of those case-specific details. At least
two nose-ringed young women—counselors or
campers, Joanna couldn't tell which—were lined

up in Andrea Petty's office. Seeming to hang on Joanna's every word and glancing pointedly at their watches, they were evidently waiting none too patiently for their turn to use the camp director's phone.

"Look," Joanna told Dick, "I just dropped Jenny off at camp. I'm still up on Mount Lemmon at the moment. Once I leave here, it'll take me the better part of three hours to get back home to Bisbee. I'll stop by the department on my way out to the ranch to see if there have been any new developments."

Putting down the phone, Joanna left Andrea Petty's office. Except for a few stragglers, the dining hall was almost deserted. Near the door, Joanna caught sight of Lisa Christman.

"I'm going to have to leave now," Joanna said. "You're sure I can't see Jenny just long enough to tell her good-bye?"

Lisa shook her head. "It's not a good idea," she said. "Jenny's already up in her cabin. I've introduced her to the other girls, and they're starting to get settled in and acquainted. The afternoon nature hike starts in ten minutes. If you were to see Jenny now, it would disrupt the whole process."

Here was another jarring transition—in the opposite direction this time—from cop to mother. It hadn't occurred to Joanna earlier as she watched Jenny walk away, lugging her bedroll, that she wouldn't be permitted to give her child a more formal good-bye.

For most people, that might not have been such

a big deal. To Joanna, it was. One month shy of her thirtieth birthday, Joanna had already been a widow for most of a year. Her husband, Deputy Andrew Roy Brady, had died without her ever having a chance to tell him good-bye. She and Andy had exchanged angry words that last morning as he left for work—words Joanna ached to take back or put right somehow. That last quarrel had left her painfully aware—far more so than most people her age—that life doesn't last forever. She had learned to her sorrow that each good-bye, however mundane or normal it might seem, had the potential of being a last one.

"But, I just . . ." she began.

Lisa, clearly as practiced at handling distressed parents as she was homesick campers, shook her head. "No, Mrs. Brady," she said adamantly. "Really. It'll be far harder on Jenny if she sees you again right now than it will be if you just leave. Remember, it's only two weeks."

Joanna wanted to argue. Still, she knew the counselor was right. "Right," she said. "Only two weeks. Thanks for the use of the phone."

With that, she headed back toward the Eagle. Around her were squeals and laughter—the sounds of girls at play. In the background from high in the trees she heard the soft sifting of wind through pine needles—the whispering pines that had given the camp its name.

You're being stupid, Joanna told herself, biting back tears. *Lisa is right. Two weeks isn't forever.*

She was in the car and about to put her key in

the ignition when the thought came to her. *I wonder if David and Katherine O'Brien had a chance to tell Brianna good-bye.*

Sheriff Joanna Brady was known for her common sense. She had the reputation of having both feet firmly on the ground. Had someone asked her straight out right then whether or not she believed in ESP, she would have told them definitely not.

And yet, in that moment, a glimmer of absolute knowledge came to her from somewhere else—from something or someone outside herself. From that moment on, despite all rational arguments to the contrary, Joanna lived with a terrible premonition, one that shook her to the very depths of her soul. Roxanne Brianna O'Brien was dead. She wouldn't be coming home again. Not then. Not ever.

Not only that, halfway down the mountain, Joanna saw the Gila monster again—or, rather, what was left of him. He had been squashed flat by oncoming traffic. The bloody, multicolored remains struck her as an omen and made her feel that much worse.

While the sudden five-thousand-foot drop in altitude sent the Eagle's interior temperature soaring, Joanna's initial outrage at David O'Brien's refusal to deal with Detective Carbajal was soon tempered by thoughts about what would happen to the man if his daughter really was dead. Losing a spouse was bad enough, but the pain of losing a child—any child, but especially one filled with so much promise—had to be hell on earth.

Emotional turmoil—not only reliving her own hurt but also anticipating what soon might be happening with the O'Briens—made it difficult for Joanna to keep her attention focused on the road. Today David O'Brien could still afford to exercise his petty little prejudices. Tomorrow, though, if his daughter really was dead, that would be a different story. Plunged into a nightmare world from which there would be no waking, David O'Brien would no longer care that Detective Jaime Carbajal was Hispanic. Joanna knew from personal experience that in the aftermath and desolation of a loved one's death, things that had seemed to be of earth-shattering importance beforehand suddenly faded into total insignificance.

Because of the heat, Joanna had dressed in shorts and an old Cochise County Fair T-shirt to drive Jenny to camp. Now, though, she wondered how that kind of casual dress might affect and offend the O'Briens. She worried that they might think Sheriff Joanna Brady wasn't paying attention; wasn't according their family's crisis the kind of respect it deserved.

Taking that into consideration, she changed her mind about stopping off at the department first thing. Instead, she drove straight home to High Lonesome Ranch. Barely pausing to greet the two dogs, Tigger and Sadie, Joanna hurried inside to shower, put on fresh makeup, and change into civilized work clothes—her most lightweight business suit, a blouse, heels, and hose.

If Bree is dead, I probably won't be able to do a

damned thing to help those poor people, she told her image in the mirror as she gave her short red hair one last shot of hair spray. *If nothing else, though, at least I'll look competent. That may be the best I can do.*

FIVE

FINISHED DRESSING, Joanna rushed out to her waiting Crown Victoria. Late afternoon sun had turned the interior into a fiery oven. Barely able to stand touching the steering wheel, Joanna turned on the air-conditioning full blast. By the time she made it out to the highway, the car was beginning to cool off some. The difference between her Eagle and the air-conditioned Ford was astonishing. *I will have to get the AC fixed this week,* Joanna told herself. *Definitely* before *I go back to pick Jenny up from camp, not* after.

Driving toward David O'Brien's place, Joanna still thought of it by its old name, Sombra del San Jose—Shadow of San Jose, named after the stately mountain that thrust up out of the Mexican desert a few miles away. That was the name the ranch had been given originally by David O'Brien's grandfather, back before the turn of the century. When David O'Brien had returned to the family digs from Phoenix several years earlier, he had renamed the place Green Brush Ranch, after the mostly dry wash bed—Green Brush Draw—that bisected the entire spread. The new name was posted above the gate, formed in foot-high, iron letters.

Despite the sign, the new name hadn't caught on with most other locals any better than it had with Joanna. They regarded it as change for change's sake. Now, knowing about David O'Brien's attitude toward Jaime Carbajal, Joanna saw the name in a whole new light. Considering his attitude toward Mexicans, no wonder David O'Brien had dropped the Spanish language name.

At the entrance to the ranch, a closed, electronically controlled gate barred her way. On either side of the gate, as far as the eye could see, stretched an eight-foot-tall chain-link fence topped by V-shaped barbed wire with a coiled layer of razor wire resting inside it. The fencing reminded Joanna of the barrier surrounding the inmate exercise yard at the Cochise County jail. It was the same stuff that encircled countless human and auto junkyards all over the country.

At the time the O'Briens had been having the fencing installed at great expense, they had been considered something of a laughingstock. Old-timers around the county had made fun of the whole concept, calling the fence David's Folly and referring to the ranch itself as Fort O'Brien. That, however, was before the dawn of the era of "Border Bandits," roving bands of mostly Sonora-based thieves and thugs who practiced home invasions, burglaries, and armed robbery on people who lived along the U.S. side of the border. Taking the grim presence of those folks into consideration, David O'Brien's fence no longer seemed foolish.

Joanna leaned out the driver's window of the Crown Victoria and punched the talk button on an intercom mounted on a post just outside the gate.

"Come on in, Sheriff Brady," a disembodied voice said as the gate slowly began to swing open. "Drive right up to the house. They're expecting you. Detective Carpenter said you were on your way."

Joanna glanced around in surprise. There was no sign of any monitoring video camera, yet there had to be one somewhere. Joanna hadn't announced her name, yet whoever was in charge of the gate knew who she was and what she was doing there.

"Thanks," she said, putting the Crown Victoria back in gear and moving forward. "I'm glad to hear they know I'm coming."

Outside the gate, on the county side of the fence, the far western end of Purdy Lane was little more than a dirt track. Inside the fence, however, the private road leading away from the gate was a smooth layer of well-maintained blacktop. Thinking of the rough, rutted track that led through High Lonesome Ranch and of the sometimes sagging barbed-wire fence that surrounded it, Joanna shook her head. *The O'Briens must have money to burn*, she told herself.

Following the winding road, Joanna reviewed

what little she knew about David and Katherine O'Brien. David, in his early seventies, was a Cochise County native and the only grandson of one of southern Arizona's more colorful pioneers. David's grandfather, Ezra Cooper, had first set foot in what would eventually become the Arizona Territory when, as a young man, he had worked as a surveyor laying out the boundaries of the Gadsden Purchase. Later, after making a fortune working for what would become the Southern Pacific Railroad and also after contracting TB, Cooper had returned to the southern part of the Arizona Territory hoping to regain his health. He had brought with him a young wife and had expected to found a thriving family dynasty on the lush grassland of the lower San Pedro Valley.

When Ezra Cooper died a few years later, he left behind a widow named Lucille, a six-year-old daughter named Roxanne, and, to his regret, no sons. Lucille's second husband, a fortune-hunting ne'er-do-well named Richard Lafferty, had so overgrazed the place that when he died of influenza in 1918, what was left of Ezra Cooper's Sombra del San Jose was little more than a mesquite-punctuated wasteland. Now, with the help of a university trained botanist and liberal applications of money, David O'Brien had gained a good deal of favorable press by systematically removing the water-hoarding stands of mesquite and returning the desert landscape to its original grassy state.

So much for David O'Brien. Joanna knew that

Katherine was David's second wife. Other than the fact that she was the middle-aged mother of an outstanding daughter, Joanna knew very little about her. Economically and socially, Green Brush Ranch and the High Lonesome were worlds apart.

Coming around a curve, Joanna encountered a Y in the road. Never having been to the place before, Joanna might have taken the wrong fork. Fortunately, an all-terrain vehicle, its original color obscured by a layer of red dirt, sat idling at the intersection. The driver—a cigar-chomping cowhand with a roll of fat around his middle—waved her on, sending her down the right-hand fork and slipping onto the roadway behind her.

A white-stuccoed ranch house appeared a moment later. Surrounded by yet another razor wire-topped fence, the house was set in a small basin, nestled in among a stately copse of green-leafed cottonwoods. Once again Joanna had to wait for an electronically operated gate to open to allow her access to the house itself.

Threading her way through a collection of several parked police vehicles and past another fiberglass-topped ATV, Joanna pulled up under a shaded portico and parked next to David O'Brien's customized Aerostar van. In front of the van sat Katherine O'Brien's distinctive Lexus LS 400—the only one like it in town. On the verandah, beyond David O'Brien's wheelchair-accessible van and next to a gurgling fountain, stood the hulking figure of Chief Deputy Richard Voland. He was talking to another man, one Joanna didn't recognize. Beside the stranger sat a huge panting German shepherd.

Voland glanced up as Joanna approached. "Afternoon, Sheriff Brady," he said. "This is Alf Hastings, Mr. O'Brien's operations manager."

Alf was a suntanned forty-something man with a cream-colored straw Resistol cowboy hat pulled low over pale blue eyes. Joanna might not have recognized the face immediately, but she did recognize the name.

In Arizona law enforcement circles, Alf Hastings was notorious. As a Yuma County deputy, he had been the focal point of one of the biggest police scandals in the state's history. He and three other deputies had been fired for systematically brutalizing a group of teenaged undocumented aliens (UDAs) who had been caught crossing the Mexican border just north of San Luis. The four officers had herded the UDAs into a van, driven them just inside the Cabeza Prieta National Wildlife Refuge, and left them there—after first beating the crap out of them and taking their water. No doubt all six of them would have died had they not been found by a feisty Good Samaritan—a spelunking retired schoolteacher from Wooster, Ohio. She had given them water, loaded them into her Jeep Wagoneer, and then carted them off to the nearest hospital.

In the resulting investigation, the cops had lost their jobs, although none of them actually went to prison. An ensuing flurry of civil lawsuits, shades of California's Rodney King, had put a big hole in Yuma County's legal contingency fund.

"So you're our local lady sheriff, are you?" Alf said with what was no doubt calculated to be an engaging grin. "Glad to meet you."

He held out his hand. Joanna shook it without enthusiasm. "I didn't know you had moved to Bisbee," she said.

"I haven't exactly," he returned. "Unless the Bisbee City limits come all the way out here. My wife and I live at the hired help's compound just a ways back up the road here. Mr. O'Brien was good enough to set aside six mobile homes for those of us who work here, except for Mrs. Vorevkin, the housekeeper. She has a room here at the house."

Hastings's pocket radio squawked to life. As the operations manager walked away to answer his summons in private, Joanna turned to Dick.

"What's he doing here?" she asked.

Voland frowned. "As near as I can tell, he's probably doing the same thing he was doing before—keeping America safe for Americans, only on a private basis, this time, not a public one."

"Have we had any complaints?"

"Not so far," Voland answered. "My guess is he's been keeping a pretty low profile."

"Did you tell him we don't tolerate that kind of behavior around here?"

"The subject didn't come up," Voland said.

"Never mind," Joanna said. "I'll tell him myself the next time I see him. In the meantime, what's going on? Any word about the girl?"

At six-four, Chief Deputy Voland towered over Joanna by a whole foot. The top of her head barely grazed the bottom of his chin. For months now, the sheriff had been aware of the possibility that her not-quite-divorced second in command might have a crush on her. Always gruff and blustery in public, his private dealings with Joanna had changed. Too much the professional to say anything directly, his feelings were betrayed by ears that reddened when she spoke to him in private as well as by sudden bouts of his being tongue-tied in her presence.

As a consequence, in her dealings with Dick Voland, Joanna always found herself walking a tightrope. Because he was in charge of the day-to-day functioning of her department, it was essential that she have a good working relationship with the man. On the other hand, she didn't want to say or do anything that would encourage him or give him the wrong idea.

"Nothing much so far," he said. "Ernie just got here a little while ago. He's inside talking to the parents. You can go on in, if you want to."

"How are the O'Briens holding up?" Joanna asked.

"About how you'd expect," Voland answered. "The mother is brokenhearted; the father is pissed. If I were Brianna O'Brien's daddy," he added, "I would be, too."

As soon as Joanna rang the bell, the O'Briens' front door was opened by a round-faced red-haired woman who spoke with what sounded to Joanna like a thick Russian accent. "I'm Sheriff

Brady," Joanna said, showing the woman her photo ID and badge. "I'd like to see Mr. and Mrs. O'Brien."

"Yes," the woman said. "Of course. This way, please."

Inside, away from the blazing heat, the interior of the air-conditioned house felt almost chill. As Joanna followed the shuffling, heavyset housekeeper across a smooth saultillo tile floor, she was struck by the scale of the house. The ceilings were high and broken by walls with clerestory windows that provided light without letting in heat. The housekeeper led the way down a long hallway that was almost twice as wide as those in most private homes. The white walls were adorned with groupings of carefully lit and lavishly framed art. Some of the pieces looked familiar. Walking past, there was no way for Joanna to tell whether or not any of the pieces were originals or whether they were simply extremely well-executed reproductions.

Surely they're not originals, Joanna thought. *No one in his right mind would bring a valuable collection of original art right here to the border. . . .*

But then, thinking about the razor wire–topped chain-link fence and the ATV-mounted security guards, the video monitoring system, and what was no doubt a trained guard dog, she reconsidered. Maybe this was original artwork after all.

At the far end of the long hallway, the housekeeper paused. "You wait," she said.

Before Joanna, set in an alcove that had clearly been designed for that specific purpose, sat an exquisite, two-foot-tall marble statue of the Madonna and Child. The baby was roly-poly and clung to his mother's waist with one chubby bare leg. The young mother's face seemed almost alive with a benevolent, welcoming smile. Her one free hand reached out in graceful, openhanded greeting to all who looked upon her. Beneath the statue sat a polished rosewood prie-dieu. On the prie-dieu lay an open Bible, an onyx-beaded rosary complete with a gold crucifix, and a single lit votive candle. The brown leather of the padded knee rest glowed with the patina of long and faithful use.

Feeling as though she were standing in a chapel, Joanna gazed up at the statue while running an admiring finger over the satin-smooth grain of the wood.

"Sheriff Brady?"

Like a child caught doing something she shouldn't, Joanna turned to face the lady of the house. The luxury automobiles parked under the covered portico, the spaciousness of the beautifully tiled hallway, the elegance of the artwork had all led Joanna to expect that Katherine O'Brien would be someone equally elegant—slender, fashionable, and maybe even a little on the delicate side.

Joanna was surprised to see before her a plain-faced and sturdy woman in her early to mid-fifties. She was dressed casually in a tank top, Bermuda shorts, and leather thongs. Her brunette hair, going gray around the temples, was drawn back in a casual, foot-long ponytail. As soon as

Joanna saw the woman she realized she had seen her before—in the grocery store and post office on occasion—without having the smallest glimmer of who she was.

"I'm sorry," Joanna apologized. "The wood is so lovely I couldn't help touching it."

Katherine smiled sadly and nodded. "I know what you mean. I've spent the better part of the afternoon on my knees there, praying. Both pieces, the prie-dieu and the statue, came from a Sisters of Silence convent in upstate New York. When the Cistercian Order closed the place down, they asked Sotheby's to auction off all the contents. The prie-dieu and the statue had both been in the mother superior's private chapel. I was glad David was able to buy them so we could keep them together."

Katherine stopped abruptly, as though the customary graciousness of telling visiting guests about her objets d'art had somehow outdistanced the painful circumstances that had brought this particular visitor into her home. "Sorry," she said. "Detective Carpenter and my husband are out back by the pool. If you'll come this way."

Katherine O'Brien led Joanna past a formal dining room and through a large kitchen where the housekeeper was busy cooking something meaty that smelled absolutely wonderful. Beyond the kitchen was an informal dining room and a family room complete with a massive entertainment unit. French doors from the family room led to a fully enclosed patio complete with black wrought iron furniture, a permanently installed canopy, a hot tub, and a lap pool. The interior wall of the patio was lined with raised flower beds that held an astonishing assortment of vividly colored, dinner plate-sized dahlias.

An empty wheelchair sat parked next to the edge of the pool. In the pool itself, a silver-haired man Joanna recognized as David O'Brien swam back and forth. Meanwhile, Detective Ernie Carpenter, overdressed as usual in his customary double-breasted suit, sat sweltering under the canopy.

As soon as Joanna and Katherine came out onto the porch, O'Brien used two swift strokes to propel himself over to a stainless steel pole that stood next to the wheelchair. Turning his back to the side of the pool, he did something that activated a whirring motor. Moments later, he emerged from the water seated on what was evidently a one-person lift. The lift stopped when David O'Brien was exactly level with the seat of the chair. Using the strong, well-defined muscles in his arms and shoulders, David swung himself from lift to chair.

A stack of terry cloth towels sat on the table. David O'Brien rolled his chair over to the table. Taking the top towel off the pile, he draped that over his deformed and useless legs. He used a second towel to dry his hair, face, and upper body.

"It's about time you got here, Sheriff Brady," he grumbled. "Maybe now you can get Detective Carpenter here to stop asking all these damn fool questions about Bree's friends and start doing something useful like actually looking for her."

"They *are* looking for her, David," Katherine

reminded her husband gently. "Detective Carpenter already told us that they have deputies and the highway patrol searching all the roads between here and Playas. . . ."

"But she didn't go to Playas!" David O'Brien exploded, pounding the table with his fist. The powerful blow sent Ernie's almost-empty glass of iced tea skipping across the surface of the table. The detective managed to catch it, but only just barely.

"What would you like us to do, Mr. O'Brien?" Joanna asked.

"Call in the FBI. Get some manpower on this thing."

"The FBI?"

"Hello, Sheriff Brady," Ernie said, nodding in greeting. He was a solidly built, beetle-browed man in his early fifties. His tie and stiffly starched white shirt were wilting fast.

"Mr. O'Brien here is under the impression that his daughter has been kidnapped." He finished his tea and returned the emptied glass to the table.

"Kidnapped," Joanna repeated. "Why? Has there been a ransom demand?"

"Nothing like that," Ernie replied. "Not so far."

"What about the pay phone call? If that wasn't an abortive call for ransom . . ." David O'Brien interjected.

"What phone call?" Joanna asked.

"The O'Briens have caller ID on their phones," Ernie said. "A call came in a few minutes ago, just about the time I got here. The monitor reported it as a pay phone call. I traced it to a location near the Kmart down in Douglas. The problem is, whoever it was hung up."

"So you didn't actually speak to anyone?" Joanna asked Katherine.

"No."

"And there was no request for ransom?" Joanna continued.

"That's true," Katherine agreed.

"But that's where ransom calls usually come from, isn't it?" O'Brien interrupted. "From pay phones so the calls can't be traced back to the kidnapper's residence or place of business."

"It could have been nothing more ominous than a wrong number," Joanna suggested. "What makes you think otherwise? Have there been kidnapping threats in the past?"

"No. Not really. But look around," O'Brien said brusquely, with an expansive gesture that took in both the patio and the opulent home beyond it. "My wife and I have money, plenty of it. What better way for someone to lay hands on some of it than by kidnapping our only daughter? It's not as though her existence is some kind of secret. Her graduation picture was plastered all over the papers a few weeks back. It's no wonder—"

Joanna glanced back at Ernie. "Any sign of violence or foul play?"

The detective shook his head. "Not that I've found so far. In addition, Brianna has evidently taken off like this on at least two other occasions. According to Mrs. O'Brien here, there have been two other similar incidents in the last few months— times when Brianna has left for the weekend without arriving at her supposed destination. Each time it's been with the understanding that she was going to visit this same girl, this"—Ernie paused to consult his notes—"this Crystal Phillips over in Playas. The problem is, Crystal's father says Brianna hasn't ever been there."

"But she keeps pretending that's where she's gone," Joanna said.

Ernie nodded. "Right. Each time, she left home late in the day on a Friday and returned Sunday evening. As long as her folks here didn't call to check up on her, everything was peachy. My expectation is that she's pulled the same stunt this time, too. She isn't lost at all. Late Sunday she's going to show up thinking everything's all fine and dandy. Only this time, she'll find out the game's up. When she comes waltzing home on Sunday afternoon, she's going to be one mighty surprised young lady."

Ernie finished his speech by hauling out a hanky and mopping his sweat-drenched brow. His theory sounded reasonable enough, and Joanna wanted it to be right. She wanted to believe that an errant Brianna O'Brien would arrive home on Sunday night in time to be read the riot act by both her outraged parents for having been AWOL all weekend long. Still, Joanna couldn't dodge the premonition that had come to her before she ever left the parking lot on Mount Lemmon—one that left her believing that Brianna O'Brien was already dead.

Standing there fully clothed with the late afternoon sun blazing down on her, Joanna was already regretting having changed clothes. The O'Briens' flower-bordered patio might have been fine if you were dressed in shorts or if you had just stepped out of a swimming pool. For people dressed in business clothing and wearing body armor, though, it was like playing dress-up in the middle of a blast furnace.

David O'Brien glared across the table at the detective. "My daughter is an honor student," he announced. "She's never lied to me about anything in her life. I can't understand why she'd start now. But since we've done our jobs as parents, how about you starting to do yours as cops?"

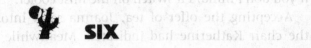

SIX

JOANNA KNEW there were lots of people in town who were intimidated by David O'Brien. It was easy to see why. He was a craggy-faced man whose suntanned arms and chest glistened with silvery hair. He had a long, hawkish nose and piercing blue eyes. He was ruggedly handsome in an aging Marlboro man kind of way. In fact, at that very moment, he reached for a pack of cigarettes that lay on the table in front of him. Watching him light up, Joanna estimated that he had to be somewhere in his late seventies—of an age when he might be more likely to be a teenager's grandfather rather than her father.

"You'd say you're on good terms with your daughter, then?" Joanna asked.

"Absolutely!"

"David, please don't shout," Katherine said quietly, giving him a lingering look Joanna noticed but couldn't quite decipher. "That isn't necessary.

And we're forgetting our manners. Won't you sit down, Sheriff Brady? This chair is still in the shade. Would you care for a glass of iced tea? And, if you don't mind, I'll switch on the mist cooler."

Accepting the offer of tea, Joanna sank into the chair Katherine had indicated. Meanwhile, Katherine herself walked over to the wall and flipped a switch. Instantly a fine spray of water settled over the patio. It was a cooling device Joanna had seen in Phoenix and Tucson at nicer restaurants with outdoor seating areas, but this was the first time she had seen that kind of setup in a private home. She would have loved to strip off her jacket, but that would have revealed that she was armed, twice over. Her Colt 2000 rested in a shoulder holster under her arm. Her backup weapon—a Glock 19—was hidden in a discreet small-of-the-back holster.

"Did you already tell Detective Carpenter what kind of vehicle your daughter is driving?" she asked.

"A red Toyota," Katherine said.

"It's a Tacoma," David added. "She could have had any kind of car, but what she wanted was a damned pickup. We gave it to her three months ago as a combination birthday/graduation present."

"Do you happen to know the license number?"

David shook his head. "Not off the top of my head, but I'm sure the registration and title are in my file. Would you like me to get them?"

Joanna shook her head. "That's not necessary. We'll get it from the D.M.V." She looked at Ernie.

"Have you checked the house to make sure nothing's missing, Detective Carpenter?"

"Not yet," he replied. "I was about to do that when—"

"Missing?" David O'Brien interrupted. "What do you mean, missing? Are you implying that Brianna would steal from her own parents?"

"I'm implying nothing of the kind," Joanna returned coolly, choosing to ignore David O'Brien's continuing bluster. "Your daughter left home yesterday, correct?"

"Yes."

"I'm merely trying to ascertain what, if anything, she took with her. Something she might have taken along may give us a clue as to her actual destination."

"I see," David agreed reluctantly.

Joanna turned to Katherine. "Would it be possible for you to show us Brianna's room?"

The woman stood at once. "Of course," she said. "I'll be happy to. Right this way."

With Katherine leading, Ernie and Joanna walked back into the welcome coolness of the house. Morosely smoking his cigarette, David O'Brien remained where he was.

"Please excuse David," Katherine O'Brien was saying. "He's not usually so on edge. You have to understand, this has all been a terrible strain on him. A shock. And the idea that something awful may have happened . . ." Pausing, she shook her head. "After what went on before, it's just . . . just unthinkable," she finished at last.

They had entered a part of the sprawling house that appeared to be a bedroom wing.

"After what happened before?" Joanna asked.

"You know," Katherine said. "If he lost Bree, too. Just like he lost his other two kids. I don't think he'd survive it."

Joanna frowned. "He had other children?"

Katherine had stopped in front of a closed door. With one hand on the knob, she hesitated before opening it. "I've always respected Bree's privacy," she said. "I've never gone into her room without permission."

"Do it just this once," Ernie urged. "I think she'll forgive you." Nodding, Katherine opened the door and let him inside, but without entering the room herself. Since the woman was staying in the hallway, so did Joanna, mulling over what Katherine had just told them.

"I thought Brianna was an only child," Joanna said a moment later.

"There were two others," Katherine said. "A boy and a girl. From his first wife."

"What happened to them?"

Katherine looked surprised. "I thought everyone knew about that."

"I don't."

Katherine sighed. "They both died," she said simply. "David and Suzanne, his first wife, were driving back to Phoenix after being down in Tucson over Fourth of July. David was at the wheel. The two kids were asleep in the backseat. David Junior was eight, and Monica five. On the road between Phoenix and Casa Grande, they got caught in one of those terrible Interstate-10 dust storms.

"David told me that he saw the dust cloud coming and was trying to make it to the next exit, but the storm got to them first. He drove over on the shoulder of the road, hoping to get out of the way of traffic. He got out of the car and was opening the passenger door to lead Suzanne and the kids to safety when a semi slammed into them from behind. The impact threw him clear of the wreckage. Suzanne and the kids were trapped in the car. The coroner said they all died on impact. I hope so, because there was a terrible fire after that—one of those awful chain reaction things. Nine people died in all, most of them burned beyond recognition.

"It was more than an hour later when someone finally found David. He was unconscious and had been thrown so far from the other wreckage that no one saw him at first. They airlifted him to Good Samaritan in Phoenix. That's where I met him. I was an intensive care nurse. I was on duty in the ICU when they brought him in. I was there when he regained consciousness."

Remembering, Katherine paused and bit her lip. "I'll never forget it. 'Where's my wife?' he asked. 'Where are my kids? Please tell me.' The doctor had left orders that he was to be told nothing, but that didn't seem right. The funerals were scheduled for the next day, and he didn't even know they were dead. So I told him.

"Later, when his doctor found out I was the one who had given David the information, the doctor tried to have the nursing supervisor fire me. It didn't work, but I quit anyway. When David left the hospital, he needed a full-time nurse, and he hired me to take care of him. Those first three or four years were awful for him. He was devastated. He felt like he had lost everything. He was suicidal much of the time. There were guns in his house. If I hadn't hidden them, I think he would have taken his own life a dozen times over."

"When did you get married, then?" Joanna asked.

"Five years later," Katherine answered. "When David finally realized that his life wasn't finished. That he wanted to live again. That he could possibly father another child."

Katherine stopped. "People say that, you know," she added. "At funerals. To the parents of dead children. They say, 'You can have another child.' Except it doesn't work out. You can never replace one child with another."

Up to that very moment, Katherine O'Brien had given every indication that she was a pillar of strength. Leaning against the doorjamb of her daughter's room, she began to cry.

"She's gone," she sobbed hopelessly. "I know it. My poor little Bree is gone, and she's never coming back."

For a time there was nothing Joanna could do but wait. She knew that words would do nothing to relieve the kind of distress Katherine O'Brien was suffering. "I'm sorry," the weeping woman mumbled at last, blowing her nose into a tissue.

"I've been trying not to fall apart in front of David, but opening the door to Bree's room was more than I could bear."

"I understand," Joanna said kindly. "Believe me, I do."

Ernie reappeared in the doorway. "Would you mind coming in here now, Mrs. O'Brien? I'd like you to look through your daughter's clothing and toiletries and try to see if anything in particular isn't here. That way, if it becomes necessary to broadcast a report to other jurisdictions, we'll be able to include a description of exactly what she might be wearing."

Joanna gave Ernie a grateful nod. Officially, Bree O'Brien's possible disappearance was not yet a missing persons case. Still, Ernie's diplomatic handling of the situation seemed to offer Katherine some comfort and give her courage.

Sighing and pulling herself together, Katherine stepped into her daughter's room. Joining her, Joanna was surprised by what she saw. The room was immaculately clean; the bed carefully made. Books on the loaded bookshelves stood with their spines aligned in almost military precision. The desktop held a formidable computer setup, but no stray pieces of paper lingered around it. In fact, the place was so unbendingly neat that, had it not been for the posters and pictures pinned to the walls and for the mound of teddy bears piled at the head of the bed, it would have been hard to tell that a teenager lived there at all.

Jenny's room stayed neat because she liked it that way, but Joanna remembered all too well the chaotic condition of her own room back when she had been Brianna's age. The place had been a pit. Once a week or so, and always uninvited, Eleanor Lathrop had stepped over the threshold into Joanna's sanctum sanctorum. Once inside, she never failed to raise hell. Eleanor, needing to exert control, had wanted the place kept spotless, while a rebellious Joanna had craved and reveled in the very disorder that drove her mother wild.

Based on that scale of value, Joanna's initial reaction was to see Brianna O'Brien's room as an indicator of a good relationship between mother and child—one of mutual respect. As always, when faced with evidence that some mothers and teenage daughters actually got along, Joanna allowed herself to indulge in the smallest flicker of envy. After all, her relationship with her own mother was still far from perfect.

"Right this way, Mrs. O'Brien," Ernie was saying. "If you'll just take a look at the closet here and tell me if you notice anything in particular that's missing—something that ought to be here but isn't."

The closet was a walk-in affair. It was big enough for both Katherine and Joanna to join Detective Carpenter inside the well-organized little room without even touching shoulders. The closet was as compulsively neat as the room. Clothes were hung on hangers. Paired shoes were carefully stacked in hanging shoe bags. A dirty clothes hamper stood in the corner, but it was empty.

"Her overnight bag," Katherine said at once, gesturing toward a foot-and-a-half-wide empty space on an upper shelf. "It's just a little carry-on. That's all she ever takes with her."

"You don't see any clothes missing?" Ernie urged.

"Her tennis shoes," Katherine said.

Ernie grimaced in disappointment. "Nothing else?"

"Not from the closet. It's summer, though. Bree spends most of the time in shorts and tank tops. Those are kept in the dresser."

Moving over to the dresser, Katherine pulled open the top drawer. "Some underwear, I suppose," she said. Closing that drawer, she moved on to the next one. "And shorts. She usually wears cutoffs and tennis shoes."

"Do you know the brands?"

"Wranglers for the jeans and Keds for the shoes," Katherine said. "And tank tops. She has several of them. They're all the same style but in several different colors, so I can't really tell you which ones aren't here."

Ernie scribbled something in his notebook. "Nightgown?"

Katherine walked as far as the bed and lifted the right-hand pillow, spilling the mound of lounging teddy bears off onto the floor. "Her nightgown's definitely missing," she said a moment later. "And her diary . . . her journal, rather," Katherine corrected. "I think of it as a diary, but Bree prefers to call it a journal. It's one of those little blank books with lots of pink or blue flowers on the cover. I forget which it is. She buys them at a bookstore in Tucson, and she usually keeps the one she's working on right here on her nightstand. She says that's the last thing she does before she falls asleep at night—writes in her journal."

Ernie made another notation. "What about the bathroom?" he said. "Would you mind checking there?"

Moving deliberately, Katherine headed there next. She stood for some time in front of the bathroom counter. "Perfume, deodorant, makeup are all gone," she said. "She's taken the usual stuff. The kinds of things you'd expect. Her hair dryer is here, but I'm sure Crystal has one Bree could borrow."

Reaching out, Katherine pulled open the top drawer in the built-in bathroom vanity. "Comb and brush," she reported. Then, frowning, she reached down into the drawer and picked something up. At first glance it looked to Joanna like a light green, oversized matchbook.

"What's this?" Katherine asked, turning the packet over. Lifting the flap revealed a layer of tiny white pills covered by a plastic shield and backed by foil. To Joanna, the packaging was instantly recognizable. It took Katherine O'Brien a moment longer.

Turning the package over in her hand, Katherine frowned as she read the label. "Birth control pills!" she exclaimed in dismay. "What on earth would Brianna be doing with these?"

Behind Katherine's back, Ernie Carpenter and Joanna Brady exchanged glances. *The usual reason*, Joanna thought. *Maybe there's a lot more rebellion going on in Brianna O'Brien's amazingly clean room than anyone—most especially her mother—ever imagined.*

Those thoughts flashed through Joanna's head, but she was careful to say nothing aloud. Keeping quiet allowed Katherine O'Brien the opportunity to arrive at those same conclusions on her own. "Why, you don't think . . ." Katherine blanched. "No. Absolutely not. Bree wouldn't do such a thing."

But clearly, Ernie Carpenter *did* think. "When we were out in the other room and I was asking about Bree's friends," he ventured, "neither you nor Mr. O'Brien mentioned a boyfriend."

Detective Ernie Carpenter had been a homicide cop for fifteen years and a deputy before that. He knew everything there was to know about murder and mayhem. Up to then, his careful handling of Katherine O'Brien had been sensitive in the extreme, but as soon as he made that statement, Joanna realized his knowledge of women was still somewhat lacking. His comment hit Katherine O'Brien hard, especially since the little green package clutched in her hand would most likely rob her of any lingering illusions about her daughter's supposedly virginal purity.

Rather than believe the evidence in her hand, however, Katherine turned on Ernie. "My daughter does *not* have a boyfriend, Detective Carpenter!" she insisted. "N-O-T. If she did, don't you think her mother would know about it?"

Not necessarily, Joanna thought, relieved to note that, at that juncture, Ernie was smart enough to keep his mouth shut.

"As for these," she continued furiously, flinging the offending package of pills back into the drawer and slamming it shut, "there's probably a perfectly reasonable explanation. Bree sometimes has terrible menstrual cramps. Maybe she's taking the pills for that. It's a common treatment. She certainly wouldn't be using them for birth control. Now, if there's nothing else, I need to be getting back to my husband."

"Mrs. O'Brien," Joanna said quickly, "would you mind if Detective Carpenter and I poked around in here for a few more minutes in case there's something we've missed?"

Having spent her outrage, Katherine took a deep breath. She considered for a moment, looking back and forth between Ernie and Joanna. "No," she said finally. "I suppose not, but still, I should be getting back to David."

"As soon as we finish in here, we'll come find you," Joanna said.

In an exhibition of self-control Joanna found astounding, Katherine O'Brien switched off her anger and turned on an outward display of good manners. "We'll probably be in the living room," she said. "We usually have cocktails there every evening. In times of crisis, David likes to stick to as normal a routine as possible. You and Detective Carpenter are welcome to join us if you like."

"Thanks," Joanna said. "But not while we're working."

Katherine walked as far as the door. She went out into the hallway, pulling the door almost shut behind her. Then she opened it again and stuck her head back into the bedroom. "One more thing," she added. "I'd appreciate it if you wouldn't mention the pills. To David, I mean. Knowing about them would only upset him. He's already very close to the edge."

"Talk about close to the edge," Ernie said, staring at the closed door as Katherine left and the latch clicked home. "What about her? And what's the big deal anyway? Would these people prefer having their daughter turn up pregnant rather than be caught taking birth control pills?"

"They're Catholic," Joanna said, as if those words alone were explanation enough. "Practicing birth control is a sin."

"Maybe so," Ernie said. "But it seems to me that there are times when not practicing birth control is downright crazy."

Going into the bathroom, he opened the drawer and removed not one but two identical containers of pills. He took out his notebook and made a note of the doctor's name and the pharmacy's address on the label.

"She got these up in Tucson," Ernie told Joanna. "The pharmacy is there, and probably the doctor is, too. Which means that she probably went to a good deal of trouble to make sure her parents wouldn't find out about them. My guess is that these two packages are for the next two months. She most likely has this month's supply with her."

Nodding, Joanna wandered over to the nearest bookshelf. There, on the second shelf from the bottom, sat a series of identical books—blue ones with streams of pink flowers spilling over the covers. Realizing these had to be the journals Katherine had mentioned, Joanna reached down and plucked the first one off the shelf. Inside the front cover was Brianna's full name—Roxanne Brianna O'Brien—written in flowing purple ink. The first entry was dated in June, three years earlier. Entries in that first volume ran from June 7 to September 12. The next volume picked up on September 13. Each volume covered roughly a three-to-four-month period. The last journal ended on October 8 of the previous year.

"Look at this," Joanna said, thumbing through the last volume. "Why did she stop?"

"Stop what?" Ernie asked.

"Keeping a journal. Bree started doing it three years ago. From the looks of it, she poured her heart and soul into these books. Each day's entry covers one to three pages, and one volume fills three to four months. Then, at the end of the first week of last October, she stops cold. But her mother just told us that Bree writes in her diary every night before she goes to sleep. So what's happened to the last eight months' worth of entries?"

Ernie came over to where Joanna was standing and squinted down at the shelf from which she had removed the volume she was still holding.

"Where'd this one come from?" he asked.

Joanna pointed. "Right there," she said.

"Bree took one with her," Ernie said decisively. "The ghost of the book's footprint is still here, in the dust at the back of the shelf behind the books. That means that, if she's continued to write her diary entries at the same pace, she may have taken two volumes along—one completed and the other nearly so."

"Why?" Joanna asked.

"Something to do with that nonexistent boyfriend maybe? But if she went to all the trouble of taking both journals along, why didn't she take the pills, too?"

Joanna thought about that for a moment. "According to Katherine, she didn't generally come into Bree's room. If she did, the books were all there on the bookshelf, in plain sight. The pills were put away."

Ernie shook his head. "None of that makes much sense to me," the detective said. "But then I'm not a girl."

"I suppose I am?" Joanna returned.

"Aren't you?"

Had anyone else in the department called Sheriff Brady a girl, she might well have taken offense. But Ernie Carpenter was a crusty homicide detective who, from the very beginning, had treated Joanna as a fellow officer—a peer—rather than as an unwelcome interloper. Their already positive relationship had solidified when the two of them had narrowly survived a potentially fatal dynamite blast. Since they were comrades in arms, Joanna was able to overlook Ernie's occasional lapses into male chauvinism.

"Look," Joanna replied, "girl or not, it doesn't take a genius to see what's going on here. Bree was far more worried about her parents' finding out what was in her journal than she was about them stumbling over her supply of birth control pills. So that's where we have to start—with whatever is in that journal."

"Great," Ernie said. "But as you've already noticed, the last seven or eight months of entries are missing."

"No problem," Joanna said. "Just because whatever Bree wrote is a deep dark secret to her family, that doesn't mean it is to everyone else. Half the students at Bisbee High School may know what's been going on. The trick is going to be getting one of them to tell us."

"Mrs. O'Brien gave me a list of all her friends," Ernie offered.

Joanna shrugged. "We can start with them, I suppose," she said. "But we'll get what we want sooner by talking to Bree's enemies. They're the ones who'll give us the real scoop."

"Enemies!" Ernie sputtered. "What kind of enemies would Bree O'Brien have? She's eighteen years old, comes from a good family, is an honor student, and was valedictorian of her class. That's not the kind of girl you'd expect to be drinking, drugging, or hanging around with gangs, which, as far as I'm concerned, is where most teenage problems and fatalities come from."

Joanna looked at Ernie. He was a man who brought to his position as detective a bedrock of old-fashioned, small-town values. His solid beliefs and common sense had seen him through years of investigating the worst Cochise County had to offer. He and his wife, Rose, had raised two fine sons, both of whom were college graduates—

although neither of the boys had followed his father into law enforcement.

"You and Rose only raised sons," Joanna said. "You probably still believe girls are made of sugar and spice and everything nice."

"Aren't they?" He turned back and once again surveyed Bree O'Brien's almost painfully neat room. "But I don't think that's the case here," he said finally.

"Me either," Joanna said.

"So who's going to give David O'Brien the good news/bad news?" Ernie asked. "Who gets to tell him that his precious daughter most likely hasn't been kidnapped but that she's probably out there somewhere, shacked up for the weekend with an oversexed boyfriend her daddy doesn't know anything about?"

"I suppose," Joanna said without enthusiasm, "that dubious honor belongs to me."

SEVEN

ANGIE KELLOGG tried calling Joanna several times during the course of the afternoon. She had known Joanna was taking Jenny to camp that Saturday morning, but Angie also knew that her friend had expected to be back home in Bisbee some time before dark. Angie was still hoping she'd be able to convince Joanna to go along on the next morning's hummingbird-watching expedition. By the time Angie had to get dressed to go to work, she still didn't have an answer.

What do I do now? she asked herself, standing in front of her closet. *Should I take along hiking clothes or not?*

In the end, she decided to pack a bag with hiking gear just in case. After all, it was early in the evening. There was still plenty of time for Joanna to call.

Picking up the phone, Angie dialed the High Lonesome one last time. "It's Angie again," she said when the machine clicked on. "Give me a call at work as soon as you get in. I really need to talk to you."

🌵 **JOANNA AND** Ernie left Brianna's room together and started back to the living room. Walking down the hallway, Joanna paused to study a collection of framed photographs that lined both walls. There were four distinctly separate groupings of pictures.

One set featured poses of a much younger and still able-bodied David O'Brien. One photo showed him in an old-fashioned Bisbee High School letterman's sweater accepting the Copper Pick trophy from the captain of the Douglas team in the aftermath of a long-ago game in which the Bisbee Pumas had beaten the Douglas Bulldogs. Another showed him standing in front of the entrance of the old high school building on Howell up in Old Bisbee. A third photo showed him in a cap and gown standing next to the fountain in front of Old Main at the University of Arizona. Beside him stood two women—one middle-aged and the other stooped, white-haired, and elderly. *His mother and grandmother,* Joanna assumed.

The first picture in the next group featured a smiling David O'Brien dressed in white tennis togs. One hand gripped a tennis racket while the other arm was draped casually across the bare, halter-topped shoulders of an attractive young woman. Seemingly unaware of the camera, she

smiled up at him with a look of undisguised ado-
ration. When Joanna saw the same woman again
in the next picture—an informal family grouping
posed around a towering Christmas tree—she
realized this had to be David O'Brien's first
family—the wife, daughter, and son who had
perished in a fiery chain reaction wreck on Interstate 10.

The little boy was a somber-faced young man
who bore an uncanny resemblance to his father.
The daughter, with an impish smile and a dis-
arming set of dimples, was a carbon copy of her
mother. It saddened Joanna to see those two
long-dead children, youngsters whose lives had
been snuffed out in a moment, leaving them no
opportunity to grow to adulthood or to experience
all the joys and sorrows life has to offer. With a
sudden ache in her heart, Joanna found herself
missing Jenny.

"This must be his first wife and their two kids,"
Joanna said quickly to Ernie, pointing back at
the Christmas picture.

The detective nodded. "And these must be
Katherine."

In the next grouping, one picture showed a
much younger version of Katherine wearing a
prom dress but standing alone, posing beside an
easy chair all by herself rather than with a male
escort. Another featured a young and smiling
Katherine proudly wearing her black-banded
R.N. cap. A third showed her beaming down at a
scowling newborn baby that had to be Brianna.

The last section, one featuring almost as many photos as the other three combined, featured Bree O'Brien herself. Among others there were shots of her on a tricycle, clasping a teddy bear under each arm. One frame held a family Christmas card featuring a toothless six-year-old Brianna along with a caption that read, "All I want for Christmas is my two front teeth." Another photo was a pose of her in a BHS cheerleading uniform. The last picture in the montage was a framed copy of Bree's senior portrait, the same one that had been featured in the newspaper prior to graduation.

Seeing the pictures grouped together like that gave Joanna the odd sensation of having all those people's lives spread out in almost instant replay fashion. The one woman and the two children had been wiped off the face of the earth, leaving behind hardly a trace—other than a few photographs—to testify to their all-too-brief lives. David O'Brien had gone from being a strappingly handsome, healthy young man to an embittered, wheelchair-bound, old one. Katherine's bright-eyed and sweetly smiling nurse's portrait was totally at odds with the dignified and sadly reserved middle-aged woman she had become. As for Brianna, there was nothing in the photos that gave any kind of hint about the existence of the double life that, Joanna was convinced, lay hidden in her missing journal entries.

After studying the pictures, Ernie must have reached the same conclusion. Pointing to the senior portrait, he shook his head. "A picture's supposed to be worth a thousand words," he said sadly. "But it makes you wonder, doesn't it?"

Joanna nodded. "It certainly does," she said.

BACK IN the O'Briens' living room, David and Katherine sat in front of a massive stone fireplace. David's wheelchair was parked on one side. Katherine's overstuffed brocade-covered chair was opposite his. Both Katherine and David held fist-sized cocktail glasses in their hands. As soon as Joanna walked into the room, Katherine's eyes sought hers. That silent, pleading look spoke volumes. *Please don't tell my husband about the pills,* it said. Her voice, however, belied the desperate message in her eyes.

"Won't you reconsider and join us?" Katherine asked. She gestured graciously toward a silver serving tray stocked with several crystal glasses, a matching ice bucket, and a selection of liquor bottles. The tray, placed well within reach, sat on an elegantly carved ebony coffee table. "Or, if you wish," Katherine continued, "Mrs. Vorevkin could bring in a fresh pitcher of tea."

David O'Brien frowned as though finding his wife's offer of hospitality somehow offensive. Polishing off the liquid in his own glass, he leaned over, slamming the crystal glass down on the tray hard enough to jangle the bottles standing there. After tossing in a couple of ice cubes, he refilled his glass with a generous serving from a half-empty bottle of Chivas Regal.

"No, thank you . . ." Joanna began.

"Stop it, Katherine," O'Brien ordered. "That isn't necessary. No sense treating these two cops like they're honored guests or long-lost relatives. They're here for business, not pleasure."

Katherine blanched at the rebuke. Wanting to make her feel better, Joanna ignored David O'Brien's rudeness and turned instead to his wife. "Your husband is right, Mrs. O'Brien," Joanna said smoothly. "Detective Carpenter and I are here on business. It's very kind of you, but it isn't necessary to treat us as guests. And, now that we're finished, we need to be going."

Katherine had been ordered to stifle, and she did so. She nodded mutely in response, holding her mouth in a thin, straight line while her eyes welled with tears. David O'Brien, however, seemed oblivious to the fact that his actions had caused his wife any discomfort. Still fuming, he turned his attention on Joanna.

"Well, Sheriff Brady," he continued brusquely, "what have you decided? Are you going to call in the FBI or not?"

"Not," Joanna replied. "I realize, Mr. O'Brien, that you're under the impression that some serious harm has come to your daughter. However, nothing we found in her room gives any indication of foul play. According to what your wife could tell us about your daughter's things, the clothing Bree packed when she left home is consistent with someone going away for a few days—of someone going away with every intention of returning. Your daughter told you she'd be back on Sunday afternoon, correct?"

"Yes, but . . ."

"How old is she, Mr. O'Brien?"

"She turned eighteen in March."

"Not a juvenile, then. She's of an age where the law allows her to come and go as she pleases, regardless of her parents' wishes. Until she misses her Sunday afternoon estimated time of arrival or until you receive some kind of threat or ransom demand, there's really nothing more we can do."

"Can or will?" David O'Brien asked.

"We've already done something," Joanna countered reasonably. "Probably more than we should have under the circumstances. Even though Brianna doesn't officially qualify as a missing person, my department has nonetheless alerted authorities both here and in New Mexico to be on the lookout for her."

"But not the FBI."

"No."

"And you have no intention of notifying them?"

David O'Brien was clearly a bully—someone who was accustomed to having his own way each and every time, no questions asked.

"As I told you earlier," Joanna said, "we won't take that kind of action unless there's some compelling evidence to indicate that a kidnapping has actually taken place."

The unwavering calmness in Joanna's answer seemed to provoke David O'Brien and make him bristle that much more. "I thought as much," he said. "But that's all right. You do your thing, Sheriff Brady, and I'll do mine."

"David . . ." Katherine began, but he silenced her once more with a single baleful glare. Again the woman subsided into her chair. She said nothing more aloud, but the fingers gripping her partially filled glass showed white at the knuckles.

Looking at the woman, the phrase "contents under pressure" suddenly popped into Joanna's head. That was what Katherine O'Brien was like. She seemed to be forever walking on eggshells around her husband, trying to keep things from him—things like learning about his daughter's birth control pills—that might provoke . . . what?

For the first time, the possibility of domestic violence entered into the equation. Joanna had been sheriff long enough to know that domestic violence was a part of all too many seemingly happy marriages in Cochise County and throughout the rest of the country as well. DV calls came from homes at all socioeconomic levels and all walks of life. David O'Brien was in his seventies, but his bare arms bulged with the muscles and sinews used to propel his nonmotorized wheelchair. His hands, callused from turning the rubber wheels, would come equipped with a powerful grip. Used as weapons, those same hands could be dangerous, although, in Joanna's opinion, the words that came from his mouth—words steeped in anger and bitterness—seemed damaging enough.

Joanna thought again of the almost obsessive neatness of Brianna's room—of the *House Beautiful* quality of the whole spacious and well-appointed place. Some people were good housekeepers by their very nature, but Sheriff Brady had learned from reading her deputies' incident reports that in some relationships keeping a clean house was a stipulation—a requirement to be met on a daily basis—in order to keep from earning a smack in the mouth. Or worse. In that kind of environment, Bree's birth control pills, her missing journal entries, and even her own AWOL status made far more sense. For that matter, so did Katherine's obvious fear of rocking the boat.

Joanna turned back to David. He was studying her with narrowed eyes, as if expecting her to cave in to his demands.

"What do you mean by your thing and my thing, Mr. O'Brien?" she asked.

"It means that as soon as I saw your department's reluctance to call in reinforcements, I went ahead and made other arrangements. I've contacted a private eye up in Phoenix. Detective Stoddard will be here by nine o'clock tomorrow morning. You may be unwilling or unable to do the job, Sheriff Brady. I'm sure my PI won't be."

"Hiring a detective is certainly your prerogative, Mr. O'Brien," Joanna returned. "It may prove to be a waste of money, however, especially if your daughter shows up on her own as scheduled tomorrow afternoon."

"Even if she does, it's my money," O'Brien said sourly.

"Of course," Joanna agreed. "And you're entitled to spend it in whatever manner you see fit. Good evening, then." She started to leave, but then stopped and turned back. "May I ask one more question?"

"What's that?"

"Have you noticed any changes in your daughter's behavior in the last few months?"

"What's this? You're asking me questions about a daughter you insist isn't really missing?"

Joanna ignored the jibe. "Has she changed?"

O'Brien shrugged. "Of course she's changed," he said. "Night to day. As though she had a personality transplant. Telling us one thing and doing another is just the tip of the iceberg." He paused long enough to glower at his wife, as though he held Katherine personally accountable for his daughter's emerging dishonesty.

"She never should have dropped out of the cheerleading squad," he continued. "That was the beginning of all this and a grave disappointment to me as well. I didn't raise my daughter to be a quitter. That's not what O'Briens do."

You mean being student body vice president and class valedictorian weren't enough? Joanna wanted to ask, but she didn't. Instead, she stifled that question in favor of another. "She just quit?"

David O'Brien might have wanted Katherine to keep quiet, but his orders weren't enough to suppress a mother's natural inclination to defend her daughter. "Miss Barker had to drop her," Katherine interjected. "It happened back in November. At the end of football season. Because Bree had been captain of the squad, there was a bit of a flap about it. You may have heard . . ."

From the moment Joanna had found her wounded husband shot and bleeding in a sandy wash her every waking moment had been preoccupied with her own concerns, with her own survival and with Jenny's. Joanna Brady had had very little energy left over to squander on anyone else's difficulties. In that kind of emotion-charged atmosphere, it was hardly surprising that a tempest centered in and around the local high school cheerleading squad had failed to penetrate her consciousness.

Joanna shook her head. "I don't remember hearing anything about it," she said.

"You're probably the only one," David said. "It happened during the Bisbee-Douglas game. One of the players from Douglas—some young Mexican kid—ended up getting hurt. Had his leg broken, I guess. Bree was upset about it beyond all reason. She walked off the field right in the middle of the game. Left the ballpark and went directly to the hospital. Naturally, the cheerleading adviser had no choice but to put her off the squad."

Joanna counted off the months in her head. November through June. Seven months. About the same length of time covered by the missing journals. "And that was when you first noticed the change in her?"

"She was moody, I suppose," Katherine said. "But that was understandable. After all, losing her position on the squad was a very real loss to her, a blow to her self-esteem. There's some grieving to be done after something like that happens.

Grieving and a certain amount of acting out. But beyond that, she was fine. It's not like it interfered with her grades or anything."

Realizing Katherine was once again attempting to smooth things over and to minimize whatever had happened, Joanna decided to press the issue. "What kind of acting out?" she asked.

"She called me a bigot, among other things," David O'Brien snarled, his face darkening with rage. From the looks of him, Bree's accusatory words might still be hanging in the charged air around him. "My own daughter called me that to my face when I tried to explain to her that some stupid Mexican having his leg broken was no reason for her to give up something she'd wanted for years—something the whole family had worked for."

Joanna couldn't help noticing the sneer in O'Brien's voice when he said the word *Mexican*. She also remembered his irrational refusal to deal with Detective Jaime Carbajal. *Maybe*, she thought, *Brianna O'Brien's assessment of her father was right on the money.*

"Are you a bigot, Mr. O'Brien?" Joanna asked.

The room grew still. Raising his bushy eyebrows, Ernie Carpenter shifted uneasily from one foot to the other. The silence lasted so long that Joanna wondered if perhaps she had gone too far, but David O'Brien didn't appear to be especially offended by the question. In fact, he seemed to like the idea that Joanna was standing up to him and pushing back.

"Are you aware that I'm from here originally?" he asked at last, favoring Joanna with an unexpected but grim smile. She nodded.

"Not just from Bisbee," he continued. "But from right here on the outskirts of Naco. My father, Tom O'Brien, died of a ruptured appendix when I was two. Growing up in a border town makes it tough for kids. On both sides. I didn't transfer to St. Dominick's in Old Bisbee until I was in the third grade. Before that I was one of the only Anglo kids in Naco Elementary. The Mexican kids down here used to beat me up every day, Sheriff Brady. Not only that, it was a Mexican driving the truck that killed my first family, smashed my legs to smithereens, and sentenced me to a wheelchair for the rest of my natural life. So believe me, if I've got my prejudices, maybe I'm entitled. That's what I told Brianna, and that's what I'm telling you."

EIGHT

NOT KNOWING what to say in response, Joanna headed for the door. As she did so, Katherine reached forward and plucked a small silver bell off the coffee table. Moments after she rang it, Mrs. Vorevkin appeared in the room. "Olga," Katherine said, "please show Sheriff Brady and Detective Carpenter out."

The housekeeper nodded in her stolid, impassive way and started down the hallway. She was standing in front of the open door waiting for them to step outside when Joanna stopped beside her. "Can you tell us anything about all this, Mrs. Vorevkin?" Joanna asked.

The woman's faded blue eyes welled with tears. "I packed the food," she said brokenly. "Just like before. I did not mean to cause trouble."

"What trouble?" Joanna demanded. "And what food?"

"A bag of sandwiches, chips, some fresh fruit,

113

and sodas," Olga answered. "She always wanted plenty of sodas, root beer and Cokes, both."

Joanna frowned. "Two kinds?"

Olga nodded. "Several of each."

"And what kinds of sandwiches?"

"Peanut butter and bologna."

"How many?"

"Five of each."

Joanna turned to Ernie. "What do you think?" she asked.

"Either Brianna O'Brien was one heavy eater or the picnic lunch was being made for more than one person."

"That's what I think," Joanna said, returning her gaze to Olga's placid face. "You were the last person here to see her?" Joanna asked.

Olga nodded.

"What was she wearing?"

Olga glanced toward Ernie. "He ask me already, but I don't remember. Too upset. She's a good girl, Brianna," the woman added after a moment. "A nice girl. A very nice girl. You find her and bring her home."

Sheriff Brady saw no point in attempting to explain the twenty-four-hour missing persons rule to Olga Vorevkin. "We will," she promised instead. "We'll do our very best."

Outside in the driveway, the only official vehicles left were Ernie's white van and Joanna's Crown Victoria. Alf Hastings, David O'Brien's chief of operations, sat on a folding camp stool next to Joanna's sedan. He was smoking the stub of a powerful cigar.

"Where'd everybody go?" Joanna asked.

Hastings shrugged. "Beats me," he said. "Call came in over the radio, and they all took off like they'd been shot out of a cannon."

Opening the car door, Joanna reached for her radio. "Sheriff Brady here," she said. "What's going on?"

Larry Kendrick, the Cochise County Sheriff Department's lead dispatcher, took the call. "We had what at first sounded like a serious explosion over in St. David. Everything's pretty much under control now, but Chief Deputy Voland didn't want to disturb either you or Detective Carpenter while you were talking to the O'Briens. Voland headed over to St. David right away, along with two other cars."

Joanna's heart constricted to hear the words *explosion* and *St. David* mentioned in the same sentence. St. David was the site of a nitrate-manufacturing plant that specialized in both fertilizers and explosives. "Not the Apache Powder Plant," she breathed.

"No," Kendrick reassured her. "It wasn't nearly that serious. It was at a farm near the river on the other side of town, off to the south rather than to the northwest."

"Any injuries?"

"None reported so far. There was a small fire. Out-buildings only. As I understand it, that's out now."

"Keep me posted anyway," Joanna said. Sliding her thumb away from the push-to-talk switch, she turned to Hastings. The man stood up, making a production of grinding out what was left of his cigar. "If you're ready to go, I'll get my ATV and lead you as far as the gate."

"That's not really necessary," Joanna objected. "I'm sure we can find our way out."

"I'm sure you can, ma'am," Hastings said, doffing his hat. "But orders are orders, and since the guy giving the orders also writes my checks, I've got no choice but to follow 'em."

Hastings ambled away, leaving Joanna and Ernie alone in the deepening twilight. "What do we do now, Coach?" the detective asked.

"Tomorrow's another day," Joanna told him. "We go home. You take off your tie, I take off my high heels, and we both put our feet up."

"You really don't want me to do anything more tonight?" Ernie asked.

Joanna shook her head. "No," she replied. "We're not going to move on this case unless and until Brianna O'Brien doesn't show up tomorrow afternoon."

"Are you sure that's wise?" Ernie asked. "It looks to me as though David O'Brien has more money than God. And clout to match. What if he decides to put you out of office?"

Joanna shrugged. "This is a free country and that's his God-given right. In the meantime, you and I are charged with providing equality under the law. That means for everybody, David O'Brien included. If we have a twenty-four-hour waiting period for every other missing person in Cochise County, then we have a twenty-four-hour waiting period for him as well."

"Sounds good to me," Ernie said, loosening his tie and setting off for his van.

Hastings rumbled up just then on his ATV. First Ernie and then Joanna fell into line behind him. At the far gate, there was a turnout along a side road that provided a stopping place just inside the fence. Hastings swerved off the roadway onto the parking strip, leaving enough room for Joanna and Ernie to drive past as the gate swung open. Checking in her mirror, Joanna saw him wait until both vehicles had cleared the gate before he let it swing shut and drove away.

Fort O'Brien, Joanna thought. *That would have been a much better name for the place. Taking all the security into consideration, Green Brush Ranch just doesn't do it.*

JOANNA HAD traveled only a mile or two back toward town when hunger suddenly asserted itself. It had been almost eight hours since her lunchtime Whopper in Benson. At that hour, the idea of going home to cook was out of the question. Instead of driving directly to High Lonesome Ranch, she headed for Bisbee's Bakerville neighborhood and Daisy's Cafe.

On that still-steamy June Saturday night, other Bisbeeites must have had much the same idea. The draw might have been the almost chilly air-conditioning in the restaurant as much as it was the food. Whatever the reason, Daisy's was jammed. People stood in clutches of two and three in the cashier's lobby area, waiting for one of the booths or tables to clear. When Daisy Maxwell, the owner, came to collect the next pair of customers, she spied Joanna standing alone.

"You here by yourself?" Daisy asked, picking up a fistful of menus.

Joanna nodded.

"There's a single up at the counter. You're welcome to that if you like," Daisy told her. "Everybody else is at least a two-top."

Collecting a menu of her own, Joanna headed for the single empty stool. She waited while Daisy's husband, Moe, finished clearing the spot of dirty dishes before she sat down. "What are you doing here?" she asked.

Moe Maxwell's usual place of employment was the Bisbee branch of the post office. His primary role in his wife's restaurant was as chief occupant of the booth nearest the door. There, ensconced with a view that included both the cash register and a tiny black-and-white TV, he would while away his weekend hours drinking coffee and visiting with whichever one of his many cronies happened to stop by.

Sorrowfully, Moe shook his head. "Don't even ask," he said, placing a glass of ice water in front of Joanna. "I was drafted. When it got crowded, Daisy said I could either go to work or plan on spending the night with old Hoop out in his doghouse tonight when we get home. That didn't leave me much of an option."

Joanna laughed. "I suppose not," she said.

"Hot enough for you?" Moe continued, half-heartedly wiping the counter.

Joanna nodded. "And wouldn't you know, the air-conditioning went out in my car today. I had to take my daughter to camp up on Mount Lemmon. Between now and when I go to pick her up, I'll have to get it fixed."

"Good luck with that," Moe said. "You'd better call for an appointment right away. Jim Hobbs is the only mechanic I know of around town who's doing that right now. People are lined up out the door. I just went through it myself a couple of weeks back, me and my old GMC. I can tell you this, it lightened my wallet by a thousand bucks."

Joanna almost choked on a single sip of water. "A thousand dollars?" she repeated in dismay. "You're kidding. To fix an air conditioner?"

Moe nodded, looking even sadder than before. "That's right," he replied. "I'm not sure I understand all the details. Has something to do with global warming and holes in the ozone. According to Jim Hobbs, one itty-bitty little thirty-pound canister of Freon costs a thousand bucks a pop these days. Jim retrofitted my truck with some new kind of compressor that uses something else. I can't remember exactly what it's called. Had a whole bunch of letters and numbers. R2D2, maybe? Anyways, the damned thing cost me a fortune, and it doesn't work nearly as well as the Freon did, either. I would have just let it go, but you know Daisy. With her hair the way it is, she can't even ride to the grocery store with the windows rolled down."

Joanna looked across the room to where Daisy was separating yet another two people from the herd waiting near the door. For thirty years, a towering beehive—one with each peroxided blond hair lacquered firmly into place—had been Daisy Maxwell's signature hairdo. The mere fact that the price of Freon had shot sky-high wasn't enough to make her change it.

Daisy delivered the two waiting diners to a nearby booth and then detoured behind the counter on her way back to the cash register. Slipping past her husband, she gave him a swift jab in the ribs with one bony elbow. "Booth six needs bussing," she told him. "So does table two."

With a long-suffering sigh, Moe picked up a wet rag and went to clear the tables.

"He'd a whole lot rather gab than work," Daisy complained, pulling a pencil out of her hair and an order pad out of her apron pocket. "If that man really was on my payroll, I would've fired him by now. Since he's working for free, though, what can I do? Now, if you know what you want, I can put the order in on my way through the kitchen. Otherwise it'll take a while for me to get back to you. We're shorthanded tonight. I didn't expect this kind of crowd."

"Chef's salad," Joanna said without bothering to look at the menu. "Ranch dressing on the side. Iced tea with extra lemon."

"Corn bread or sticky bun?"

"Definitely sticky bun," Joanna answered.

"You got it," Daisy said, and hurried off.

The tea came within less than a minute. Stirring in sugar, Joanna became aware of the music playing through the speakers situated at either end of the counter.

Reba McEntire sang of a lonely woman living through the aftermath of a painful divorce. The lyrics were all about how hard it was to sleep in a bed once shared with a no-longer-present husband. Regardless of the cause of that absence—death or divorce—Joanna knew that the loneliness involved was all the same, most especially so at bedtime, although mealtimes weren't much better.

Determined to shut out the words, Joanna sat sipping her tea and observing the people in the room through the mirror on the far side of the counter. Unfortunately, she could see nothing but couples. Pairs. Men and women—husbands and wives—eating and talking and laughing together. In the far corner of the room sat a young couple with a toddler in a high chair. The child was happily munching saltine crackers while the man and woman talked earnestly back and forth together.

Struck by a sudden jolt of envy, Joanna forced herself to look away. It reminded her too much of the old days when Jenny was at what Andy had called the "crumb-crusher stage." It had been a period during which every meal out—whether in a restaurant or at someone else's home—had included the embarrassment of a mess of cracker crumbs left around Jenny's high chair.

Right about now, Joanna thought, *I'd be so happy to have a few of those crumbs back again that I wouldn't even complain about having to clean them up.*

🌵 **BY THE** time Joanna's salad came, the hunger she had felt earlier had entirely disappeared. She picked at the pale pieces of canned asparagus and moved the chunks of bright red tomato from side to side. It was easy to feel sorry for herself, to wallow in her own misery and self-pity. Butch Dixon, a man she had met up in Peoria when she went there to attend the Arizona Police Officer's Academy, had made it quite clear that he was more than just moderately interested in her. But Joanna didn't think she was ready for that. Not yet. She was glad to have Butch as a friend—as a pal and as someone to talk to on the phone several times a week—but it was still too soon for anything beyond that, not just for Joanna but also for Jenny.

"Mind if I sit down?"

Joanna looked up to see Chief Deputy Richard Voland standing with one hand on the back of the now-vacant stool next to her.

"Hi, Dick," she said. "Help yourself."

She was grateful Daisy's was a public enough venue that Voland's ears didn't turn red as he eased his tall frame down onto the stool. Opening a menu, he studied it in silence for some time before slapping it shut. "Batching it is hell, isn't it?" he grumbled. "Ruth maybe had her faults, but she was one helluva cook."

Ruth Voland, Dick's soon-to-be-ex-wife, had taken up with their son's bowling coach from Sierra Vista. Their divorce was due to be final within the next few weeks. As that day loomed closer, Chief Deputy Voland was becoming more and more difficult to be around.

"You're right," Joanna agreed. "It's not much fun, but thanks to people like Daisy Maxwell, neither of us is starving to death."

Voland nodded morosely. "Hope you don't mind my tracking you down. Dispatch said you were stopping off to have dinner. I needed to grab a bite myself."

Daisy came to take his order. Joanna waited until she left before speaking again. "So what's up over in St. David?"

"Killer bees," Voland answered. "It was unbelievable."

"Killer bees?" Joanna repeated. "I thought there was some kind of an explosion."

"That's right. There was. A lady by the name of Ethel Jamison found a swarm of killer bees up under the roof of a tool shed. Her great-grandson is down visiting from Provo, Utah, for a couple of weeks. He offered to take care of them for her. So he and a buddy of his logged onto the Internet, consulted some kind of cyberspace *Anarchist's Cookbook*, and blew the place to pieces, bees and all. Except they didn't quite get all the bees. Like this one, for example," Voland added, pointing to an ugly red welt on the back of his hand. "And this one, too." A second vivid welt showed itself on the back of his neck, just above his wilted shirt collar.

"I wasn't the only one who got stung, either," Voland added. "A couple of the volunteer firemen did, too. Naturally, the two boys didn't."

Dick's coffee came. He stopped talking long enough to add cream and sugar. "So what's happening on the O'Brien deal?"

"Nothing," Joanna said.

"But I thought . . ."

"Brianna O'Brien may not have gone where she *said* she was going," Joanna told him, "but she's not yet officially missing. According to her parents, she's not due back until tomorrow afternoon. If and when that deadline passes, we'll make an official missing persons determination."

"You're going to wait the full twenty-four hours?" Dick Voland asked. "David O'Brien will have a cow."

"He's already having a cow, so I don't see what difference it makes."

"David O'Brien isn't someone I'd want to get crosswise with," Voland warned. "From a political standpoint if nothing else. With his kind of money, he can make or break you."

Joanna gave her chief deputy a sidelong glance. "I'm surprised to hear you say that, Mr. Voland," she told him. "Aren't you the same guy who was out on the stump during the election, trying to get people to vote against me?"

Voland ducked his head and shrugged self-consciously. "Maybe I changed my mind," he said while his ears glowed bright red.

It was Saturday night. Knowing small-town gossipmongers might read far more into this casual dinnertime meeting than it merited, Joanna picked up her ticket and slid off her stool.

"I'd better be going," she said. "See you Monday."

"Right," Dick returned. "See you then."

NINE

JOANNA WENT out to the Crown Victoria and drove north toward the traffic circle where Jim Hobbs's auto repair shop was located. Remembering Moe Maxwell's advice that she put the Eagle in the shop for repairs as soon as possible, she glanced off in that direction. To her surprise, even after nine o'clock on a Saturday night, the lights were still on at Jim's Auto Repair. One of the two garage bay doors was still open.

Instead of heading out toward the ranch, Joanna drove on around the circle and pulled in beside Jim's cherished 1956 Chevy BelAir. Jim himself was hanging over the front fender of a Honda Civic. He straightened up when he heard Joanna's car stop and sauntered out of the garage, wiping his greasy hands on a rag.

"It's you, Sheriff Brady," he said, grinning when he recognized Joanna. "I thought it would be Margo come to tell me to get the hell home.

But since I'm working on my mother-in-law's car, I don't figure I'll be in too much trouble. What can I do for you?"

"It's the air-conditioning on my Eagle," Joanna began. "It went out on the way to Tucson today. Moe Maxwell says I'll need to get in line for an appointment, so I thought I'd check."

The congenial grin disappeared from Jim's face. "It's a setup deal, isn't it? A sting. As soon as I got the call, I figured it would be something like this. Sorry, Sheriff Brady. I'm all booked up for air-conditioning work. I won't be able to get around to you for a month or so, maybe even longer."

"A month?" Joanna echoed. "That long? Right in the middle of the summer?"

"Too bad, isn't it," Jim returned coldly. "But like I said, it might even be longer than that." Then, as if dismissing her, he turned and headed back into the garage.

For several moments Joanna sat there wavering in confusion. Jim Hobbs had done lots of work for her over the years. She had no idea what had provoked him or why she would deserve such an abrupt dismissal. Something was wrong. Not wanting to leave the misunderstanding hanging, Joanna climbed out of the Crown Victoria and followed him into the garage.

Jim's Auto Repair had arisen from the ruins of a defunct gas station, one that had become a permanent casualty in the EPA's ongoing war against leaky gasoline tanks. Anyone walking into the orderly but run-down building would have known at once where Jim Hobbs's priorities lay.

The grungy cinder block walls, the fly-specked dirty glass, and the cracked cement flooring might have all been seventy-year-old original construction, but there was nothing old or lacking in the gleaming tools and up-to-date equipment lining the walls.

Walking inside, Joanna stood for a long time watching Jim in silence while he studiously ignored her. "All right, Jim," she said at last, trailing him over to a metal tool chest where he slammed a wrench into one of the drawers. "What's going on?"

"I'll tell you what's going on," he growled, turning on her and poking the air between them with one of his stubby fingers. "That weasely Sam Nettleton character over in Benson gives me a call this afternoon and tells me he's got a cool deal on some really cheap Freon if I want to go in with him on it. Well, here's the real scoop, Sheriff Brady. I didn't bite, so you can call off your dogs and forget it. I've got twenty thousand bucks tied up in legally approved equipment to do air-conditioning work the right way. The reason I'm as busy as a one-armed paperhanger right now is that hardly anyone else in the county has bothered to invest in that new equipment—including Mr. Sleazeball Sam Nettleton. If you think you're going to waltz in here and find me using illegal Freon—"

"Wait a minute, Jim," Joanna said. "Hold on. I don't have any idea what you're talking about. I stopped in here to see about getting my Eagle fixed because I almost roasted to death driving Jenny up to Mount Lemmon today."

Jim looked suddenly abashed. "You mean Sam Nettleton didn't try to sic you on me?"

"The person who sent me here is Moe Maxwell. I saw him in Daisy's just a few minutes ago, and he said you had fixed the air-conditioning on his GMC. I don't even know Sam Nettleton. From the sounds of it, though, maybe I should. Care to tell me about him?"

Now Jim looked downright embarrassed. "I shouldn't," he said. "But the whole deal makes me so damned mad."

"What deal?"

"Years ago, the tree huggers in Washington, D.C., got all hot and bothered about holes in the ozone. They fixed it so Congress passed some laws designed to fix 'em. The holes, I mean, not the tree huggers. The first guys the feds went after for chlorofluorocarbon use were the big industries. Now they're coming after us—the little guys. It turns out that Freon is bad for the ozone, and Freon just happens to be what makes most pre-1995 air conditioners run. The U.S. isn't producing R-12 Freon anymore. Newer cars use R-134A. Dealers have to have proper, EPA-approved equipment to work on that or on any other R-12 substitute.

"Some of those supposed substitutes are so bad the cars blow up. Like the two little old ladies who burned to death up on I-40 last summer. Some shyster mechanic over in Gallup had filled up their compressor with something that was more butane than it was anything else."

"Let's get back to Sam Nettleton," Joanna urged. "Who is he? What does he do?"

"He runs an outfit called Sam's Easy Towing and Wrecking up in Benson. He's the kind of guy who gives every other mechanic in the universe a bad name."

"And what's his connection to Freon?"

"Like I said, the U.S. is out of the R-12 business, but other countries are still making it. If they can figure out a way to ship it here, there's a ready black market. Arizona has lots of pre-1995 automobiles that are still on the road. Here in the desert, air-conditioning is a necessity rather than an option. A thirty-pound container of Freon that would have cost thirty bucks a few years ago now sells for nine hundred."

Joanna whistled. "No wonder there's a black market."

Jim nodded. "No wonder."

"Why did Nettleton call you?"

"Who knows? My guess is he needed someone to go in with him on it, someone who could bring along some cash. I've got a reputation for doing more automotive air-conditioning work than anyone else in the county, so he probably figured I could use it. If I bought it at his price and charged the usual markup for the real stuff, it would be a regular gold mine—for a while anyway. Until somebody got wise. But like I told Nettleton on the phone, if the EPA inspectors come in and find me using illegal Freon, I'm out of business, just like that. I'm not going to risk it. And I've been standing here all night, working and stewing about it."

"When's Nettleton's cut-rate Freon supposed to be here?" Joanna asked.

"Sometime soon, I guess," Jim said. "He told me he's got to have the money by Monday noon at the latest."

"He didn't say where the shipment was coming from?"

Hobbs shook his head. "No, but you can pretty much figure it out. It's gotta be Mexico. Maybe all the old drug dealers have switched over and are carrying Freon these days instead of heroin and cocaine." He paused for a moment. "So do you still want me to work on your car?" he asked somewhat sheepishly.

Joanna grinned at him. "As a matter of fact, I do. It's like you said, we're talking necessity here."

"What do you think happened to it?"

"It sounded to me as though the compressor died."

"You want it retrofitted to run on R-134A?"

"That must be the stuff Moe Maxwell calls R2D2. Is that what you did to his GMC—retrofitted it?"

Jim Hobbs nodded.

"Well," Joanna said, "if it's good enough for Daisy Maxwell's beehive, it's good enough for me. When can you do it? I'd like to have it sooner than a month or two if that's possible."

"Okay, okay," Jim said, realizing she was teasing him. "We'll get it done a little sooner than that. Come on into the office. I'll have to check the book."

BACK IN her Crown Victoria Joanna headed east on Highway 80, but again, instead of going straight on out to the ranch, she turned off at the Cochise County Justice Complex. After all, no one was waiting for her at home. *Is that why I'm finding a hundred reasons not to go there?* she wondered.

After a few seconds of reflection, Joanna shoved that unwelcome thought aside, convincing herself, instead, that the real reason she was stopping off at the office was because something Jim Hobbs had said was still niggling at her. Joanna realized that what Hobbs had suggested about drug smugglers switching over to Freon was indeed true. As head of law enforcement for a county with eighty miles of international border inside her jurisdictional boundaries, Sheriff Brady was a member of the MJF—the Multi-Jurisdiction Force—an organization designed specifically to combat border area criminal activities. As such, she was well aware that, after heroin and cocaine, Freon had now moved to number three on the DEA's list of illegal substance smuggling headaches.

Bearing that in mind, Joanna felt obliged to share whatever information she had gleaned with other members of the MJF. Before opening her mouth, however, she wanted to know more specifics. She pulled into the lot at the back of the building, parked in her reserved spot, and then let herself into the office through a private door outfitted with a keypad lock. Once inside, she settled down at her desk, turned on the computer, and logged onto the MJF web site.

As soon as she typed in the word *Freon,* she hit pay dirt. For the next twenty minutes she learned more about the lucrative trade in illicit R-12 smuggling than she ever would have thought possible, including the fact that the Drug Enforcement Agency was now working jointly with the U.S. Customs Service to put a stop to it. When she finished, she picked up the phone and dialed a Tucson number for Adam York, the DEA's local agent in charge, who had become both a colleague and a friend.

"So where are you this time?" Joanna asked when he answered. York's job took him all over the state and even all over the country at times, but through the magic of call-forwarding, his Tucson number always seemed to work.

"Believe it or not," he said, "I'm just sitting here by the pool with a drink in one hand savoring the idea of a Saturday night at home. How about you? You're not in Tucson, are you?"

"I wish," Joanna said. "I'm busy, reading up on Freon."

"Freon. How come?"

"There's a possibility I may have stumbled onto a smuggling operation down here."

Joanna heard Adam York's glass hit a table. The sound of it told her she had the man's undivided attention. "Who?" he asked urgently. "Where?"

"I heard tonight that some guy up in Benson was about to pick up a big load of cut-rate Freon. I thought you might be interested."

"You bet I am. Who is he?"

"His name's Sam Nettleton. Runs a place called Sam's Easy Towing and Wrecking in Benson. I just ran a copy of his rap sheet. Everything from drunk and disorderly to assault. He's also had a number of consumer complaints for exorbitant towing charges. Does this sound like somebody you'd be interested in?"

Over the next few minutes, Joanna gave Adam York a complete rundown on the situation, including Sam's offer to bring Jim Hobbs in on buying what was evidently an illegal shipment of coolant. York listened all the way through.

"This Nettleton guy sounds like a pretty small fish," the DEA agent said when she finished. "But small fish often lead to bigger fish. We've been investigating a big air-conditioning contractor up in Phoenix for months now. So far we haven't been able to put together anything solid. It's not likely the two cases are related, but that's always a possibility. Let me do some checking and get back to you. Is Monday soon enough?"

"Monday will be fine, I guess," Joanna said. "But it may be too late. Remember, that's when the alleged shipment—whatever it is—is supposed to arrive. Nettleton told Jim Hobbs he had to have the cash by noon on Monday in order to pay for it."

"I'll get back to you on this tomorrow, then," Adam promised. "If not in the morning, then tomorrow afternoon for sure. If I can manage it, I'll figure out a way to put this guy under surveillance. What about the fellow who told you about him? What's his name again?"

"Jim Hobbs," Joanna told him. "He runs an auto repair shop here in Bisbee."

"Do you think he'd mind talking to one of my investigators?"

"Are you kidding? He's so pissed about what Sam Nettleton is pulling, I'd be surprised if he wasn't willing to take out an ad in the paper."

Joanna gave Adam York Jim Hobbs's telephone numbers. While the DEA agent's moving pencil made scribbling sounds over the phone, she added, "Sorry about screwing up your peaceful weekend at home."

"Don't worry about it," York said. "Happens all the time. Besides, look who's talking," he added. "It's ten o'clock on a Saturday night, and here you are calling me from the office."

"Don't tell me," Joanna said. "Caller ID. Right?"

"It would have to be," Adam York said with a chuckle. "I'm sure as hell no psychic."

WHEN JOANNA left the office an hour or so after she arrived, she found that the outside temperature had dropped some. Turning off on Double Adobe Road, she noticed that, off to the southeast, at the southernmost corner of the vast Sulphur Springs Valley, there were a few muted flickers of light on the distant horizon. Lightning. The first storms of the summer monsoon season were trying to make their way up into the Arizona desert from the Gulf of California.

Traditionally, summer rains always arrived just in time to throw a wet blanket on Bisbee's Fourth of July fireworks celebration. But Independence Day was still more than two weeks away. In the meantime, Joanna expected there would be more days of scorching summer temperatures accompanied by the added complication of gradually increasing humidity.

She had barely turned off onto the High Lonesome's dirt track of a road when Tigger, a clownish golden retriever/pit bull mix—and Sadie, a leggy bluetick hound—bounded into the moving glow of headlights to greet the car and race the Crown Victoria back to the house. When Joanna parked and opened her door, the dogs raced around to the far side of the vehicle in a frenzied but futile search for Jenny.

"Too bad, guys," Joanna told them. "No Jenny tonight. Sad to say, you two are going to have to make do with just me for the next little while."

Out of habit, Joanna had switched off the cooler when she had left for Green Brush Ranch late that afternoon. Now, at ten o'clock at night, the inside of the house felt overheated, especially when compared to the far more moderate temperatures outdoors. Once Joanna turned on the old swamp cooler, she knew it would take an hour or more for it to work its magic. In the meantime, she stripped off her work clothes in favor of shorts and an old T-shirt. Then, pausing only long enough to take messages off the machine, she collected her new cordless phone, a tablet, and a pen and went outside onto the front porch. Settling into the swing, she began returning calls.

Eva Lou Brady, Joanna's mother-in-law, had called early in the afternoon to invite Joanna to come to dinner after church on Sunday. One of the organizers of the Fourth of July parade had called to see if Sheriff Brady would be willing to step in as grand marshal now that Bisbee's mayor, Agnes Pratt, had been sidelined with an emergency appendectomy. There were also two separate calls from Joanna's friend Angie Kellogg—one from home and one from work.

The parade call couldn't be returned until Monday, and Angie would be at work until two o'clock in the morning. The call to Joanna's in-laws was different. Jim Bob and Eva Lou Brady usually went to bed right after the local news ended at ten-thirty, so she called them back immediately. Jim Bob Brady answered the phone.

"How'd it go?" he asked. "You get Jenny dropped off at camp all right?"

The hours between then and Joanna's last glimpse of Jenny seemed to melt away. The image of her daughter trudging dejectedly away from the car with her camp counselor caused a sudden tightening in Joanna's throat. "It was fine," she managed, speaking around a lump in her throat that made speech almost impossible. "It would have been better if the air-conditioning in the Eagle hadn't given out on us along the way."

"Did you get it fixed?" Jim Bob asked at once. "Is there anything you need me to do?"

Her in-laws' unfailing helpfulness and generosity never failed to warm Joanna. "Thanks, Jim Bob," she said. "I've already made an appointment with Jim Hobbs to have it fixed."

"Good. What about dinner tomorrow, then?" Jim Bob asked. "Eva Lou doesn't want you to get too lonely out there all by yourself."

"Dinner would be great," Joanna told him. "What time?"

"One. One-thirty."

"I'll be there," Joanna said.

Ending that call, she dialed the bar in Brewery Gulch. Angie Kellogg answered, speaking over the din of talking people and blaring jukebox music. "Blue Moon. Angie speaking."

"It's Joanna. You called?"

"Yes," Angie said. "I wanted to ask a favor, but it doesn't matter. He's already here."

"Who's already there?"

"The parrot guy. He came to take me for a hike tomorrow morning. To see some hummingbirds. I was going to ask you to come along."

"No kidding. The parrot guy? The one from the Chircahuas? What was his name? Hacker, isn't it?"

"That's right," Angie said. "Dennis Hacker."

"And the two of you are going on a hike? That's great."

Angie's voice sounded a little more hopeful. "Could you maybe come along with us?" she asked. "We're going to leave here right after I get off work."

At two o'clock in the morning? Joanna thought. "Sorry, Angie," she said. "I just can't make it. I'm already beat as it is. I've got to go to bed and get some sleep. Not only that, I just made arrangements to have an early dinner with Jim Bob and Eva Lou."

"Oh," Angie said. "Well, I guess I won't go then, either."

"What do you mean you won't go? You love hummingbirds."

"It's just that . . ."

"It's just what?"

"I don't know if I want to go with him all by myself."

Joanna thought back to her one meeting with Hacker. He had come to the Cochise County Sheriff's Department to give a statement in regard to another case. Jenny had been in the office for Take Our Kids to Work Day, Cochise County's modified version of the national Take Our Daughters to Work Day. While there, she had encountered the tall, gangly, and loose-jointed Englishman in the hallway. Afterward, Jenny had come dashing into her mother's office.

"Mom," she had babbled breathlessly, "you'll never guess who's out there in the hall. It's the Scarecrow from the *Wizard of Oz*."

Smiling at the memory, Joanna addressed Angie. "What's the matter?" she asked. "Why don't you want to go out with him? I've met him. He seems like a nice enough guy to me."

"That's just it," Angie said defensively. "I don't know what to think. What if he turns out to be too nice for me or else . . ."

"Or else what?" Joanna asked.

"Well," Angie returned defensively, "what if it turns out to be like the old days? What if we go on a hike to see the birds but he really thinks we're going out there for something else?"

"You wrote him a letter, didn't you?" Joanna asked.

"Yes. He claims that's why he came to see me after all this time—because of the letter."

"What do your instincts tell you?"

"Half one way and half the other."

Joanna smiled. "It sounds like a date to me, Angie," she said kindly. "A regular, ordinary, old-fashioned date for two people to get together and do something they're both interested in. If I were you, I'd go."

"Would you really?"

"Yes."

"I've gotta go," Angie said. "Someone's asking for a drink."

"Have fun," Joanna told her. "Call me tomorrow and tell me how it turned out."

"Okay," Angie said with a dubious sigh. "I will."

TEN

JOANNA PUNCHED the button that ended the call. Putting the phone down on the swing beside her, she picked up the tablet and pen and began to write.

Dear Jenny,

I had to go in to work this afternoon for a little while, so I've only just now come home. If it weren't for Mr. Rhodes stopping by to feed the dogs on a regular basis, they'd be living on the same kind of crazy schedule I am.

It's almost eleven o'clock at night, and it's too hot to be inside, so I'm writing this on the front porch. Even the dogs think it's too hot. They're both lying here beside me, panting like crazy. They didn't much like it when I came home and you didn't get out of the car. Tigger especially couldn't quite believe it.

141

I just took a message off the machine asking me if I could serve as grand marshal of Bisbee's Fourth of July parade. I don't know if you heard about it, but Mayor Pratt had an appendectomy last week. She isn't going to be up to riding in a parade. I'd be happy to sub for her, but I don't happen to own a horse. I was wondering if you'd consider lending me Kiddo for the day.

Joanna paused, holding the pen to her lips. Jenny had begged for a horse for her tenth birthday. Joanna had resisted, only to be overruled by Grandpa Jim Bob, who had purchased the horse on his own. In the months since, though, Joanna had seen the almost magical changes having a horse to care for had wrought in her grieving daughter. Somehow, taking responsibility for an animal who had lost its former master had helped the fatherless Jennifer Ann Brady immeasurably. There were times when it seemed to Joanna that Jenny was making far more progress at working through her grief than her mother was.

I stopped by Jim Hobbs's place tonight and made an appointment to have the Eagle fixed. You'll be happy to know that by the time I come pick you up, we'll once again have a fully working air conditioner.

Joanna paused again. She had already decided to say nothing at all about work or about the type of case that had occupied the whole of her Saturday afternoon. There was no point in mentioning Brianna O'Brien's disappearance. Chances were the missing teenager would show up safe and sound the next afternoon. In that case, if she had been off somewhere fooling around with a boyfriend, the less said, the better. On the other hand, if David O'Brien was right and his daughter had fallen victim to some awful fate, then word of that would come soon enough for everyone—Jennifer Brady included.

With a shock, Joanna realized that Jenny, at ten, was a mere eight years younger than Bree. Determinedly thrusting that disturbing thought aside, Joanna returned to her writing.

Grandpa and Grandma Brady have invited me over for dinner tomorrow after church. I think they're afraid that with you gone for two weeks, I'll dry up and blow away or starve to death.

Speaking of drying up, I can see lightning way off in the distance to the south, somewhere down in Sonora. Maybe the summer rains will get here a little early this year—sooner than the Fourth of July. But not so soon, I hope, that they spoil any of your time at camp.

I guess that's all for now. It's so hot inside the house and so nice out here on the porch that I think I'll do what we used to do on hot summer nights when Dad was alive. Remember how we'd bring those old army cots out here and sleep on the porch? That way, you'll be camping out tonight, and so will I.

Love,
Mom

Joanna addressed an envelope, sealed the letter inside it, and then carried the letter, the phone, and her writing materials back inside. The three old army cots were stowed in the back of Jenny's closet. Joanna dragged one out, brought her pillow and a set of sheets, and returned to the porch. For tonight, at least, she wouldn't be dealing with Reba's double bed problem.

She was on her way back outside for the last time when the phone rang. That late at night, there were only two real possibilities—something had happened at work, some new emergency that demanded the sheriff's attention; or else, things had quieted down enough at the Roundhouse Bar and Grill up in Peoria and Butch Dixon had found a spare moment to give her a call.

"Did you get Jenny off to camp safe and sound?" Butch asked. "How did it go?"

Glad to hear the sound of his voice, Joanna slipped onto the chair beside the telephone table and tucked her feet up under her. "It went fine," she said, giving Butch the benefit of only the smallest of white lies. "No problems at all."

Later, lying there on the porch, waiting to fall asleep and watching the intermittent flickers of lightning, Joanna reviewed what had gone on during the day. One of the things that stood out in her mind was Ernie's objection to Joanna's use of the word *enemies* in conjunction with Bree O'Brien. Having raised only sons, Ernie was more familiar with little boy kinds of disputes—ones that included straightforward fistfights and uncomplicated rock throwing.

Joanna, however, was acquainted with the kinds of insidious, ego-damaging warfare traditionally practiced on young women by other young women. Joanna Lathrop Brady had been there and done that. Her nemesis at Bisbee High School had been a girl named Rowena Sharp.

Popular and smart and blessed with two doting parents, Stub and Chloe Sharp, Rowena had been everything Joanna Lathrop wasn't. In fact, now that she thought about it, Bree O'Brien reminded Joanna of Rowena. Going through adolescence is tough enough, but Joanna Lathrop had also been dealing with the loss of her father. For some reason, Rowena had singled Joanna out as the object of unmerciful torment and contempt. Not only that, Rowena's gal pals had risen to the occasion and joined in the fun, not unlike a flock of cannibalistic chickens pecking to death some poor wounded and defenseless bird that had happened to wander into their midst.

Joanna never knew what she had done to merit Rowena's scorn, but it was something she had been forced to endure, day in and day out. There had been bitchy remarks about "Miss Goody Two-shoes" in the girls' rest room and the cafeteria lunch line. There had been numerous and undeniably deliberate pushings in the hall and gym when Joanna's back was turned to open her locker. It wasn't until late in their senior year that things had changed ever so slightly.

Rowena had been one of two contenders for the position of salutatorian, but she was having a terrible time grasping the basics of chemistry. On her own, she would have earned a solid B in the course, but a B wouldn't have done enough for her GPA. She had persuaded one of her friends—a girl who worked in the principal's office during second period—to lift a copy of Mr. Cantrell's final exam. Word of the pilfered exam had traveled like wildfire through the senior class. Even Joanna heard about it, and she alone had tackled Rowena on the issue.

"Why cheat?" Joanna asked. "Why not just take the grade you've earned on your own?"

"Because it won't be good enough," Rowena shot back. "Because if Mark Watkins is salutatorian instead of me, my parents will just die."

Not wanting to be saddled with more "Miss Goody Two-shoes" remarks, Joanna had kept her mouth shut. Rowena Sharp received her illicit A and graduated second in their class, with Mark Watkins coming in a close third. As for Joanna, she could never look at that page in her senior yearbook without feeling a stab of guilt whenever she saw Rowena's smiling face staring back out at her.

The last time Joanna had seen Rowena Sharp Bonham had been at their ten-year class reunion, where the printed bio had announced that Rowena was an attorney practicing law in Phoenix. Clearly, the passage of time hadn't helped Rowena forget any more than it had helped Joanna. When they encountered one another in the buffet line, Rowena had cut Joanna dead.

Good riddance, Joanna thought as a surprisingly cool breeze wafted over her, letting her drift off to sleep. *As Eva Lou would say, good riddance to the bad rubbish.*

🌵 **LONG AFTER** midnight, Francisco Ybarra sat in the kitchen of his darkened home, keeping company with a bottle of Wild Turkey and worrying.

Frank wasn't much of a drinker. Nonetheless, he poured himself another glassful of bourbon. The hundred-proof liquor warmed his gut as it went down. Maybe eventually sleep would come, but right now he was still wide awake.

Frank's worries had two separate sources—his ailing wife, Yolanda, and Pepito. Hector had told him about the blond girl in the red truck, about how she had come by the station the previous afternoon and about how today Nacio had been in a foul mood all day long. Frank's nephew had left the station after first lashing out at Hector. When he had returned to the station much later in the day, Hector claimed Pepito hadn't been worth a plugged nickel.

Hector had long ago alerted Frank Ybarra to the existence of the girl in the red pickup truck—the one who came by the station, usually when Frank wasn't there and sometimes even when he was. He knew about her long blond ponytail, her long tan legs, and her cute little ass. Frank was sure she had to be the same girl from Bisbee, the one Yolanda had been all over Pepito about last winter.

Frank had known from very early on about what was going on, but he had decided to let it go—to allow the affair to run its own course—because he was confident Pepito would get over it eventually. Now he wasn't so sure.

From outside the house, came the sound of familiar tires crunching the gravel of the back alley. A pair of glowing headlights dissolved into darkness. Not moving, not reaching for the light, Frank Ybarra sat in the dark and waited, listening for the telltale creak of the iron gate and for Nacio's limping steps on the wooden planks of the back porch.

Stealthily, almost as though he were willing the sometimes fussy lock to silence, Nacio's key clicked in the keyhole. The door opened. Almost simultaneously, the overhead light came on. Illuminated in the glaring fluorescent glow, Ignacio Ybarra was a bruised and bloodied mess. His scraped and scabby face looked as though it had been dragged along a sidewalk. Underneath the torn material of a ragged shirt, Frank glimpsed a layer of bandages encircling the boy's chest.

"What happened?" Frank asked, even though he thought he already knew the answer.

The door was still open when Nacio saw his uncle. He turned and would have fled back into the night, had Francisco Ybarra not stopped him. "I asked you, what happened?"

"I got in a fight," Nacio said, slipping unconcernedly onto a chair and trying to sound casual. "A guy beat me up."

Uncle Frank stood up, a little unsteadily, and

walked around the table to the far side of Nacio's chair. He stared down at his nephew for a moment, then, walking with great dignity, Frank returned to his chair. He had seen beatings before. He knew what they looked like.

"What guy?" he asked, his face going still and cold. "An Anglo?"

Nacio nodded.

"Which one?"

"Just a guy," Nacio answered. "I can't say."

"The hell you can't!" Uncle Frank returned savagely, pounding the table with his fist. He realized then he was more than a little drunk. "You can tell me, and you will. People can't get away with this kind of shit anymore. You tell me who it was who did this. I'll call the cops."

"No," Ignacio insisted. "No cops."

"Why not, Pepito?" Frank's voice grew softer suddenly, almost cajoling. Nacio was the little boy he had raised from an infant, the one he loved almost as much or maybe even more than his own son. The fact that once again someone had hurt his beloved Pepito shook Francisco Ybarra to the core. His fury was made that much worse by the fact that it could so easily have been prevented. Frank knew that he himself should have put a stop to Nacio's dangerous romance. If nothing else, he should have told his wife about it. Yoli would have handled it.

"Were you doing something wrong?" Frank asked gently. "Something you shouldn't?"

Nacio's chin trembled. His Adam's apple wobbled up and down with the effort of speaking.

"No," he replied. "I wasn't doing anything wrong. But still, no cops."

He stood up then, walked over to the light, and switched it back off. "I'm going to bed, Uncle Frank. We can talk about this in the morning."

Feeling sick, Frank Ybarra waited until the door swung shut before he reached for the bottle. This time, though, instead of pouring another drink, he grasped the bottle by the neck. Holding it in one knotted fist, he stood up and staggered as far as the back door. After wrenching open the door, Frank hurled the bottle as far as he could into the inky darkness of the backyard. The bottle splattered against the brick wall of the garage and splintered into a thousand pieces.

Frank stood for a moment longer, leaning against the doorjamb while his chest heaved and he fought with the knowledge that his worst fears had been realized. One of the reasons he hadn't told Yoli about the girl was his firm belief that Pepito could take care of himself. Evidently, Frank had been wrong about that, too. Nacio might have tried to spare his uncle some of the gory details, but Frank was convinced he already knew them anyway. This was exactly the kind of shit Yoli had been worried about when she herself had warned Pepito to stay away from the girl.

Ignacio Salazar Ybarra wasn't the first Hispanic boy to have the crap beaten out of him for messing with an Anglo girl, and he sure as hell wouldn't be the last. But now, with Yoli so sick—in the hospital and facing surgery on Monday morning—how on earth would Frank ever be able to tell her?

HAVING DENNIS Hacker hanging around in the bar made Angie nervous. Not that he did or said anything out of line. Not that he was obnoxious. He just sat there, chatting with the other customers, drinking coffee, and watching her. By last call, he had settled in with Archie and Willy at the far end of the bar, where the three entertained one another telling tall tales about the Huachucas and the Peloncillos. They were on such good terms that Hacker bought the two old men their last round of the evening.

All night long, Angie had waffled back and forth, wanting to go and not wanting to go. Now, though, at ten minutes before one and after the man had waited for her for hours, it was too late. She couldn't very well tell him that she had changed her mind and wasn't going.

Hacker, Willy, and Archie were the only customers left in the bar when Angie went into the back room to lug out the four locking wood panels that slipped into slots in the bar's front to cover the supply of liquor. "Those look heavy. Would you like me to help you with them?" Dennis Hacker offered.

"It's all right," Angie said. "I can manage."

"Hey, Angie," Willy said. "This Brit knows all about birds. All kinds of birds. If you don't believe me, just ask him."

"Finish your drink, Willy," she ordered. "You, too, Archie. It's closing time."

"What about him?" Archie whined.

"He's drinking coffee," Angie pointed out. "There's no law against drinking coffee after hours, only booze. Besides, he's with me."

Archie's toothless face collapsed in on itself. "You mean like a date?" he asked. "You're not going to put her in that fancy damned Hummer of yours and pack her off, are you?" he demanded. "Angie's the best thing that's ever happened to this place."

"What'd she say?" Willy asked.

"This guy's her boyfriend," Archie groused. "That's why he can stay and we can't."

Flushing with embarrassment, Angie collected their glasses. "Out," she ordered. "Time to go."

Still grumbling, the two old men helped one another off their respective stools and shuffled toward the door. They shared a basement room in an old, moldering rooming house two buildings up the street, so Angie knew they were in no danger of driving a car. At the door, Archie turned around and shook an admonishing finger in Dennis Hacker's direction.

"Remember," he warned, "don't you go carrying her off. Angie's ours. We saw her first."

Once they were out, Angie pushed the door shut and locked it behind them.

"I think they like you," Dennis Hacker said.

Angie rolled her eyes in exasperation. "I guess they do," she agreed.

Still nursing his coffee, Dennis Hacker waited

while Angie finished her closing time chores, washing the last of the glasses and ashtrays and sweeping the floor. She took her time—far longer than she needed—but at last there was nothing left to do.

"Are you ready, then?" Dennis Hacker asked.

"I have to change."

She disappeared into the back room and returned a few minutes later wearing hiking boots, jeans, and a flannel shirt.

"You look great," Dennis said. "We'd better go. Those hummingbirds will be up bright and early."

ELEVEN

ANGIE KELLOGG had seen Hummers in news broadcasts about the Gulf War, only they had been called Humvees back then. Lately she had even seen a few television commercials about them, but she had never seen one in real life, and she had certainly never expected to ride in one.

Once Dennis Hacker helped her climb inside, she was surprised by how spacious it was. Between her bucket seat and the driver's was a wide flat expanse of tan leather that was almost as big as her kitchen table. Climbing in himself, Dennis caught her looking across the space between them. "That's the air-conditioning unit," he explained. "Behind that's the drivetrain. That's what makes Hummers so hard to tip over."

"Right," Angie said, not letting on that the word *drivetrain* was a total mystery to her.

Dennis turned the key and the engine growled to life. Angie thought it felt like being inside some huge animal—like being swallowed by a tiger, maybe.

"The ride isn't all that wonderful on the highway," Hacker continued, as he expertly maneuvered the vehicle out of what Angie thought was far too small a parking place. "But it's great for the kind of work I do and for getting around in the backcountry." He paused and looked questioningly at Angie. "You're sure it's all right to leave your car here on the street like this? It wouldn't be any trouble to drop it off at your house."

Angie wasn't at all sure she wanted Dennis Hacker to know where she lived. "Oh, no," she said lightly. "It'll be fine right here."

As they drove out of town, Dennis kept up an easy line of patter, telling Angie about his five years of working almost exclusively with parrots and reintroducing them to former habitats in the Southwest.

"The parrots are usually fine," he told her. "It's people who cause problems. That's where I am now, over in the Peloncillos. Before I bring in any birds, I have to negotiate a peace treaty with the local ranchers and the environmentalists both. The odd thing about the Peloncillos is that it seems to be one of the few places in Arizona where those two opposing sides are starting to work together. Just because they evidently have a jaguar or two down there now, though, doesn't mean they'll let my parrots in."

"What could the ranchers possibly have against a few parrots?" Angie asked.

Hacker shrugged. "There's always the concern

that as soon as the birds show up, someone will pull some endangered species stunt that will also endanger the ranchers' time-honored grazing rights. Believe me," he added, "when cowmen and tree huggers go to war, it's easy for a guy like me to get caught in the middle and end up wearing a bullet in my chest."

"A real bullet?" Angie asked nervously.

Dennis Hacker's answering smile didn't hold much humor. "Unfortunately, yes."

He went on to tell Angie how his grandmother's interest in birds had been passed on to him. Leaning back in the upright seat, Angie was happy to listen. Only when Dennis Hacker's story ran down and he began to ask questions about her own background did Angie Kellogg grow uneasy once more.

"Where did you go to school?" he asked.

She knew this incredibly intelligent man had attended Cambridge University in England before coming to the United States and picking up graduate degrees in zoology from both Stanford and UCLA. Angie was a high school dropout. Since leaving school, what education she had achieved had come through reading books.

"Ann Arbor," she said.

"What did you study?"

Angie lost it then. For a moment she could think of nothing to say. "Education," she managed finally.

"Why are you a barmaid, then?" he asked.

"I tried teaching but I didn't like it," she said lamely.

She was relieved when the conversation wandered back to birds once more, with Dennis telling her about the wonderful displays at the Arizona/Sonora Desert Museum up in Tucson, especially the hummingbird compound. "It's a shame you haven't been there yet. Maybe that's where we should go next. I'd love to take you."

With lightning flickering far to the south, they left Douglas on what Dennis explained was the Old Geronimo Trail. "That's where he surrendered, you know," Dennis told her.

"Where who surrendered?"

"Geronimo," he said. "That famous old Apache chief. He surrendered in Skeleton Canyon, just down the mountain from where we'll be watching the hummingbirds."

Dennis Hacker's travelogue continued as they drove east. Angie was feeling at ease when the Hummer turned off one dirt road, bounced past something that looked like a walled-in cemetery, and came to rest beside a small, two-wheeled camper/trailer.

"What's this?" she asked suddenly wary as Dennis switched off the motor.

"Home sweet home for the next little while," he answered cheerfully. "Come on in. It's time for breakfast."

"But I thought we were going on a picnic," Angie objected. They were miles into the wilderness. Since leaving Douglas an hour earlier they hadn't seen a single other vehicle. Dennis Hacker seemed nice enough, but the idea of going into this little house with him alone . . .

He came around to Angie's side of the Hummer, opened the door, and then held out a hand to help her down. "There's plenty of time for us to eat before we head up the mountain. Besides, I can fix a much better breakfast here than I can over a campfire. It also means we won't have to carry food and cooking utensils in our packs. Come on."

Hacker's gentlemanly gesture of extending his hand didn't leave Angie much choice. Feeling trapped and scared and wishing she hadn't come, she allowed herself to be led toward the trailer. There was no telling what he could do to her alone out here in the wilderness like this. Angie Kellogg had been with some pretty scary guys in her days as a hooker, but she had always been on her own turf in the city. If one of the johns or a pimp came after her there, all she'd had to do was run outside, screaming for help and knowing that, eventually, help would come. Here there was no one. If Hacker turned on her, what would she do?

Angie looked longingly back at the road, back the way they'd just come, but Dennis Hacker didn't relinquish her hand. "That's Cottonwood Creek Cemetery over there," he said, leading her forward. "It's an interesting place, but there's not much to see in the dark. I'll take you there later, after we come down the mountain. Here's the step. Be careful."

Opening the door with one hand, he guided her up a wooden stair. "Stay right here until I turn on the light."

The light turned out to be a butane-fueled light

fixture that hung over a tiny kitchen table. "Sit," he told her. "As you can see, this place is too small for two people to stand at once, so if you'll sit and supervise, I'll cook."

Angie eased herself into the little breakfast nook and peered around. The place was indeed tiny, but it was also neat as a pin. As she sat down, she caught a glimpse of a well-made bed in a loft tucked up over a built-in desk. The paneled walls glowed warm and golden in the softly hissing light.

"How do bacon and eggs sound?" he was asking. "And do you prefer coffee or tea? I've become Americanized enough that I drink coffee most of the time, but I still like to have a nice cup of tea first thing in the morning."

"Tea will be fine," Angie managed.

Watching as he bustled around the trailer—getting out pots and pans, setting a pot of water to boil—Angie noticed that Dennis was so tall he had to stand with his neck bent to keep from bumping his head on the ceiling. "Doesn't that bother you?" she asked. "Having to hold your head that way?"

He shrugged. "I'm used to it. In order to get a higher ceiling, I would have had to go for a bigger caravan—"

"Caravan," Angie interrupted with a frown. "What's that?"

Hacker stopped peeling potatoes long enough to grin at her. "Sorry. I mean trailer. That's what you Yanks call them. This one happens to suit me. The short wheelbase makes it possible for me to take it almost anywhere I want to go."

Within minutes, Angie was enjoying the delicious aroma of frying bacon and sipping strong, hot tea from a beautifully delicate bone china cup and saucer. The pattern on the cup showed a long-legged blue bird standing, regal and serene, among exquisitely painted pink and orange flowers. When her bacon, eggs, and hash browns (homemade, from scratch) showed up a little later, the food was arranged on matching and equally beautiful crane-decorated plates. The silverware was a mismatched jumble, but the dishes themselves were elegant and beautiful.

"Where did you get this wonderful china?" Angie asked.

Dennis Hacker smiled. "It's called Kutani Crane," he told her. "It's Wedgwood. The set was a gift from my grandmother. Sort of a congratulatory gift for getting this job. It meant I didn't have to go back home and sign up to work in my father's shipping business."

"Your grandmother must have chosen that pattern because she knew you liked birds," Angie said. "That was thoughtful of her."

Dennis laughed out loud. "No," he said. "Grandmum chose it because *she* likes birds. Remember who got me interested in birds in the first place. Come on now. Eat up. It's getting late. We'll need to hit the trail pretty soon. I'll just leave the dishes in the sink and do them when we get back."

They were almost ready to leave when a phone rang. "A phone?" Angie asked in surprise when she heard it ringing.

Dennis nodded apologetically. "Sorry," he said. "Speak of the devil. That's probably Grandmother right now. She's never quite gotten the hang of the time change. She usually rings up early Sunday mornings before I go out to take care of the birds. She likes to keep tabs on me."

Angie tried not to listen as Dennis chatted with his grandmother. The idea of someone calling all the way from England to visit on the phone with someone sitting in a camper parked in the middle of nowhere in the Arizona desert seemed strange to her. But then, the things Angie Kellogg did would probably seem strange to most other people, too.

While Dennis was busy talking, Angie contented herself with examining an old framed but faded photo hanging on the wall between the table and the desk. In brown and sepia-tinged tones, it showed an endless line of hundreds of men dressed in heavy winter gear and loaded with huge packs climbing what appeared to be an almost vertical snow-covered mountain.

"My great-grandfather took that," Dennis explained when he got off the phone. "It's called *Climbing Chilcoot Pass*." He took the picture off the wall and handed it over to Angie so she could examine it more closely.

"Where's Chilcoot Pass?" she asked.

"Alaska. These guys were all part of the Klondike Gold Rush. The shortest way to get from the States to the gold in Yukon Territory was over this mountain pass from Skagway, then down Lake Bennett and the Yukon River both."

"They look like ants," Angie said. "How come they're all carrying so much stuff?"

"The Canadian authorities were worried that the miners were totally unprepared for the hardships of a Yukon winter. They didn't want half of them dying of hunger, so they sent Mounties out to patrol the border and make sure no one crossed into Canada without at least a year's worth of supplies—literally, a ton of supplies per man. That's what these guys are doing—hauling their supplies up and over the mountains in hopes of striking it rich."

"Did he?" Angie asked, handing the picture back. "Your great-grandfather, I mean. Did he strike it rich?"

"In a manner of speaking, he did," Dennis said. "He'd always been something of a black sheep—an adventurer. Over the years, this particular picture has actually made him famous in some quarters. But the Yukon got to him in the process, made him a believer. He lost all of his grubstake and most of his toes before he finally wrote home and asked for help. His father paid for his return passage to England. In exchange, he had to shape up and go into the family business the way everyone thought he should have done in the first place."

Dennis stopped and glanced at his watch. "Come on now," he said. "It is getting late."

Outside, the sky was just beginning to lighten into a pale gray. Once again, Dennis handed Angie up into the vehicle, closing the door behind her the way a gentleman might treat a lady or like someone handling one of those delicate bone china cups back inside the trailer.

For Angie, who had never before experienced that kind of treatment, it was a strange sensation. It made her feel all funny—both good and bad at the same time—as though she didn't quite deserve it. Still, she was gratified to realize that, despite all her worries beforehand, nothing at all had happened. She and Dennis Hacker had eaten breakfast together and enjoyed it. The food had been delicious and the conversation fun. He hadn't made a pass at her. Hadn't tried to get her into bed. In fact, there hadn't been a single off-color remark. In her whole life, Angie Kellogg never remembered having quite such a wonderful time.

"With all this cloud cover, it should be a glorious sunrise," Dennis told her. "And just wait till you see all those hummingbirds. They're unbelievable."

THE RED Miata convertible came screaming down Highway 80, ignoring the speed signs, almost missing the curve. Joanna, merging into traffic from the downtown area of Old Bisbee, switched on her lights and siren and fell in behind the other car.

In actual fact, that part of Highway 80 was inside the Bisbee city limits and, as such, outside the jurisdiction of the Cochise County Sheriff's Department. Since this was a dream, however, jurisdictional boundaries didn't apply. In real life,

Sheriff Joanna Brady had never once made a traffic stop, but in the dream landscape, that didn't matter, either.

"Pull over," she announced in a voice that reverberated as though being broadcast through a huge megaphone. "Pull over and step out of your vehicle."

Ignoring the order, the driver of the Miata shot forward, racing down the grade onto the long flat stretch of highway that runs along the edge of Lavender Pit. Generations of speeding drivers have given that part of Highway 80 the unofficial name of Citation Avenue. The driver of the speeding convertible seemed determined to do her part to help maintain the legend, but Joanna wasn't about to be outdone. This was hot pursuit, and she was determined to pull over the speeding motorist.

With Joanna's Crown Victoria right on the Miata's back bumper, they raced down through the back side of Lowell and then onto the traffic circle. Around and around they went, time and again. Suddenly, for no apparent reason, the Miata simply stopped. As Joanna approached the vehicle, weapon in hand, the driver's side door popped open and a woman stepped out. She was tall and blond, wearing a miniskirt and a pair of impossibly high heels.

"Hands on your head," Joanna ordered.

"You can't do this to me, Joanna Brady," Rowena Sharp Bonham screeched. "You can't pull me over like a common criminal. I won't stand for it. I wasn't doing anything wrong."

"Yes, you were," Joanna told her calmly. "You were cheating."

She woke up then, laughing. For a moment she was disoriented by waking up outside the house rather than in her own bedroom, but that momentary jar gave way to a feeling of well-being. Mourning doves cooed their early morning wake-up calls. Across the Sulphur Springs Valley, dawn was tinging the sky a vivid orange. But something was different.

For weeks now, clouds had drifted up from the south each afternoon, bringing with them the tantalizing promise of much-needed rain. By morning they would retreat back into the interior of Mexico without leaving behind a trace of moisture. This time, though, the clouds were still there, billowing up in tall, puffy columns above the far horizon. From miles away across the thirsty desert came the welcome scent of an approaching storm.

Joanna had grown to adulthood with a desert dweller's unbridled delight in the prospect of a summer rainstorm. What she wanted to do more than anything that morning was to sit on her porch and watch the storm build. She wanted to track the wind and surging clouds of dust as they marched across the desert just ahead of the rain. She wanted to sit back and watch jagged flashes of lightning electrify the entire sky, and to listen to the rolling drums of thunder, but first, she wanted to make a pot of coffee and read the Sunday paper. In order to do that, she'd have to collect the paper from the tube down by the cattle guard.

She went inside. The house had been dreadfully hot when she came home the night before. To counteract the heat, she had left the swamp cooler running all night long. Overnight, both indoor and outdoor temperatures had dropped enough that now the house seemed almost chilly. The first thing she did was switch off the cooler. As soon as she did so, she was startled by how quiet it was. Far too quiet.

Don't stand around dwelling on it, she told herself firmly. *Do something.*

Throwing on a pair of jeans and one of Andy's old khaki shirts, she hurried into the kitchen to start the coffee. Then, after stuffing a carrot into her pocket and with both dogs trailing eagerly behind, she walked out to the corral.

In the last few months, since Bucky Buckwalter's horse Kiddo had come to live on High Lonesome Ranch, one of Jenny's weekend duties had been to ride the horse down to the end of the road to bring back the Sunday paper. Before Kiddo's arrival on the scene, Joanna herself would have driven down in the Eagle. This morning, while water dripped through the grounds in the coffeemaker, Joanna decided to take the horse herself and go get her newspaper.

As soon as the nine-year-old sorrel gelding heard the back door slam shut, he came to the side of the corral and peered eagerly over the fence. Ears up, whickering, and stamping his hooves, he shook his blond mane impatiently while Joanna stopped in the tack room long enough to collect a bridle. When she came into the corral, Kiddo gobbled the carrot and accepted the bridle without complaint.

"I'll bet you miss Jenny, too, don't you?" Joanna said soothingly, scratching the horse's soft muzzle once the bridle was in place. "That makes four of us."

Joanna had worried initially that Kiddo would be too much horse for Jenny to handle, but the two of them—horse and child—had become great friends. Jenny had taken to riding with an ease that had surprised everyone, including her mother. She preferred riding bareback whenever possible. Girl and horse—both with matching blond tresses flowing in the wind—made a captivating picture.

Joanna herself was a reasonably capable rider. For this early morning jaunt down to the cattle guard, she too rode bareback. The sun was well up by then. On the way there, she held Kiddo to a sedate walk, enjoying the quiet, reading the tracks overnight visitors had layered into the roadway over the marks of her tires from the night before. A small herd of delicately hoofed javelina—five or six of them—had wandered down from the hills, following the sandy bed of a dry wash. In one spot Joanna spied the telltale path left behind by a long-gone sidewinder. There were paw prints left by a solitary coyote. She saw the distinctive scratchings of a covey of quail as well as the prints of some other reasonably large bird, most likely a roadrunner.

Butch Dixon—a city slicker from Chicago— had come to visit the High Lonesome and had marveled at how empty it was.

It isn't empty at all, Joanna thought. *I have all kinds of nearby neighbors. It's just that none of them happen to be human.*

Coming back from the gate, with the folded newspaper safely stowed under her shirt, Joanna gave Kiddo his head. They thundered back down the road with the wind rushing into Joanna's face. It was an exhilarating way to start the morning.

No wonder Jenny liked Kiddo so much. It was almost like magic. On the back of a galloping horse it was impossible for Joanna Brady to remember to be sad.

TWELVE

ANGIE AND Dennis arrived in the meadow off the south fork of Skeleton Canyon just as the sun came up. Settling into a rocky cleft, Dennis reached into his backpack and pulled out two pairs of powerful binoculars, one of which he handed to Angie. "There's no real trick to this," he said. "You just have to be patient. They'll show up eventually."

As promised, the hummingbirds appeared half an hour later. There they were, hundreds of them, hovering in vivid color against an overcast sky. "The dark green ones with the black bills are Magnificent Hummingbirds or *Eugenes fulgens*," Dennis explained. "The lighter greens—chartreuse almost with the orange bills—are called Broad-billed or *Cynanîhus latinostris*. The ones with distinct red caps are male Anna's—*Calypte anna*."

Enchanted but also self-conscious that he knew so much more than she did, Angie held the binoculars glued to her eyes. "And the ones with the purple throats?" she asked.

"Male Lucifers—*Calothorax lucifer*. I spotted some Black-chinned in here the other day, but I don't see any of them now."

Angie watched until her arms grew tired of holding the binoculars. When she took them down, she was surprised to find Dennis Hacker looking at her rather than the birds. Nervously, she cast around for something to say. "It doesn't seem fair that the males are always so much prettier than the females," she said.

"That may be true for birds," Dennis told her, "but it certainly isn't true of humans."

Embarrassed, Angie looked back at him. "What's that supposed to mean?"

He grinned. "It means you're beautiful," he said. "You're willing to hike a mile and a half uphill to watch birds at six o'clock in the morning. You're interested in my parrot project. What else is there? I think I'm in love."

Not knowing how to reply, Angie put the binoculars back to her eyes and said nothing.

"I'm serious, you know," Hacker continued. "I told my parents once that I was going to marry the first woman I ever found who was as interested in birds as I am."

In the few hours they had spent together, Angie had found Dennis Hacker to be pleasantly likeable, but she could tell from the way he spoke that he was serious. There was no point in letting things go any further.

"Look," she said, "this is silly. You don't know anything about me."

"But I do. You're a hard worker. You're kind to old drunks. You're a woman of your word. All day long yesterday, I was afraid you'd stand me up."

Angie smiled. "I almost did," she said.

"But the point is, you didn't. You're here. Maybe you don't believe in love at first sight, but I do."

That was it. "Look," she said forcibly, "you think I'm a woman of my word, but I already lied to you. When you asked where I went to school, I know you meant where did I go to college. I've never even been to Ann Arbor. I went to high school in a place called Battle Creek, but I didn't graduate. When I ran away from home, I took the name Kellogg after the factory my father worked in back home. I don't have a degree in teaching. I'm an ex-hooker. The job in the Blue Moon as a bartender is the first real job I've ever had."

Not knowing what kind of reaction to expect, she stopped and waited. It wasn't long in coming. A grin creased Dennis Hacker's face. "You're kidding!"

"I'm not."

Angie Kellogg couldn't possibly have anticipated what happened next. Dennis's initial grin dissolved into gales of laughter. He laughed until the tears rolled down his cheeks and he had to hold his sides. "That's the funniest thing I've ever heard," he gasped at last.

But Angie didn't think it was funny. She put down the binoculars and stood up.

"Where are you going?"

"I'm leaving."

"Come on, Angie. Let me explain."

Angie Kellogg wasn't interested in explanations. Without a glance over her shoulder, she bolted away from him, heading back down the mountain the way they had come. Dennis, shaking his head and still chuckling, took his time packing up. He returned the two pair of binoculars to their separate cases and then put them and the bottled water he'd brought along back in his backpack. He had no doubt that he'd meet up with Angie back at the truck. Once she realized what he was laughing about, Dennis knew it would be all right.

Hefting the pack onto his back, he started after her. On the way up, he had followed a meandering path that had kept the rise in elevation from being quite so steep. For going back down, though, and because he wanted to reach the Hummer about the same time Angie did, he set off straight down the mountain.

Which was how, half an hour later, Dennis Hacker stumbled onto the wrecked remains of a smashed red pickup.

AFTER RUBBING Kiddo down, feeding him, and returning him to the corral, Joanna went back to the house. By then the coffee was ready.

She poured herself a cup and was headed for the porch when the phone rang.

"Sheriff Brady?" Tica Romero, one of the departmental dispatchers, was on the phone. "We've got a problem."

"What's that?"

"A one-car fatality rollover has just been reported in the Peloncillos. Off the road up in Skeleton Canyon. A hiker reported the incident. Called it in on his cell phone. At least one person is dead, but it's pretty rough country. There could be more bodies and they just haven't found them yet. The guy who found it gave me a description and a license number."

"And?"

"I thought you'd want to know right away. It's a red Toyota Tacoma," Tica replied. "Registered under the name of David O'Brien. Isn't that the missing person case—"

"Yes, it is," Joanna interrupted. "Any ID on the victim?"

"Not so far. The body must have been thrown free in the accident. The vehicle fell on top of it. There won't be any way to tell exactly what's underneath until we get a tow truck in there to move the vehicle."

Joanna's throat constricted. Her right hand shook so badly that she had to put down her coffee cup in order to keep from spilling it. The O'Briens' worst fears and Joanna's niggling premonition were both coming true. Brianna O'Brien was dead, but there could be no notification made to the parents waiting at Green Brush Ranch until after the sheriff's department had some additional confirmation.

Joanna turned at once to the enlarged map of Cochise County that she had tacked to the wall over her living room phone. There were two forks to Skeleton Canyon. The south fork ran virtually north and south and was entirely inside Cochise County. The north fork ran east and west and crossed over into New Mexico.

"You're sure this is our deal and not Sheriff Trotter's over in New Mexico?" Joanna asked. She couldn't help hoping the wrecked truck would end up being someone else's problem instead of hers.

"It's ours, all right," Tica answered. "It's the south fork, not the north. And the truck isn't all," she continued. "Mr. Hacker says—"

"Mr. Hacker?" Joanna asked. "You mean Dennis Hacker, the parrot guy?"

"I don't know anything about parrots, but that's the name he gave. Dennis Hacker. Do you know him?"

"Yes. What does he say?"

"That one of your friends is missing up there as well. Her name is Angie Kellogg. Hacker says that in all the confusion of finding and reporting the accident, she wandered off some place by herself. He says she's out there alone without any food or water. He's asking for help organizing a search party."

Angie missing? Joanna wondered. *How could that be?* With a sinking feeling, she remembered her conversation with Angie the night before—

remembered how Angie had been concerned about going on what had essentially been a bird-watching blind date. Joanna also remembered all too clearly that she, Joanna, had been the one who had urged Angie to put her concerns aside and go.

"Tica," Joanna said, "can you patch me through to Mr. Hacker? I want to talk to him."

"Sure thing, Sheriff Brady. Hang on."

"Mr. Hacker," Joanna said seconds later, "this is Sheriff Brady. What's happening?"

"Angie disappeared," he said.

"How did the two of you get separated?"

"We had a little misunderstanding," Hacker said. "She took off. I discovered the wreck while I was following her back down the mountain. I thought for sure she'd go straight back to the truck, but I'm here now, and there's no sign of her. She isn't here and hasn't been, as far as I can tell. I tried to backtrack up the trail. She must have missed one of the turns along the way."

Misunderstanding, Joanna thought grimly. *Right*.

"So where are you now?"

"At the north entrance to Skeleton Canyon. The one off Highway 80."

"And where's the wrecked truck?"

"Just below the ridge between Hog Canyon and the south fork of Skeleton."

"Can we get a wrecker to it?"

"It won't be easy. It's twenty yards off the nearest trail in strictly four-wheel-drive terrain. It's going to be bad enough just getting the body out, to say nothing of the wrecked pickup. What about Angie, though? Will you notify Search and

Rescue? From what Angie told me, I don't think she's ever been out in the mountains by herself before. I'm afraid—"

"Exactly how long has she been gone?" Joanna interrupted.

"An hour now, maybe more."

"Just hold on, Mr. Hacker. I know Angie Kellogg personally. She's a friend of mine, and one thing I can tell you about her is that she's got plenty of common sense. We've got people on the way. There'll be sirens and lots of noise out there. I'm sure she'll be able to follow the sounds and find her way back down the mountain."

"But . . ."

"No buts. I'm on my way myself. I'll be there as soon as I can. You wait right where you are so you can guide us in when we get there."

Joanna ended the call and then immediately dialed back to the department and shifted into an all-business mode. "Tica," she said, once the dispatcher was on the phone, "who all have you called?"

"You were number one," Tica answered. "That's the standing order. The detectives are next, and then Dr. Winfield." George Winfield was Cochise County's newly appointed coroner.

"What about Dick Voland?" Joanna asked.

"I can call him, but are you sure you want me to? He's supposed to be off today unless there's some kind of real emergency. I think he has tickets to take his boys up to Tucson for a Toros game this afternoon."

"Don't bother him, then," Joanna answered.

"You notify the detectives. I'll call Doc Winfield. I have both his home and work numbers programmed into my phone. If I call him instead of having you do it, it'll save time."

After punching the proper number, Joanna waited through the automated dialing sequence and two rings.

"Hello."

Joanna had expected a male voice to answer, but the person speaking into the phone was definitely not Doc Winfield. In fact, the woman who answered sounded very much like Joanna's mother, but that couldn't be.

Quickly, without saying anything, Joanna disconnected the call. Of course, Eleanor's number, along with several others, was also programmed into the phone. Maybe Joanna had simply punched the wrong button, although that seemed unlikely. She tried again, this time taking special care to punch the right one—George Winfield's nine rather than Eleanor's five.

"Hello," Eleanor Lathrop answered again, a bit more forcefully this time.

"Mother?" Joanna asked. "Is that you?"

"Of course it's me," Eleanor said. "Who else would you be calling at this ungodly hour of the morning? The phone rang a minute or so ago, but no one was there when I answered. Was that you, too?"

"Mother," Joanna interrupted, "I wasn't calling you. I was trying to reach George Winfield. What are you doing at his house at seven o'clock on a Sunday morning?"

"I'm not at George's house," Eleanor returned stiffly. "I'm right here in my own bed trying to catch up on my beauty sleep."

"But I dialed George's number and got you. Twice," Joanna pointed out.

"Oh, that," Eleanor said. "I see. Well, he must have forwarded his calls here, then. He does that sometimes in case someone needs to get hold of him."

Joanna took a deep breath. "I think this is one of those times. You'd better put him on."

Dr. George Winfield was a relative newcomer to town. An attractive widower from Minnesota, he had somehow managed to hook up with Eleanor Lathrop within months of arriving in Bisbee. Joanna knew the two of them had been going out together for some time, but she couldn't quite imagine her straitlaced mother actually allowing a man to spend the night in her home. It was hard enough for Joanna to picture George Winfield in her mother's life. To imagine him now in Eleanor's cozy little house on Campbell Avenue and in the double bed that had once belonged to both Joanna's parents was unthinkable.

Still, she had no choice when George's sleep-distorted voice came on the phone. "Hello? Joanna? What's up?"

For a moment she couldn't answer. Joanna had lectured herself on the subject more than once. It shouldn't have been that big a deal. Eleanor Lathrop had been widowed for a long time. After being left to raise a sometimes difficult and headstrong teenager, she certainly deserved to find some personal happiness. And George *seemed* nice enough. There was no logical reason why Eleanor's resumption of dating should have thrown her daughter for such a loop, but it had. And, months later, it continued to do so. No matter how hard Joanna tried, she still couldn't get over or around her own personal objections. Was it a matter of not being able to accept her mother as a sexual being? Or, on a far more basic level, was it nothing but jealousy?

"Joanna?" George repeated. "What's going on?"

"There's been a car wreck up in Skeleton Canyon," Joanna said. "A pickup truck. According to the guy on the scene there's at least one body trapped under it, maybe more."

"Where the hell is Skeleton Canyon?" George Winfield demanded. "Is that a real place, or did you make it up?"

Joanna thought about the complications of trying to explain to a newcomer how to find the entrance to Skeleton Canyon or even how to get to the Peloncillos themselves. She also thought about what Dennis Hacker had said about the rugged terrain. The coroner's official vehicle was nothing more than a modified hearse. That wouldn't cut it.

"Skeleton Canyon is real enough, but I'm not going to try to give you directions over the phone. Meet me at the Double Adobe turnoff on Highway 80 just as soon as you can. I'll drive you there. That'll be easier for all concerned."

"All right," George said. "But I'll need to jump in the shower first."

"Fine," Joanna said impatiently. "I'll shower,

too. But meet me as soon as you can. And bring your hiking boots."

"Hiking boots? Why?"

"Because the body's twenty yards off the nearest trail down a mountainside," Joanna said. "We'll most likely have to do some hiking."

"Thanks for the warning," George said. "I'll have to do the best I can."

Abandoning her now-cold cup of coffee, Joanna headed for the shower herself. Minutes later, with her hair still damp, and dressed in boots and hiking attire, she headed outside and stopped cold in front of the Crown Victoria. The low-slung patrol car wouldn't cut it in Skeleton Canyon any better than George Winfield's hearse.

Unlocking it, she picked up the radio. "I'm going to be out of radio contact," she told Tica Romero. "I'll be in my Eagle. It doesn't have a radio or air-conditioning, but at least it has four-wheel drive." She was about to end the contact when she remembered it was Sunday.

"When you have a chance, Tica, I'll need you to call a few people for me. My in-laws are expecting me to drop by after church for dinner. I'll need you to let Jim Bob and Eva Lou know I most likely won't make it."

"And the other call?"

"Make that one to Reverend Marianne Maculyea of Canyon Methodist Church," Joanna said. "Tell her I won't be coming to Sunday school or church today. Let her know why. Mari's a friend of Angie Kellogg's, too. She and Jeff will both want to know what's going on."

Joanna had barely stopped the Eagle on the shoulder of Highway 80 when Ernie Carpenter's van went flying by. Fifty yards down the road, it almost stood on its nose as Jaime Carbajal, driving in Ernie's stead, jammed on the brakes. Pulling a quick U-turn, the van came back to the spot where Joanna was parked. After yet another U-turn, the van pulled in behind the Eagle, and both detectives climbed out. For a change, even the usually dapper Carpenter was already dressed down to crime scene-appropriate attire.

"What gives, Sheriff Brady? Do you need help?"

Joanna shook her head. "I'm waiting for George Winfield. He's still a little short when it comes to Cochise County geography. I wasn't sure he could find his way to Skeleton Canyon on his own."

Ernie nodded. "The guy's still pretty much of a greenhorn. I hope he gets a move on, though. Looking at those clouds over there, we may not have much time."

"You two go on," Joanna told them. "Winfield and I will be along as soon as we can."

"Are you sure you're all right, Sheriff Brady?" Ernie asked. "Tica told us about Angie Kellogg being missing as well. I know she's a friend of yours."

"Thanks, Ernie," she said. "I'm okay and I'm sure Angie will be fine. She'll find her way out. Once you get out there, though, you might want to turn on your siren. It'll make it easier for her to know where you are."

"Right," Ernie said. "Will do."

The two detectives started away. "Detective Carbajal?" Joanna called after them.

"Yes, ma'am?"

"Remember," she said, leveling a reproving look in his direction, "sirens yes, but whoever was in that pickup is already dead. You're not out to set land speed records here. This isn't a hot pursuit situation, and I don't want it treated as such."

With a meaningful glance at Ernie, who had no doubt been urging him on, Jaime nodded. "Right, Sheriff Brady," he said. "I'll be sure to slow it down."

THIRTEEN

ERNIE AND Jaime had just pulled away when George Winfield arrived in the converted hearse that doubled as his coroner's wagon. When George walked up to the window of Joanna's Eagle, he was carrying an Arizona map that he had unfolded and was holding at arm's length. His left cheek bore a faint smudge of lipstick that was, no doubt, Eleanor's.

"Ellie says Skeleton Canyon is somewhere over here in the Pelon . . ." He paused. "How do you say it? The Pelonsillios?"

He pronounced the word in true gringo fashion with the word *silly* taking the place of the two silent *l*s. The sound of it grated on Joanna's ear. So did his use of Joanna's father's pet name for her mother. The lipstick didn't help.

"It's Spanish," she explained, without bothering to cover up her irritation. "That means you don't pronounce the double *l*. It's Pelon-si-yos."

George shook his head. "I'll never be able to say all these god-awful Spanish and Indian words. Whatever happened to good old American English?"

"You mean like Minnesota?" Joanna asked testily. "Or maybe Illinois?"

Realizing he had stepped in something but unsure what it was, Winfield regarded her warily. "I guess we'd better get started."

"I guess we'd better," Joanna said.

Winfield went back to the hearse and removed a heavy leather satchel, which he lugged over and loaded into the back of the Eagle. By the time he climbed into the rider's seat, Joanna already had the engine running.

The turnoff to the north entrance of Skeleton Canyon was at a crossroads presuming to be a village that called itself Apache. From Double Adobe Road to the turnoff was a good fifty-five miles. The drive took them east across the southern end of the Sulphur Springs Valley and then north through the San Bernardino Valley. Most of the time on a drive like this, Joanna would have been frustrated by the vastness of her jurisdictional boundaries. Six thousand two hundred and forty square miles was a big area to cover, but today the miles flew past far too fast for her to even think about it.

Absorbed in her own thoughts, Joanna was thinking not only about the tragedy of Brianna O'Brien's death, but also about her own culpability with regard to whatever was going on with Angie Kellogg. Joanna had thought Dennis

Hacker was inviting Angie on a harmless, old-fashioned date—the kind of innocent, hand-holding thing old people sometimes use to regale their kids, grandkids, and great-grandkids. Wrong. Not in this case.

Joanna knew something about the abuse Angie Kellogg had endured as a child. And she knew a little about her life as a prostitute in L.A. It was hardly surprising that someone with her background would worry that maybe the Bird Man's intentions weren't all they were cracked up to be—that he was interested in something besides hummingbirds. Considering what had happened, Joanna had little doubt who had been right and who had been wrong.

Thinking about the realities of Angie out walking around, unprepared, in the wild, rock-strewn landscape that made up the Peloncillos, Joanna glanced at Doc Winfield's feet. Despite her warning advice, he was nonetheless wearing a pair of thin-soled, highly polished loafers.

"Are those the only shoes you have along?" she asked.

"Unfortunately yes," he said. "I'm not much for hiking. I haven't quite gotten around to buying any hiking boots yet."

"What about water?" she asked. "I don't suppose you brought along any of that, either."

"I brought along my crime scene kit."

"But no water to drink?"

"No."

Joanna sighed. "That's all right. I have two canteens in the back. I'll give you one to use. That's what happens to city slickers when you turn them loose in the desert. If you don't watch them every minute, pretty soon they turn themselves into potato chips. When you're working out in the sun, especially with the humidity going up like it is right now, heatstroke can sneak up and catch you unawares."

"Is that why they call the place we're going to Skeleton Canyon?" Winfield asked. "Because people died out there?"

Joanna nodded.

"Of thirst?"

"They were mostly murdered," Joanna answered. "You ever hear of the Clanton gang?"

"As in Wyatt Earp?"

"Before they tangled with him, the Clantons ambushed a band of Mexican gold smugglers here in the Peloncillos. According to legend, the Clantons made off with a shipment of stolen gold, only to be caught by the survivors a few miles away. In the ensuing fight, a few more people died and the gold disappeared. It's still supposed to be out there somewhere."

"Amazing," George Winfield murmured.

"The Peloncillos have always been a haven for smugglers. It's a mountain range that's almost impossible to patrol. The Baker Wilderness Area, between Skeleton Canyon and the international border, is supposed to be closed to vehicular traffic. Unfortunately, smugglers don't necessarily pay any attention to the edicts of the Environmental Protection Agency *or* the U.S. Forest Service."

"Amazing," George Winfield said again, settling

back in his seat and staring out the window at a landscape that was waist-high in yellow grass. "I can't believe I'm living in a place where those names are part of history and not just something that used to turn up in Saturday matinees. Coming here I thought this would all be real desert, maybe even sand dunes. This almost looks like wheat."

Joanna considered explaining to him how Anglos had encouraged the spread of mesquite, which had killed off the native grasses, but she let it go. *Let him learn some of that stuff on his own*, she thought.

They drove in silence for several more miles before George spoke again, clearing his throat as he did so. "By the way, Joanna, has Ellie said much of anything to you about . . ." He paused. "Well, about us," he finished lamely.

There he was, using the name Ellie again to bring up a topic Joanna wasn't at all eager to discuss. "Not really," she returned coolly. "Why?"

"She hasn't happened to mention that we're . . . er . . . married?"

Joanna turned to look at him and in the process ran the right-hand tires onto the shoulder of the road. She had to struggle with the steering wheel for a moment before the Eagle returned to the sun-cracked pavement.

"Married?" she demanded, her face pale. "You can't be serious!"

George shook his head. "I wouldn't kid around about something like this. I've been telling her for weeks now that she needed to let you know.

In case you haven't noticed, your mother's a little stubborn. We eloped, Joanna. Last month. We got married in a little chapel up in Vegas. I've booked an Alaskan cruise for our honeymoon in August. I wanted you to know about it before then."

Joanna couldn't think of a single word to say in reply. George hurried on. "I hope you're not too shocked. At our ages, you know, it's hard to tell how much time we have. And your mother and I are just alike. High-fidelity and low-frequency, if you know what I mean."

He chuckled at his own joke and then looked at Joanna to see if she was laughing. She wasn't. They were approaching the turnoff to Skeleton Canyon. With her chin set and her eyes staring straight ahead, Joanna jammed on the brakes. She swung the Eagle onto the gravel road with such force that, had George Winfield not been wearing his seat belt, he would have come sliding into her lap.

"I guess you're a little angry about this," he murmured a little later.

"Angry?" Joanna repeated. "Whatever makes you think that?"

"I suppose that's why Ellie was so reluctant to tell you in the first place. She was afraid you'd react this way."

In front of them a trio of three black-tailed deer gracefully leaped across the sandy track, clearing the barbed-wire fences on both sides as though they didn't exist and then disappearing into the waist-high grass. Seeing them gave Joanna a chance to gather her resources. The last thing she ever wanted to do was react just the way her mother said she would. If Eleanor had thought Joanna was going to be angry, then, by God, angry was the last thing she'd be!

"I'm surprised," she said carefully. "Surprised and shocked, but not angry."

George Winfield sighed. "That's a relief, then," he said. "What about your brother? What do you think he'll say?"

Bob Brundage, Joanna's long-lost brother, was another one of Eleanor Lathrop's little secrets. Born out of wedlock before D. H. Lathrop and Eleanor married, Bob had been put up for adoption as an infant. Joanna had first learned of his existence at Thanksgiving the previous year, when he had tracked down his birth mother after the deaths of both his adoptive parents.

"I have no idea what Bob will say," Joanna replied, curbing a desire to snap. "You'll have to ask him yourself."

"I thought we'd invite him and his wife to the reception," George continued.

"What reception?"

"The one we'll have when we get back from the cruise. Maybe in September sometime. That'll be fun, don't you think? Nothing too fancy. Maybe just a little get-together at the clubhouse out at Rob Roy Links. That's where we went on our first real date, you see."

"I'm sure it'll be a ball," Joanna said. "I can hardly wait."

They came around a sharp curve where the road was blocked by a barbed-wire gate. Parked in front of the gate was a battered green Range Rover. A slender woman in a dark blue dress and wearing huge, wraparound sunglasses stood next to the vehicle, studying a map.

Joanna rolled down her window. "Excuse me," she called. "Would you mind moving out of the way? We need to get past."

The woman looked up. "Maybe you can help me. I'm looking for Skeleton Canyon, but when I came to this gate, I was afraid I had missed a turn. Am I going the right way?"

Leaving the Eagle idling, Joanna climbed out. "I'm sorry," she said, pulling out her badge. "I'm Sheriff Brady. There's been a serious accident up in Skeleton Canyon today. A fatality. We're expecting emergency vehicles in and out of here on this road. If you don't mind, it would probably be better if you could postpone your visit to some other time."

"But that's why I'm here," the woman replied. "Because of the accident. I heard about it on my police scanner and came straight on out." She reached into her purse and pulled out an ID wallet of her own that she handed over to Joanna.

"Frances G. Stoddard," the identification card said. "Private Investigator."

Suddenly, a day Joanna Brady was convinced had already bottomed out got that much worse. "You're David O'Brien's private eye."

"Bingo," Frances Stoddard said with a smile. "You can call me Frankie. Everybody else does. What was your name again?"

"Brady," Joanna said wearily. "And you can call me Sheriff."

If Frankie Stoddard was offended by Joanna's brusque reply, she certainly didn't let it show. "Glad to meet you, Sheriff," she said. "I understand you've been traveling in a vehicle with no radio, so you probably don't know what's going on."

"What now?"

"If this is the right road, two of your officers are up ahead. Stuck in a wash. They've called for a wrecker to come get them out. I have a winch on the Rover. I thought if I could get up to where they are . . ."

Joanna closed her eyes and shook her head. *From bad to worse and worse again.*

"Come on," she said to Frankie. "If you can move your vehicle out of the way, I'll go first. And if you can winch them out, I'll be eternally grateful. Otherwise, we'll be stuck here half the day without getting anywhere near where we're supposed to be."

At the turnoff in Apache, the road to Skeleton Canyon had been a fairly generous gravel affair that soon dwindled to dirt. On the other side of the closed gate, however, it was comprised of two rocky tracks with foot-high grass growing up in the middle. A few hundred yards beyond the gate, the road opened out again into a wide, sandy wash. Ernie Carpenter's van sat stuck in the middle of it, mired in sand up to the hubcaps.

Ernie sat on a nearby rock, wiping the sweat off his forehead. As soon as Detective Carbajal saw Joanna, he came hurrying up to her Eagle. "Sorry about this, Sheriff Brady," Jaime apologized. "I thought I had enough momentum going into the wash to get us through. The sand just reached out and grabbed us."

There was no sense in ripping into him about it. "Tell you what, Jaime," Joanna said. "Load what you can of Ernie's equipment into the back of this. The lady behind me, Frankie Stoddard, is a private detective working for David O'Brien. She says she has a winch, and she thinks maybe her Range Rover can haul you out of here. Meantime, I'll take Doc Winfield and Ernie on up the line to see if we can make it to the accident scene."

"Sure thing, Sheriff Brady," Jaime said. "I'll get right on it."

Twenty minutes later, Joanna was ready to set out again with George Winfield in the front seat and with Ernie scrunched into the backseat along with as much of his equipment as would fit. Shifting into four-wheel drive, she negotiated the wash with no difficulty.

"Who was that lady?" Ernie asked again. "The one with the Range Rover?"

"Her name's Frankie Stoddard," Joanna answered. "She's David O'Brien's private eye."

"Great," Ernie muttered.

"That's what I say," Joanna said.

ANGIE KELLOGG heard the sirens. Sitting in a thicket of mesquite, she watched the drama below. She saw an agitated Dennis Hacker bound off the hillside and into the little clearing where the Hummer was parked, saw him look around anxiously for her, heard him calling her name and talking on his cell phone, but Angie didn't move. She was too hurt. Too angry.

It wasn't that she liked Dennis Hacker that much. She had seen him just the two times. What was important about him, though, was what he represented. Joanna Brady, Marianne Maculyea, Jeff Daniels, and Bobo Jenkins had all tried to convince Angie that she could leave her past behind and live a normal life. And it had seemed to her in the past few months that she was doing so, that she was succeeding. She had made some friends at work. At home, she was learning to deal with neighbors, some of whom she liked and some she didn't.

The former included Effie Spangler, Angie's spry, octogenarian neighbor, who despite her years and having a working clothes dryer in her laundry room, nevertheless preferred drying her wash on a clothesline. The latter included Richard, Effie's obnoxious husband, who always seemed to find something to do in the backyard whenever Angie was sunbathing and who never failed to complain that her bird feeders were bound to attract rats.

For Angie, there was much to be proud of. There was a normalcy and a regularity to her existence now that would have astonished her family back home in Battle Creek. Some of that normalcy included things her parents themselves had never achieved. For instance, Angie's snug little house in Galena was completely paid for. She had a job and a car and insurance premiums. She had her own driver's license and her very own voter's registration card. All of those achievements should have said she was real.

Yet, in spite of all that, once she told Dennis Hacker the truth, he'd had the nerve to laugh at her. That hurt like hell.

She heard him now, calling her name. "Angie, Angie. Where are you?"

I'm up here, she thought determinedly, *and I'm not coming down.*

From her vantage point high on the hillside, she could see north to a road—a paved highway of some kind. Every ten minutes or so a vehicle would pass slowly in one direction or the other. She knew this wasn't the road she and Dennis had taken from Douglas early that morning because what Dennis had called Old Geronimo Trail had been dirt most of the way.

That's what I'll do, she told herself, watching a pickup wend its way along that same paved road. *When he finally gives up and leaves, I'll walk down there and hitchhike home.*

But what would she do when she got there? Stay or go? Work her heart out to get along, knowing all the time that as soon as people knew the real story, they would reject her out of hand? What was the use of fighting it? Maybe she should leave for a while, go someplace else. She'd have to give Bobo notice, of course. Give him a chance to find someone to take her place, but that probably wouldn't be all that hard.

Just then, with that thought barely formed in her head, she felt a whirring past her ear. A high squeak shrilled in her ear as a beautiful, multi-colored Lucifer Hummingbird settled on a branch not five feet from where Angie was sitting. He was close enough that she could see the distinctive downcurved bill, the rich purple feathers on the underside of his throat, and the bronze-green hues from crown to rump. Although Angie was careful not to move, he stayed for only a few seconds, then he was off, buzzing down the mountainside.

It was like a fairy tale. It seemed almost as if the beautiful bird had given her permission to go. She stood up as he disappeared from view.

"Good-bye," she whispered aloud. "I'm leaving, too."

FOURTEEN

STANDING ON the edge of the ridge, Joanna looked down on the shattered remains of the pickup far below. It lay on its top, parallel to the road, with a spray of silvery glass shards glittering around it. "Where's the body?" she asked Dennis Hacker, who was standing beside her.

"Under the cab," he replied. "I couldn't see it, but I know it's there."

"How?" Joanna asked.

Hacker nodded skyward toward three vultures circling lazily high overhead. "A little bird told me," he said. "When I got closer, I could figure it out for myself."

Joanna turned to Ernie Carpenter and George Winfield, who had been walking back and forth along the cliff, trying to determine exactly where Brianna had run off the edge and why. Now they stood nearby, conferring in low voices.

"No sign of braking or skidding. No sign of her

meeting another vehicle and being forced off the cliff."

"What happened, then?" George asked.

Ernie shook his head. "The only thing I can figure is she came around the rock face too close to the edge and tipped off. But if she was in four-wheel drive, with two wheels still on the track, she should have been able to correct and get back up on the trail—unless she was drunk or sound asleep, that is."

"Who'd go to sleep driving in a place like this?" George asked, looking around. "Maybe she did it on purpose."

"Maybe," Ernie agreed.

"What next?" Joanna asked, inserting herself into the discussion.

"Mr. Hacker says the body is caught under the cab. If that's the case, we may have to tip the truck over to get at it," Ernie said.

"But won't that run the risk of rolling it further down the hill?" Joanna objected.

"It's possible, so before we do anything rash, I'd suggest we climb down and take a closer look."

Detective Carpenter and George Winfield set off, with Ernie leading the way and with George slipping and sliding in his wake. *I warned him to bring along decent shoes*, Joanna thought, hoping he wouldn't break a leg or his neck in the process.

"But what about Angie?" Dennis Hacker was saying. "Is anyone looking for her?"

"Why don't you tell me what happened?" Joanna said.

"We were up in the meadow, watching the

hummingbirds and having a great time, when we started talking. I guess I hurt her feelings, but I didn't mean to. She took off down the mountain. I haven't seen her since."

"Exactly how did you hurt her feelings?"

"You're a friend of hers," Hacker said. "Does that mean you know about her background?"

Joanna met the man's troubled gaze, staring back at him without flinching. "If you're asking me whether or not I know Angie Kellogg is a former prostitute, the answer is yes. I know all about it. She told me."

"She told me, too," Hacker continued with a pained expression on his face. "I'm afraid I did something unforgivable. I laughed."

"You did what?"

"I laughed. Look, I can explain . . ."

"I don't think I'm interested in your explanations, Mr. Hacker," Joanna said coldly. "But I can certainly see why Angie left. She wasn't physically injured in any way the last time you saw her, was she?"

"No, she was fine—"

Joanna cut him off. "I'm sure, from what you say, that she probably *is* fine. And I have no doubt that she'll find her own way home."

"But it's getting hot. She didn't take any water with her. If she drinks water from the stream, there's no telling what will happen. She could come down with giardia—or worse."

"Thank you for your help in finding the pickup, Mr. Hacker," Joanna said, dismissing him. "Dispatch has your cellular number, don't they?"

"Yes."

"How about if you go home and look after your parrots. We'll give you a call when we find her."

Joanna knew she was being curt, but she didn't care. Why should she? She was so angry with Dennis Hacker right then that she could have spit. How dare this arrogant asshole with his sixty-five-thousand-dollar off-road wonder and vanity plates that said BRDMAN laugh at Angie Kellogg? How dare he make fun of someone who, against terrible odds, was struggling to gain a toehold in the regular world?

"But, Sheriff Brady . . ." Hacker began, flushing beet red under his tan from the top of his khaki collar to the roots of his straw-colored hair.

Joanna was glad to see that flush, gratified that her words had hit home. Dennis Hacker deserved to be embarrassed. "You'll have to excuse me now," she said. "My people and I have an accident to investigate."

Leaving Dennis Hacker alone and stewing, Joanna followed Ernie Carpenter and George Winfield down the cliff face. Even with proper hiking boots, getting down was no easy task. Just below the ridge, the empty camper shell clung to a rocky outcropping like the dead husk of a molted and long-gone cicada. A few steps farther down the hill, Joanna realized that however long ago the accident had happened, the summer heat had done its worst. Within fifteen feet of the wreck, Joanna's nostrils filled with the ugly stench of rotting flesh. Dennis Hacker was right and so were the vultures. There could be no doubt someone or something was dead.

By the time Joanna reached the shattered truck, both Ernie and George were wearing face masks over their mouths and noses. Both of the truck's doors were missing, and the two investigators were peering into the cab of the pickup through the missing uphill door. When Joanna joined them, George Winfield fumbled a third mask out of his pocket and handed it over. She accepted the mask gratefully and put it on at once—not that it did much good.

"What gives?" she asked.

George pointed to a boulder that was perched beside the top of the cab. "No sign of any survivors," he said. "That rock down there on the other side of the engine is what stopped it. The problem is, with the truck's center of gravity up in the air like this, we can't be sure the rock is strong enough to hold it secure."

"So what do we do?" Joanna asked. "Try to get it back on its wheels?"

Ernie nodded. "We sure as hell can't do any investigating this way. I'm worried about tipping it, though. On this kind of steep grade, depending on the momentum and what it hits going down, it could still roll a long way. Hopefully, though, we'll accomplish two things—uncover the body so George here can get at it, and have the truck come to rest against something solid enough that we can actually get inside."

"The grass around here is tinder dry," Joanna observed. "Any danger of starting a fire?"

Ernie shook his head. "Fortunately, I don't smell any leaking fuel. If it didn't catch fire when it came rolling down the hill with the engine running, it isn't going to burn up now."

Hearing the sound of falling rocks and pebbles behind her, Joanna turned in time to see a block and tackle fall to the ground behind her. Moments later Dennis Hacker came sliding after it, carrying a crowbar. Without a glance in Joanna's direction, he walked up to Ernie. "If you're going to try to move the truck, I thought these might come in handy," he said.

He paused for a moment and surveyed the situation. "I don't think that boulder's enough to hold it. Want me to try prying it out of the way?"

"Sure," Ernie said. "Let's see what happens."

Since Ernie had already agreed, there wasn't much point in Joanna's objecting. Besides, compared to Ernie Carpenter and George Winfield, Dennis Hacker was a hulk of a young man. Somewhere in his thirties, he was a good twenty years younger than the detective and twenty-five or so younger than the coroner. Not only that, he was in tremendously good shape.

"Be careful," was all Joanna said, then she stood aside and watched. It took several grunting, muscle-bulging efforts before Hacker sent the boulder crashing down the steep face of the mountain, cracking like a rifle shot as it bounced against other rocks along the way and finally rolling out of sight into the underbrush.

The worry had been that with the rock out of the way, the truck itself might slip loose from its precarious mooring and come rolling down on Hacker. It didn't. Moments later, the four of them, all wearing disposable rubber gloves, were once again uphill from the wreck.

Joanna expected it would take a good deal of effort to move the truck. Her assumption was that they would have to rock it back and forth to get it moving, sort of like pulling a gigantic tooth. In actual fact, they pushed far too hard. The first shove sent the truck tumbling while the pitch of the steep hillside, momentum, and gravity all worked together to do the rest. The Tacoma rolled first onto its side and then up onto its flattened tires. It tottered there briefly and then went right on rolling, careening down the hill twice more before it came to rest, upright again, against a scrub oak.

"Way to go," Ernie panted. "That tree should hold it."

But by then Joanna wasn't listening. She was looking down at her feet, staring at the pitiful lump of smashed flesh that had once been Brianna O'Brien. She lay facedown on the rock-strewn hillside. Her long blond hair fanned out around her, parted by a jagged bloody gash that ran almost the whole length of her head. Her face had been crushed almost flat.

For Joanna, though, the worst part wasn't the awful physical wounds visible on the broken and rapidly decomposing body. She had expected those. They went with the territory of accident investigation. What Sheriff Brady hadn't expected was the fact that Brianna O'Brien wasn't dressed the way her mother had predicted she would be. Bree wasn't dressed at all. She was, in fact, stark naked.

Faced with that horrifying full view of Bree O'Brien's mangled and naked corpse, Joanna's knees went weak beneath her. She had to fight to control the wave of nausea that rose in her throat.

"I'm going to need my stuff," George Winfield was saying as he picked his way across the mountain's steep grade all the while struggling to maintain his balance.

"I'll go get it for you," Dennis Hacker offered at once, wiping the perspiration off his brow. "Tell me where it is."

Joanna reached into her pocket and pulled out her car keys. "Thanks," she said, handing them over. "It's the brown leather satchel in the back of the Eagle."

While Dennis Hacker climbed back up the cliff, George Winfield knelt beside the body, close enough to look but without touching anything. In the meantime, Ernie set off down the mountain after the truck. Given an option, Joanna followed Ernie.

In the process of falling the first time, the camper shell had been knocked loose. There was debris scattered all over the hillside. Careful not to touch anything, Joanna picked her way through it—past the battered cooler that had spilled out its cache of sandwiches and smashed and empty soda cans. Past an unfurled bedroll and an air mattress that was still fully inflated. Past broken camp stools and a still-zipped cloth suitcase that trailed clothing out of its torn side.

Joanna was sidestepping the suitcase when she saw a book. The cover—blue with a cascade of pale pink flowers—matched the others she and Ernie had seen in Brianna O'Brien's bedroom. "Ernie," she called, "here's the journal."

Ernie had pulled out a camera and was already taking photos of the battered wreck. "One journal or two?" he called, without bothering to look over his shoulder.

"Only one so far," Joanna replied. "The other one's probably around here somewhere. Is it okay if I pick this one up and look at it?"

"You're wearing gloves, aren't you?"

"Yes."

"Go ahead then, if you want to," he said.

Fully aware that the person who had last touched the book was dead, Joanna approached the journal reverently, almost as though it were a holy relic. Dropping down onto a nearby rock, she opened the front cover. Written in the same girlish hand Joanna remembered from the other volumes, this one covered the period of time between October 9 of the previous year and this year's March 4.

"It's the completed one," Joanna called to Ernie.

"Well then," Ernie replied impatiently between squeezes on his camera's shutter, "go look for the other."

By then Dennis Hacker had returned from the Eagle with George Winfield's equipment satchel.

Taking out an evidence bag, Joanna slipped the book inside. Then she began to comb the hillside, searching for the missing book. It was hard, hot work. She went to what appeared to be the edge of the debris field—the camper shell—and started there. At the end of half an hour she was too hot and winded to continue.

"Your face is all red," George Winfield observed, glancing in her direction. "Better have some of that water of yours. I'd hate for you to have a heat-stroke."

"Thanks," Joanna said. She heeded his advice immediately. Sinking down next to the evidence box, she helped herself to water from her canteen. As she did so, the journal was right there, sitting in plain sight, tempting her. Finally, handling it with the gloves on, and being careful to touch only the edges, she slipped it out and opened it, turning to the last entry first.

The entry for March 4 was written at the very bottom of the page. It consisted of only five words, written in a hurried, careless, and almost illegible scrawl: "My mother is a liar."

So is mine, Joanna thought. Remembering what was going on with Eleanor Lathrop and George Winfield, she couldn't help empathizing with the hurt made almost visible by Brianna O'Brien's angry scribble. Since that was the last sentence written at the bottom of the last page, there was no further explanation about what kind of lie Katherine O'Brien had told her daughter. No additional explanation was necessary for Joanna

Brady to know exactly how Brianna must have felt when she wrote those words—betrayed, hurt, and left out.

Glancing at the journal again, Joanna realized it was possible Bree had written more on the topic. Perhaps the entry continued in the next volume—the one that was still missing.

Still too hot to return to the ground search for the missing diary, Joanna spent a few more minutes scanning the preceding entries. From what was written there, she was able to gather that at the time Katherine O'Brien had been out of town, off on some kind of extended trip. Nothing Joanna could find in the days immediately preceding the March 4 entry gave any indication that there was anything amiss. One entry said that Bree was hoping to pull off a special surprise in honor of her mother's birthday, but there was nothing to explain exactly what the surprise was to be or whether it had anything to do with the unvarnished anger in those last few words.

Remembering that David O'Brien had mentioned the previous November as the time things had changed so for Brianna, Joanna thumbed back to the last week in November and the first few days of December. A few minutes later, after closing the book and returning it to the bag, she made her way down to where Ernie Carpenter was meticulously examining the interior of the truck.

"Find anything?" he asked.

"We now know the name of the boyfriend. Ignacio Ybarra, the football player from Douglas who was injured during the Bisbee/Douglas game."

Ernie stopped what he was doing. "The one Brianna O'Brien got kicked off the cheerleading squad over?"

"One and the same."

"We'd better go talk to him. Anything else?"

"The last entry is intriguing. It says, 'My mother is a liar.'"

"That's all?"

"That's it."

Ernie frowned. "It sounds as though there's a possibility that we're dealing with two liars here—like mother like daughter."

"It does sound that way," Joanna agreed. Just then she heard the noisy clamor of what must have been several approaching vehicles. "I'd better go up and see who's here."

"Go ahead," Ernie told her. "I'll keep working. If Jaime's finally dug himself out of that sand trap, tell him to get his ass down here. I need him to establish a grid and start bagging up some of this evidence. I don't like the sound of that thunder. I want this stuff out of here before it rains, not after."

Up until then, Joanna had been so preoccupied with what was going on that she hadn't paid any attention to the weather. Now, though, she looked up. Earlier the sky had been simply overcast. Now it was threateningly so. A storm was definitely brewing. Not only would they need to gather the evidence as quickly as possible, Joanna

realized, they would also need to get all the vehicles back across that enormous wash before the
rain arrived. Then, with a sudden pang of guilt,
Joanna realized she had spent more than an
hour too busy to give the missing Angie Kellogg
a single thought.

Hurriedly, she scrambled back up to the top
of the ridge. The crest looked like a traffic jam.
Vehicles were parked single file behind Joanna's
Eagle. First came Ernie's van, followed by a
wrecker from Willcox big enough to haul semis.
Bringing up the rear was Frankie Stoddard's
Range Rover. Dennis Hacker's Hummer, which
once had been parked directly behind the Eagle,
now was nowhere in sight.

Jaime Carbajal met Joanna at the lip of the
cliff. "Sorry it took so long, Sheriff Brady. We
ended up having to wait for the wrecker after all."

"That's okay. Hurry, though. Ernie wants you
down there on the double, establishing a grid
and bagging evidence. What about Mr. Hacker?"

"We ran into him about half a mile back. He's
off searching for Angie Kellogg."

"No one's heard from her or seen her?" Joanna
asked.

"Not so far."

Looking at the sky and worrying that she had
waited too long, Joanna hurried over to Ernie's
van and commandeered the radio. "Tica," she said
when the dispatcher answered. "Where are the
guys from Search and Rescue?"

"They're on the way," Tica responded.

"Tell them we've got an inexperienced hiker

lost out here in the Peloncillos, and it looks like a big storm is coming. If they need something of Angie's to give the dogs her scent, have them get in touch with her boss, Bobo Jenkins, at the Blue Moon up in Brewery Gulch."

By the time Joanna got off the radio, Frankie Stoddard was standing directly behind her. "So what gives?" the private investigator asked. "Is it her?" she asked, nodding in the direction of the wreck.

Joanna nodded. "We're pretty sure," she said. "Pending positive ID, of course."

"And she just ran off the cliff here?"

"That's how it looks."

For a long moment, Frankie stood with her arms crossed, staring down at the wreck. "I know it's your job to notify the parents," she said at last. "But I'd guess you're going to be tied up here for quite some time. If you'd like, I could drive back into town and tell the O'Briens that there's been a fatality accident out here and the victim is most likely their daughter."

Notifying the O'Briens was a task Joanna had been dreading from the moment she looked over the edge of the cliff and saw the smashed red pickup far below. "Once we get the body back to town, we'll need them to come do an official identification, but you're sure you wouldn't mind telling them initially?"

Frankie Stoddard shook her head sadly. "Mr. O'Brien hired me to find his daughter," she said. "It looks as though I have."

❦ FIFTEEN

THE NEXT several hours passed in a blur of activity. While awaiting the arrival of the Search and Rescue unit, Joanna stayed on the scene of the accident investigation. Overhead, the sky went from merely overcast to dark and threatening. The constant and ominous rumble of thunder to the south put real urgency into the race to gather evidence.

Joanna, along with Jaime Carbajal, worked at combing the steep hillside, bagging, logging, and labeling the debris they found there. She kept hoping one of them would stumble over the second volume of Brianna's journal, but so far it hadn't been found. Joanna and Jaime had just been joined by two additional deputies, Lindsey and Raymond, when Ernie called Joanna over to the truck.

"I'm about to give the wrecker operator the all-clear to haul this away, but I wanted you to take a look first," he said, motioning Joanna in the direction of the truck's interior. "See anything strange?"

Joanna looked inside. At first glance, there was nothing to see. The truck was absolutely empty. With both doors missing and both the windshield and back window broken out, there was nothing loose, including the driver, that hadn't been shaken out during the truck's roll down the mountain. On the gray leather headrest of the driver's seat was a single smear that looked like blood, but that single stain was all there was.

Joanna had been there when the truck was removed from the body. She had seen the terrible laceration on the back of Brianna's skull, a blow so severe that it had left part of her brain exposed. With a wound like that, there should have been blood. Lots of it.

"Where's the spatter?" Joanna asked.

"Precisely," Ernie returned. "You're definitely starting to get the hang of this."

Joanna appreciated her investigator's unsolicited compliment, but there was no time to savor it. "So what?" she asked. "You're saying Brianna was already dead when the pickup went over the edge?"

"It's a possibility," Ernie said. "A distinct possibility."

Joanna felt yet another emotional hole open up and swallow her. On Saturday afternoon David O'Brien had expressed his fear—no, his firm belief—that something terrible had happened to his daughter. He had wanted Joanna to call in the FBI immediately. Had she done so? No. Instead, Sheriff Joanna Brady had taken refuge in the twenty-four-hour missing persons cop-out. She had done nothing. She wondered now if the outcome would have been any less fatal had she made a different decision.

"What about the other journal?" Joanna asked. "It's not out on the hill. We've searched every inch of it. I thought maybe it might be inside here, under the seat or behind it."

Ernie shook his head. "Believe me, this cab is clean as a whistle. So maybe whoever killed her took the book with him. Maybe she had written something in it that was incriminating."

Joanna nodded, remembering the last entry in the other journal. "My mother is a liar."

While Ernie went off to confer with the tow truck driver, Joanna returned to the spot at the bottom of the cliff where Doc Winfield had just finished zipping the body bag closed. As the two deputies loaded it into a basket, George turned to Joanna.

"I'm worried about trying to maneuver the body up that trail. Looks to me as though it's going to be next to impossible. Do you think Mr. Hacker would mind if we used his block and tackle?"

Joanna wasn't much interested in what Dennis Hacker would or wouldn't mind. "He left it here," she said. "He must have meant for us to use it."

While Winfield attached the come-along to the basket, one of the deputies took the rest of the block and tackle back up the cliff. Even with Detective Carbajal and the two deputies to apply muscle, pulling the body up was still a tricky process. The face of the ridge wasn't smooth. More than once the basket got hung up, once on a clump of mesquite and another time it wedged in underneath a jagged outcropping of rock. The second stall was far more serious than the first. With Doc Winfield on his hands and knees at the edge of the cliff shouting instructions, Joanna had to work her way out onto a narrow ledge far enough to pry the basket loose. The storm was almost on them by then. Sand and grit flew in her eyes, and the force necessary to set the basket free also threatened to knock Joanna off her precarious perch. It took half a dozen tries before the basket swung free and disappeared overhead.

"Good work," Ernie said, stretching out a hand to pull Joanna back to the relative safety of a newly made path. "It's a wonder you didn't break your neck."

Joanna was standing there catching her breath when she heard Doc Winfield's shout. "Hey, Ernie. Come on up. There's something here you need to see. Quick, before the wind blows it away."

Grumbling, Ernie did as he was told, with Joanna close on his heels. When Joanna reached the top and could see, George Winfield was still on his hands and knees, staring intently into a scraggly clump of yellowed grass. "What's this look like to you?" he asked.

Wedging his way between Jaime and one of the deputies, Ernie Carpenter dropped to the ground beside Winfield. The detective, too, stared into the grass. "I'll be damned!" he exclaimed a moment later.

Joanna, coming up behind the group, was almost run over by Jaime, who was heading for the van at a gallop. "What's going on?" she asked.

"Ernie'll need a set of hemostats," he said. "I'm going to get them, along with the evidence log and the tape measure."

"And evidence bags," Ernie called after him. "I'm all out of the small ones."

Catching up with the others, Joanna peered over Ernie's shoulder and saw nothing. "What did you find?" she asked.

"A hair," Ernie answered. "A single strand of long blond hair."

"You're thinking the same thing I am, aren't you?" George Winfield said. "That she was dead long before she hit the ground."

Ernie nodded. "I'm afraid so," he said.

ANGIE KNEW the storm was brewing. She was out on the flat now and traveling at an angle toward the road, but behind her in the mountains and to the east of them, she could see a black torrent of rain falling from the sky. She had always been afraid of thunderstorms. One of the girls in her first grade class in Battle Creek had been hit and killed by lightning at an outdoor barbecue. There was nothing for it, though, but to keep walking.

A chill wind shrieked through the three-foot-tall grass. Lightning forked across the sky and thunder rumbled all around her. Angie wore jeans and boots and a long-sleeved shirt, but nothing waterproof. She hadn't expected to be out in the rain on foot. She hadn't expected to be in the desert alone.

The wilderness was still a frightening and alien place to her. Watching the desert birds was wonderful, but there were other desert dwellers that weren't nearly so pleasant. She had heard, for example, that snakes and Gila monsters came out in advance of rain storms. Archie McBride had told her that, and Willy had backed him up. They both claimed that a Gila monsters bite could kill you within a matter of minutes. A lot of what Archie and Willy said was so much bullshit. It was possible they had just been teasing her with more of their tall tales. Still, out there all by herself, with the wind whistling and the grass bent almost double, it seemed likely that they had told the truth.

In the course of hours of waiting and walking, Angie Kellogg had moved beyond being hurt. Now she was simply mad. "Damn you anyway, Dennis Hacker," she shouted into the screeching wind. "Go ahead and laugh. See if I care."

"YOU THINK it's hers, then?" Joanna asked, watching Ernie fight the windblown hair into an equally windblown glassine bag.

"Who else's would it be?" he asked. "As soon as we can get the body transported, we'll have to search the rest of the area up here, just in case. And we're going to have to hurry. The storm's almost here. Get her loaded into that truck on the double."

"Truck?" Joanna asked.

Ernie nodded. "Deputy Raymond brought along his pickup. He can take her back to Bisbee in that."

Joanna looked at Matt Raymond's Ford F-100 parked four vehicles down the hill. Then she looked back at the basket and the body bag. "No," she said.

"What do you mean, no?" Ernie countered.

"Just what I said. We're not going to haul Brianna O'Brien's body back to town in the bed of a pickup truck like she was a sack of potatoes or a bale of hay. Put her in my Eagle."

That announcement stunned the little group gathered around the body basket into total silence. Joanna caught the questioning look George Winfield leveled in her direction. "Are you sure?" he asked.

"I'm sure," she said. "Load her up."

As Deputies Raymond and Lindsey hurried to comply, Joanna turned back to the others. "Doc Winfield and I will go on ahead. The rest of you, don't spend too much time looking for evidence. It looks like this storm's going to be a doozy. It's the first one of the season, so most of the water should soak in, but I don't want anybody taking any chances with that wash." She aimed the last sentence directly at Jaime Carbajal, who grinned apologetically.

"Don't worry, Sheriff Brady," he said. "I've learned my lesson. Besides, if we get into any trouble, the wrecker's already here."

"I don't even want to think about it," she said. With the storm boiling in from the south, the possibility of vehicles getting stuck was one consideration. What was far worse, however, was the thought of Angie, out by herself, lost and afraid in a storm of that magnitude. She knew nothing at all about the desert. If a fully loaded vehicle couldn't stand up to a flash flood, what would happen to her if she made the mistake of stepping into a raging, water-filled wash?

I don't want to think about that, either, Joanna told herself. She had summoned Search and Rescue and made sure they were doing their job. For now, that was the best she could do.

THE RAIN hit long before Angie made it to the road. Within seconds she was soaked to the skin. Her hair was plastered down around her face. The downpour was startlingly cold. *Looking like this, I'll never catch a ride,* she thought despairingly as she ducked through the strands of barbed wire that stood between her and the narrow ribbon of pavement. Angie was enough of a hitch-hiking veteran to know that most drivers wouldn't stop for someone who was soaking wet. Why would they want to put some muddy bedraggled wreck into a perfectly clean and dry car?

Still, what choice did she have? Treading carefully, she picked her way across the rain-slick blacktop and positioned herself on the far side of the road. Through the pouring, slanting raindrops, no vehicles were visible as far as she could see in either direction. It looked as though it was going to be a long damned wait.

She stood in the rain for what seemed like a very long time. Peering blindly off to the east, she didn't even hear the car bearing down on her from the west until it was almost upon her. When she did hear it, she turned just in time to see a VW bug flash by. It looked like Marianne Maculyea's car. Sea foam green was the right color, but . . .

A few feet beyond where Angie stood the VW's brake lights flashed on. Skidding dangerously back and forth across the center line, the car came to a stop and then the backup lights came on.

Angie ran forward, meeting the vehicle just as Marianne rolled down the window. "What are you doing here?" Angie asked.

"What do you think? That I'm out for a Sunday ride?" Marianne asked. "I'm looking for you. I came as soon as I could get loose from coffee hour. Climb in. You're soaking wet."

Summoning as much dignity as she could, Angie walked around to the far side of the car and got inside. "I knew they were looking for me," she said. "I heard the sirens, but I didn't want them to find me."

"Why not? It's pouring rain."

Angie's eyes filled with tears. "Because Dennis Hacker made fun of me," she said. "I told him who and what I was and he laughed."

Reverend Marianne Maculyea put the VW into a sharp U-turn and then shifted back up to speed. "Maybe you'd better start at the beginning," she said kindly. "Tell me about Dennis Hacker. I don't know who this guy thinks he is, but he sounds like a creep in need of having his lights punched out."

It took several minutes for the body and Doc Winfield's satchel to be loaded into the Eagle. After that a series of several backing maneuvers were necessary before Joanna could turn the Eagle back down the ridgeline. In the rearview mirror, she saw the investigators scouring the ground where the body had been hauled up over the cliff. She was just picking her way past Ernie's van when the detective came huffing up behind her.

"On the way back to Bisbee, Jaime and I will stop by and see this Ignacio Ybarra down in Douglas."

Joanna nodded. "You think you'll be able to find him all right?"

"Are you kidding? Half of Jaime's relatives live

in Douglas. Finding him won't be a problem. What about going to see the O'Briens? Do you want us to handle that, too?"

Joanna considered his offer. She had already done one cowardly thing by letting Frankie Stoddard handle the initial notification, which, by rights, should have been a function of the sheriff's department. It would have been all too easy to let Carpenter and Carbajal go and take the brunt of David O'Brien's wrath. Easy, but not fair. Joanna had been the one who had insisted on following procedure. Regardless of whether or not the twenty-four-hour rule had made any difference in Brianna O'Brien's survival, it was only right that Joanna should take the heat for that decision.

"After I drop the body off at the morgue, I'll go home, clean up, and change. Call me as soon as you get in. We were the ones who went out to see the parents yesterday. We should be the ones to go there today."

Ernie gave her a half-assed salute that was at once both mildly teasing and respectful. "Right, Chief," he said. "I'll give you a call as soon as we hit town."

As he backed away from the car, Joanna started to roll up the window. Then she thought better of it. Instead, she left it down. The smell of moisture sweeping across the parched desert was a welcome antidote to the smell of decaying flesh that leaked through the thick folds of the body bag and permeated the air.

"I appreciate this," George Winfield said as they started down the mountain. "The truck might have done the job, but you're right. It wouldn't have shown the proper respect."

"What about the autopsy?" Joanna asked. "How soon can you do it?"

"Tomorrow," Winfield answered. "Unless you need it sooner."

"No," Joanna said. "Tomorrow will be fine. You'll be able to tell when she died?"

"Friday, between nine and ten," George said confidently.

Joanna was impressed. "You can tell that just by looking at the body?"

George Winfield shook his head. "No, by looking at her watch," he said. "It stopped at nine fifty-one on Friday, June fourteenth. It could have been broken during the initial attack or during the plunge off the mountain. I'd say from the condition of the body that disposal took place within an hour or so of time of death."

"I see," Joanna said. In a way, she was relieved. It salved her conscience a little to know that Brianna had already been dead long before Joanna herself had taken refuge in the twenty-four-hour rule. What she had or hadn't done once she and Ernie had been summoned to Green Brush Ranch would have made no difference in whether or not Bree O'Brien survived.

By the time the Eagle neared the big wash, the storm was starting in dead earnest. First came hard, wind-driven drops that pounded into the dry earth and sent up little puffs of powdery dust. Then came a cloud of needle-sharp hail while jagged forks of lightning crackled across the sky. After that, the sky seemed to open up and the rain fell in torrents. The laboring windshield wipers couldn't come close to keeping up. Lack of visibility forced Joanna to slow to a crawl.

"Unbelievable!" George shouted over the roar of the wind, rain, and thunder. "I've been here for months and never knew it could storm like this."

Going into the big wash, Joanna stopped at the crest of the hill to examine the roadbed. The process of extricating the van had torn it up, leaving great gouges in the sand. If the wash started running, those deep, gaping holes would fill first. Peering through the windshield, she spotted a new set of tracks that detoured around the damaged roadway. Deciding those had most likely been left by Frankie Stoddard leaving and the two deputies coming, Joanna followed them. She heaved a sigh of relief when they were safely across.

Winfield looked behind them. "Are those washes really dangerous? I keep suspecting that all the flash flood nonsense is so much hooey—something old-timers tell new arrivals just to scare their pants off and keep 'em in line."

"They're not nonsense," Joanna told him. "When you see a sign that says DO NOT ENTER WHEN FLOODED, don't. A wash like the one back there can fill up with water in less than a minute. In fact, in less than sixty seconds it can swallow a car."

"How can that be?" George asked. "It doesn't look that deep."

"The sand liquefies in the water," Joanna explained. "What looks like a foot-deep little drop right now can turn into a six- or seven-foot killer during a storm. People drown in them all the time."

"No shi—" Winfield stopped himself. "No kidding," he corrected.

Joanna looked across the seat at George and smiled. In the last several hours, they had worked so hard together and in such a focused, purposeful manner, that all personal considerations had somehow melted away. They had been sheriff and coroner working together as professionals. Now, his small verbal slip brought the personal back into view.

"It's all right if you use the word *shit* around me," Joanna assured him. "You don't have to edit what you say and you certainly don't need to apologize. I'm a big girl. I've heard it all before."

"It's just that . . ."

"That's one of the differences between my mother and me," Joanna continued. "On occasion, with enough provocation, I've been known to use that particular expression myself and a few that are worse. I don't believe, however, that any of those words have ever passed Eleanor Lathrop's lips. As far as I know, she's never moved a whit beyond a heartfelt 'My stars and garters.'"

George smiled and nodded. They reached the fence then. Joanna waited while George climbed out into the driving rain to open the gate. When he stepped back inside, he was soaked to the skin.

They were almost to the turnoff at Apache before he spoke again. "Why do you call her that?" he asked.

"Why do I call my mother Mother?" Joanna asked.

"No. Why do you call her Eleanor?"

Until George pointed it out, Joanna wasn't even aware of it. She had to think about her answer for some time before she gave it. "I've always called her that," Joanna said.

"Do you call her that to her face, or is it just when you speak of her to other people?" George persisted.

Again, Joanna considered her reply. "I don't suppose I've ever called her that to her face," she admitted honestly. "But it is how I talk about her, and it's how I think about her, too. As Eleanor."

"I see," George said, nodding thoughtfully and rubbing his chin. "So what you're saying is that it's not so much a matter of disrespect as it is a matter of distancing."

And because the questions and George Winfield's resulting conclusion came far too close to home, Joanna had to lash out at him.

"She tried to hold me too close," Joanna snarled. "She tried to smother me."

For a long time after that, while they traversed the rest of the gravel track into Apache and then for several miles after they turned onto the blacktop, they drove through the curtain of pouring rain with neither of them saying a word.

"Ellie isn't doing it anymore," George Winfield said at last. "I believe she's willing to let you go, Joanna. Isn't it about time you did the same?"

SIXTEEN

BY THE time they reached Douglas, Joanna realized she had been wrong in her assumption about
that first storm of the season. The rain wasn't
soaking in after all. Water came down in such a
swift deluge that there wasn't time for soaking.
The dips on Highway 80 northeast of Douglas
were already trickling with water that, Joanna
knew, could turn into a torrent at any time once
runoff from higher elevations drained into the
gullies and washes.

In Douglas proper, the highway's railroad
underpass was closed—for good reason. Years
earlier, the highway department had painted
markers on the wall in foot-long increments in
order to measure and warn otherwise unsus-
pecting motorists of the water's dangerous and
potentially lethal depth. Joanna was surprised to
see that the water filling the Southern Pacific
underpass—murky, reddish brown stuff topped

by a foamy white froth—had already topped the four-foot mark and was still rising.

"Now I see what you mean," George Winfield murmured as the Eagle sat idling next to the yellow-and-black sign that stated the all-too-obvious—DO NOT ENTER WHEN FLOODED.

Southeastern Arizona's summer thunderstorms are often fierce but brief. For some reason, this one, after that first incredible outburst, had now settled into a steady downpour. George Winfield's clothing, still damp from getting out to open the gate, made the windows inside the Eagle keep steaming up. Unfortunately, because the air-conditioning compressor wasn't working, neither was the defroster. As they waited in the detour line to be routed around the flooded underpass, Joanna thought she glimpsed Marianne Maculyea's 1960s vintage VW far ahead of them.

Seeing the car reminded Joanna that Marianne hadn't shown up in Skeleton Canyon. Had she been there with the Search and Rescue Unit looking for Angie, Joanna surely would have heard about it. Something serious must have come up in Bisbee, Joanna reasoned. It wasn't like Marianne not to show up in person when one of her friends and/or parishioners was in trouble.

Thinking of Angie reminded Joanna once again of just how wrong she could be. And how often. This supposedly welcome rain storm was turning into a veritable flood. Instead of spending an un-authorized weekend with her boyfriend, Brianna O'Brien was dead—at the hands of person or persons unknown. And Dennis Hacker, who had struck her as a nice man, had turned out to be a jerk instead.

You're batting a thousand, old girl, Joanna told herself. *Just keep it up.*

❦ **AT THE** Double Adobe turnoff, Joanna stopped to let George Winfield into his own vehicle. "Do you want to transfer her into my van now?" he asked before opening his door. "That way you could go straight home from here."

Joanna shook her head. The rain was still falling. The coroner's office up in Tombstone Canyon was housed in a former funeral home that came complete with a covered portico. "I'll take her the rest of the way to your office," Joanna told him. "That way she won't get wet, and neither will your satchel."

"Thanks, Joanna," George told her, climbing out. "See you there."

The usually dry creek in Mule Gulch was running bank to bank where it crossed the highway, and there were fallen rocks and muddy debris on the roadway in the high cuts between there and Bisbee. Wanting to report the hazard and summon someone to clean it up, Joanna reached for her radio. For the dozenth time that day, it wasn't there. Her ability to communicate with Dispatch was at home in the Crown Victoria, parked in the yard of High Lonesome Ranch.

That does it, she thought. *Budget or no budget, I'm getting a cellular phone.*

It was almost four in the afternoon as Joanna made her way up Tombstone Canyon. That wasn't easy, either. The deluge had washed what looked like at least one vehicle down Brewery Gulch. It was stuck in the subway, a massive storm drain designed for just such occasions. Driving past emergency vehicles and personnel out in the downpour trying to pull whatever it was out, Joanna couldn't help being grateful that this latest incident, whatever it might be, was inside the Bisbee city limits rather than outside. That made it someone else's problem, not hers.

She realized then that she was hungry. Not just hungry—starving. She'd had nothing to eat all day long. She had missed Eva Lou Brady's Sunday dinner, which had probably been something wonderful like a pork roast or fried chicken. Health-conscious badgering might have persuaded the Colonel to change a few things at KFC, but there had been no change in Eva Lou's philosophy of what was appropriate fare for Sunday dinner.

Fantasizing about that missed meal, Joanna failed to notice the black Lexus parked by the curb just down the street from the coroner's office. Joanna was sitting in the Eagle under the portico and waiting for George to pull in behind her when someone tapped on the window beside her head. She looked outside to see the grief-ravaged face of Katherine O'Brien.

Joanna opened the door. In the more than two hours she had been in the car with the body, Joanna's olfactory senses had somehow become deadened to the stench. Only when she opened the door and moved into the fresh air could she tell the difference. The evil cloud that came out of the Eagle with her sent Katherine reeling backward, gagging and holding her mouth.

"That's not . . ." she wailed, shuddering and pointing at the mud-encrusted back gate of Joanna's wagon. "It can't be . . ."

"Mrs. O'Brien," Joanna said quickly. "What on earth are you doing here?"

"I had to come and see for myself," Katherine said. "Miss Stoddard told us that it didn't look good, but I had to know for sure. I had to know what really happened."

Seeing the Lexus now, Joanna squinted through the rain. "Where's your husband, Mrs. O'Brien? Is he waiting in the car?"

Katherine shook her head. "I came by myself. I told him I was going up to St. Dominick's to light a candle and pray. He doesn't know I'm here."

"And you shouldn't be," Joanna admonished. "Dr. Winfield wasn't planning to try to ID the body until after it's been properly taken care of for evidence reasons."

"It?" Katherine said, her voice rising until it verged on hysterics. "You're calling my daughter an 'it'? And what's she doing stuffed in the back of a station wagon like that?"

Thank God Deputy Raymond didn't drive up with the body in the back of his pickup, Joanna thought.

Just then Doc Winfield pulled in behind the Eagle. "What's going on?" he asked.

"This is Katherine O'Brien," Joanna explained.

"She came to find out what's happened to her daughter."

George Winfield's clothing was still plastered to his body. The man was a mess. Still, with a look of total and grave concern, he reached out and took Katherine O'Brien's hand, grasping it firmly. "I'm so sorry, Mrs. O'Brien," he said, his voice softened by genuine warmth and dignity both. "It will take some time for me to prepare things so you can actually view your daughter. If you wouldn't mind going inside to wait, I'll come get you as soon as possible."

Taking Katherine by the arm, he escorted her to the door while Joanna stood there waiting. She knew George Winfield had been a doctor once, an oncologist, before he had left that field to study forensic pathology. As she watched Katherine O'Brien lean against him, taking comfort from whatever he was saying to her, Joanna realized she was seeing a demonstration of bedside manner in action—an impressive demonstration at that.

Joanna knew the body was far too heavy for her to manage on her own. During the next few minutes, she occupied herself with hauling George Winfield's equipment case out of the back of her Eagle. In less than five minutes, the coroner reappeared. He was dressed in clean, dry scrubs and wearing a lab coat. He was also pushing a gurney.

"If you can help me load her onto this," he said, "I'll be able to handle things from here."

"What about Mrs. O'Brien?" Joanna asked.

"Do you want me to have her go home and come back later?"

Winfield frowned. "I'm not used to having family members waiting outside quite this soon," he said. "But you could just as well let her stay. The face is so badly mangled from being squashed flat by the falling truck that there isn't that much that will soften the blow. Not only that, if the mother can't positively identify her by sight, then we're better off knowing now that we'll have to get the dental records."

Joanna nodded. "Do you want me to wait with her?"

"If you don't mind," George Winfield said, "that would be a big help."

Painfully aware of her own scruffy appearance—of her dirty clothes and dusty hiking boots—Joanna Brady ventured inside. The Cochise County Coroner's Office was housed in quarters once occupied by Dearest Departures, a bankrupted discount funeral home. George Winfield had stowed Katherine O'Brien in a small, darkened room that had probably been intended to function as a private chapel. Katherine sat on one end of an upholstered love seat, weeping quietly into a hanky. Joanna walked over and sat down beside her.

"You probably shouldn't do this alone," Joanna said tentatively. "Would you like to have someone go out to Sombra—" She stopped and corrected herself. "—to Green Brush Ranch and bring your husband here to be with you?"

Katherine O'Brien shook her head. "I'm a trained nurse," she said. "It's better if I do it."

Joanna nodded. "All right, then," she said.

Katherine blew her nose. "Tell me about Ignacio Ybarra," she said.

"I didn't think you knew anything about your daughter's boyfriend," Joanna returned. "That's what you told us yesterday."

"I didn't," Katherine said. "Not then. Frankie Stoddard picked up the name earlier by listening to radio transmissions on her police scanner. As soon as she mentioned the name, I recognized it. He's the football player from Douglas—the one who was injured in the Bisbee-Douglas game."

"The one your daughter quit the cheerleading squad over?"

Katherine nodded. "That's him," she said.

"My mother is a liar." Unbidden, the words from the last entry in Brianna's journal came back to Joanna in a rush. *What kind of liar?*

There were lots of ways to lie, Joanna realized. Eleanor Lathrop had lied, not by spinning some outrageous fib but by keeping silent. By marrying George Winfield on the sly and then by not mentioning it to anyone, not even to her own daughter. That was what Ogden Nash and the Catholic church would have called a sin of omission rather than a sin of commission. So what kind of untruth on Katherine's part had so offended her own daughter that Brianna had retaliated by weaving her own web of lies?

"Are you aware that two of your daughter's journal volumes are missing from her room?"

"No," Katherine replied. "I had no idea."

"One was found at the crash site. The second—the current one—wasn't there."

"So it is her, then, isn't it," Katherine said doggedly, her tears starting anew. "I kept hoping and praying it might be some other truck. There are lots of those around, you know. I saw one just like it on my way uptown. But the journal . . ." She shook her head. "That pretty well settles it. How did it happen? The accident, I mean. Tell me. I need to know."

Joanna sighed. With no certain confirmation from the autopsy, it was still way too early to discuss the possibility that Bree's death might prove to be a homicide rather than an accident. Still, as long as Frankie Stoddard continued to monitor all departmental radio transmissions, it wouldn't be a secret for long. Joanna nonetheless decided to try.

"The truck ran off a cliff out in the Peloncillos," she said. "It turned over several times. It looks as though Brianna was thrown clear. When the truck finally came to rest, she was crushed underneath it. Under the cab."

Katherine closed her eyes. "She died instantly, then?"

Joanna shook her head. "I don't know," she said. "Dr. Winfield is the only one who can answer those kinds of questions. That's why he needs time to collect evidence."

"Yes," Katherine said. "Of course."

"Tell me something," Joanna said. "Yesterday, when your husband wanted me to notify the FBI, he raised the issue of a possible kidnapping. Is there anything in your husband's business dealings that would lend itself to that kind of scenario?"

The change in Katherine's demeanor was abrupt. "What exactly do you mean by that?" she demanded. "And what does a question like that have to do with my daughter driving her truck off a cliff?"

She's doing it again, Joanna thought, watching in fascination as Katherine O'Brien seemed to collect herself and make an almost instant transformation into a tigress defending her young or den. It was the same kind of almost schizophrenic behavior she had exhibited the day before when Ernie and Joanna had been interviewing her. One moment she had been falling apart. The next, in a daunting display of willpower, she had pulled herself together and assumed the role of gracious hostess. This time she came out swinging in her absent husband's defense.

"It's just curiosity more than anything," Joanna assured her quickly. "Obviously, your husband has made a good deal of money over the years . . ."

"He was in real estate," Katherine returned. "Real estate and construction both. He was a major player in the development of Paradise Valley up in Phoenix. Over the years, he diversified enough so that when it was time to sell out and come down here, he was able to make a good deal of money—funds that are still coming in, by the way. If you're asking me whether or not my husband hangs out with lowlifes who would do this kind of thing—a kidnapping, I mean—I'll tell you right here and now that he doesn't. David O'Brien may be a little overbearing at times, even unreasonable occasionally. But my husband is a highly principled man. If you don't believe me, there are any number of people you could ask. Wally, for instance."

"Wally?"

"Wally Hickman," Katherine O'Brien said. "Years ago, before Wally went into politics, he and my husband were business partners."

Joanna took a deep breath. "You mean Governor Hickman," she asked.

Katherine O'Brien nodded. "You know him, don't you?"

"Not personally."

"Well, I do, and so does David. Wally and his wife, Abby, are good friends of ours."

Sheriff Joanna Brady suddenly had visions of this tragic but seemingly obscure little incident in the Peloncillos taking on statewide proportions. *I'll have to get hold of Frank Montoya and bring him up to speed,* she told herself in a mental note. Montoya, her chief deputy for administration, also doubled as her department's public information officer. Not if but when the case turned into yet another media hot potato, Frank would be the one who had to handle it.

Joanna decided to back away from the kidnapping line of inquiry. "You said a moment ago that your husband can be unreasonable at times. If you'll pardon my saying so, I did happen to notice some evidence of that yesterday when Detective Carpenter and I were at the house talking to you."

"So?" Katherine asked defensively. "There are lots of unreasonable people in the world. If you think of all that's happened to David over the years, I believe he has more grounds than most for being difficult."

"He made that quite clear himself," Joanna said. "But considering his attitude toward Hispanics, what do you think he would have done had he known his daughter was secretly involved with someone like Ignacio Ybarra?"

"What any right-thinking parent of a rebellious teenager would have done, Sheriff Brady. He would have grounded her for the rest of her life."

Before Joanna could think of another question, George Winfield appeared in the doorway. "Mrs. O'Brien?" he said. "You can come in now."

Taking Katherine by the arm, he led the two women into a spotless lab. "I must apologize for having to show you your daughter in her current condition, but . . ."

Katherine swallowed hard. "That's all right," she said. "I understand."

Having been away from the awful smell of decaying flesh long enough to clear her nostrils and lungs, Joanna once again had to fight to keep from gagging. The basket was gone. The body bag lay on a gurney. The bag was unzipped only far enough to allow an unobstructed view of the terribly mangled face.

Katherine walked forward far enough to glimpse it, then she stopped. Sagging against Doc Winfield, she nodded. "It's her," she whispered.

"You're sure?"

"Yes. I recognize the birthmark on her neck."

"Very well." Winfield went to the head of the table and covered the bag with a clean white sheet. "Wait," Katherine said. "What about her jewelry? Along with the truck, her father gave her a diamond ring for her eighteenth birthday. I'm sure he'll want to have that back, and her class ring as well."

Winfield pulled out a form and consulted it. "I've inventoried both of those items on the personal effects form," he said. "Along with her purse, wallet, watch, and the earring as well, but for the time being, I'll have to hold on to all of them. The watch we'll most likely have to keep indefinitely."

"Why's that?"

"It might prove helpful in setting the time of death. Everything else you'll get back, of course, once the investigation is complete, but—"

"What kind of earring?" Katherine interrupted.

"It's a single pearl," Winfield answered. "Looks to be of pretty good quality. The other one must have fallen off somewhere. The only reason this one wasn't lost as well was that the post was smashed flat."

"I don't want it," Katherine said at once. "The

earring or the watch. Just give me the two rings. Those are all I care about."

"But, Mrs. O'Brien—"

"The watch is a cheap Timex. It's of no consequence whatever. The earring is different. Brianna had her ears pierced just a few weeks before school was out," Katherine said. "It caused a good deal of heartache in our home because her father disapproves of pierced ears. On anyone, but most especially on his daughter. He forbade her to wear the earrings in the house. In fact, he gave her strict orders to get rid of them. It would hurt him terribly to learn that she had disobeyed him. His heart will be broken as it is."

"You don't understand, Mrs. O'Brien," Winfield interjected. "Once personal effects are no longer required for evidentiary reasons, I'm required to turn them over to victims' families. If I were to keep any items that had appeared on inventory sheets, I would be in clear violation. If it was reported, I'd be out of a job."

"Very well," Katherine said. "If that's the case, when the time comes, I'll make sure I'm the one who collects Bree's things. That way I can take care of it myself. You won't have to have anything at all to do with it." She backed toward the door. "Is that all? Can I go now?"

"Yes," George said. "Thank you so much for your help. Please accept my condolences and extend them to your husband as well."

Katherine nodded. "Thank you," she said. "I will."

Joanna followed Katherine from the lab as far as the outside door. "Mrs. O'Brien?"

"Yes." Katherine O'Brien stopped with her hand on the doorknob. "You'll have to forgive me, Sheriff Brady," she said. "I can't answer any more questions, not right now. Since it's confirmed, I must go home and tell my husband."

"Yes," Joanna said. "I understand. Later on this evening, when Detective Carpenter gets back to town, he and I may need to come back out to the house to see you and Mr. O'Brien."

"That'll be fine," Katherine said. "We'll be home."

She left then. Joanna turned back to the lab. Inside, the discarded bag lay on the floor and George Winfield was in the process of draping a sheet over the naked body. He looked up at Joanna. "Is there something else?" he asked.

"What do you think about her?" Joanna asked, nodding toward the door.

"You mean about Katherine O'Brien?"

Joanna nodded. "She may have been a nurse once, but how could she be so cool, so calculating?"

"Shock affects different people different ways," George replied. "Some people collapse in hysterics. For others, it's just the opposite."

"Oh," Joanna said. Instead of leaving, though, she stood there lost in thought, considering the many mystifying faces of Katherine O'Brien. Was her surprising reaction to her daughter's death shock, as George suggested, or was it something else entirely?

"Is that all?" George asked at last as if impatient to be rid of Joanna so he could go on with his work.

The question startled Joanna out of her contemplation and back into the present. "When you do the autopsy, be sure you check to see whether or not Brianna was raped."

Winfield nodded. "That's all part of the autopsy protocol—looking for semen, hairs, and other evidence of rape." The coroner paused. "You think she might have been?" he asked. "Of course, given the fact she was naked, it's certainly possible."

Joanna nodded.

"And if she was," George added wearily, "I suppose her father won't want to know about that any more than he would about the earring."

"You're right," Joanna said, closing the door behind her and leaving George Winfield to deal with his grisly tasks. "I don't suppose he would."

SEVENTEEN

JOANNA LEFT the coroner's office at five. The rain had finally let up by then, but when she got to High Lonesome Ranch, the creek beds were still running too deep for her to risk crossing them even with four-wheel drive. Instead, famished now and feeling filthy as well, she headed back to town.

She considered going to her mother's place but quickly decided against it. She wasn't yet ready to walk into Eleanor Lathrop's house and encounter George Winfield's shaving kit on the bathroom counter. And she wasn't ready to discuss it, either. Instead, she drove to her in-laws' duplex on Oliver Circle, where she could be relatively sure of her welcome.

Stopping the Eagle in front of the Bradys' walkway, she stepped out into the cool, rain-freshened air and realized that the smell of deteriorating flesh was still with her—still clinging to her hair and clothing and to the car's upholstery as well. Hoping time and open windows would help, she rolled them all down before going inside. When Sadie had gotten into a skunk once, Andy had used one of his mother's time-honored remedies—he had washed the dog in tomato juice. *Maybe Eva Lou will have to do the same thing to me*, Joanna thought grimly, climbing the steps.

If Joanna's mother-in-law noticed the odor, it wasn't apparent in Eva Lou's greeting when she opened the door. "Why, Joanna," she said, her face beaming in welcome. "What on earth are you doing here?"

"Hoping to bum a meal, a shower, and use of your washer," Joanna said sheepishly. "I've spent all day at a crime scene. I'm a mess and need a shower in the worst way. I tried to go home to clean up, but the washes out at the ranch are still running. So I came here to throw myself on your mercy."

"Why, of course," Eva Lou agreed. "You come on inside and make yourself at home. I saved you some leftovers, and it won't take any time at all to run those clothes of yours through the wash. You can wear my robe in the meantime."

By the time Joanna was out of the shower, the washer was running full steam and a plate of micro-waved chicken dinner was waiting for her on the kitchen table. Beside it sat a platter stacked with mouthwatering slices of ruby-red tomatoes fresh from Jim Bob's garden.

"The gravy came out a little too thick today for some reason," Eva Lou apologized, hovering as Joanna took her first bite of mashed potatoes.

"The gravy," Joanna declared, savoring that first mouthful, "is absolutely scrumptious."

Jim Bob poured himself a cup of decaf and wandered over to the table. "Did I hear you say you've spent all day on a crime scene?"

When Andy had signed on as a Cochise County deputy sheriff, his father had taken on the unofficial role of the department's Monday morning quarterback. Retired from his job as a foreman in Bisbee's copper mines, Jim Bob Brady had enjoyed backstopping his son's handling of various cases, analyzing what had worked and what had gone wrong, making suggestions that were based on common sense rather than proper police procedures. Now that his widowed daughter-in-law had assumed the job of sheriff, Jim Bob was at it again.

Had Joanna's mother been the one asking those kinds of probing questions, Joanna most likely would have felt Eleanor was prying. With Jim Bob, though, it was . . . well, different.

"A possible crime scene," Joanna corrected. "In Skeleton Canyon. At this point it could still go either way—as an accident or as a homicide."

"Anybody we know?" Jim Bob asked.

Katherine O'Brien had already positively identified her daughter's body. There was no need to withhold information pending notification of next of kin. "You may know her," Joanna answered. "The victim's name is Brianna O'Brien."

Eva Lou paled visibly upon hearing the name. "Not that nice girl who was valedictorian of the senior class!" she exclaimed.

"Unfortunately, yes."

"What happened?" Jim Bob asked.

"Brianna was evidently out in the Peloncillos east of Douglas four-wheeling it. Sometime over the weekend, she went off a cliff. It turns out my friend Angie Kellogg was out there, too, hiking and bird-watching with a friend of hers. The friend is the one who actually discovered the body. In the process of notifying us, though, Angie herself got lost. When Doc Winfield and I left the mountains to bring the body back to town, Search and Rescue was still looking for Angie."

"You mean to tell me that poor girl was out there all by herself, walking around in that awful storm?" Jim Bob asked. "I have two-point-six inches showing in my rain gauge right here in the yard. No telling what it was like in the mountains. Some places around are reporting more than that—up to three inches in Sierra Vista. And it said on the news a little while ago that Tucson is a mess, too, with flooded streets and power outages all over town."

Jim Bob's unwelcome weather report went straight to the heart of Joanna's own guilt where Angie was concerned. And Jenny, too, for that matter, staying up on Mount Lemmon in Camp Whispering Pines' canvas-topped cabins. Joanna pushed her chair back and started for the phone. "I should probably call the department and check in. Hopefully they've found Angie by now. I've been driving the Eagle all day, so I've been without a radio."

"You stay right where you are," Eva Lou ordered. "You can call *after* you finish eating."

Obeying Eva Lou's edict, Joanna settled back onto her chair, but from then on, with Angie foremost in her mind, even Eva Lou's crisp chicken and Jim Bob's juicy hand-grown tomatoes had a cardboard taste to them. Whatever had happened to Angie, it was all Joanna's fault.

While his daughter-in-law ate, Jim Bob sat quietly nearby thoughtfully sipping his coffee.

When the food was gone and with her now-clean clothes transferred to the dryer, Joanna helped herself to the Bradys' kitchen wall phone. "What's the latest?" she asked after identifying herself to the duty clerk.

"Things are hopping. We've got fender benders and road washouts as well as spotty phone and power outages all over the county."

"I'm sure. Who's working Dispatch?"

"Kendall Evans and Larry Kendrick are both on tonight. Want me to put you through to them?"

"This is Sheriff Brady," Joanna said to Kendall a moment later. "I've been out of radio contact most of the day. What's going on?"

"Where are you?" Kendall asked. "Ernie Carpenter has called in several times looking for you."

"I'm at my in-laws' place here in Warren bumming a meal. I'm sure you have the number displayed on your screen. Where's Ernie?"

"He and Detective Carbajal got stuck on the wrong side of a dip east of Douglas. They had to wait until the water went down. They're in Douglas now, talking to someone. Will you be at the same place for a little while?"

"It looks that way," Joanna answered. "I'm having my own version of the same problem. I can't go home until the creek goes down. I'll probably be here for another hour at least. When you catch up with Ernie, remind him that his radio currently has big ears. He shouldn't say anything about the Peloncillo situation that he doesn't want broadcast nationwide."

"Right," Kendall said.

"Next, what's happening with Search and Rescue?"

"They all went home. They may not be there yet, but they're on their way."

"What did they do?" Joanna asked. "Call off the search on account of weather?"

"You mean the search for Angie Kellogg? Oh, no. She's fine."

"They found her, then?"

"Search and Rescue didn't find her but somebody else did. Here it is. Marianne Maculyea, the report says."

Joanna breathed a sigh of relief as Kendall Evans continued. "She was found walking along Highway 80. Reverend Maculyea loaded her in the car and hightailed it back to Douglas hoping to beat the worst of the storm. She called from the first available phone booth to let us know Ms. Kellogg was safe."

"That's great," Joanna breathed.

"The problem is, Sheriff Brady," Kendall continued, "we're real busy right now. There are two other calls coming in. I've got to go."

"Sure. I'll be here if you need me."

Emptying the dregs of his coffee into the sink, Jim Bob announced he was going into the living room to watch *America's Funniest Home Videos.* Even though the dishes were done and put away, Eva Lou, looking troubled, seemed reluctant to leave the kitchen.

"So young," she said sadly after her husband disappeared into the living room. "So terribly young. Brianna O'Brien was a smart girl who should have had a whole wonderful future ahead of her. Here she is gone." When Eva Lou paused, Joanna could see the older woman was struggling to control herself.

"Not only that," she added, "I know exactly what her parents are going through right now. I'll never forget how it was when that first call came in about Andy. I just couldn't believe it. Hearing about that poor girl and her family brings it all back to me as clearly as if it happened yesterday."

Joanna nodded. It was the same for her. Each time she witnessed some new family descending into the hellish pit of losing a loved one, she, too, was sucked along, back into the awful abyss of Andy's death. Other people's pain mingled with her own, and neither seemed to lessen that much with time. Joanna didn't bother explaining any of that to her mother-in-law. She didn't have to. Eva Lou Brady was dealing with exactly the same thing.

"Do you know the O'Briens?" Joanna asked, more to make conversation than anything else.

Eva Lou shook her head. "Not personally. I know of them, though. Babe Sheridan goes to St.

Dominick's, you know. She says they're nice people. Mr. O'Brien is all crippled up, but Babe said something about Katherine going off on missions for two weeks at a time. Medical missions, I believe she said, where a team of doctors and nurses go into out-of-the-way places and provide medical services for the poor. They do corrective surgeries—the kinds of procedures that wouldn't be available otherwise. I believe Katherine O'Brien is a trained nurse. It takes a real giving person to do that—and a whole lot of gumption, too."

"It certainly does," Joanna agreed.

For a few minutes, Joanna and Eva Lou sat together in silence. "How's your mother doing?" Eva Lou asked finally. "I've barely seen her these past few weeks. She must be awfully busy."

"She's been busy all right," Joanna returned dryly. "She's married."

Eva Lou put down her coffee cup. "She's what?"

"Married," Joanna repeated. "She and George Winfield eloped when they went to Vegas."

"Why forevermore!" Eva Lou Brady said wonderingly. "Good for her. Good for both of them. What wonderful news!"

In the face of her mother-in-law's evident enthusiasm, Joanna had the good sense and grace to stifle any further negative comments of her own. Besides, just then Jim Bob called to his wife from the living room.

"Hey, Eva Lou, the last commercial just ended. Come on now or you'll miss it."

Eva Lou excused herself and went to join her

husband in front of the blaring television set. Left on her own in the kitchen, Joanna dialed Frank Montoya's number, alerting him to the Brianna O'Brien situation and bringing him up to speed as much as possible. Then she tried dialing her own number, hoping to use her answering machine's remote feature to retrieve her own messages. Nothing happened. The phone rang and rang, but the answering machine wouldn't pick up.

Frustrated and unwilling to go into the living room to watch TV, Joanna picked up the yellow pad Jim Bob and Eva Lou kept on the kitchen table next to the phone. Since she was just passing time, why not write today's letter?

Dear Jenny,

For a long, long time, "Dear Jenny" were the only words that appeared on the paper. *Where should I start?* Joanna wondered. *How should I begin?*

This afternoon's storm was a real corker. The washes are running at home, so I'm writing this from Grandma and Grandpa Brady's house. I tried calling for messages a little while ago, but the answering machine isn't working, so maybe our phone is out of order as well. I hope the storm didn't catch you out somewhere on a hike. If it did, you probably got soaked.

You've only been gone for a day and a half, but it feels much longer. And it turns out that there's all kinds of news. The most important of which has to do with Grandma Lathrop.

As you know, she's been going out with that Dr. Winfield. Well, you'll never guess what happened! It turns out that they've been doing a little more than just "going out." Dr. Winfield and I were working on a case together today and he told me that they're married. He said they eloped last month when they took that trip up to Las Vegas. They're planning on a honeymoon cruise sometime in August. So, not only do you have a new grandfather, I have a new stepfather as well.

Joanna paused long enough to reread what she had written, hoping that it sounded breezy enough—breezy and nonjudgmental. After all, she didn't know how George Winfield would measure up in the stepfather department, but he might be perfectly fine as a grandfather. Joanna didn't want to write anything that would prejudice Jenny against him.

The animals are all fine. At least, they were fine when I left the house this morning, and I'm sure they still are. I've been off investigating a crime scene most of the day. The storm that blew through late this afternoon didn't make things any easier.

Oh, I almost forgot. Search and Rescue had to be called out today to look for Angie Kellogg. She and a friend went bird-watching up in Skeleton Canyon. They got separated, somehow, and Angie was lost for several hours. She found her way out, however. Dispatch just told me that Marianne found her and brought her home safe and sound.

The telephone rang. "I'll get it," Joanna said before Jim Bob made it out of his easy chair. "That's all right," he said. "It's probably for you anyway."

And it was. "Sheriff Brady?" Ernie Carpenter asked. "What big ears?"

"Frankie Stoddard and her police scanner."

"That's right," he said. "I forgot all about her. It's a good thing I'm calling on a phone then."

"Why? What's happening?"

"Jaime and I just made arrangements for a deputy to come pick up Ignacio Ybarra and bring him in for questioning. I'll ride back to the department in the patrol car with them while Jaime drives the van."

Joanna was stunned. "Brianna's boyfriend? You think he had something to do with what happened to her?"

"Wait until you see him," Ernie said grimly. "He looks like hell. Claims somebody beat him up, but he won't tell us who it was or where it happened."

"If you're bringing him to the department, I'll meet you there."

Joanna put down the phone.

Oops, I've gotta go. I'll have to mail this tomorrow along with Saturday's letter as well. You'll probably get them both on the same day—Tuesday, I hope.

Love,
Mom

Joanna didn't even bother trying to go home a second time. Once her clothes finished drying, she dressed, said her good-byes and thank-yous to her in-laws, and drove straight to the department. Jaime Carbajal wasn't there with the van yet, and neither was Ernie Carpenter. Waiting in her office, Joanna decided to give Angie Kellogg a call and see how she was doing. To her surprise, there was no answer at Angie's house in Galena.

That's odd, she thought. *Maybe she's working.*

Except, when Joanna dialed the Blue Moon, no one answered there, either.

Concerned, Joanna finally tried calling Jeff and Marianne's parsonage up Tombstone Canyon. Marianne herself answered.

"Mari," Joanna said, "it's me. I'm looking for Angie. I just wanted to make sure she's all right, but I can't find her. She isn't at home and she isn't at work, either."

"You've called the right place," Marianne Maculyea said cheerfully. "She's here all right, but she's in the tub right now, trying to soap her troubles away."

"She's okay, I hope," Joanna said. "She's not still upset about Dennis Hacker laughing at her, is she?"

"No," Marianne said. "I'd say Mr. Hacker is pretty far down the list of concerns at the moment. She's a lot more upset about her car."

"Her car!" Joanna exclaimed. "What happened to that?"

"When she and Dennis Hacker went birding

this morning, he picked her up at work. She left her Omega parked in Brewery Gulch, sitting out in front of the Blue Moon. This afternoon, when a four-foot wall of water came pouring down the gulch, not only did it shut down all the telephone service in Brewery Gulch, it also picked up Angie's car and carried it right along with it. Washed it down into the storm drain under Main Street."

"Oh, no," Joanna murmured.

"Oh, yes," Marianne continued. "With the fire department's help, a tow truck finally managed to pull it out, but I'm worried that it's wrecked for good. The engine was completely under water. Not only that, it went nosefirst down into the drain. The whole front end is bashed in—the grill, the hood, and both front fenders. Angie's just sick about it."

So was Joanna. From what Marianne was saying, the Omega would probably end up being totaled. Although Angie had been extraordinarily proud of her little Omega, it was, nevertheless, a seventeen-year-old vehicle. As an inexperienced driver who had never before carried auto insurance, Angie Kellogg was in a high-risk/high-premium group. She carried the state-mandated coverages, especially liability, but her policy included nothing that would repair the physical damage.

"She's staying with us for tonight, at least," Marianne continued. "Jeff and I didn't think she should be alone after all she's been through today. As for tomorrow, I don't know. It's too far for her to walk from her house back and forth to work. We'll have to work something out."

"Other than her car, though, she's all right?" Joanna asked.

She had heard Dennis Hacker's lame version of what had gone on in Skeleton Canyon earlier that morning. But all day long, whenever she had thought about Angie Kellogg, Joanna had worried and wondered if that was all there was to it, or had there been something more? Dennis Hacker might have looked like the boy next door, but then so had Ted Bundy.

"She's fine," Marianne said. "She was wet to the bone, chilled, and hungry when I picked her up. Jeff gave her a little shot of medicinal brandy when I got her home and then he fed her some supper. He also administered a brotherly talk about some men being such incredible bums that women shouldn't waste a minute of their time on them. By the time Jeff finished with her, I think she was feeling better. Once she's done soaking in the tub, she'll probably be ready to go night-night right along with the girls."

"Give Jeff Daniels a hug for me," Joanna said. "He's one of the nicest people I know."

"I'll be glad to tell him," Marianne said. "I happen to think so, too. In the meantime, can you tell me anything about what else was going on out in the mountains today? I've heard all kinds of awful rumors that Brianna O'Brien is dead."

"I don't know who your sources are," Joanna

said. "Unfortunately, they're right. Brianna O'Brien *is* dead. Her mother identified the body a little while ago."

"That's dreadful," Marianne breathed. "An accident of some kind?"

"We don't know that yet," Joanna told her. "And we won't, not until after Dr. Winfield conducts the autopsy."

There was a long pause while neither woman said a word. "Are you all right?" Marianne asked at last.

Marianne Maculyea knew Joanna all too well. There was plenty of reason for Joanna *not* to be all right, but before she could go into any of it, including telling Marianne about Eleanor Lathrop's latest caper, Joanna's other line started ringing.

"Sorry, Mari. There's another call. I've got to go." She punched the other line. "Yes?"

"Excuse me, Sheriff, but there's a man out here named Burton Kimball. You know, the attorney. He says Detective Carpenter is bringing in one of his clients. Mr. Kimball is supposed to be present for the interview. I talked to Dispatch. They didn't know anything about it. Kendall Evans said I should talk to you."

"Thanks," Joanna said. "I'll be right out."

EIGHTEEN

TALL, BROAD-SHOULDERED, and with his brown hair going gray at the temples, Burton Kimball stood in front of the lobby display case examining the photographs featured there—pictures of all the previous sheriffs of Cochise County, up to and including Sheriff Joanna Brady. Except for hers, all the black-and-white photos were formal portraits of the "lawman" variety—pictures of solemn, upright men staring back at the camera with unsmiling disdain. All of the men sported some variation of cowboy getup. A few of the portraits even included horses.

Joanna's picture was different. Cropped from an ordinary snapshot and then enlarged, it showed her as a smiling child, dressed in a Brownie uniform and posing with her Radio Flyer wagon stacked high with cartons of Girl Scout cookies.

"The Women's Club did a great job of putting this display together, but how come most of these guys look like they have a corncob stuck up their butts?" Burton asked Joanna when she walked up beside him.

After a day filled with thorny complications and unrelenting tension, Cochise County's leading defense attorney's comment was so unexpectedly lighthearted and welcome that Joanna burst out laughing. "Probably because they did," she replied. Still smiling, she offered him her hand. "How's it going, Burton? I understand you're waiting for a client."

He nodded and looked around. "I take it they're not here yet?"

"Not so far. You're welcome to wait in my office if you like."

She led him through a security door and down the long hallway to the suite of private offices at the back of the building. Joanna's was in the far back corner. "Have a chair," she invited as they entered.

Gratefully, Burton sank down on the long leather sofa that, along with the oversized desk and all the other furnishings, were hand-me-downs dating from the administration of Walter V. McFadden, Joanna's immediate predecessor. Folding his arms behind his head, Burton leaned back into them. "Tell me," he said. "How's Ruby Starr holding up? Is she still cooking up a storm around here?"

In local law enforcement circles, Burton Kimball had a reputation for attracting an oddball and sometimes difficult clientele. Ruby Starr qualified on both counts. She and her husband had come to Bisbee with the intention of opening a fine dining establishment. The husband had been supposed to provide the business expertise while Ruby was expected to do the cooking. Their partnership and marriage both had come to grief in a domestic dispute that started with Ruby going through the house and nailing her husband's discarded dirty clothes to the hardwood floor. The battle had escalated into a sledgehammer-to-windshield finale that had put Ruby Starr in the county jail charged with criminal assault.

She just happened to be there—with Burton Kimball on retainer as her attorney—when the jail's previous cook made off in the middle of the night, taking with him all the fixings for the jail inmates' Thanksgiving dinner. In an act of civic generosity, Burton and his wife had provided dinner, replacing the missing turkeys and other necessary ingredients as well. Ruby Starr had been drafted out of her jail cell to do the cooking. She had done such an admirable job that, upon her release, she had been offered the jail cook's job on a permanent basis. Seven months later, she was still there.

Joanna smiled. "Ruby's doing fine," she answered. "Now the only inmates who complain about the food are the ones who weren't here before and who don't have any idea how bad it can be. One of our repeat offenders usually sets the griper straight in a big hurry."

After a few minutes of small-town talk about whose kids were doing what over the summer, Joanna steered the conversation toward the business at hand. "How do you know Ignacio Ybarra?" she asked.

"I hardly know him at all," Burton admitted. "His uncle, Frank, and I played football at the same time. Not exactly together, since we were on opposite teams. Still, we knew one another by reputation. Over the years, I've done some work for Frank, including legalizing Frank and Yolanda's informal guardianship of their nephew—Frank's sister's son—Iggy."

"That's what they call him, Iggy?"

Burton shook his head. "No, I picked that up from reading a newspaper article about his football exploits. His family calls him Pepito."

The phone rang just then and Joanna answered. "They're here," she told the attorney moments later.

Burton Kimball rose to his feet and smoothed his jacket, switching at once from his at-ease demeanor to something far more businesslike. "If it's at all possible, I'd like to meet with my client in private for a few minutes before we go into one of the interview rooms."

"Certainly," Joanna said. She rang the desk clerk. "Tell Detective Carpenter to bring Mr. Ybarra into my office. Mr. Kimball would like to speak to him in private."

Joanna stood up. "I'll go into the outer office to wait." She started toward the reception room door and then paused, glancing at the private door from her office that led back outside to the parking lot.

Burton Kimball seemed to read her mind.

"Don't worry, Sheriff Brady," he said. "Ignacio Ybarra won't take off. I give you my word."

Nodding, Joanna went out and closed the door. In the reception area, she met Ernie and Ignacio Ybarra as they entered the room. The young man was taller than Joanna expected—well over six feet. He was dark-haired, dark-eyed, and good-looking, except for the fact that his face was covered by a series of scrapes and ugly bruises. He held himself stiffly, as though his whole body hurt.

"How do you do, Mr. Ybarra," Joanna said.

Anxiously, Ignacio peered around the room. "I thought Mr. Kimball was supposed to be here," he said.

"He is," Joanna responded. She pointed toward her closed office door. "In there. He's waiting to speak to you. You may go in."

With a glance over his shoulder at a fuming Detective Carpenter, Ignacio Ybarra walked past them both and into the sheriff's private office while Joanna turned to her outraged detective.

"We don't have to do this," Ernie grumbled. "Allowing them a private conversation isn't required by law. And why leave them alone in your office? What if Ybarra takes off?"

"He won't," Joanna said. "It may not be a legal requirement, but giving them the opportunity to confer in private is an act of common decency. Burton told me that he barely knows his client. Why shouldn't we give them a chance to introduce themselves?"

"You're telling me Kimball claims he doesn't

know him?" Shaking his head, Ernie broke off in disgust. "I doubt that. When we picked Ybarra up, he just happened to have Burton Kimball's home telephone number on him. In a pencil-written note in his shirt pocket. That doesn't much sound like strangers to me. And when he made his single phone call, all Ybarra had to do was tell Burton Kimball his name and the attorney says he'll be right here. Which he is, by the way."

"That's all that was said, Ignacio Ybarra's name?"

Ernie consulted his notes. "That's right. Ybarra says, 'It's me, Mr. Kimball, Ignacio Ybarra,' and then he hangs up. Burton Kimball drops everything on a Sunday night and scoots right over here. Yup, I'm sure they're strangers." The sarcasm in Ernie's voice wasn't lost on Joanna.

"So you're saying Burton Kimball had already been alerted to some coming legal difficulty long before you and Jaime showed up at Ignacio's house?"

"You bet. Mr. Ybarra may have put on an Academy Award-worthy performance when we told him Brianna O'Brien was dead, but it isn't going to wash with me. And neither is his cock-and-bull story about some guy he didn't know beating the crap out of him."

"What do you think *did* happen?" Joanna asked.

"My guess is that he and Brianna got into some kind of beef. It turned physical. He ended up killing her, but with her giving almost as good as she got. Then, realizing what he'd done, he decided to run the truck off the cliff and try to make it look like an accident."

"Without any clothes on?" Joanna raised an eye-brow. "Do you have anything at all to substantiate that theory, Ernie?"

"Not so far," he grunted, "but I'm working on it."

The door to Joanna's office opened and both Burton Kimball and a subdued Ignacio Ybarra walked into the reception room. "We're ready now," the attorney announced. "Where are we going to do this? One of the interview rooms?"

"How about right here?" Joanna suggested. "It's certainly more comfortable than anywhere else, and bigger, too."

They settled into places, with Ignacio and Burton Kimball seating themselves in the two matching captain's chairs. Ernie assumed the love seat, while Joanna leaned against the front of her secretary's desk.

Ernie didn't waste any time. "All right, Mr. Ybarra. May I call you Iggy?"

Ignacio shrugged. "I like Nacio better, but Iggy's okay."

"Very well, Nacio. Why don't you tell us in your own words exactly what your relationship was to the dead woman."

Ignacio Ybarra winced at the words. His face paled. "We were in love," he said softly. "We wanted to get married someday."

"Did Brianna's parents know anything about that?" Ernie asked.

"Probably not," Nacio said.

"Why's that?"

Ignacio's eyes met and held Ernie's. "Because we didn't tell them. They wouldn't have approved," Nacio said.

"Because Mr. O'Brien doesn't like Mexicans?"

"I guess," Nacio said quietly. "But I'm an American. I was born in Douglas."

"All right," Ernie said. "Now, why don't you tell us what happened last Friday?"

"Bree and I were supposed to go away together," Nacio said. "To the Peloncillos, but when she came by to meet me, I told her my aunt got sick and ended up in the hospital in Tucson. I was going to have to work Friday night and Saturday morning both. I thought Bree would just go back home. Instead, she decided to go on up to the mountains by herself to wait for me. That way, she said, she could reserve our camping place, and I could come up on Saturday whenever I got off. That's the last I saw her."

"And you let her go? Just like that?"

"Bree did what she wanted," Nacio said. "I didn't have any choice."

"So tell us about Saturday," Ernie continued. "Did you go to the mountains to meet her?"

"Yes," Nacio said. "I went where Bree was supposed to be, but she wasn't there. She had been, but she must have left."

"How do you know that?"

"Because I found part of her earring. It was lying in the dirt."

Joanna had been standing quietly to one side,

listening. Mention of the earring jarred her out of her self-imposed silence. "What kind of earring?"

"A pearl," Nacio said as tears suddenly welled in both eyes. "The earrings were a graduation present to her from me."

Remembering Katherine O'Brien's surprising response upon hearing about the existence of that one earring, Joanna thought she understood it better now. It wasn't just a matter of David O'Brien's being offended by pierced ears. It had as much or more to do with who had given Bree the pearl earrings in the first place.

"Where is it now?" Joanna asked.

"I lost it again."

"Where?"

"I don't know," Nacio murmured.

There wasn't a person in the room who didn't believe Ignacio Ybarra's barely audible answer was a lie. Ernie Carpenter pounced on it at once. "You expect us to swallow that?" he demanded. "You know exactly where you found it but you can't tell us where you lost it again?"

Nacio shook his head. Ernie's glower proclaimed he was unconvinced, but Nacio said nothing more.

"So," Ernie continued a moment later, "you went up to the mountains. When Brianna wasn't there, what did you think?"

Nacio shrugged. "I thought maybe she was mad at me."

"Why?"

"Because I was so late. I thought maybe she got tired of waiting and just went home."

"What did you do then?"

"I went back home, too. I went to work, actually. I kept thinking she'd come by and see me there, but she didn't."

"Let's go back to the camping bit. Where was that, the spot where you usually stayed?"

"Up in the Peloncillos," Nacio said. "Along the creek."

"In Skeleton Canyon?"

"I'm not sure which canyon is which out there. They all sort of run together, but where we camped is in a little clearing. It's just off the road, but hidden from the road. Easy to get to but hard to see."

"You didn't have to go four-wheeling it to get there?"

"No," Nacio said. "Not at all."

Standing outside the fray as the questions droned on and on, Joanna's attention began to wander. She was going more by her impressions of how Nacio answered—of his manner in doing so—rather than by his specific replies. Joanna had the sense that, for the most part, Ignacio Ybarra was telling the truth—that he had loved Brianna O'Brien and was devastated by her loss. He spoke of her with the bewildered pain of someone who can't quite come to terms with what has happened, of someone who wants nothing more than to awaken and discover what he thought had happened was nothing but a bad dream.

"When you went sneaking around on these camping trips," Jaime was saying when Joanna tuned back into the conversation, "where exactly did you sleep?"

"Usually in the back of Bree's pickup on an air mattress."

"With a bedroll?"

"Two," Nacio said. "One on top and one on the bottom. We zipped them together."

"But we found only one bedroll at the scene today," Jaime said casually. "Where do you suppose the other one went?"

"I have no idea. Someone must have taken it."

"They took it, all right," Jaime said. "They took it because it was soaked in blood. We're convinced Brianna's killer used that other bedroll to wrap up the body and move her around."

Jaime reached into his pocket and pulled out one of the evidence bags. "See this?" he said, handing it over to Nacio. "We found that stuck on a clump of brush near where Brianna's truck went over the edge of the cliff. What does it look like to you?"

Nacio looked at it. Then, as his face took on a deathly pallor, he let the bag drop to the floor. Groaning, he buried his hands in his face and began to sob, his shoulders heaving. By then, Burton Kimball was on his feet.

"All right, you guys. That's enough of this. No more questions. Either book my client or let him go, but there'll be no more questions tonight." Bristling with anger, he bent down and retrieved the bag. "What the hell is this?" he demanded, handing it back to Jaime.

"It's a piece of material," Jaime returned. "We found it snagged on a clump of cat claw at just about the same spot where Brianna's truck went off the cliff. It looks like it could be from the inside lining of a bedroll. Not only that, I wouldn't be surprised if that spot on it didn't turn out to be a splotch of blood matching the victim's."

Burton Kimball's jaw clenched with anger. "You had no business showing him that," he snarled at Jaime. Then Burton wheeled on Ernie as well. "Let's cut to the chase, Detective Carpenter. Are you arresting my client or not?"

"Not at this time," Ernie returned mildly. "But he's not to leave the area. We're going to be questioning all his associates. If Mr. Ybarra knows what's good for him, he'll have a sudden flash in the memory banks about what exactly happened to his face and ribs. If he wants us to believe that he didn't get those injuries as a result of a physical confrontation with Brianna O'Brien, then he'd better come up with some other plausible answer, along with some witnesses to back it up."

"Come on, Ignacio," Burton Kimball said. "Let's get out of here."

"I'm free to go then?" Nacio asked. He sounded dazed, as though he couldn't quite believe what was happening.

"Evidently," Burton said. "For the time being at least."

Taking his young client by the arm, Kimball exited the room. The reception area was quiet for some time after they left.

"I figured showing him the cloth would provoke some kind of reaction," Jaime said. "Did I go too far?"

Rubbing his forehead, Ernie shook his head. "You were pushing it, maybe, but you did get a reaction. What do you think?"

Jaime shrugged. "Maybe she was trying to break up with him. Maybe they got in a fight over that."

"Maybe. How about you, Sheriff Brady?" Ernie said, turning to Joanna. "What's your opinion?"

"I wish we had that missing journal," she said. "If we could read that, we'd have a better idea of what was really going on."

"We'll find it all right," Ernie said grimly. "I'll bet we find that missing bedroll, too."

"You want me to go to work on getting a search warrant?" Jaime asked.

"Not tonight," Ernie replied. "Tomorrow's another day."

"Right," Jaime said. "I'll get after it first thing in the morning."

Ernie turned again to Joanna. "What about the O'Briens?" he asked. "Should we drive out to Green Brush Ranch and talk to them tonight?"

Wearily, Joanna shook her head. "As you said, Ernie, it's late. Tomorrow's another day."

They all left the department a few minutes later. On the drive home, Joanna found she was so exhausted that she had trouble staying awake. Coming through the cuts on Highway 80, she was dismayed to see orange emergency lights flashing at the intersection of High Lonesome Road and the Double Adobe cutoff.

"What now?" she muttered. "Not an accident, I hope."

When she reached the lights, however, she discovered not one but two utility crews. "What's going on?" she asked, rolling down her window.

"We've got a fried transformer here," the foreman told her. "It melted some wires as well. None of the people up High Lonesome have power right now, but we should have it back on within a couple of hours."

"Great," Joanna said. "The perfect ending to a perfect day."

The dogs met her, as usual, halfway up the drive. The water had drained out of both creek beds, leaving both crossings rocky and muddy and devoid of the usual tracks, but passable nonetheless. It was eerie, though, driving into the yard without having the motion detector turn on the floodlights. Joanna wasn't looking forward to the silence, either.

It's going to be quiet, she thought. *Way too quiet.*

But when she stepped out of the Eagle, she was assailed by the noise of what sounded like the bleating of a herd of a thousand sheep. *Colorado River toads,* she realized with a smile of relief. The night wasn't going to be quiet after all.

The frogs' noisy squawking was one of the sounds of summer. That first rainstorm always awakened hordes of hibernating toads and set them their brief but frenetic mating trail. Their raucous racket never failed to cheer Joanna. It meant that after months of dry days and endless blue skies, the rains had returned, bringing with them the promise of life begun anew.

Joanna knew that once she went inside, the walls of the house would cut off the toads' welcome, cheery song. *That settles it,* she told herself, making up her mind. *I'm sleeping out on the porch again tonight.*

NINETEEN

STANDING IN front of her closet on Monday morning, Joanna was faced with the usual problem of what to wear. Had she managed to go shopping on Saturday afternoon, she might have had a few more choices. As it was, she settled on a three-piece hunter green pantsuit that was coming up on the end of its useful life. It was an old standby that dated from her previous career in the insurance business. She had worn it until she was tired of it. Most likely so was everyone around her.

The phone in the outer office was ringing as she walked in the door to hers. "It's Adam York," Kristin Marsten, her secretary, announced over the intercom once Joanna made it as far as her desk. "Do you want me to put him through?"

"Sure," she said. "Hello, Adam," she added a moment later. "You're certainly up and at 'em bright and early this morning."

"You call this bright and early? What do you mean?" Adam replied. "I've been working all weekend—ever since you called on Saturday. In fact, I tried like hell to reach you yesterday evening. The phone rang and rang, but there was no answer. Your machine never picked up, either."

"Sorry about that," Joanna apologized. "I was out all day in a car with no radio. Then, last night, a storm came through and knocked out a transformer just up the road, shutting off the electricity for several hours. It also seems to have put a permanent glitch in my answering machine. Even with the power back on this morning, I couldn't make the thing play back messages or record a new one."

Adam York laughed. "Sounds like it's about time to toss out that outdated machine and sign up for something civilized like voice mail."

"I'll look into it," Joanna told him. "Now, what have you got for me?"

"Here's the deal. As I told you the other night, the guys up in Phoenix have been working overtime on a big-time Freon-smuggling case. I checked with them. No one on that case thinks your Benson guy is related to what's going on in Phoenix. They agree with me that he sounds like more of a small-time, independent operator than a big one. The Phoenix case revolves around a major air-conditioning contractor up there, not some seat-of-the-pants tow truck operator. All the same, as of six o'clock this morning, both Sam Nettleton and Sam's Easy Towing and Wrecking are under twenty-four-hour surveillance."

"Great," Joanna said. "How'd you manage that?"

Adam York laughed. "There are a few advantages to being the agent in charge, you know. If we come up with anything concrete, we'll let you know right away."

"I appreciate it," Joanna said. Glancing out into the reception area, she saw both her chief deputies pacing back and forth, waiting for their early morning briefing. "Thanks for keeping me posted, Adam. I have to go. Duty calls. There are people outside waiting for me."

"Sure thing," Adam told her cheerfully. "But don't bother thanking me. If this lead turns into something, we should be thanking you. You're the one helping us, remember?"

Putting down the phone, Joanna motioned Deputies Voland and Montoya into the room. Wrangling as usual, they assumed their customary chairs. "What's the deal?" Joanna asked.

"We took another big hit in the overtime category again this weekend," Frank Montoya complained. "Nobody around here seems to listen or believe me when I tell them a budget crunch is coming. It's going to nip us in the butt. We can't keep squandering our resources this way, day after day, week after week."

"You call that squandering? We had a homicide, for one thing," Voland reminded him. "We also got hit by a record-breaking storm—one that played havoc with roads and traffic all over the county. Of course, we had to use overtime. What do you expect?"

"I'll tell you what I expect. If we keep splurging on overtime at the same rate we have been lately, my computer model says payroll will hit empty two weeks prior to the end of the fiscal year. What's going to happen then?"

"Nothing much," Dick Voland said easily. "We'll have ourselves an old-fashioned SDC with the board of supervisors."

"An SDC?" Frank Montoya asked with a frown. "What's that?"

"A stare-down contest," Voland replied with a sardonic grin. "First guy to blink loses."

Montoya, chief deputy for administration, was not amused. "That's no way to run a department," he said.

"And neither is this," Joanna told them firmly. "Quit bickering, both of you. You sound like a wrangling old married couple. Let's go to work. Yesterday's overtime charges aren't Dick's fault, Frank. He wasn't even in town when the storm hit. On the other hand, Frank is right about the budget shortfall. Every week he gives me a computer printout that shows where we are and where we're going. At the moment we're running six-point-seven days short of being able to meet basic payroll at the end of the fiscal year. That's a serious problem. Everybody from patrol right through jail staff is going to have to do something to fix it. Now let's—"

The intercom buzzed. Shaking her head in annoyance, Joanna pushed the button. "What is it, Kristin?" she demanded. "We're having a briefing in here. Can't it wait until—"

"There's someone here who insists on seeing you, Sheriff Brady," Kristin said. "His name's Ignacio Ybarra."

"You mean he's here to see one of the detectives, don't you?" Joanna asked.

"No. He says he wants to see the sheriff. Right away."

"Where's Detective Carpenter?"

"He still hasn't come in this morning."

"And Detective Carbajal?"

"He's on his way up to the courthouse to see Judge Moore about a search warrant."

Joanna considered for a moment. "Does Mr. Ybarra have Burton Kimball along with him?"

"The lawyer? No," Kristin answered. "He's here alone."

"Ybarra," Dick Voland said, glancing down and scanning his briefing sheet. "Isn't he the prime suspect in the O'Brien case?" Joanna nodded, and Voland rose to his feet. "If you want me to, Sheriff Brady, I can handle this for you. . . ."

"He asked to speak to me, Dick," Joanna said firmly. "I'll talk to him myself."

"Without Ernie?"

"You heard Kristin. Mr. Ybarra asked for me. He didn't ask for you or Detective Carpenter or even for Detective Carbajal."

"But—" Voland began.

Joanna cut him off. "I'm quite capable of passing along whatever information is given to me, Dick. Now, if it's all right with you two, we'll continue our briefing in the conference room as soon as I finish up with Mr. Ybarra."

The two chief deputies left immediately after that, although Dick Voland was still grumbling about it under his breath as he walked out the door. Joanna punched the intercom button once more. "All right, Kristin," she said. "You can send him in now."

Ignacio Ybarra entered the room looking awful. His eyes were red-rimmed and puffy. His coloring was gray. Dark circles under his eyes said he hadn't slept. Once through the doorway, he paused and glanced warily around the room as if expecting to see other people.

"Have a seat, Mr. Ybarra," Joanna said. "And relax. There's no one else here but us—no hidden microphones, no nothing. Are you sure you wouldn't like to have your attorney present when you speak to me?"

Ignacio shook his head and eased himself onto a chair, grimacing with pain as he did so. "No," he said. "This is all right."

"What can I do for you, then?" Joanna asked.

Nacio took a deep breath. "I came to talk to you about Bree's earring."

"The one you found and then lost again?"

The young man nodded. "I only found part of it," he said. "The pearl."

"What about it?" Joanna asked.

"You know something about that earring, don't you, Sheriff Brady?"

Once again, Joanna thought back to Katherine O'Brien's surprising reaction to the one remaining earring—to the fact that the dead girl's mother wanted to have nothing to do with it. Nodding,

Joanna kept quiet and waited for Ignacio Ybarra to speak again. Instead, he sat in an uncomfortable and lengthening silence, staring down at his hands.

Joanna wasn't quite sure what to do next. Here was a murder suspect who had willingly walked into her office. He must have come there with the intention of volunteering some bit of information he hadn't been prepared to share earlier in the presence of his attorney. Now, though, he had frozen up. He seemed unable to say anything at all much less what he had come to say.

Sitting there, Joanna Brady regretted that she wasn't more experienced at interrogating suspects. What she had done instead, however, was live on the High Lonesome long enough to recognize the sometime necessity of priming a pump. In order to elicit any information from this obviously guarded and wary young man, she would have to share some bit of intelligence herself.

"I know her parents didn't approve of them," she said quietly.

Ignacio's troubled brown eyes met hers. The pained hurt in that look—the all-consuming grief—was almost more than Joanna could bear. Katherine O'Brien's way of grieving had been far more decorous and controlled—grief under glass, almost. Ignacio's pain was much closer to the surface and written over every inch of him. Joanna Brady had been through her own terrible loss. She recognized there was no fakery in Ignacio Ybarra's hurt, no pretense. Regardless of how Brianna O'Brien had died—at her lover's hands or someone else's—that Monday morning, Ignacio was suffering. His heart was broken.

"They told you that?" he asked at last.

"Mrs. O'Brien did," Joanna replied. "She said her husband disapproved of Brianna's wearing earrings."

"Did she tell you how much they didn't like them?"

"What do you mean?"

"Mr. O'Brien hit Bree," Ignacio said quickly. "Did her mother tell you about that, too?"

Joanna shook her head. "No," she said.

"Well, he did," Ignacio declared, rushing on. "He caught her wearing the earrings in the house and told her to take them off. She told him they were her ears, that she should be able to decide what she would and wouldn't wear on them. That's when he slapped her—hard, right across the face. It happened the week before graduation. She had to wear makeup all week to keep the bruise from showing."

Joanna let her breath out. *I wasn't wrong,* she thought. *There was an undercurrent of violence in that compulsively clean house. And in Bree's room as well.*

"Did her parents know about you?" Joanna asked gently a moment later. "Did they know that's where the earrings came from?"

Ignacio shook his head. "I don't think so," he said. "She was afraid to tell them."

"Why?"

He shrugged. "Bree was afraid of what her father might do if he discovered his daughter was involved with an Hispanic."

"Afraid he'd do something to her or to you?" Joanna prompted.

"Maybe both," Ignacio replied after a pause.

"She was afraid he'd hurt you?"

"He did," Ignacio said simply.

Joanna sat bolt upright in her chair. "He did what?"

"Mr. O'Brien hurt me. At least, one of his men did."

Joanna could barely believe her ears. "Wait a minute. You're telling me that one of David O'Brien's men beat you up? When? Where?"

"Saturday night," Ignacio said haltingly. "It happened right outside the gate to Green Brush Ranch. I went there hoping to catch sight of Bree. I thought if she had gone home, maybe I could spot her truck and know she was all right. I wanted to talk to her—to apologize for being late. I didn't see her truck, though. All I saw were police cars. I was afraid something had happened to her."

Fully alert, Joanna listened with every cell of her body. Ignacio was a homicide suspect. If what he was saying was true—if he had gone to Green Brush Ranch hoping to catch sight of the victim—that would mean he still thought she was alive almost twenty-four hours after Brianna's shattered Timex had stopped ticking for good at 9:51. On Friday, not Saturday. That would also mean Ignacio Ybarra hadn't killed her. The question was, however, was he telling the truth?

"When was this again?" Joanna asked.

"Saturday. I went there in the late afternoon,

after I left the station. I was hiding outside the gate in a clump of mesquite when some guy saw me—one of Mr. O'Brien's security guards, I guess. He's the one who beat me up."

"You're saying the man who beat you up came from Green Brush Ranch?" Joanna asked.

"He must have," Ignacio replied. "I didn't see exactly where he came from. All I know is, he snuck up on me from behind. I didn't see him until he was on top of me. But that's where he went afterward—back through the gate to Green Brush Ranch. Another guy on an ATV drove up to the gate. He waited just inside the fence. After the one guy finished with me, he walked across the road and went inside the gate. The two of them rode away together, back up the drive toward where the house must be."

"Where the house must be," Joanna repeated thoughtfully. "You've never been there?"

Ignacio shook his head. "Bree made me promise that I wouldn't go. I think she was worried something like this might happen."

"Like what?" Joanna asked. "Tell me exactly what happened."

"This guy came up behind me—an older guy."

"What did he look like?"

"I couldn't see him too well in the dark, but he was tall and skinny. Tan. Wearing a cowboy hat."

Unbidden, the image of Alf Hastings flashed across Joanna's mind, but she brushed it aside. "Go on," she said.

"Like I said, it was after dark," Ignacio said. "I may have dozed off for a minute. All I know is, out of nowhere I heard someone walk up behind me. I tried to stand up, but I had been in the same position for so long that my legs were asleep. When I tried to stand up, they collapsed under me. I fell forward, right on my face. I had managed to make it as far as my hands and knees when the guy kicked me in the gut. He was wearing pointed cowboy boots, and the toe caught me in the solar plexus. It knocked the wind out of me. I fell down again. The next thing I knew, he had me by the hair, pulling it out by the roots."

Ignacio paused, as if remembering the attack were almost as painful as living through it the first time.

"So?" Joanna urged.

"I must have blacked out for a minute. When I came to, he was talking to me. 'You're a big one for a greaser,' he was saying. 'But you know what they say about that. The bigger they come, the harder they fall, right?' I didn't answer. I tried to turn around so I could get a better look at him, but he shook me so hard, I was afraid he was going to break my neck. 'Did you hear me?' he said again. 'You're supposed to answer when somebody speaks to you.'

"He shook me again—the kind of shake a coyote might give a rabbit in order to break its neck. That's when I decided a rib was broken. One at least. According to Dr. Lee, it turns out to be three."

"Dr. Lee over at the Copper Queen?" Joanna asked. She was taking notes now, writing as fast as she could.

Ignacio nodded. "He was my doctor last fall

when I got hurt up here playing football. And that's where I went after this happened—to the hospital to see Dr. Lee."

"Go on then," Joanna said.

"'What're you doing here, greaser?' the guy says. 'Casing the joint? Trying to figure out how you and your buddies can get inside and steal some of Mr. O'Brien's stuff?' I tried to tell him that I didn't care about the O'Briens' stuff, but he didn't believe me. He must've thought I was one of the border bandits."

"What happened next?" Joanna urged.

"He let go of my hair. When I fell back down, it hurt so bad, I was afraid I might have ruptured a lung. I was still dealing with that when he burned me."

Joanna caught her breath. "Burned you?"

Ignacio nodded. "I heard him strike a match and then I smelled cigar smoke. The next thing I knew, he burned me—right between my shoulder blades. I could smell that my shirt was on fire. I rolled around on the ground, trying to put it out. All the time, he's talking to me. 'Just pass the word along to all your thieving friends down there across the line,' he said. 'Tell 'em Mr. O'Brien has a few surprises for anyone who comes around here trying to steal his stuff.' By the time I finally got the fire out, the guy was already crossing the road to where the other guy was waiting on the ATV."

Listening to the story, Joanna felt almost physically ill as she recalled some of the almost forgotten details of the Alf Hastings case over in Yuma

County. There wasn't a decent police officer in the state of Arizona who hadn't been ashamed of what had happened to the young illegals who had fallen into his clutches. They had been beaten and left to die. Now that Ignacio Ybarra mentioned it, Joanna thought she remembered that the young men had also been tortured and burned.

She stood up. "Would you excuse me for a moment?"

Ignacio nodded. "Sure," he said.

Joanna stalked out into the outer office. She picked up Kristin's phone and dialed Frank Montoya's extension. As a recent law enforcement graduate of the University of Arizona, he was also the most computer literate.

"Does the name Alf Hastings ring a bell?" she asked when he answered.

"Not right off," Frank responded. "Should it?"

"He was the deputy over in Yuma County who was the ringleader in that police brutality case with the four young UDAs. I want you to run Hastings's name through the computer database. Bring me a copy of everything you get back."

"What are you after specifically?" Frank asked.

"I want to hear from some of the other investigating officers," Joanna told him. "I'm looking for an MO. I want to know exactly what was done to those kids."

"Any particular reason?"

"Yes," Joanna said. "Alf Hastings is living in Cochise County right now and working for David O'Brien. Unless I'm mistaken, I have one of Hastings's most recent victims sitting here in my office. My major concern is that there may be others we don't even know about."

"I'll get right on it," Frank told her.

Taking Kristin's phone book from the shelf behind her desk, Joanna located the number for the Copper Queen Hospital. It was morning office hours at the clinic, so Joanna had to pull rank before she was finally put through to Dr. Lee directly.

Dr. Thomas Lee was a Taiwanese immigrant in his mid-thirties who had come to Bisbee straight out of medical school. He had initially planned to stay long enough to pay off his school loans. The loans were all gone now—had been for over a year—but still he stayed on.

"Sheriff Brady," Dr. Lee said, when he came on the phone. "Can I help you?"

"I have a young man in my office right now," Joanna told the doctor. "Ignacio Ybarra. Do you know him?"

"Nacio? Yes, of course."

"I need to ask you a question about him."

"Sheriff Brady, you know I can't reveal—"

"Please, Dr. Lee. I need to ask just one or two questions. Did you see him this weekend?"

"Yes."

"When was that?"

"Saturday," Dr. Lee said. "Saturday night. He came to the emergency room."

"You treated him then?"

"Yes."

"Is there a possibility that Ignacio's injuries had been received the night before?"

"You mean on Friday instead of Saturday? Absolutely not!" Dr. Lee exclaimed. "He was bleeding. Dirt was still in the wounds."

"Thank you, Dr. Lee," Joanna breathed. "That's all I need to know."

"But you must tell me," Dr. Lee objected. "Why are you asking such questions? Has something happened to Nacio? Is there anything I can do to help?"

"You already have," Joanna told him. "I thought Ignacio was telling me the truth. Now I know for sure."

Putting down the phone, she went back into her office. Ignacio Ybarra was still sitting in the same place with his head lowered, his shoulders bent. Sorrow exuded from every pore.

Moving with a confidence she hadn't felt before, Joanna returned to her desk. Ignacio looked up as she came by. Joanna sat down and met his questioning gaze.

"Nacio," she said kindly, "why didn't you tell us any of this last night?"

The young man ducked his head. "I don't know," he said. "I guess I was too scared. I didn't think anyone would believe me."

"So why are you here now?"

"I've thought about the pearl for two nights now. I want it back, Sheriff Brady. I gave it to Bree because I loved her, and I want it back for the same reason. It's all I'm ever going to have to remember her by." He broke off, burying his grief-contorted face in his hands.

Joanna waited several moments while the

young man sat there sobbing. "You must have loved her very much," she said at last.

Ignacio nodded, but it took several seconds longer before he was under control enough to speak. "Bree and I thought that someday we'd be able to be together. We were going off to school in September. With us in Tucson and with both our families here, how much could they have done to stop us?"

Plenty, Joanna thought, thinking about how much grinding criticism her disapproving mother had heaped on Joanna's and Andy's marriage over the years. For good or ill, Ignacio Ybarra was never going to have to face those kinds of issues with David and Katherine O'Brien.

"You lost the pearl during the beating, then?" she asked. "Is that what you're telling me?"

"Yes," Ignacio murmured. "I'm sure that's when it fell out of my shirt pocket. It's bound to be there, right across the road from the gate. I'm sure I can find it again, but if I go back on my own to look for it, he'll send somebody after me again. That's why I came here this morning, Sheriff Brady. To ask for help. If I go there with a deputy, no one will bother me."

"Do you want to file charges against him?" Joanna asked.

"Against the man who beat me up?"

"Yes."

Ignacio seemed to consider the possibility. "I hadn't thought that far ahead," he admitted. "I just wanted the pearl back, that's all."

"If you have broken ribs, we're talking about a

serious assault here," she told him. "Whoever did this to you shouldn't be allowed to get away with it."

"But I barely saw him," Ignacio objected. "It was dark. I may not be able to identify him."

"Don't worry about it," Joanna said grimly. "I have a pretty good idea of who he is."

Before Joanna had a chance to turn back to Ignacio, there was an impatient knock at the door. "Come in," she called.

The door burst open and Detective Carpenter strode into the room. "What exactly is going on here?" he demanded, glowering first at Joanna and then at Ignacio. "I thought I was the detective on—"

"Good morning, Ernie," Joanna interrupted. "I'm so glad you could join us. I need you and/or Detective Carbajal to take Mr. Ybarra's statement. I believe Nacio has been the victim of a serious assault at the hands of one of David O'Brien's employees. Afterward, you'll need to search the area opposite the outside gate to Green Brush Ranch to see if you can find Brianna O'Brien's missing pearl earring, which was lost in the course of that attack. I'm sure Mr. Ybarra will be able to show you where it happened. I'm waiting for some information from Yuma County. If what I suspect pans out, sometime early this afternoon you and I should pay a visit to Green Brush Ranch."

Ernie started to object, but something in the authoritative way Joanna had spoken stopped him cold.

"Jaime Carbajal is up at the courthouse trying

to obtain a search warrant," Joanna continued. "Call him off that and have him go with you. Now, get going."

Without another word, Ernie turned on his heel and started for the door. Once there, he turned and looked back into the room. "Coming, Mr. Ybarra?" he asked.

Slowly, Ignacio Ybarra rose to his feet. He stepped toward Joanna's desk, holding out his hand. "Thanks," he said quietly, as they shook hands. "Thank you for believing me. I think what Mr. Kimball said about you was right."

"Why?" Joanna asked. "What did he say?"

"He said that he'd met a lot of sheriffs in his time but that you were the only one who knew how to listen with your heart as well as your ears."

"Thank you," Joanna said.

May it always be so.

TWENTY

AN HOUR later, while Joanna was busy reading Frank Montoya's computerized printout on the police brutality case in Yuma, Kristin called in on the intercom to announce that Dr. Winfield was on the phone.

The prospect of talking to the coroner threw Joanna off center. Officially, Doc Winfield was the coroner, but he was also Joanna's new stepfather. Picking up the handset, she wasn't sure how to speak to him on the phone. Winfield settled the whole issue by handling the entire transaction on a strictly professional basis.

"I still have some toxicology tests to do, and those take time—weeks even," he told her. "But the preliminary results are these. The victim was struck on the head, repeatedly. The weapon was a heavy blunt object of some kind, but what actually killed her was drowning."

"Drowning?" Joanna asked.

"In her own blood. Her rib cage was completely crushed. Both lungs filled with blood. That's what killed her."

Joanna shivered. Drowning in your own blood seemed like an appalling way to die. She forced herself to sound dispassionate. "Any signs of defensive wounds?" she asked.

"None," George Winfield returned. "It looks to me as though she was naked when the attack came and as though her assailant came at her from behind. There are contusions and abrasions that look as though they happened prior to death."

"Like she was running, maybe?" Joanna asked. "As though she was trying to get away?"

"Maybe."

Joanna didn't want to ask the next question, but she had to. "Was she sexually assaulted?"

"No," George Winfield answered. "Given the circumstances of a naked victim, that's something I would have suspected. But there's no sign of sexual violation at all."

"What about pregnancy?" Joanna asked.

"Negative on that, too. Her birth control pills must have been working."

"Good," Joanna said. Those things seemed like insignificant details, but Joanna was glad that they were blows David and Katherine O'Brien would be spared.

"Anything else?" Joanna asked.

"That's all so far. This should be typed up by noon in case you want someone to come get it."

"Thanks, George," Joanna said. "I appreciate the advance notice."

She had no more than put down the phone when it rang again. "We've got it," Ernie said.

"Got what?" Joanna asked.

"The pearl."

"You found it, then?"

"Looks like. With the rainstorm and all I didn't think we'd ever find it, but we got lucky. It was right where Ignacio said it would be. Maybe he was telling the truth after all."

Having already talked to Dr. Lee, Joanna didn't need any more convincing, but she was happy to have Ernie Carpenter's concurrence.

"What do we do now?" he asked.

"While I was sitting here waiting, I've been reading up on Alf Hastings's background," Joanna said quietly. "He sounds like a hell of a nice guy. You'll never guess what he liked to do to undocumented aliens besides kicking the crap out of them."

"What?"

"He liked to burn them," Joanna answered. "With the lit end of a cigar. Either between the shoulder blades or else on the genitals. On one of those four kids, he did both."

The phone line went so silent that for a moment Joanna thought Ernie Carpenter had hung up on her. "Ernie?" she asked. "Are you there?"

"Yeah," he said. "I'm here."

"What's going on?"

"I'm thinking about Ignacio Ybarra," Ernie Carpenter said. "I guess he's one lucky guy."

"Lucky? How do you figure? He just lost a girl he cared about very much. He—"

"Right, but he only got the shoulder blade treatment," Ernie interjected. "From my point of view, that's luck."

As soon as Sheriff Brady stopped long enough to think about it, she had to agree.

"I guess I'd better go on over to the ranch and have a chat with Mr. Hastings," Ernie said a moment later.

"Alone? Where's Detective Carbajal?"

"He left a few minutes ago. I had him take Nacio back over to the hospital. He was here with us when we found the pearl. I had planned to take him out to the Peloncillos this afternoon and have him show us where he and Brianna usually camped. Considering yesterday's storm, there's probably not much to find, but I wanted to give it a try. The problem is, as soon as he saw the pearl, the guy fell to pieces. He even blacked out for a while. It may have just been the heat, but with his ribs the way they are, I didn't want to take any chances. I told Jaime to take him over to the hospital and to stay with him there. If he comes around later on, Jaime will take his statement."

"If Detective Carbajal's not there with you," Joanna said, "who's going to be your backup when you go see Alf Hastings?"

"I'll call in and have Dispatch send me out a deputy," Ernie replied.

"No," Joanna said, standing up and reaching for her purse. "Don't do that. I can be there in ten minutes flat. Alf Hastings is a worm. There's nothing that'll give me greater pleasure than seeing his face when he realizes we've dug him out of the dirt."

🌵 **"Do you** think you'll be able to fix it?" Angie Kellogg's lower lip trembled as she asked the question.

Hurt by Dennis Hacker's derisive laughter, Angie had come back to Bisbee intent on simply packing up and leaving town. That plan had been derailed twice over. For one thing, Angie's Omega had been washed down Brewery Gulch, drowned and smashed almost beyond recognition. But that misfortune had brought into focus the other thing that made the thought of leaving town almost impossible. For the first time in her life Angie Kellogg had friends, real friends—Jeff Daniels and Marianne Maculyea, for example.

At the moment, Jeff—with the twin girls strapped into car seats in the backseat of the VW—was giving Angie a ride to work after viewing the crushed remains of the Omega in the fenced backyard of Jeff's new business venture, Jeff's Auto Rehab.

For years Jeff Daniels had played the role of stay-at-home spouse, backstopping his minister wife's career. Their recent adoption of twins, Ruth and Esther, had thrown a severe financial wrench into the works, especially in view of the fact that Esther had a heart condition that would eventually require surgical correction.

With money perpetually tight, Jeff had always kept the family's two aging vehicles—a '63 VW and an even older International—in pristine driving condition. Over time, his reputation for taking meticulous care in restoring vintage automobiles had spread. Working more as a hobbyist than anything else, he had restored several antique autos. The twins' arrival from China, complicated by Esther's ongoing medical difficulties, had brought home the necessity for Jeff Daniels to give up his house-husband status and look for work outside the home. Torn between the need for an additional paycheck and the difficulty of finding and paying for child care, Jeff had opted for opening a business of his own.

Within days of making that decision, the opportunity to rent a defunct gas station had fallen into his lap. Its location, half a mile up Tombstone Canyon from the parsonage, was ideal, and the bargain basement rent had seemed an answer to a prayer.

Jeff had begun the process by remodeling the office area into a combination nursery/playroom for the girls. Only then had he turned his hand toward the actual work space. Now, several months later, having found a number of clients with, as Jeff said, more money than sense, he was hard at work restoring several old cars, including a venerable Reo that belonged to a retired three-star general from Fort Huachuca.

Angie Kellogg's battered Omega had been towed to the fenced lot behind Jeff's garage, where it was parked next to the '52 DeSoto that was scheduled for Jeff's ministrations once he finished work on the Reo.

"Yes, we will," Jeff told Angie reassuringly. "I've already made a list of the parts we'll need. If we're lucky, I'll be able to find most of them in wrecking yards up in Tucson or Phoenix. Once we get the parts assembled, it's just a matter of putting the pieces together, priming, and painting."

"Will it be very expensive?" Angie had already discovered the sad reality that the physical damage to her vehicle wasn't going to be covered by her insurance policy.

"If you're worried about how much it's going to cost," Jeff said, "you could always come help me and do some of the work yourself."

"Me?" Angie asked in surprise. "Work on a car?"

"Why not?"

"I never have. I don't know anything about it."

"You can learn. It doesn't take a genius to do priming and painting. Besides, as I recall, you didn't know all that much about bartending when Bobo Jenkins hired you to work at the Blue Moon."

"No," Angie agreed after a moment's consideration. "I guess I didn't."

"Speaking of which," Jeff said, pulling up in front of the Blue Moon, "here we are. Right on time, too. Now, do you want either Marianne or me to come get you when your shift ends?"

"No, thanks," Angie said. "I'll be off early tonight. I can walk back up the canyon to your place. It's not that far. And it's a whole lot less than the four miles out to Galena."

"Well, okay," Jeff said reluctantly. "But if you change your mind, the offer still stands."

Angie's eyes filled with tears. "I don't know how to thank you."

"You already did," Jeff said.

As Angie moved to open her door, a howl of protest erupted from the backseat. "Me go, too! Me go, too," Ruth screeched, holding out her pudgy little arms, begging to be picked up and taken along. Angie Kellogg was Ruth Maculyea-Daniels's all-time favorite baby-sitter. Angie's leaving always provoked a noisy squawk of objection.

Angie leaned into the backseat and blew the girls a pair of kisses. "You can't come, Ruth," she said. "Not right now. I have to go to work. I'll see you tonight."

"Read me a story?"

"Right," Angie said with her first smile of the day. "When I get there, I'll read you a story."

As she opened the door to the Blue Moon, she heard the phone ring. Behind the bar, Bobo Jenkins looked at his watch. "It's for you," he said without bothering to pick up the receiver. "It's a good thing you're on time. This guy's been driving me crazy all morning."

"What guy?" Angie asked.

"You tell me," Bobo replied. "Just answer the phone."

"Angie?"

Dennis Hacker's clipped English accent was instantly recognizable. "Angie," he repeated. "Are you all right? I've been worried sick. I've been dialing your home number all night and all morning, too. Where have you been?"

Angie's initial pleasure at hearing his voice turned almost immediately to anger as she remembered his hurtful laughter once again. "I can't talk right now," she said. "It's time for my shift to start."

"But first you have to let me explain," Dennis said. "You must let me tell you what it was that set me to laughing."

"There's nothing to explain," Angie returned coldly.

"But there is. It's because of my great-grandmother, you see. I wanted to tell you about her in person, but I'm meeting with members of the Peloncillo Ranchers' Association later on this afternoon. It's taken weeks to put the meeting together, so I can't leave for Bisbee until it's over—sometime between four and five. What time do you get off work?"

"I don't see what your great-grandmother has to do with me—" Angie began her objection with every intention of hanging up, but Dennis Hacker didn't let her.

"Wait, please," he interrupted. "You don't understand, Angie. Great-grandmother Hacker has everything to do with you. That's what's so funny. She was a working girl, too. From Nome. If it hadn't been for her kindness, my great-grandfather would have died during the winter of 1898. He was terribly sick with pneumonia, so sick that he let the fire go out in his cabin. That's when the frostbite got him and he lost all those toes. For some reason, Caroline took pity on him. She nursed him back to health as much as possible. Eventually, his father relented and brought him back home to England to finish his recovery. As soon as he was well, he sent for her, brought Caroline to England, and married her.

"She was a runaway—a jilted bride from a good San Francisco family who had turned to prostitution as an alternative to going back home. Her upbringing in the States was such that no one in England ever knew about her real background, except for my grandmother, who still has the letters the two of them wrote back and forth.

"I just found out about all this a few weeks ago when I went home because my grandmother was so sick. She had me take the letters out of her strongbox and let me read them. I'm sure she thought she was dying and if she didn't tell me then, she wouldn't have another chance."

Angie was listening, trying to make sense of the words while Dennis Hacker hurried on. "The letters probably ought to be in a museum somewhere, but I have them with me. I want to show them to you. Can I come see you tonight? After you get off work?"

"I don't know," Angie said dubiously. "Really, I . . ."

"Listen, Angie. What I'm trying to tell you is that if a working girl from Nome was the apple of my great-granddad's eye, then you're good enough for me. Much too good, most likely. End of story."

Blushing furiously, Angie looked up and down the bar. Everyone in the room was staring at her. The place was deathly quiet as all the weekday morning regulars waited to see what would happen.

"You don't mean that," Angie objected. "You barely know me."

"Just try me," Dennis Hacker returned. "I think you'll be surprised."

"I've got to hang up now," Angie said.

"Can I see you tonight? We'll have dinner together. We can talk."

"I don't think so," Angie said.

"Can I call you, then, after the meeting? I don't know what time I'll get away from there, but maybe you'll change your mind by then and agree to see me."

"I'll be working," she objected. "It'll probably be busy."

"I won't take long," Dennis pleaded. "I promise. Now tell me what time you get off so I don't miss you."

Taking a deep breath, Angie relented. "Six," she said.

"Good. I'll be sure to call before then."

Angie put down the phone. At the far end of the bar, Archie McBride and Willy Haskins exchanged knowing smirks.

Archie McBride shook his grizzled head and

raised his nearly empty glass. "Damn those Boy Scouts anyway!" he said.

MRS. VOREVKIN led Ernie and Joanna through the house and showed them into a darkened study. David O'Brien was seated at a desk with only a single small reading lamp lighting the curtain-shrouded room.

"Why are you bringing them in here?" he demanded irritably of the housekeeper. "I thought I told you all inquiries were to be directed to Katherine."

"Mrs. O'Brien isn't here right now," Olga said. "She had to go uptown to the mortuary, remember?"

"Oh, all right," O'Brien responded. "Come on in, then. What is it you want?"

Maybe it was only a trick of the dimmed lights, but the man hunched behind the desk seemed far less formidable than the arrogant swimmer Joanna had met on Saturday. Events in the two intervening days had taken their toll. By late Monday morning, all of David O'Brien's seventy-odd years showed in the sun-etched lines of his craggy face. Even his peevish verbal response to Mrs. Vorevkin lacked some of his previous stridency.

"We asked to speak directly with you," Joanna put in.

"I suppose it's just as well you're here." O'Brien sighed. "I understand there have been deputies out front by the gate most of the morning, Sheriff Brady. What's going on? Brianna's been dead for days. Isn't it a little late for you to come prowling around now?"

"We're investigating another case," Joanna said. "An assault. In fact, we're actually looking for Alf Hastings. We'd like to ask him some questions about the incident."

"What incident is that?" O'Brien asked. "And what do you want with Alf?"

"Has Mr. Hastings told you anything about what happened outside the entrance to your ranch on Saturday night?"

As they spoke, David O'Brien began sounding more and more like his old self—condescension, arrogance, and all. "You mean the one with the wetback he found sneaking around outside the gate? Fending off interlopers who are trying to gain access to my property is Alf's job. Of course he told me about it. He gave me a full report."

"Did he tell you this alleged wetback's name?"

"His name?"

"Ignacio Ybarra."

At once the fight went back out of David O'Brien. "Him?" he asked hoarsely. "Brianna's boyfriend?"

Joanna nodded.

"What was he doing here?"

"He claims he was looking for your daughter," Joanna said. "She wasn't where he expected to find her. He was worried about her."

"And I suppose you believe that?" David O'Brien asked.

"Until we hear Mr. Hastings's version of what went on, I don't know what to believe," Joanna told him.

"In any case, you won't be able to talk to Alf today. He's out of town. Today's his day off. He asked for tomorrow off as well. He said he had some pressing business out of town. He left the ranch early this morning. I don't expect him back before tomorrow night."

"You don't know where he was going?"

O'Brien shook his head. "I have no idea. What my employees do on their own time is none of my business."

"Would his wife know?"

"Maggie? Maybe."

"Where would we find her?" Joanna asked.

"If she's home, she's most likely down in the workers' compound. First trailer on the right-hand side of the road."

"We'll go see her, then," Joanna said.

"Suit yourself," O'Brien said with a wave of his hand. Dismissed, Ernie turned and left the room while Joanna hovered in the doorway. Thinking both his visitors had left the room, David O'Brien hunched back over his desk and buried his face in his hands. His shoulders heaved. A strangled sob escaped his lips. Joanna didn't like the man, but she couldn't help being moved by such abject despair.

"Mr. O'Brien?"

At the sound of Joanna's voice, he started but didn't lower his hands or look in her direction. "What?"

"Please accept my condolences about your daughter. I know how much it must hurt . . ."

"Thank you," he mumbled almost inaudibly.

Warned by some guiding instinct, Joanna glided away from the door and moved back into the room. She didn't stop until she was standing directly in front of the desk. In a pool of golden lamplight she saw a single piece of paper—and a pen, a Mount Blanc fountain pen. Years of working over the counter in the Davis Insurance Agency had made Joanna Brady adept at reading words that were written upside-down. What she saw scrawled across the top of the single piece of paper chilled her. "To whom it may concern."

"I thought you told me the other day that O'Briens aren't quitters," she said quietly.

O'Brien dropped his hands and glared up at her, his vivid blue eyes probing hers. "What do you mean?"

"I mean that suicide isn't the answer. It never is."

Hurriedly, David O'Brien covered the revealing paper with his hands. "What would you know about it?" he asked.

"When my husband died, I felt the same way. As though I couldn't possibly go on."

"No, you didn't, Sheriff Brady," David O'Brien interrupted. "You couldn't have felt exactly the same way. You lost a husband. That's different from losing a child. I've done that before. Twice. I've had three children, and I've outlived all three."

"There must be a reason."

"Oh, there's a reason, all right," he conceded

bitterly. "I tried to outwit God, and this is what it got me. As far as I can see, I've got nothing left to live for."

"What about your wife?"

"What about her?" He shrugged. "Katherine's had one foot out the door all these years. With Brianna gone, there's no reason for her to stay. And there's no reason for me to hang around, either. I built all this for my daughter," he added. "If I can't give it to her, what's the point?"

"There may be another answer," Joanna told him. "One you've missed so far. The problem is, suicide is a permanent solution. If you're dead, you'll never have a chance to find out what that answer might be. Talk to a counselor, Mr. O'Brien. Or to Father Morris from St. Dominick's. You need some help."

"What I need is for you to get out and leave me alone," David O'Brien said wearily. "You don't know what you're talking about."

Ernie met Joanna at the door. "What happened?" he asked. "I got all the way to the door before I figured out you weren't right behind me. What's going on?"

"Where's Mrs. O'Brien?"

"I'm pretty sure she's home now. The Lexus was just driving into the yard when I started back to find you."

"Good," Joanna said grimly. "We'd better have a word with Katherine before we go see Maggie Hastings."

"Why?" Ernie asked. "Is there a problem?"

"There will be if someone doesn't do something to prevent it," Joanna replied. "Unless I'm mistaken, David O'Brien is right on the brink of blowing his brains out."

"What are you going to do about it?"

"I'm going to tell his wife."

As it turned out, they met up with Katherine O'Brien in the entryway. She had just come in the door and was depositing her keys and purse on a gilded entryway table. She was dressed in a sedate navy blue shirtwaist dress. There was makeup on her face. Her graying hair was swept up into an elegant French twist. The cumulative result made Katherine O'Brien far different from the casually attired, makeup-free woman Joanna had met on two previous occasions. The one thing that remained constant, however, was Katherine O'Brien's ironclad emotional control.

"What's going on, Sheriff Brady?" Katherine asked. "I saw two sheriff's cars out in the drive. Has something happened? Did you catch Bree's killer?"

"No," Joanna said hastily. "Nothing like that. We're here on another matter—to see your husband about Alf Hastings. But Mrs. O'Brien, I must warn you, I think your husband is taking your daughter's death very badly."

"Of course he's taking it badly," she returned. "It isn't the kind of thing you take well."

"I believe your husband is suicidal," Joanna added. "You need to talk to him about this. Or find him some help, someone to talk to—a priest or a counselor. Unless you want to be planning two funerals instead of one."

Katherine O'Brien seemed to draw back. Her eyes narrowed, her fists clenched. "God helps those who help themselves," she said.

The woman's brusque response was so different from what Joanna expected—so different from the concerned and hovering helpmate Katherine had appeared to be previously—that Joanna was momentarily taken aback. "What do you mean?"

"Just that. I mean David's a grown-up. If he wants to find someone to talk to about this, he'll have to find help for himself. It's not up to me."

"But isn't—"

"Look," Katherine interrupted, her eyes blazing with anger, "I spent eighteen years of my life walking a tightrope and running interference between those two. While Brianna was here, nothing she did ever quite measured up. No matter what, she wasn't good enough to suit him. If he's going to go off the deep end now that she's gone, it's up to him. He'll have to come to terms with his own guilt for a change. I'm finally out of the middle, and I have every intention of staying that way."

Looking at Katherine, Joanna couldn't help remembering David O'Brien's words. *Katherine's had one foot out the door for years.* Was that what was going on here, then? Was this one of those cases where an incompatible couple had stayed married for the sake of a child? And, now that the child was gone, did that mean the marriage was over? Unfortunately, in trying to help David O'Brien, it seemed Joanna had only succeeded in pouring oil on the flames.

She decided to take one last crack at smoothing things over. "We all have to learn to live with the consequences of our actions," she said.

Katherine nodded. "I figured that out a long time ago," she said. "David never has. Now, if you'll excuse me." She turned toward the kitchen. "Olga," she called, "I'm going to go lie down for a little while. Please don't let me sleep past three. I have a four o'clock appointment with Father Morris."

Left alone in the foyer, Joanna and Ernie let themselves out the front door. "Whew!" Ernie exclaimed, once the door closed behind them and they were alone on the verandah. "What the hell was that all about? Katherine O'Brien isn't what I'd call your typical grieving mother."

"Maybe there's no such thing," Joanna said thoughtfully. "Come on. Let's go see Maggie Hastings."

TWENTY-ONE

TAKING TWO separate cars, Ernie and Joanna drove back up the road to the Y that led off through the lush grass to the Green Brush Ranch employee compound. It consisted of five separate fourteen-by-seventy mobile homes. They were set in a slight hollow, out of sight from both the road and the main house. The mobile home sites were newly carved from the desert. The trailers were surrounded by raw red dirt punctuated by baby landscaping of reed-thin trees, tiny cacti, and leggy clumps of youthful oleander.

The first trailer on the left-hand side of the road was flanked by a six-foot-high chain-link dog run. As soon as Joanna stopped her Crown Victoria and stepped outside, the German shepherd she had seen on Saturday threw himself against the gate, barking and growling.

Ernie, joining Joanna beside her car, gave the

dog run's fierce occupant a wary look. "Let's hope to hell the damned thing holds," he said.

The dog was still barking furiously when a woman opened the door in answer to Ernie Carpenter's knock. "Yeah?" she said, holding on to the doorjamb with both hands and swaying unsteadily on her feet. "Whad'ya want?"

"Maggie Hastings?" he said, opening his wallet and displaying his ID. "Would it be possible to speak to you for a few moments? Could we come in?"

Maggie Hastings was a disheveled, dark-haired woman in her mid-to-late forties. Her graying, lackluster hair was pulled back in a greasy ponytail. She wore a soiled man's shirt over a pair of too-tight shorts. She was also quite drunk.

Stumbling away from the door, she allowed Joanna and Ernie to enter. "Whaz this all about?" she slurred.

The room's curtains were tightly closed. The difference between the interior gloom and the brilliant exterior sunlight left Joanna momentarily blind. The stench of booze combined with a lingering pall of cigar and cigarette smoke was so stifling that Joanna could barely breathe.

"Sorry the place is such a mess," Maggie muttered, kicking something aside. "Haven't had a chance to pick up today. Waddn't 'xactly expecting company."

From the sound, Joanna suspected that the invisible object was an empty bottle of some kind. As her eyes adjusted to the dim light, she was shocked by the disarray. To the outside world, Alf Hastings presented a neat, well-pressed countenance. It was hard to believe that his starched khaki uniform could have emerged from such filth. The living room wasn't merely a mess. It was a disaster. Empty bottles—gin mostly, but some beer as well—littered the newspaper-strewn floor. The dining room table, visible from the living room, was covered with stacks of dirty dishes, milk cartons, margarine containers, and bread wrappers—several days' worth at least. A line of what seemed like mostly can-and-bottle-filled garbage sacks lined one side of the room, marching from the kitchen doorway toward the front door.

Remembering all too well how many bugs the new cook had rousted from what supposedly had been a clean jail kitchen, Joanna shivered. No doubt there were plenty of well-fed but currently invisible bugs hiding in this very room.

Turning her back on her visitors, Maggie staggered as far as the end of the couch and then fell onto it. She picked up a remote control and muted the droning television set, turning an afternoon talk show into a wordless pantomime of moving lips and wagging heads. She stared at it with such avid interest, however, that Joanna wondered if she even remembered that someone else was in the room.

"This is about your husband," Joanna said.

Maggie Hastings's eyes never wavered from the set. "What about him?" she asked.

"Do you know where he is?"

"Work." Maggie's reply was little more than a grunt.

"No, he's not," Joanna told her. "Mr. O'Brien told us your husband went away for a day or two."

"Well, that's news to me," Maggie said with a noncommittal shrug. "If he was going somewhere, don't you think he'da told me?"

Not necessarily, Joanna thought. *And even if he did, who's to say you'd remember?* "This is serious, Mrs. Hastings," she said aloud. "Do you have any idea where he might be?"

The firmness in Joanna's question somehow must have penetrated Maggie Hastings's drunken haze. "Why all the questions?" she asked, finally glancing away from the television set for the first time. "Whaz going on?"

"On Saturday night, a young man was severely beaten outside the gate to Green Brush Ranch," Joanna replied. "Not only was he beaten, but burned, too, with the lit end of a cigar."

Joanna said no more than that, but it was evidently enough. Maggie Hastings's response was instantaneous. Her face seemed to collapse. Her mouth went slack while her eyes brimmed with tears. "Oh, no," she wailed. "Not that. Not again."

"What do you mean?"

"I can't believe it. How could he? What if we lose this job, too?" Maggie whispered brokenly but with far less drunken slurring. "And the roof over our heads, too, just like the other time. You don't know what it was like then. We lost everything—our house, our furniture, our friends. Stevie will kill him when he finds out. He'll just plain kill him."

Overcome with a combination of emotion and

booze, she fell into a long series of racking sobs. For several minutes, she was totally incapable of speech. Joanna had no choice but to wait until the sobs subsided before she could ask another question. "Who's Stevie?"

Maggie took a ragged breath, blew her nose, and wiped her eyes. "Stephan Marcovich," Maggie answered. "Alf's cousin up in Phoenix. He's an old friend of the O'Briens. He's also the one who arranged this job for us. If it hadn't been for Stevie, once the lawyers got done with us, we'da been sunk. We had no place to go. Alf couldn't find a job anywhere in Yuma, not even flipping burgers. It was like we had a disease or something. We were one step away from living on the street when Stevie sent Alf here. Oh, my God. And now he's done it again. I can't stand it," she wailed. "I just can't."

Once more Maggie's voice trailed off into a torrent of hopeless tears.

"Mrs. Hastings, would your husband's cousin have any idea where Alf might be?"

Blowing her nose again, Maggie shook her head. "I don't think so," she said. "If I don't know where he is, how would Stevie?"

"Just the same, can you give us his number?"

"Stevie's? Up in Phoenix?"

Joanna nodded. "Please," she said.

"I guess so." Unsteadily, Maggie Hastings hoisted herself off the couch, then she wobbled across the room and staggered down a short hallway. For several minutes, Joanna and Ernie could hear her in a room down the hall, mumbling and cursing.

Finally she returned, carrying a frayed business card.

"Here it is!" she announced triumphantly, handing it over to Joanna. "Alf says I never can find anything in all this mess, but he's wrong, you know. There's a system around here. He just doesn't understand it, that's all."

She belched then, spewing a cloud of stale gin throughout the room. "Can I get you something?" she asked.

Looking down at the card, Joanna barely heard her. "Air Conditioning Enterprises," the raised print said. "Stephan J. Marcovich, President."

"No," Joanna managed, coming to her senses. "Nothing, thank you. We've got to go."

As soon as the door opened and they stepped out into the fresh air and light, the dog resumed its barking. "What's going on?" Ernie asked as they headed toward the cars. "You look like you've seen a ghost."

In a way, Joanna had seen a ghost—her father's. She was remembering a breakfast from long ago. Her father, D. H. Lathrop—only a deputy back then—had been working on a case. "When it comes to homicide," he had announced over his bacon and eggs, "there ain't no such thing as coincidence."

"Isn't," Eleanor had returned at once, correcting his grammar as usual. She was forever doing that, trying to weed out the remnants of her husband's Arkansas childhood. "There isn't any such thing," she added for good measure.

It was one of the few times Joanna could remember her mother's habitual corrections riling her easygoing, even-tempered father. "Ellie," he had said, banging his coffee cup back into the saucer. "It would be nice if, just once in your life, you'd listen to what I mean instead of picking apart whatever I say."

With that, he had stood up and stalked out of the house.

"Well?" Ernie pressed. "What's going on?"

"I'm remembering something my father said years ago," she told him, handing over the card. "He told me once that, in a homicide case, there's no such thing as coincidence."

"I'd have to agree, but . . . ."

"Did I mention anything to you about Jim Hobbs being offered the opportunity to get in on an illegal Freon buy? The guy trying to put the deal together was Sam Nettleton."

"Nettleton? The scuzzball towing operator from up in Benson?"

"Right."

Ernie shook his head. "You didn't say a word to me about it."

"Sorry. With everything else that happened, it must have slipped my mind. But I did call Adam York about it. He said the DEA is investigating a big Freon-smuggling deal up in Phoenix, something involving one of the big refrigeration contractors. So here we have a Cochise County Freon case, supposedly unrelated to theirs, and a Phoenix air-conditioning contractor connected, however loosely, to one of our homicides. What do you think?"

Ernie handed Joanna back the card. "You're right," he said. "There's no such thing as coincidence. What are you going to do about it?"

"As soon as I have some lunch, I'm going back to the office to call Adam York. What about you?"

"I'm supposed to meet Rose uptown. After that, I'll run by the coroner's office to see if George has that official copy of the autopsy typed up for us by then."

Joanna nodded. "Good deal," she said. "I'll see you back at the office right after that. I don't know about you, but I can do a whole lot better job of strategic planning on a full stomach than I can on an empty one."

On her way back to the office, Joanna stopped long enough to grab a hamburger. She sat alone in the midst of Daisy's noisy lunchtime clatter, letting her thoughts wander back to Green Brush Ranch. What had happened to Bree was an appalling tragedy, but it seemed to Joanna that there were other tragedies looming there as well. She had read somewhere that the death of a child was one of the most difficult marital storms for a couple to weather. From what she had seen that afternoon from both David and Katherine O'Brien, Joanna didn't hold out much hope for the long-term survival of their marriage.

Leaving the restaurant, she glanced off to the south. A series of tall columns of cumulus clouds was rising up on the far horizon. Another afternoon storm was brewing. If this one turned out to be as bad as yesterday's, there'd be another big bite in the overtime department. Frank Montoya would have a fit.

Back at her desk, Joanna immediately tried calling Adam York, but he didn't answer his phone. Following his voice mail directions, she left her number on his pager. Even so, it was almost forty-five minutes before he answered the page and called her back. In order to contain her impatience, Joanna had buried herself in that day's pile of paperwork and correspondence.

"Just how mad are you?" the DEA agent asked as soon as Joanna picked up her phone.

"Mad?" she repeated. "Why would I be mad?"

"D.C. went over my head on this one," he said. "I couldn't help it. It's all gone down since I talked to you this morning. I tried to call you about it the minute it happened, but you weren't available, and it was too complicated—"

"Adam," she interrupted. "What the hell are you talking about?"

"The Freon deal. We've been in touch with the guy you told me about, the one in Bisbee."

"Jim Hobbs?"

"Right. He's agreed to make the buy. Somebody was supposed to meet him in Benson just a little while ago to give him a briefcase full of marked bills."

"Wait a minute," Joanna fumed. "Are you telling me that you people are initiating a sting operation in my jurisdiction without anyone letting my department know beforehand?"

"Unfortunately, yes. Joanna, I'm sorry. As I said, I did try calling you earlier to let you know.

If you had a damn cell phone, maybe I could get through to you once in a while. Ever since that one attempt, I've been shut up in meetings. This case is all coming together so fast—"

"What case?" Joanna interrupted. "With Air Conditioning Enterprises, you mean?"

Adam York stopped in mid-sentence. "What did you say?"

"With Air Conditioning Enterprises," Joanna repeated, reading from the card Maggie Hastings had given her. "Stephan J. Marcovich, President."

"How the hell did you do that?" Adam York demanded. "This was supposed to be totally hush-hush. Nobody is supposed . . ."

The undisguised shock in Adam's voice told Joanna that she had indeed made the right connection. Stephan Marcovich did have something to do with the DEA's Freon deal. "It's like you told me the other day, Adam," she reminded him, not worrying if she sounded a little smug. "Little fish lead to big fish, remember?"

"But what . . . ?"

"Hush-hush or not, maybe it's time we traded info," Joanna informed him. "I've got a homicide case down here—a young girl, eighteen years old, who was murdered and dumped off the side of a cliff out in the Peloncillos east of Douglas sometime over the weekend. We didn't get a positive ID until late last night. My public information officer has been dealing with the press about it all morning, so it'll probably be headlines statewide by late this afternoon."

"Why?" Adam York asked. "What makes a

week-end homicide in Cochise County headline news all over Arizona?"

"Because the girl's name is O'Brien."

"So?"

"And her parents, David and Katherine O'Brien, are good friends of the Hickmans—as in Wally and Abby."

"I don't think I want to hear this." Adam groaned. "You mean as in Governor Wallace Hickman?"

"One and the same."

"Damn!"

"And I wouldn't be the least bit surprised," Joanna continued, "if we don't find out that Mr. Stephan J. Marcovich wasn't part of the governor's circle of acquaintances as well."

Adam York sighed. "We already know he is. A major contributor besides. That's why we're trying to keep this thing quiet. What's his connection to the O'Briens?"

"Marcovich's cousin is a man named Alf Hastings, who happens to work for David O'Brien. You remember Alf Hastings, don't you?"

"Remind me."

"He used to be a deputy sheriff over in Yuma County. He got drummed out of the corps on a charge of police brutality. Now this same Alf Hastings is David O'Brien's chief of operations. Translation: junkyard dog/bodyguard. According to Hastings's wife, Maggie, Alf's cousin—Stevie, as she called him—arranged for the job when Alf couldn't get work anywhere else. The dead girl's Hispanic boyfriend went out to the O'Brien place hoping to catch sight of his missing girlfriend. Instead, Alf Hastings beat him up. We're investigating it as an assault case, but he could develop into a suspect in our homicide and into a possibility for your smuggling case as well."

"Have you talked to this Alf guy?"

"Not yet. He's not at work today," Joanna told him. "According to his boss, he won't be at work tomorrow, either. And nobody—his wife included—seems to know where he is. But let me tell you something about the O'Brien place, Adam. It's called Green Brush Ranch, and it's situated smack on top of the Mexican border. In fact, the property line runs along the border for miles, from Naco west all the way to the San Pedro River. Over the past couple years, under the guise of reestablishing the grassland, the owner has turned the whole place into an armed camp, complete with razor wire all the way around the perimeter and with ATV-mounted guards and guard dogs patrolling the property line."

There was a long silence on the other end of the line. "In other words, what you're telling me is that no law enforcement folks have been allowed inside."

"That's right."

"Which would make for an ideal smuggling operation."

"Right again." Joanna agreed.

Ever since she had read the words on Stephan Marcovich's business card, the same ugly theory had been germinating inside Joanna's head. Now that she had confirmation from Adam York that

Marcovich was indeed the air-conditioning contractor in question, she was almost sure of it. The seed of the idea was there, but she had yet to voice it aloud. She felt self-conscious at the idea of laying it out in front of Adam York. Would the DEA agent find it as chillingly believable as she did, or would he simply toss it aside?

"Let me run this past you, Adam. If either David O'Brien and/or his wife is involved in this smuggling deal, what do you think the chances are that one of them had something to do with their daughter's death?"

"What makes you think that?" Adam responded at once.

Relieved that he didn't laugh outright at her theory, Joanna continued. "I had a chance to look through the girl's diary," she said. "Through one of them, anyway. Brianna O'Brien was one of those faithful diarists. She's been keeping a journal for several years now. The last entry stuck with me. 'My mother is a liar,' it said. My guess is that both her parents are liars, not just her mother.

"When Ernie and I were out at the house earlier today, I saw the father writing what looked like a suicide note. The mother is pissed as hell— at the father. Not only that, she said something that I've been thinking about ever since. She said her husband has never lived with the consequences of his actions. The way she said it set off all my alarms."

Again the telephone line went quiet. Joanna suffered through the silence, expecting the DEA agent to tell her she had a far too vivid imagination.

"The liar comment is the very last entry in the journal?" Adam asked at last. "The final one the girl made before she died?"

"No. It was the last entry in the next-to-last volume. It was written months ago. The problem is, the volume Brianna O'Brien has been writing in since then—the one that might contain any telling details—is missing. It isn't in her room. It wasn't at the crime scene, either."

"As in maybe somebody got rid of it," Adam York muttered.

"The same thought that occurred to me," Joanna said.

"Unfortunately," Adam continued, "this Freon thing is a multimillion-dollar business. If our suspicions are correct, Stevie Marcovich, otherwise known as Marco, runs an operation that will be right up there with the six-million-dollar bust we made in Florida a year ago. If the O'Briens are involved and their own daughter was expendable, I'd say Sam Nettleton up in Benson is in way over his head. So is Jim Hobbs, for that matter."

"What do we do about it?" Joanna asked.

"For one thing," Adam said, "I'm canceling the sting operation as of right now. How soon can your detectives be in Benson?"

Joanna glanced at her watch. One forty-five. "Ernie Carpenter is probably still up the canyon at the coroner's office. With luck I can possibly have him there by two-thirty. The same thing goes for Jaime Carbajal. Why? What do you have in mind?"

"I think somebody should go see Sam Nettleton and lay the cards on the table. We'll let him know his ass is on the line. Maybe we can scare him into springing with what he knows."

"And if he doesn't?"

"Then we're no worse off than we were before."

"Except you may have blown your chance to nail Marcovich," Joanna said.

"Right," Adam returned. "But considering there are innocent lives at stake, that's a chance I'm willing to take. I'm on my way to Benson, too, but I'm coming from Casa Grande. I don't know if I'll make it there before all hell breaks loose."

"Do me a favor," Joanna said.

"What's that."

"Tell your people that Nettleton comes here first for questioning."

"Joanna—"

She cut off his objection. "You owe me, Adam. This is my turf. As far as I'm concerned, my homicide takes precedence over your sting."

"Okay," Adam York agreed reluctantly. "I suppose you're right. I'll let them know."

The moment Joanna was off the telephone with Adam York, she called Dispatch and told the operator who answered to locate both Detective Carbajal and Detective Carpenter and send them off to meet up with the DEA task force in Benson. Once that was done, there wasn't much more for Joanna to do except sit and wait. She was tempted to go racing off to Benson right along with everyone else. After a moment's consideration, though, she decided against it. That wasn't her job. It was why she had detectives. Besides, Cochise County or not, the Benson operation was the DEA's deal. Adam York would be in charge of that one—of his officers and Joanna's as well.

Sit and stay, she told herself firmly. *No need for a second commander in the field. All that would do would be to gum up the works.* She stopped long enough to eye the ever-growing mounds of paper that littered her desk.

Especially, she added, *when I've got more than enough to do right here.*

TWENTY-TWO

DURING JOANNA'S term as sheriff, paperwork had become the bane of her existence. No matter how often she did it—no matter how hard she tried to keep up—it continued to roll across her desk in a perpetual stream. It struck her that it was just like trying to keep up with housework at home, where there was always another pile of dirty laundry to wash or another load of dishes to do. It was a drudgery aspect of police work that somehow never quite made it into the phony TV world of quirky cops and equally fantastic crooks duking it out in exotic high-speed car chases.

She had barely made a dent in the pile labeled "Thursday" when Chief Deputy Frank Montoya tapped on her half-open door and let himself into her office. Frowning, he eased his lanky frame into one of the chairs opposite Joanna's desk.

"What's wrong?" she asked.

"It's that obvious?" he returned.

"From a mile away," she said with a smile. "Now, what is it and how bad?"

"The usual," he said. "It's going to be another big-time media blitz, including all the out-of-towners."

"Great." Joanna groaned. "Just what we need."

Frank nodded. "I've been doing this job long enough that I should be getting used to it. At least by now I pretty well know all the players—as in which reporters are trustworthy and which ones should be run out of town on a rail."

"That sounds ominous," Joanna said.

"It is. I happen to have in my possession a preview of Marliss Shackleford's column for tomorrow's *Bisbee Bee*."

"What do you mean a preview?"

"Just what I said. Ken Dawson, the publisher over at the *Bee*, sent along a copy of tomorrow's column just in case you have any comment."

Despite the fact that Joanna and Marliss both attended Canyon Methodist Church, the two of them had never been friends. Since Joanna's election, their already thorny relationship had deteriorated even further. Marliss never failed to publicly point out whatever she thought to be Joanna's official shortcomings.

Joanna reached for the paper Frank was holding in front of him. "That bad?" she asked.

"It's not good," Frank muttered as she turned her attention to the words on the paper.

With eighteen-year-old honor student Brianna O'Brien dead by what officials are calling homi-

cidal violence, it remains to be seen how much responsibility Sheriff Joanna Brady must shoulder for the girl's untimely death.

As late as Saturday afternoon Sheriff Brady reportedly refused to call in the FBI to search for Brianna even though the girl's father, retired Paradise Valley developer and Naco native David O'Brien, specifically requested that she do so.

Although it is doubtful summoning the FBI at that point would have spared the recent BHS graduate's life, the question remains about why Sheriff Brady was so reluctant to request the involvement of other law enforcement agencies to help with this unfortunate situation.

At a time when the criminal element is able to leave a trail of destruction that crosses both state and international boundaries, can Cochise County afford a sheriff who regards herself as a female version of the Lone Ranger?

Think about it, Sheriff Brady. How about a little more cooperation and a little less ego-mania?

Her head buzzing with anger, Joanna tossed the paper back to Frank. "How dare she? That's garbage and Marliss knows it. Brianna O'Brien was dead long before I *refused* to call in the FBI."

"You know that and I know that," Frank agreed. "Unfortunately, everybody else—other reporters included—may take this stuff as gospel. I think you should make some kind of official comment. In fact, I've even drafted a couple . . ."

"The Lone Ranger?" Joanna continued, almost as though she hadn't heard him. "I've never been a lone damned ranger. And here she is, putting that in the paper when, even as we speak, my department is up to its ears in the middle of a joint operation with the DEA."

After that, Joanna fell silent. "So," Frank asked. "Do we send a response or not?"

What Joanna really wanted to do in response was get in her car, drive uptown to the *Bee*'s office on Main Street, grab Marliss by the front of her shirt, and shake her until her teeth rattled. That, of course, was a rotten idea. Struggling to get a grip, Joanna thought about it. As for a written response, any mention of the joint operation ran the risk of blowing the Freon deal and possibly the murder investigation as well. Much as Joanna personally would have liked to drop Marliss Shackleford down the nearest mine shaft, Joanna knew that just wasn't possible—not without jeopardizing too many other things.

"Not," she said. "Thank Ken for sending it over. That was very evenhanded of him for a change, but we'll let the column go as is. With no comment."

"Wouldn't it be better if you said something?" Frank asked.

"No," Joanna said. "In this case, I think we'll let our actions speak for themselves."

"All right," Frank conceded. "Have it your way."

Once Frank left her office, Joanna continued to fume. She found herself second-guessing her decision. Between that and wondering what was going on in Benson, it wasn't too surprising that she couldn't concentrate on paperwork anymore. No matter how hard she tried, she couldn't force herself to proofread a densely worded letter from her to the board of supervisors. The sentences on the page simply didn't make sense. They kept becoming entwined with Marliss Shackleford's Lone Ranger comment and with the single sentence from Brianna O'Brien's diary that Joanna had come to regard as the dead girl's haunting last words. "My mother is a liar."

Finally, giving up on her third attempt at reading the letter, Joanna put it aside, along with the remainder of that day's untended correspondence. Abandoning all pretense of staying on task, Joanna leaned back in her oversized chair and stared out the window.

When Joanna had come into her office an hour or so earlier, the sky outside her window had been brilliantly blue. Now that same blue sky was pockmarked with puffy white, gray-bottomed clouds. On the ground below, swiftly moving shadows from those same clouds glided silently over the desert landscape like so many circling vultures. Watching the shadows, Joanna found herself once again thinking about Brianna O'Brien's mother, the liar.

Determined to do something constructive, Joanna stood up and headed for the evidence room. Buddy Richards, the evidence room clerk, greeted her with a welcoming smile that Joanna knew was far more pleasant than it should have been. Buddy was one of the recalcitrant old-timers who had much preferred things the way they were. Months after the election, Buddy still wasn't happy about having a woman for a boss.

"What can I do for you, Sheriff Brady?" he asked from behind his manufactured grin.

Buddy was a former deputy who, as a result of a bull-riding accident on the amateur rodeo circuit, now had a right leg two inches shorter than the left. When he had been offered a disability retirement, Joanna had hoped he'd take it, thus ridding her of one more detractor. Unfortunately, Buddy had refused the offer, claiming he'd much rather "gimp around the evidence room than be put out to pasture."

"Ernie Carpenter should have turned in a book with regard to the O'Brien case," Joanna told him. "Do you happen to know whether or not it's been dusted for prints?"

"Looks like," Buddy replied, consulting his computer screen.

"Could I see it, then?"

Richards frowned. "According to the rules, I'm only supposed to release it to one of the officers on the case."

Joanna looked the man directly in the eye. "What do you think I am, Mr. Richards?" she asked. "Chopped liver?"

"I'll get it right away," he said.

Once the book was in her hands, Joanna took it straight to her office. Out on the mountain on Sunday afternoon, she had scanned through most of the journal. Now, with nothing to do but wait, she took the time to read it more thoroughly. More than once, the words Brianna had written brought tears to Joanna's eyes.

Bree had filled the pages with teenaged joy

and anguish both. She had spent full pages ago-
nizing over the extent and seriousness of Ignacio
Ybarra's football injuries. Using the journal as a
sounding board, she had also poured out her dismay at the callous attitude exhibited by the other
girls on the cheerleading squad who had once
been her friends. Not only did they not share her
concern for the injured player, they had ostra-
cized her for leaving the squad. It was only in reading the journal that Joanna learned how Bree,
once arguably the most popular girl in school, had
been forced to come to grips with life as a social
outcast.

In that emotional snake pit, it wasn't surprising that she had invested so much of herself in a
new and forbidden relationship with Ignacio. Iso-
lated and alone, she had turned to him for solace.
No wonder the friendship between them had
quickly blossomed, first into romance and later
into love.

Joanna discovered some references to a brief
summer school connection between them that
was little more than a stolen kiss or two. Had they
never seen one another again, that brief encounter would have been dismissed as mere puppy
love. Their second interaction, however, had been
far different. Even from a distance, Joanna Brady
couldn't help but be moved by the youthful but
undeniable passion that had flowed so freely out
of Bree's heart and onto the pages of her journal.
The outpouring was made all the more poignant
by Joanna's knowing the rest of the story. Ignacio
Ybarra had returned Bree's feelings. Now he was

left alone, trying to find a way to survive the loss of that ardent first love.

Not only did the journal provide a detailed road map of Bree's feelings, it also offered a faithful account of the resourceful young couple's meetings, of how they had arranged at least one of their secret assignations. It also told about where they went and what they did on the first of their unauthorized weekends together. It wasn't until Joanna reached the last week in February that she found an item that had nothing at all to do with Ignacio Ybarra. It was something Joanna remembered reading on her first scan of the journal, but with everything that had been going on at the time, she had missed the entry's possible significance.

As per usual Mom is going to be out of town over her birthday. I don't know why she insists on being gone right then. She always gives some lame excuse like she doesn't care for birthdays or that after a certain age they don't matter that much anyway. And she always says it wouldn't be fair to interrupt what the whole group is doing for some kind of birthday celebration.

Before, I've gone along with her wishes and haven't done anything about her birthday until she gets back home. But this time I've made up my mind things are going to be different. I've found the most wonderful birthday card—the perfect one—and I don't want to have to wait and give it to her after she gets back home. I know that one of those companies like FedEx or UPS—the

*ones who advertise that they can deliver anything
anywhere—will be able to get it to her on time.
All I have to do is figure out in advance exactly
where she'll be. After that, the rest will be easy.*

Joanna stopped reading and once again stared
out the window. The clouds that earlier had merely
dotted the sky now had coalesced into an omi-
nously dark and unbroken gray canopy. Across
the parking lot, gray sticks of ocotillo, already
edged with new green leaves sprouting in the aftermath of yesterday's rain, tossed wildly back and
forth in a brisk breeze.

Just as Joanna had suspected earlier, another
fierce summer thunderstorm was on its way,
bringing with it wind, dust, and rain. *Not to mention flash floods and more overtime,* Joanna thought.
But as she continued to stare out the window,
her budget concerns were overtaken by another
consideration—by the glimmer of a hunch that
was more gut instinct than anything else.

Under normal circumstances, Joanna would
have turned that hunch over to her investigators.
With both her detectives otherwise occupied, she
decided to follow through on it herself. Picking
up her phone, she dialed the records clerk. "Cindy,
can you get me driver's license information for
Katherine O'Brien?"

"Sure, Sheriff Brady," Cindy Hall responded.
"Do you have a middle initial or date of birth?"

"Negative on both of those," Joanna told her.

"What about address?"

"Purdy Lane," Joanna replied. She waited

during the silence for the several seconds it took for the computer to hook into the state's vehicular database and to kick out the needed information.

"All right," Cindy said finally. "I think I've got her. Middle initial is V. Maiden name was Ross. What else would you like to know?"

"Date of birth, for starters," Joanna said.

"March four," Cindy answered. "And the year is 1942. Anything else?"

March four, Joanna thought. *The same day as the entry that said Katherine was a liar. Are the two somehow related?*

"Any arrests or convictions?" Joanna asked.

"None at all," the clerk answered.

Putting down the phone, Joanna considered her next move. Finally, picking up the receiver again, she dialed her in-laws' number. She was relieved when Eva Lou answered the phone. That way Joanna could ask her question directly without having to go through Jim Bob.

"Why, good afternoon, Joanna," Eva Lou said. "How are you doing today, and what have you heard from Jenny?"

Joanna laughed. "Nothing so far. This is Monday. She's only been there since Saturday, remember?"

"I suppose that's true," Eva Lou conceded. "It seems much longer."

Joanna nodded. It seemed that way for her as well.

"If you write to her," Eva Lou continued, "be

sure to tell her that Grandpa and I miss her terribly."

"Will do," Joanna agreed. "In the meantime, I need your help. Last night you were telling me something about Katherine O'Brien. About her mission work."

"Oh, yes. That poor woman," Eva Lou said. "My heart just aches for her."

"Who was it who told you about Mrs. O'Brien's going on missions?"

"That would have been Babe," Eva Lou answered at once. "Babe Sheridan. She also attends St. Dominick's. Why do you need to know?"

"It's nothing," Joanna said. "I have a couple of questions is all." Minutes later, Joanna was on the phone with Babe Sheridan at the water company's customer service desk, where she had worked ever since her husband's death in a mining accident some thirty years earlier.

"What can I do for you, Sheriff Brady?" Babe asked.

"I'm curious about Katherine O'Brien," Joanna said, trying to make the inquiry seem as casual as possible.

"Isn't it terrible about their daughter?" Babe said at once. "It's bad enough to lose a husband, but a child? I hear the funeral mass is going to be on Thursday afternoon. I'm planning on taking half a day off so I can attend."

"Yes, it is terrible," Joanna replied, "but I'm not calling about that at the moment. I wanted to ask you about the mission work Katherine does. I have a friend who's interested in doing some medical mission work as well, but this doesn't seem to be the right time to ask the O'Briens about it."

Joanna's story was a bold-faced lie, but it worked. "Oh, of course not," Babe Sheridan agreed at once. "They shouldn't be bothered at a time like this. Now, let me see. I don't quite remember the details or even the name of the organization. It's not Doctors Without Borders, but it's something like that. I'm terrible with names. Whatever it is, it operates out of Minneapolis. I could probably find out for you if you want me to."

"No," Joanna said quickly. "I'll give my friend the information and let her do her own searching. If she's that interested in going, she should do her own research, don't you think?"

"I suppose so," Babe replied. "But still, if you need me to help out . . ."

"You've been a help already," Joanna assured her. "I'll let my friend take it from here."

When she finished that call, she considered for only a moment before dialing Doc Winfield's office. Since he was from Minnesota and also a doctor, Joanna thought he might know something about such an organization. When his voice mail message announced he was out of the office until five, Joanna looked up the area code for Minneapolis and dialed the number for information, asking the directory assistance operator for the number of the Minneapolis public library. It took several minutes before she was put through to a reference librarian who was willing to help.

"I've never heard of any such organization," the librarian said once Joanna finished explaining what was needed. "The medical association might know about it, though, and if it's possibly church-related, the diocese might know as well."

For the next half hour, Joanna followed one blind lead after another. If a medical mission operation was working out of the Minneapolis/St. Paul area, someone was doing a terrific job of keeping it a total secret—something that didn't seem the least bit likely. An organization setting out to save the world would want everyone to know about it—for fund-raising purposes if nothing else. Of course, the simplest thing to do would have been to call Katherine O'Brien herself and ask for the name and number, but Joanna knew better than that.

Instead, she called Phoenix information. After receiving yet another number, she dialed Good Samaritan Hospital and asked to be put through to the director of nursing. While waiting for someone to answer, Joanna tried to piece together a timetable. Brianna O'Brien had been eighteen years old when she died. Joanna remembered Katherine's saying that she and David O'Brien hadn't married until five years after she stopped working at Good Sam. That meant that the records Joanna needed would be twenty-three to twenty-five years old, if they still existed at all. She didn't hold out much hope.

Moments later a woman's voice came on the line. "This is Barbara Calderone, the director of nursing," she said. "How can I help you?"

"My name is Joanna Brady. I'm the sheriff of Cochise County. We're trying to learn something about a nurse who worked at Good Sam a number of years ago. I was wondering—"

"How many years ago?" Barbara Calderone interrupted.

"More than twenty."

"It's highly unlikely that we'd still have records from that long ago. We're computerized now. It's much easier to keep track of the nurses who come and go. The problem is, few of our records go back that far unless there was some kind of special circumstance. What was her name? In those days, of course, I'm assuming the nurse was a woman."

"Ross," Joanna said. "Katherine V. Ross."

"One moment."

Over the phone line came the familiar sound of a clicking keyboard as Barbara Calderone typed something into a computer. "That's odd," she said. "Is her birthday March 4, 1942?"

"Yes," Joanna replied, fighting to contain the excitement in her voice.

Barbara Calderone sounded mystified. "I don't know why, but the name's still here, even after all this time, along with a DNH designation. There's a notation that indicates all inquiries are to be directed to the legal department."

"DNH?" Joanna asked.

"Do not hire," Barbara Calderone explained. "In this business, before we hire someone, we run his or her name, Social Security number, and date of birth through the computer just to be sure we're not rehiring someone who's already created some kind of difficulty for us, which this Katherine Ross certainly must have done. I have to say, this is one of the oldest DNH designations I've ever seen. Most of the time, records that turn up that way are for people who've developed inappropriate relationships with their patients. Or else ones who have developed difficulties with prescription medications—particularly other people's prescription medications," she added meaningfully. "But then, I suppose you know all about that."

"Right," Joanna responded. She was surprised that she had made it this far with Barbara Calderone without some demand as to Joanna's legal right to make such inquiries. Still, she wasn't about to turn down the information.

"Could you connect me with the legal department, then?"

"Sure," Barbara Calderone replied. "Hold on. I'll transfer you."

The man Joanna spoke to there, a Mr. Armando Kentera, wasn't nearly as loquacious as Barbara Calderone had been. "We do have a file on Ms. Ross," he conceded, "but, without a properly documented court order, that's all I can tell you. We're dealing with privacy issues here, Sheriff Brady. I can't give out any further information than that."

From the tone of Mr. Kentera's voice, Joanna knew there was no sense arguing. Thanking him, she ended the call and then dialed the Copper Queen Hospital, asking to be put through to Ignacio Ybarra. He answered after the second ring.

"This is Sheriff Brady," Joanna told him. "How are you feeling?"

"Better," he answered. "It's nothing serious. Dr. Lee says I just got overheated. They're letting me out. One of my cousins is coming to pick me up. Detective Carbajal wanted to take me up to the Peloncillos this afternoon to look at the campsite. I tried to get back to him, but the office said he had been called away to something else."

"That's right," Joanna said.

"Tell him if he wants to go tomorrow, he should give me a call."

"Right," Joanna said. "I will. Tomorrow will probably be plenty of time, but in the meantime, Ignacio, I could use your help with something else."

"What?"

"It's about Bree's journals."

"What about them?"

"I read the final entry in one of them," Joanna said. "The one volume we were able to find. The words were 'My mother is a liar.' Do you know anything about that?"

"I guess so. Her mother was always leaving home. About twice a year she'd go away for two weeks or so, sometimes even longer. She told Bree she was doing some kind of mission work, but Bree found out that wasn't true."

"You mean Katherine wasn't off doing medical mission work when she told Brianna that's what she was doing?"

"Right."

"Where was she, then?"

"I don't know," Ignacio replied. "If Bree ever found out, she never told me."

Joanna recognized the wary reluctance in Ignacio's voice. "She did find out something, though, didn't she?" Joanna prodded. "What?"

"That her mother couldn't have gone off on any medical missions. She wasn't a nurse anymore. She didn't have a license."

"Thank you, Ignacio," Joanna told him. "That's all I need to know."

Minutes after talking to Ignacio Ybarra, Joanna had Kristin Marsten fax an official inquiry to the Arizona State Department of Licensing. The reply returned with an alacrity that Joanna found astonishing. Katherine V. Ross had lost her right to be a nurse at the request of her former employer—Good Samaritan Hospital. Her license had been permanently revoked.

She had been implicated in the wrongful death of a patient—one Ricardo Montaño Diaz—who had died as a result of an accidental overdose of medication. The hospital had settled the resultant legal suit by making a sizable monetary payment to the dead man's family. There was no mention of criminal charges being brought against the nurse. However, as her part of the settlement with the Diaz family, she had agreed to give up the practice of nursing. Just to make sure, however, the hospital had gone to the extraordinary measure of making sure her license was revoked.

Having gleaned that much information from the first page of the multipage fax, Joanna almost put it aside without glancing at any of the subsequent pages. Halfway down the second page, though, the words *dust storm* leaped off the page.

Mr. Diaz, it turned out, had been critically burned in a fiery, dust storm-related accident on Interstate 10 when the loaded semi he was driving had plowed into another vehicle, trapping and killing a woman and two children. David O'Brien's first wife and his first two children.

Outside her window, a long fork of lightning streaked across the darkening sky, followed immediately by the crack and rumble of nearby thunder. Joanna barely noticed. She turned loose the pages of the fax and let them flutter onto her desk.

"*My mother is a liar,*" she said to herself. *And probably much worse besides.*

The words *wrongful death* could conceal a multitude of sins, everything from involuntary manslaughter to aggravated first-degree murder. *How had this death happened?* Joanna wondered. *And who was ultimately responsible?*

The hospital had paid the claim, or at least the hospital's insurer had. Katherine O'Brien, nee Ross, had lost her nursing license as a result of what had happened, so presumably she had been held primarily accountable. Had she acted alone? What about David O'Brien, her future husband, who most likely had been a patient in the same hospital at the time of Mr. Diaz's death?

While Joanna stared off into space, her mind kept posing questions. What if, after all these years, while trying to figure out where to send her mother's birthday card, Brianna O'Brien had somehow stumbled across the same information? What if she had confronted her parents about the roles they had both played in the other man's death?

With a storm in her heart that very nearly matched the one blowing up outside her window, Joanna sat at her desk and considered. To everyone who knew them, Katherine and David O'Brien appeared to be a fine, upstanding couple. Supposing Bree, having discovered bits and pieces of their darker past, had threatened to expose them. Would they have killed their own daughter to keep that secret from becoming public knowledge?

After all, if the simple disobedient gesture of wearing a forbidden pair of earrings had merited a slap in the face, how would David O'Brien have responded to something much more serious?

🌵 TWENTY-THREE

SITTING THERE thinking the unthinkable and wondering whether or not the O'Briens were capable of murdering their own daughter, Joanna was startled out of her terrible reverie a few minutes later when the intercom buzzed once more. "Detective Carpenter is on the line," Kristin announced.

"What gives?" Joanna asked, picking up the phone. "Are you bringing Nettleton in?"

"Sending him," Carpenter replied. "Nettleton, that is. Detective Carbajal picked him up for transport just a while ago. We arrested him on suspicion of possession of stolen property."

"Stolen property?" Joanna echoed.

"That's right. We found a '92 Honda that was reported stolen two days ago in Tucson. It was hidden in a shed at the very back of his lot. It hadn't quite made it through his on-prem chop shop. Once we get around to tracking VINs on some of the other pieces of vehicles we found out on Sam's back forty, there may be more besides."

"Wait a minute," Joanna interrupted. "You're talking Vehicle Identification Numbers? I thought this was about Freon. What's going on, Ernie? Why is Jaime bringing in the suspect instead of you?"

"Because I'm on my way to Willcox," Ernie answered. "Along with the boys from DEA. Adam York is going to meet us there."

"Willcox?"

"The DEA guys put the fear of God in Nettleton. He gave us a name," Ernie explained. "Aaron Meadows."

"Who's he?" Joanna asked.

"He's the guy who's supposedly selling the stuff to Nettleton. He's an ex-con lately out of Florence. He grew up just outside Willcox. You probably don't remember this. It's before your time, but his grandparents once ran a combination gas station/ cattle rest east of there."

"What's Meadows's connection to all this?"

"He went to prison for smuggling years ago. Drugs back then. Chances are, that's what he's doing again—smuggling, only now the payload is Freon rather than drugs. I'm in the process of having Dick Voland issue an APB. Meadows drives an '89 Suburban. With any luck, he shouldn't be too hard to find."

Joanna considered for a moment. With Ernie Carpenter totally focused on the Freon situation, it seemed like a bad time to bring up anything more about the O'Briens. Mentioning an almost-twenty-year old wrongful death case in Phoenix would simply muddy the waters for an officer who was already neck-deep in a complicated joint operation. There would be plenty of time to discuss the Diaz case with Ernie once the dust had settled and the damned Freon situation had finally come to a head.

"Keep me posted," Joanna said at last. "What about deputies? Will you need more?"

"That's handled. Dick Voland's already put out the word for all uncommitted deputies to head for Willcox. With them and the guys from the DEA we should have a full contingent."

"Be careful," Joanna warned. "You're wearing body armor?"

Ernie laughed. "Are you kidding? After what we paid for this outfit, Rose won't let me out the front door without it. She's determined we're going to get our money's worth."

"If nagging is all it takes to get you to wear it, good for Rose," Joanna returned.

She put down the phone and looked outside just as a storm-spawned dust devil tore through the parking lot. Wind-driven rain came moments later, slanting down to the ground with such ferocity that for a few minutes even Joanna's Crown Victoria, parked right outside the window, was totally obscured from view.

Ernie was right. If the storm lasted for very long, it would indeed be another gully-washer. All her life, Joanna had delighted in these spectacular downpours. But as sheriff, she couldn't help seeing them through the nagging prism of her fiscal and budgetary responsibilities. What had once been a welcome summertime diversion now meant nothing more than another hit in the overtime department. She didn't have to be a fortune-teller to gaze into the next morning's briefing and see exactly what would happen. Both her chief deputies would be there, and Frank Montoya would be pitching his usual fit.

She leaned back in her chair and closed her eyes, shutting out the tumult outside her window and deliberately turning off the turmoil within. Reinforcements were headed for Willcox, which meant there was no need for her to go traipsing up there. Besides, by staying behind, she would be on hand when Detective Carbajal brought Nettleton in for questioning.

Opening her eyes again, she glanced at her watch. Five of four. In a while she'd call Doc Winfield and ask him about the medical missionaries. Jaime wouldn't arrive with his prisoner for the better part of an hour. Before then, maybe Joanna could finally make some progress on her paperwork.

Resolutely reaching for the stack, she forced herself to handle the first thing she touched—the board of supervisors letter. Next came a governmental treatise—a thick, bound notebook of bureaucratic doublespeak containing the latest federal mandates and guidelines concerning the care and feeding of prisoners.

With the very best of intentions, Joanna opened it and began to read. Halfway through page five, she nodded off and fell fast asleep.

GETTING OFF the phone at noon, Angie Kellogg had turned to find her customers hanging on her every word. All afternoon she faced a barrage of good-natured teasing about her car's going for a ride without her. The jokes were made easier to endure, however, by the fact that Angie's loyal customers were also determined to do something about it. She was surprised and touched to see that while her back had been turned, someone had placed an empty gallon jar on the end of the bar with a label affixed to it reading "Let's fix Angie's Omega." By two that afternoon the jar already contained several crumpled bills and a collection of loose change.

The Blue Moon's easy camaraderie made those unsolicited donations possible. It also gave rise to teasing of a more personal nature. All afternoon, Archie McBride and Willy Haskins kept up a running interrogation about what had gone on with Angie's "Boy Scout."

"Are you gonna see him again?" Willy asked.

Angie, wavering between hoping Dennis Hacker would call and never wanting to see him again, shook her head. "I don't know," she said.

"He seemed like one of those real gentlemen. Was he nice to you?"

Angie considered for a moment before she answered. Yes, Dennis Hacker had been nice to her—right up to the time he hurt her feelings. Now, mulling over his phone call, which had obviously been an apology, she didn't know what to think. It was stupid for her to believe that Dennis Hacker had actually fallen for her after seeing her only one or two times. And yet, those things did happen. Or did they? Was that kind of instant romance something that happened only in the movies?

"He didn't try to take advantage of you, now, did he?" Archie pressed solicitously. " 'Cause if'n he did, me an' ol' Willy here'll take care of him the next time he walks through the door. Right, Willy?"

"What?" Willy asked.

"Never mind," Angie said with a laugh. "You'll do no such thing."

Feeling better, Angie went back down the bar to serve another customer. It was nice to have champions even if they were nothing more than a pair of broken-down, toothless old miners.

About three o'clock the Blue Moon's swinging door banged open and in walked the last person Angie Kellogg ever expected to see there—the Reverend Marianne Maculyea. "What are you doing here?" Angie asked.

"I brought you something." Marianne reached into her pocket and pulled out a set of car keys, which she deposited on the bar directly in front of Angie.

"What are those?"

"The keys to the truck," Marianne answered. "The International may not be a thing of beauty, but it's totally dependable. Jeff and I talked it over. He'll borrow a car from one of his clients until we can get your Omega back on the road.

In the meantime, it doesn't make sense for you to be stuck walking. This way you can come and go as needed."

For Angie, this latest kindness was almost overwhelming. "But what about—"

"No buts," Marianne interjected. "This is how it is. It's parked right outside the door."

"Thank you," Angie said. That was all she could manage.

From then on, the rest of the afternoon seemed to crawl by. Customers came and went. By four o'clock, Angie was sneaking periodic checks at the clock behind the bar. Would Dennis Hacker call or not? Finally, when the phone rang at four-fifty, she leaped to answer. "Hello?"

"Hi, Angie," he said. "I'm back."

Angie had been waiting eagerly for the call. Now that he was on the line, she found herself drowning in confusion with no clue as to what to say. "How was the meeting?" she stammered.

"Fine," Dennis said. "First rate. How about you? And what about dinner?"

Angie glanced down the bar to where Archie and Willy were listening to her every word. "I guess that'll be fine," she said.

"Great," Hacker responded cheerfully. "I came back to the house to wash up. Unfortunately, it's been raining like crazy out here, which means the washes are probably up again. The Hummer will make it through just fine, but it may take a little longer—"

He stopped in mid-sentence. The phone seemed to clatter onto some hard surface. When Dennis

Hacker spoke again, he sounded angry. "Who are you?" he demanded. "What are you doing here? What do you want?"

"Who are you talking to?" another voice, a male one, returned just as angrily. "Get your hands up in the air. I heard you talking. Who else is in here with you? Where are they?"

"There's nobody here. I'm alone," Dennis answered.

In the background Angie could hear some shuffling and banging as though someone were searching the trailer.

"Dennis?" she asked hesitantly after a moment. "Can you hear me? What's wrong? What's going on?"

"Oh, it's the phone," the unidentified voice said. "Hang it up."

She heard a noisy crash. "Dennis?" Angie said after that. "Are you there? Are you all right?"

In answer, there was nothing but silence.

JOANNA, AWAKENED from her momentary snooze and still unable to contact Doc Winfield, was back plowing through the federal mandate when her private phone rang. It was a line that came directly through to her desk, bypassing both Kristin and the switchboard.

Like working mothers everywhere, Joanna had worried about Jenny's being able to get through to her quickly in case of some pressing emergency. Emergencies aside, the sheriff had been self-conscious about nonemergency calls as well. It was embarrassing when a phone call asking what was for dinner came through departmental channels. That went for the social calls that came to Joanna's office as well.

Not many people had that private number—notably Jenny, both sets of grandparents, and Marianne Maculyea. In addition, there was that solitary male friend up in Phoenix—Butch Dixon. As she reached for the ringing phone, Joanna found herself hoping he might be the one who was calling now. She hadn't spoken to Butch for several days—not since the day she'd driven Jenny to camp. It surprised her to realize how much she had missed talking to him.

"Joanna?" Eleanor Lathrop announced curtly. "It's me."

At the sound of her mother's voice, Joanna felt a flash of disappointment followed almost immediately by a spurt of anger. She had meant to have it out with her mother—to have a real coming to God about what Eleanor and George had been up to behind Joanna's back. But she had wanted to have all her emotional ducks in a row beforehand. Unfortunately, Eleanor had the drop on her.

"Hello, Mother," Joanna said guardedly. "How're things?"

"I've been waiting by the phone all day long, hoping you'd call."

Going on the offensive was one of Eleanor's typical ploys. *Why should I do the calling?* Joanna wondered. After all, since Eleanor had been sitting on news of her recent elopement, it made sense that her fingers should have been doing the dialing.

"I haven't had a chance to call anyone," Joanna lied. "It's been a zoo around here."

"Well," Eleanor returned, "it hasn't been any too pleasant for me, either."

Joanna closed her eyes and steeled herself for one of Eleanor Lathrop's infamous tirades. It didn't come. "I've been afraid to call you," Eleanor continued, her voice sounding suddenly tentative and tremulous. "I didn't know if you'd even be willing to speak to me."

Joanna's eyes popped open in astonishment. "You were afraid to call me?" she asked.

"Well, yes," Eleanor allowed. "I was worried about what you'd think. Of George and me. Of what we've done. I was afraid you'd be furious."

Now that Eleanor had brought up the topic, Joanna's emotions came to a swift boil. Of course Joanna was furious! Why wouldn't she be? How could Eleanor get married, for God's sake, without even letting her own daughter know? Once again, though, the very fact that Eleanor expected anger and recrimination was enough to force Joanna into sweetness and light.

"Furious?" Joanna repeated innocently. "Why on earth would I be furious?"

It was Eleanor's turn to sound surprised. "You mean you're not? George said you were fine about it, but I didn't believe . . . ."

"I'm disappointed maybe," Joanna conceded. "Hurt that you didn't trust me enough to share the good news, but I'm certainly not furious. You've lived alone for a long time. You've more than earned whatever share of happiness you can find."

Eleanor gave an audible sigh of relief. "You don't mind, then?"

"George Winfield's a nice man," Joanna said, remembering the compassionate way he had dealt with Katherine O'Brien. "A considerate man. Not half bad, for a snowbird."

"A snowbird," Eleanor replied. "Why, I don't know what you mean—" She stopped. "Joanna Lee Lathrop Brady," she added indignantly. "I believe you're teasing me, aren't you?"

Joanna laughed. "By virtue of being newly-weds, you and George automatically leave your-selves wide open to teasing. Now tell me, when are you two going to let this cat out of the bag in public? George told me you're going on an Alaskan cruise in August. If you haven't made an of-ficial announcement by then, people are going to talk."

"I don't know," Eleanor said. "George was talking about doing something in September. I've been thinking more about that long Fourth of July weekend. With four days, maybe your brother and Marcie could come out from D.C."

Joanna's brother. If Bob Brundage came out for the celebration, it would mark only the third time Joanna had ever seen the man. It seemed somehow appropriate, however, that he would show up now as a grown man to help celebrate his biological mother's second marriage.

"What kind of party were you thinking of?" Joanna asked.

"I don't know," Eleanor said, sounding uncertain again. "I just wanted to have a little reception of some kind. Something small and tasteful. George seems to think we should do the whole thing. Have a ceremony, repeat our vows, cut a cake, and everything. What do you think, Joanna? Doesn't that seem a bit much? What would someone like Marliss Shackleford think about such a thing? And besides, at this late date, where would we ever find a place to have it?"

The very idea of Eleanor Lathrop's flying in the face of small-town convention somehow tickled Joanna's fancy. As for Marliss Shackleford, she could mind her own damn business.

"You could have it at my place," Joanna heard herself offering. "We could hold the ceremony out in the yard and follow it up with an old-fashioned barbecue."

Once again Eleanor was taken aback. "You'd do that?" she asked. "For me? You mean you wouldn't mind going to all that trouble?"

"It's no trouble, and of course I wouldn't mind," Joanna said. "If a daughter won't lend a hand when her mother gets married, who will?"

Eleanor swallowed. When she spoke again, she seemed near tears. "Nothing would please me more, but you understand, I'll have to talk all this over with George first."

"Certainly," Joanna said. "And if you're looking around for someone to do the ceremony, you might give Marianne Maculyea a call."

There was a sudden flurry of activity out in the lobby. Even through the closed door Joanna heard the sound of raised voices. "She's on the phone," Kristin was saying. "You can't go in there."

"But the Fourth of July is a holiday," Eleanor objected. "Wouldn't Marianne mind having to work that day?"

"Call her up and find out," Joanna said.

Just then Joanna's door burst open and a distraught Angie Kellogg appeared in the doorway. Her blond hair was dripping wet. Her face was flushed. She was still wearing the striped, oversized blue-and-white apron she generally wore while working the bar of the Blue Moon. Behind her trailed an indignant Kristin Marsten accompanied by Chief Deputy Voland.

"Joanna," Angie blurted, wrenching her upper arm away from Dick's restraining hand. "Please, I've got to talk to you."

Startled by all the activity, Joanna had taken the phone from her ear. "Mother," she said hastily back into the phone. "Someone's here. I have to go." She turned back to the melee in the doorway just as Dick Voland grabbed hold of Angie again and started leading her back into the reception area.

"Look," he was saying, "I don't care who you are. You can't just barge in here—"

"Dick," Joanna interrupted, "it's all right. Let her be. Come in, Angie. What's wrong?"

Angie darted away from Dick Voland and came dripping across the carpet to Joanna's desk. "It's

Dennis," she gasped. "Something terrible has happened to him."

"Dennis?" Joanna asked. "What's going on?"

"I don't know. Not for sure. I was talking to him on the phone when someone broke into his trailer. It sounded like whoever it was had a gun. I tried calling back, but there was no answer."

Dick Voland let go of Angie's arm and backed off a little. "Dennis who?" he asked.

"Dennis Hacker," Joanna told him. "The parrot guy." She turned back to Angie. "Tell us what's going on. Where did this happen, and when?"

"Out in the mountains. Right around five."

Joanna shook her head. "There are lots of mountains around here, Angie. Which ones? The Huachucas? The Chiricahuas?"

Angie shook her head. "I don't remember exactly. It's someplace around where the body was, I think."

"In the Peloncillos?"

Angie's face brightened. "Yes," she said. "That's it."

Joanna knew that the Peloncillos wandered back and forth across the Arizona/New Mexico line from the far southeastern corner of the state all the way north to Graham County. "Do you know where in the Peloncillos?" she asked, hoping to narrow the scope of the problem.

"Not exactly," Angie said. "I can show you, but I can't tell you how to get there. It was near a cemetery, though—a cemetery with a wall around it."

"That would have to be Cottonwood Creek

Cemetery," Dick Voland supplied. "That's the only one I know of in the area that fits that description. Sheriff Brady's busy right now. Why don't you come out to the desk sergeant and give your information to him?"

The bedraggled young woman shot the chief deputy a baleful look. With the notable exception of Joanna Brady, Angie Kellogg had no use for cops. She seldom came near the Cochise County Justice Center because it brought back too many painful memories. In Angie's past life, working the streets of L.A., there had been lots of crooked cops who, in exchange for certain services rendered, had been willing to forget making an arrest. Joanna knew nothing short of sheer desperation would have driven Angie this far into enemy territory.

"Dick," Joanna said, "is Deputy Carbajal back from Benson yet?"

"I believe so. He drove into the sally port a few minutes ago. He's probably over in the booking room right now."

"Call the jail," Joanna ordered. "Tell him that you and I and Miss Kellogg here are heading for the Peloncillos. He should follow ASAP. I'll take Angie with me in the patrol car. You can follow in your Blazer. That way, if we need to do any off-roading, we'll have the Blazer to do it in."

"Wait a minute," Voland objected. "If what she says is true and we're dealing with some kind of hostage situation, you can't possibly bring a civilian along. That's crazy."

"You heard what Angie said," Joanna returned.

"She can show us how to get there. She can't tell us. If we have to go driving around looking for the right spot, no telling how much time we'll lose. In a situation like this, minutes mean the difference between life and death."

"But—"

"No buts!" Joanna snapped, cutting him off. "I've got an extra Kevlar vest for her—one I keep in the trunk. If Dennis Hacker is in the kind of trouble Angie says he's in, that's the best we can do. Let's get going."

Voland shook his head, but he said nothing more. Outside the building rain poured down in the kind of downpour Jim Bob Brady would have called "raining pitchforks and hammer handles." It was only a matter of a few feet from Joanna's private entrance across the open sidewalk to her covered parking place. Even so, by the time she reached the Crown Victoria, she was drenched. Angie Kellogg, wet to begin with, was even more so. Joanna went around to the trunk, dragged out the Kevlar vest, and gave it to Angie.

"Put it on," Joanna ordered.

"Do I have to?" Angie asked.

"Yes, you do. It's the only way you're going along."

Without another word, Angie began strapping the vest into place while Joanna slipped the gearshift into reverse and switched on both lights and siren. "What happened?" she asked as the car shot through the parking lot.

"What do you mean?" Angie returned. "I already told you what happened."

"Not all of it," Joanna said. "The last I heard, you were so mad at Dennis Hacker that you were ready to walk home eighty miles in a storm every bit as bad as this one."

"I guess I was wrong about him," Angie admitted thoughtfully.

"Wrong?" Joanna echoed. "I thought you said he was making fun of you, laughing at you."

The rain was falling hard enough that even with the windshield wipers working on high Joanna could barely see the road ahead. She found herself sitting forward and squinting, but that didn't help.

"He did laugh," Angie replied. "I think now he was really laughing at something else, not me." She glanced at the speedometer. "You have the siren on. Can't we go any faster?"

"Not with all the water on the roadway," Joanna said. "We'll end up hydroplaning."

"What's that?"

"It means you're driving on the surface of the water instead of on the pavement. That's how people lose control of their vehicles in rainstorms. No traction."

"Oh," Angie Kellogg said.

They were quiet for a minute or two until Joanna spoke again. "You're sure whoever broke into the camper had a gun?"

"I'm not sure," Angie said. "It sounded like it. I heard somebody tell Dennis to put his hands up."

"Were there any guns in the trailer to begin with?" Joanna asked. "Did Dennis Hacker have any weapons of his own?"

"If he did," Angie answered. "I didn't see them."

Struck by the hopelessness of it all, Angie Kellogg's toughness and strength seemed to give out all at once. Pressing herself into the far corner of the car, she began to cry.

Joanna Brady ached to comfort her friend, but all she could do right then was keep on driving.

TWENTY-FOUR

WHEN THE speeding Crown Victoria finally reached the eastern outskirts of Douglas on Highway 80, Angie looked around at the sodden desert landscape and shook her head. "This isn't the way we went Sunday morning," she said. "It's how Marianne brought me back that afternoon, not the way Dennis took going."

Joanna immediately heeled the Crown Victoria into a sharp U-turn and headed back to the nearest intersection where she could cross over to Geronimo Trail, the only other route that led from Douglas to the Peloncillos. As they drove past Dick Voland's Blazer, Joanna caught a glimpse of the pained expression on her chief deputy's face. He was shaking his head in disgust. It made her glad they weren't in the same vehicle. She didn't want to hear his "I told you so."

Even though the storm seemed to be over and there was water standing along the road, the dips across Geronimo Trail were just beginning to run with trickles of water. Joanna knew full well that just because the rain had stopped didn't mean the danger of flash floods was past. It would take time for the runoff to drain out of the desert's higher elevations and into the lower washes. Once that happened, they could quickly become impassable.

Holding her breath each time, Joanna rushed through one dip after another with the wary expectation that at any time a solid wall of water could come crashing out of nowhere and sweep them away. Dick Voland's four-wheel-drive Blazer would be far less susceptible than Joanna's Crown Victoria. Still, the bottom line was clear. If the water did come up suddenly, no one else would be able to make it through until after the flooding receded. That meant that if Dick and Joanna found themselves in some kind of difficult situation, calling for reinforcements wouldn't be an option. Sheriff Brady and her chief deputy would be on their own. Which also meant, Joanna realized, that there was a real possibility she was placing Angie Kellogg in grave danger.

"Sheriff Brady?" The radio squawked to life with the voice of the head dispatcher.

"What is it, Larry?" Joanna returned.

"Ernie Carpenter just called in from Willcox. He says to tell you he's got some good news and some bad news."

"Give me the good news first."

"They found Alf Hastings's Jeep Cherokee parked behind Aaron Meadows's place just east of Willcox."

"Great. What's the bad news, then?"

"Nobody's home. Aaron Meadows's Suburban is among the missing, and so are both Meadows and Hastings."

"Can you patch me through to Detective Carpenter?" Joanna asked.

"Sure thing. Hang on."

Joanna came to the next dip, the place where Cottonwood Creek crossed Geronimo Trail. Here a foaming river of rushing water crossed the road. Realizing the depth might be dangerously deceptive, Joanna stopped at the crest of the dip and put her Ford in reverse, then pulled off onto the shoulder.

Ernie's voice came through the radio. "What are you doing, Sheriff Brady?"

"Changing cars, it turns out," Joanna told him. "The water's too deep for the patrol car. From here on, we'll have to ride with Dick Voland."

"But where are you?"

"On our way to the Peloncillos. There's some problem with Dennis Hacker."

"The parrot guy?"

"One and the same," Joanna answered. "What are you doing?"

"Same old same old," Carpenter replied. "What we've done all afternoon—hurry up and wait. Adam York has a guy flying down from Tucson with a search warrant. In the meantime, there's nothing much to do but hang around here and see what happens. If you need backup, we could probably spare . . ."

"Don't even bother," Joanna said. "The way

the water's running out here, we'll be lucky to get through in the Blazer. Just be sure you keep me posted on whatever's going on up there."

"Will do," Carpenter replied.

"So does this mean Hastings and Meadows are in it together?" she asked.

"Beats me," the detective returned. "Your guess is as good as mine."

"Great," Joanna said.

By the time Joanna put the radio back away, Dick Voland was standing outside her window. With his feet planted wide apart and with his arms folded across his chest, he gazed into the turbulent water and shook his head. Joanna climbed out of the Crown Victoria.

"What do you think?" she asked.

"If we had a lick of sense, we'd give up this wild-goose chase right here and now."

"It's not that much farther," Joanna told him.

"It is if we get washed down-river." Voland snorted.

"Put it in four-wheel drive," Joanna said. "From here on, we're riding with you."

Voland looked down at her. "I suppose that's an order, isn't it?"

"Not necessarily," she replied. "If you like, you can hand over your car keys and stay here."

"You're going in no matter what?"

Joanna nodded. "No matter what. Angie Kellogg thinks a man's life is in danger, and so do I."

Dick Voland shook his head. "Get in, then," he snapped. "Get in, both of you. I'll drive."

Joanna held her breath as Voland four-wheeled

it through the next two washes, both of them running bank to bank. Twice the Blazer lost its footing and floated downstream half a car length or so before it once again hit the ground firmly enough to regain forward momentum.

Once back on the roadway, Voland shot Joanna a disparaging glance. "All I can say is, this better be serious enough to justify almost drowning. Besides, with everything going on up in Willcox, we should both be headed up there instead of out into the boonies someplace."

Joanna wanted to argue with him about it—to try to explain the idea that the very fact Angie Kellogg had come to them for help was an indication of the seriousness of the situation. She decided against it. Chief Deputy Voland might be pissing and moaning, but he was also driving in the right direction.

"There'll be time enough for Willcox later," Joanna replied mildly. "After we make sure Mr. Hacker is okay."

"Right," Voland muttered.

Ahead of them, the clouds over the Peloncillos seemed to break apart, revealing a patch of brilliantly blue sky. Moments later, a breathtakingly beautiful double rainbow appeared, arching across the eastern horizon. Big Hank Lathrop had always told his daughter that there was a pot of gold at the end of any rainbow, but especially double ones. A grownup Joanna no longer believed that parental myth any more than she believed in Santa Claus or the Tooth Fairy. For today, though, more than a pot of gold, Joanna welcomed the rainbow's promise that the storm was truly over. Eventually the washes would quit running. Life would return to normal—whatever that was.

"There it is," Angie called from the backseat.

Ahead of them, a road veered off to the right. Beyond the junction, the wet rock walls of Cottonwood Creek Cemetery glowed damp and shimmery in the late afternoon sun. On the far side of the cemetery, tucked into a clearing, sat a small camper-trailer.

"Doesn't look like anybody's home," Dick Voland commented, turning right off Geronimo Trail and then pausing to take stock of the situation. "What kind of vehicle did you say he has?"

"A Hummer," Joanna said.

"As in sixty to ninety thou?" Voland asked with a whistle. "How does a guy who raises parrots for a living come up with that kind of cash? He must be one hell of a grant writer!"

"I don't know where Dennis Hacker gets his money," Joanna said. "Now, stop here and let me out."

Voland stepped on the brakes. "Here? What for?"

"So I can look at the tracks and try to figure out what's going on."

"But . . ." Voland began.

Without waiting long enough to hear his objection, Joanna climbed out of the Blazer and slammed the door. She had lived at the end of a solitary dirt road long enough to have taught herself the rudiments of tracking, of reading whatever messages were left behind in the dust and mud.

Kneeling over the still-damp dirt track, she saw that the storm had washed it clean. On the blank slate left behind, only one set of tire tracks was visible. The storm had blown up from Mexico, circling from east to west. Because Joanna had no way of knowing how long ago rain had ended on this particular stretch of roadway, it was impossible for her to tell which direction the tracks were going—in or out. The wide wheelbase made her suspect that the tracks had been left by Dennis Hacker's departing Hummer, but there was no way of knowing for sure.

Finished with her initial examination of the roadway, Joanna walked back to the Blazer. "Angie, didn't you say Mr. Hacker called you from home?"

Angie nodded. "Yes. On his cell phone. He was telling me he was about to leave for town when whoever it was came bursting inside."

Joanna looked at Dick Voland. "There's only one set of tracks showing," she told him. "Depending on when the rain ended, they could either be coming or going. Since the Hummer isn't anywhere in sight, I'd say going. You drive on in as far as the trailer. Try to stay far enough off the roadway itself that you don't disturb any of the tracks."

"What are you going to do?" Voland asked.

"Walk," Joanna said. "Something may give me a clue as to which way he was going or how long ago he left."

"Wait a minute," Voland objected. "What if they're still in there?"

"With the Hummer gone, I doubt it," Joanna returned. "But that's a risk we're going to have to take."

"Wait," Angie said. "I'll come with you."

"No you won't," Joanna told her. "You'll stay in the back of the Blazer until either Dick or I give the word that it's safe. Understand?"

Nodding, Angie subsided back in the seat. Joanna slammed the door on Dick Voland's next volley of objections and turned her attention back to the tire tracks. They were easy to follow. They led directly around the cemetery and toward the little boulder-free clearing where the trailer was parked. Halfway there, a second set of tracks—from the same tires—suddenly overlaid the first.

Joanna held up her hand and signaled for Dick to stop the Blazer long enough for her to sort out what had happened. The original set continued on toward the trailer. The second set—definitely more recent than the first—headed off toward the south. Motioning Dick to stay where he was, Joanna walked closer to the trailer. She was concentrating so hard on the tracks that only a hint of movement registered in her peripheral vision. Because she was already filled with apprehension, the movement, combined with a sudden whack of metal on metal, was enough to send her diving for cover behind a boulder, drawing her Colt 2000 as she did so.

At once, Voland killed the engine on the Blazer. In the sudden hush that followed the whack came again. "Did you see something?" Dick asked a moment later as, nine-millimeter in hand, he dropped to the ground beside her.

Feeling stupid, Joanna didn't want to answer. "It's the door," she said. "The open door to the trailer blowing in the wind."

"Cover me," Voland said. "I'll go on up and check it out."

"No," Joanna said. "We'll both—" She stopped short. Had she not been looking at Dick Voland just then, she might have missed it entirely. "Look!" she said, pointing.

"Look at what? I don't see anything."

"Footprints," she said. She crawled around her chief deputy to examine the set of footprints that had been left in the soft sand. They looked as though they had been left by a pair of worn sneakers, and they led directly from the brush toward the trailer. The prints from the right foot were distinct and clear. The ones made by the left foot were blurry, less defined. A foot or so off to the left of them was a third track of some kind—a round hole poked in the dirt at regular intervals.

"Whoever left these tracks may be hurt."

"What makes you say that?" Voland asked.

"He's using a cane or a crutch," Joanna said. "Most likely a cane."

Voland eyed her quizzically. "How can you tell?"

In order to handle the livestock chores on the High Lonesome, Joanna had found it necessary to have a hired hand. An octogenarian neighbor of hers, Clayton Rhodes, had volunteered for the job. The previous winter, though, after slipping on an ice-glazed pile of cow dung, Clayton had been forced to use a cane for almost two weeks. During that time, Joanna had noticed the tracks he had left behind on trips from his pickup to the barn, to the house, and back again. Those tracks and these were inarguably similar.

"Experience," she said, without pausing to explain. "Come on. Let's check out that trailer."

"Wait a minute," Voland warned. "Don't forget a gunman inside that trailer can shoot through those aluminum walls as easily as shooting through pop bottles."

"Right," Joanna said. "So what do you suggest?"

"Split up and stay low."

Joanna crept forward, following the tracks, while Voland moved off to the left. The tracks on the ground were easy enough to follow. They led directly to the wooden step outside the trailer's open door. There they disappeared.

"Mr. Hacker," Joanna called, ducking behind a tree trunk little more than a few feet from the door. "Are you in there?"

Joanna waited for the better part of a minute, but there was no response other than the intermittent whack of the door on the trailer's metal siding. She watched while Voland circled around until he was behind the trailer. Finally, when he signaled, they both moved forward.

They arrived at the trailer almost simultaneously, with her approaching one of the front windows just as Voland's face appeared in one at the back. "Looks like nobody's home," Voland called.

Still taking care to dodge the footprints, Joanna walked close enough to the trailer to poke her head in through the door. The interior of Dennis Hacker's camper looked as though it had been hit by a cyclone. Shards of broken glass were everywhere, along with shattered pieces of molded black plastic that looked as though they had once been part of a cell phone. There were also several reddish stains that resembled smears of blood.

Sickened, sure that she had once again arrived at the scene of a crime too late to do any good, Joanna backed away. "If you're looking for signs of a struggle," she called back to Dick, "here they are."

While Voland hurried around the trailer to peer in through the door, Joanna walked away, following two new sets of footprints. Now the person wearing the sneakers had been joined by someone else, by someone wearing what Joanna surmised to be hiking boots. Traveling together, the two pairs of prints headed around the trailer in a counterclockwise direction before disappearing into a vehicle—the same wide-tracked vehicle whose tracks Joanna had followed before.

"I'll go back to the Blazer and radio for a crime scene technician . . ."

Joanna knew Dick Voland was speaking to her, but she barely heard him. If the vehicle—presumably Dennis Hacker's Hummer—had left the trailer with two passengers instead of one, maybe Joanna and Dick Voland weren't too late after all.

"Come on," she called urgently to Dick. "Go get the Blazer. They're headed south."

"Together?" Dick asked, jogging up behind her.

"That's my guess."

Voland started toward the Blazer. Then, to Joanna's annoyance, he turned and came back. "What about the girl?" he asked.

"Angie?" Joanna returned. "What about her?"

"She got us here," Voland said. "I'll give her that much, but if we're heading into an armed confrontation . . ."

Without bothering to listen to the rest of the sentence, Joanna knew he was right. As an officer of the law, her duty was to keep civilians out of danger rather than leading them into it. She nodded. "Tell Angie to wait in the cemetery. Have her duck down behind that rock wall and stay there until we come back."

"With pleasure," Voland replied. He hurried away.

Thinking that settled the issue once and for all, Joanna turned back to the tire tracks. She had gone no more than a few yards when she heard running footsteps pounding behind her. "Joanna, wait," Angie called. "Let me come, too."

Annoyed that Dick Voland hadn't stated the case plainly enough, Joanna turned to face her friend. "Look, Angie," she said sharply, "you can't come with us. It's too dangerous."

Angie stopped in her tracks. Behind her came the Blazer with a smiling Dick Voland at the wheel. A single glimpse of the man's face was enough to let Joanna know that he hadn't tried to stop Angie, not really. If he had, he would have and she wouldn't be there. No, letting her go had been a deliberate ploy on Dick Voland's part. He was testing Joanna again, wanting to know whether or not she was tough enough to call the shots and make the right choice between friendship and duty.

Except this time there was no choice to make. As sheriff and as a sworn police officer, Joanna Brady's responsibility was blazingly clear—to serve *and* protect. "Go back," she said.

"Why should I?" Angie objected. "I'm wearing a bulletproof vest."

"You may have a vest," Joanna conceded, "but that still leaves a whole lot of you unprotected and exposed to danger, which is unacceptable. You brought us this far, Angie. We're grateful for that, but there's no telling what's up ahead. We're armed. You're not."

"But . . ."

"No buts," Joanna insisted. "What if there's a shootout? What if, in trying to take care of you, we can't protect Mr. Hacker? Your being in the way at a critical moment could make all the difference—the difference between life and death. Go now, please."

Angie's shoulders sagged. Her face crumpled. "All right," she agreed. "I'll go back. I'll wait in the cemetery, just like you said." Dejectedly, she turned back while Joanna headed for the idling Blazer.

"Good work," Dick Voland said as she climbed inside.

Aware he had intentionally set her up, Joanna was in no mood to be gracious. "Shut up and drive," she said.

SITTING ALERT and on edge, Joanna concentrated on not losing the trail. Twice she made Dick stop the Blazer long enough for her to get out and make sure the tire tracks hadn't veered off the road.

"I'm sorry," Voland said a mile or so south of the Cottonwood Creek Cemetery when Joanna climbed back into the Blazer for the second time and fastened her seat belt.

"Sorry about what?" she asked.

"About not giving your friend more credit. The whole way out from Bisbee, I kept thinking this was nothing but some harebrained wild-goose chase. Until I saw the trailer, that is. The whole thing sounded so goofy. Including the idea that anybody camping out here would have a working cell phone . . ."

The radio came to life once more with Larry Kendrick making an addition to the Aaron Meadows APB. Now Meadows was wanted for questioning in regard to the murder of Roxanne Brianna O'Brien. By the time the dispatcher had finished his transmission, Joanna had the radio microphone in her hand.

"Larry, this is Sheriff Brady. What's going on?"

"Glad you called in," Larry replied. "You're the next person I was going to contact. Ernie wants me to let you know that while they were searching Aaron Meadows's house, they found—"

"The missing journal?" Joanna interrupted.

Kendrick paused. "How did you know?"

Before Joanna could answer, the Blazer rounded a curve. Ahead of them lay the rain-swollen stream with what looked like a crippled brown-and-tan Suburban parked crookedly on the rocky bank while another vehicle—curtained by a rooster tail of muddy water, roared across the ford and bounced up the other side. Only when it regained the roadway was Dennis Hacker's Hummer clearly visible.

"There they are!" Joanna shouted.

"There who is?" Kendrick was asking. "What's happening?"

"Hang on," Dick Voland shouted as he sent the Blazer speeding toward the water. "This could be rough."

The Blazer plunged forward and dropped, bucking and shying, into the rocky streambed while Joanna held on for dear life. Once they hit firm ground on the far side of the water, Voland pounded the gas pedal all the way to the floor. The gradually receding flood had left behind a slick coating of muck on the roadway. The tires lost traction briefly, sending the Blazer into a sickening skid. But Dick Voland was nothing if not an experienced driver. With two deft twists of the wheel, he cut the skid and sent the Blazer racing after the Hummer.

As they drove past the Suburban, seconds before the Blazer roared into the water, Joanna had managed to catch a glimpse of the muddied license plate on the back of the Suburban. It carried the same numbers that had been broadcast as part of the APB for Aaron Meadows.

"Sheriff Brady," Larry Kendrick insisted urgently. "Come in, please. What's going on?"

"Call Ernie back," Joanna shouted into the radio. "Tell him we've just spotted that missing Suburban. It's parked and, most likely, disabled. But the two suspects got away. We're in close pursuit, heading east/southeast. The suspects are driving a dark green Hummer."

Joanna closed her eyes and thought about Dennis Hacker. Was he dead already, or was he still alive and in the Hummer along with Meadows and Hastings?

"It's possible they've taken a hostage," she added into the radio. "The name of the hostage is Dennis Hacker, the parrot guy. I'm pretty sure the Hummer is registered in his name."

Joanna stared out the windshield at the Hummer, which seemed to be gaining distance on them with every passing moment. She turned back to Dick Voland. "Do you know where this road ends up?" she asked.

Without taking his eyes off the road, Dick shook his head. "I'm not sure. Probably at the Mexican border, if not before."

"And how far are we from the line?"

"Thirty miles or so. Maybe less. In a Hummer, though, it's not going to matter if the road ends or not. He'll be able to go wherever he damned well pleases."

Nodding, Joanna switched on the microphone once more. "Larry," she told the dispatcher. "Can you find a way to put me through to either Adam York or Ernie Carpenter?"

It took several bone-jarring minutes. Twice during the wait Dick Voland managed to bring the Hummer briefly into view. "Can you tell how many people are in there?" Joanna asked.

Voland shook his head. "There's too much mud on the windows. I can't see a thing."

"Sheriff Brady? Adam York here. What's up?"

"How'd you get that search warrant from Tucson to Willcox so fast?" Joanna asked.

"In a helicopter."

"Where is it right now?"

"The chopper? Getting ready to head back to Tucson. Why?"

"I need it," Joanna answered. "In the Peloncillos. We've got a pair of armed and dangerous suspects making a run for the Mexican border."

"I know we have a mutual aid agreement, but—"

"Mutual aid nothing!" Joanna cut in. "This is your case, too. Aaron Meadows's Suburban is parked a mile or so back. We've just crossed Sycamore Creek and are heading south and east from Cottonwood Creek Cemetery. Ernie Carpenter will be able to tell you where that is. We're in a county-owned white Blazer. The suspects are in a dark green Hummer. They've got a hostage in there with them. Tell Ernie it's the parrot guy. I believe at least one of the suspects is wounded. Chances are, the hostage is as well."

"Damn!" Adam York muttered. "Do you want us to call for other backup?"

"You can call all you want, but I believe you two are it," Joanna told him. "The way the washes are running right now, I doubt anyone else will be able to get here. That's why I asked about the chopper."

"Hang in there, then," Adam York told her. "Ernie and I are on our way. We'll be there as soon as we can."

TWENTY-FIVE

FOLLOWING THE speeding Hummer, Dick Voland's Blazer rumbled south. After winding past the crumbling remains of what had once been an adobe ranch house, the road deteriorated to little more than a rutted cow path that led back up into the Peloncillos, heading from there on down into the Guadalupe Mountains and the Baker Canyon Wilderness Area.

"If he decides to really go off-roading on us, we're screwed," Voland told her. "I've heard those Hummers can handle a sixty percent grade if need be, and he's got at least eight more inches of ground clearance than I do. In any kind of rough terrain, I don't think the Blazer can keep up."

Sitting in the rider's side, Joanna had been remembering the last time she had been stuck in the boonies with a potentially explosive situation. That had been up in the Chiricahuas in the dead of night. She had made a call for backup and had been assured help was on the way, but when push came to shove, Joanna had been entirely on her own.

Dick Voland wasn't all that easy to work with at times, but right then she was glad to have him. She was especially thankful for his more than capable driving. "If the driving had been left up to me," she said, "the guy probably would have lost us a long time ago. In the meantime, all we have to do is keep him in sight long enough for the helicopter to show."

"If it shows," Voland muttered. "When it comes to calling for reinforcements, I don't have much faith in the feds."

Up to a point, Joanna agreed with him. But if the feds were one thing, Adam York was something else. She had total confidence in the man's ability to deliver.

"Don't worry," Joanna said. "They'll be here. After all, we're after these guys because they may have killed somebody. The DEA wants them for smuggling Freon. When it comes to the availability of crime-fighting resources, holes in the ozone are a higher priority than holes in people's bodies—to some of the folks from D.C., anyway."

"If you ask me, that sounds like the tail wagging the dog," Voland grumbled.

Despite the seriousness of the moment, despite the fact that they were even then in a hot pursuit chase with lives hanging in the balance, Joanna found herself laughing.

"What's so funny?" Voland demanded after the Blazer lurched around two more curves and then launched itself into space across another bone-jarring dip.

His question sobered her, made her recognize what was most likely something close to stress-induced hysterics.

"Nothing," she said finally. "This job is turning me into a total pragmatist. I'm in favor of what works—whatever that may be."

In the space of little more than a mile, the relatively flat desert gave way to foothills and a mile after that to genuine mountains. The twisting trail seemed more appropriate for mountain goats than it did for vehicular travel. Part of the time, Joanna was able to keep their quarry in visual contact. Most of the time she and Voland kept track of the Hummer's progress by following the faint tracks left in the rock-strewn roadway. Once back on the mountain grades, progress was much slower.

"What if they make it to Mexico before we catch them?" Joanna asked as she peered anxiously into the sky, hoping to see some sign of Adam York's helicopter. With the clouds gone and the sky washed clean by rain, there was nothing overhead but limitless blue that was gradually giving way to pale stars and evening shadow.

"Then we get Frank Montoya to see what kind of a peace treaty he can negotiate with the *federales* down in Sonora so we can get them to track the crooks down and ship them back."

They traveled in silence for a little while before Joanna took the microphone out of its holder. Calling in to Dispatch, she asked Larry Kendrick to notify authorities in both New and Old Mexico, telling officers in those jurisdictions that assistance might be required.

After all, Joanna thought, *cooperation is the name of the game.*

By the time she finished with the radio, they had left the streambed far below and were climbing up and out of yet another canyon. In the process, they crossed two broken fence lines. There were padlocked gates on each of them designed to keep out unauthorized interlopers. The driver of the Hummer had ignored the No Trespassing signs and had circumvented the locks by simply plowing through the barbed wire, popping the strands and knocking out fenceposts. Since the fences were already down anyway, Dick Voland followed suit.

Half a mile beyond the second fence, they found themselves in the middle of a small herd of panicked goats.

"Those don't look like mountain goats to me," Voland said.

"They're not," Joanna told him. "They're feral—domestics that have gone wild after being left behind by a disgruntled goat farmer. It happened when the federal government took back his land in order to create the Baker Wilderness Area. They're thriving out here because there are very few natural predators left."

"If they don't get the hell out of my way," Dick Voland growled, "I'll be happy to introduce them to an unnatural predator—me."

Once the Blazer made it through the herd of panicked and milling goats, there was no sign of the Hummer. "Where did they go now?" Dick demanded.

"Let me out again," Joanna said. "I'll walk around and see if I can pick up the trail."

She found it, eventually, but it took time—time they didn't have. The sun had disappeared completely. Dusk had deepened even more before Joanna once again spied the Hummer's distinct tracks leading off through knee-high grass. As she climbed back into the Blazer, Joanna scanned the sky once more. There was still no sign of Adam York's helicopter.

This time the tracks led off across rugged terrain where there was no hint of a road. Voland had to pick his way slowly, concentrating on every move, while Joanna tried to keep track of the Hummer's fading trail. They were both so engrossed in their own responsibilities that they were caught unawares by the springing of a well-calculated trap.

In Spanish, the word *peloncillos* means "little baldies." These mountains had been given that name because of the distinctive volcanic outcroppings and knobs on top of almost every hillock, ridge, and mountain in the range. The Hummer's driver had led them up to the crest of one of those knob-crowned ridges. Still following the trail, the Blazer rounded a semi-truck-size boulder only to have the Hummer, headlights doused, roar out from behind that same rock.

The enormous, almost-armor-plated front end of the Hummer smashed into the Blazer on the driver's side, tipping the smaller Chevy over onto its side and sending it tumbling down a steep bank. As the Blazer tipped to the right, the shoulder belt clamped tight across Joanna's clavicle and ribs while the seat belt grabbed across her abdomen and pelvis. With debris from the cargo space raining down around her head, she felt something whack her in the face. For a time, she thought she had blacked out. Then, when she could see again, she realized her temporary blindness had come from having the explosively opening air bag inflate in her face.

By then the Blazer had come to rest. Looking across the seat, Joanna was horrified to see Dick Voland, limp and unmoving, slumped over the airbag-covered steering wheel. Joanna tried the door, but it was jammed. She was starting to climb out the window when a shotgun blast shattered the twilight. A scatter of buckshot slammed into the side of the Blazer and rattled through the surrounding rocks and underbrush.

Joanna instinctively reached for her Colt. Then, seeing Dick's shotgun still fastened in place between them, she wrested it out of its clamp. *Let's fight fire with fire*, she thought grimly.

"All right," she shouted, cupping one hand to her lips in hopes of making her voice carry better. "You'd better give yourselves up. Now. Before someone else gets hurt."

The answer to her challenge came in another well-aimed blast from the shotgun.

Joanna fumbled open the glove box, found a box of extra shotgun shells, and shoved those into her pocket. Dick Voland still hadn't moved, but there was no time to check on him. With her chief deputy unconscious, Joanna knew she had no choice but to try to draw the suspects' fire—to lead them away from the helpless officer before they could come down the ridge and finish him off.

Needing a decoy, she clambered over the backseat and found a loose gym bag full of clothes. Holding the gym bag ready at the window, she called out again.

"We've got reinforcements on the way. You'd better give up while you still can."

It sounded like empty saber-rattling, even to her, but when the echoing cliffs of the Peloncillos played the last word back to her, "can . . . can . . . can"—it sounded more like a bad joke.

Joanna waited until the last echo died away. Then, heaving with all her might, she threw the gym bag out the window. Closing her eyes to avoid losing her night vision, she sent the bag tumbling down the embankment. It landed with a satisfying thump that sounded very much like a falling human body. The shooter—there seemed to be only one—must have been convinced as well. Another shotgun blast sent a hail of pellets pounding into the brush at almost the same spot where the bag had landed.

The diversion was enough to give Joanna a chance to slip out through the Blazer's shattered passenger window. She sank to the ground and picked up a handful of rocks and gravel. "Do you hear me?" she demanded. "We know who you are, and we know you killed Brianna O'Brien. Give up while there's still time."

Hoping to keep the gunman off base by having to keep watch in more than one direction, Joanna tossed her handful of rocks and gravel near where the bag had landed and away from herself and Dick Voland. Again, the still twilight was shattered by yet another shotgun blast. With the gunman focused on more distant opponents, Joanna decided to attempt a frontal attack. That strategy would work only so long as she didn't kick loose some rocks and gravel of her own, giving away her position.

Once the latest shotgun blast stopped reverberating through the rocks and mountains, Joanna heard the welcome but distant rumble of Adam York's helicopter. The chopper was still too far away to do any good. The pilot seemed to be moving back and forth in a grid pattern. That probably meant they had temporarily lost the trail and were trying to find it again.

Joanna realized suddenly that while she was sitting frozen, listening to the approaching helicopter, up on the mountain, her armed opponent was probably doing the same thing. Counting on the helicopter to distract him, Joanna risked crawling a few more yards back up the steep hillside. She stopped and ducked behind a lush clump of bear grass. From there she threw another fistful of rocks off to the right.

This time there was no answering shotgun blast. *He's getting smarter*, Joanna thought despairingly. *Smarter and that much more dangerous.*

As the helicopter drew nearer, she could see the widening beam from a searchlight as the helicopter pilot and passengers scanned the darkened landscape. With the chopper that close at hand, Joanna suspected that another flash from the shotgun would be visible from miles away. With any luck, it would draw someone's searching eyes in the right direction. The problem was, the shooter hadn't fallen for Joanna's latest gravel ploy. In order to draw his fire, she'd have to come up with something a little more realistic.

After a moment's consideration, she shrugged her way out of her jacket, blouse, and bulletproof vest. Once she had her bra off, she slipped the vest, blouse, and jacket back on. Reaching down, she felt around for a few small rocks. Feeling a little like a modern-day David battling an armed and dangerous Goliath, she tucked three small rocks into one cup of the bra to give it some added weight. Then, swinging the bra around her head, she sent it sailing through the air.

Months of throwing the Frisbee for an absolutely inexhaustible Tigger served Joanna in good stead. She managed to get some real lift on the thing. The bra sailed up into the air. Some fifteen yards to the right, it was blown out of the sky by another roar from the shotgun.

With her own ears ringing from the blast and suspecting that the gunman's would be equally affected, Joanna risked another foray up the hill, this time making for the cover of a lumpy boulder just below the crest of the ridge.

As Joanna expected, the helicopter, drawn by the sudden flash of light, headed straight for them. She was close enough to the top of the embankment now that she could hear someone speaking. "God damn it," he mumbled. "Damn it all to hell!"

She was close enough, too, to hear the sound of hurrying footsteps—footfalls that moved away from her rather than toward her. The sound told her that the gunman was most likely retreating, scurrying back toward the Hummer. Joanna remembered the cane and the smears of blood she had seen in the camper. That meant the shooter was probably wounded. By now Joanna was fairly certain the man was alone. She had some confidence that she could outmaneuver him as long as they were both on foot. Once he regained his vehicle—once he was driving and she was on foot—the odds would change dramatically. For the worse.

She needed to keep him from gaining that advantage, but how? Maybe she could use Dick's shotgun to put a hole in the monster Hummer's metal-shrouded radiator, but she wasn't sure that would work. Besides, she couldn't risk taking a head-on shot at a vehicle that might have a hostage imprisoned inside.

At that moment, Joanna had no way of telling whether or not Dennis Hacker was still alive. Nevertheless, if there was even the smallest possibility he was, Joanna had to do her best to rescue the man without putting his life in even more jeopardy.

Clutching the shotgun in the crook of her arm, Joanna scrambled up the bank. She ducked behind another boulder. She was just raising the shotgun into firing position when the Hummer's huge engine rumbled to life. Headlights flashed on in her eyes. Joanna had surfaced slightly to the left of where the Hummer was parked. Now, with the headlights temporarily blinding her, Joanna heard rather than saw the Hummer come straight at her. Convinced the driver had somehow caught sight of her and was going to try to run her down, Joanna hunkered back down behind the rock.

In the process of dodging back, the shotgun somehow slipped from her sweaty grasp and went skittering down the rocky slope. The Hummer roared past Joanna within bare inches of her face. There was no time to go searching for the fallen shotgun. Instead, she fumbled inside her jacket and drew the Colt. Without making any pretense of staying under cover, she scrambled out from behind the rock and assumed a two-handed shooting stance. She fired off three shots in rapid succession. The first two missed their marks entirely. One ricocheted off metal and the second zinged off a nearby rock. The third one, though, scored a direct hit on the Hummer's right rear tire.

Joanna's slender hope was simply to puncture a tire. She knew in advance that it wouldn't put the Hummer out of business, but she thought that it might at least slow the driver down and give the backup team a chance to catch up. Instead, the tire decompressed so quickly that it made the truck lurch sharply to the right. First the back passenger wheel and then the front one slipped off the edge of the ridge. With the engine whining in protest and with all four wheels spinning uselessly in the air, the Hummer slowly pitched over on its side and went tumbling down the mountain, following almost the exact same path taken minutes earlier by the falling Blazer.

Joanna waited until the clatter of sheet metal on rocks grew still. Realizing with horror that there were now only a matter of feet separating the gunman from the still helpless Dick Voland, she went slipping and sliding back down the mountainside herself. By then, drawn by flashes of gunfire, the helicopter was moving into position directly overhead. A searchlight came on, illuminating the whole area, making it almost as bright as day. The light was welcome, but the ungodly noise of the chopper drowned out everything else.

Clambering down over rocks and through skin-shredding clumps of bear grass, Joanna made for a spot directly between the two wrecked vehicles. The Hummer and the Blazer had come to rest less than twenty yards apart. There was no sign of movement in either vehicle. Almost sickened by the thought of it, Joanna wondered if Dick Voland was still alive. The unwelcome notion snaked into her head, but she didn't allow it to stay there.

Kneeling on the ground, she steadied her gun hand with the other one and strained to see and hear through the darkness. With the noisy chopper hovering above her, it was hard to tell for sure, but every once in a while, Joanna thought she heard the sound of voices or maybe just a single voice.

Rising to a crouch, she scrambled a few feet closer to the Hummer. "Come out," she ordered, counting on the clattering echo of the noisy helicopter engine to help disguise her exact position. "Give up and come out with your hands up."

This time she definitely did see movement in the Hummer. Slowly, a male figure materialized out of the shadowy wreckage. As the wandering searchlight once again flooded the area with artificial light, Dennis Hacker's bloodied face was thrown into stark relief. He took two or three tentative steps away from the Hummer and then sank to the ground, cradling his face in his hands.

Heedless of her own safety, Joanna hurried to his side. "Are you all right?" she shouted over the helicopter's roar.

Hacker nodded wordlessly. The man didn't seem badly hurt. He was dazed and confused, but the blood on his face seemed to be coming from what looked to be a superficial scalp wound.

"And the gunman? Where's he?"

The injured man pointed a shaky finger toward the Hummer. "He's in there," Hacker managed.

"One or two?" Joanna demanded.

"What?" Hacker returned uncomprehendingly.

Joanna shook her head. There wasn't time for explanations. "Stay low," she warned him, pushing Hacker down far enough that he was protected by an outcropping of rock. "Stay there until I give you the all-clear."

With that, she turned her attention back to the

Hummer. Suddenly the helicopter beat a retreat. In the silence left behind, Joanna heard a pitiful voice call to her from the darkness.

"Help," a man's voice begged. "Please help me. I'm trapped. My arm is stuck, and I can't get it out."

Realizing the very words themselves might be a trap, Joanna stayed where she was. "Throw out your weapons," she ordered.

"I don't have any weapons," the man whined. "Please. It's my arm. It's caught between the truck and the ground or something. You have to help me. Please."

Warily, Joanna crept forward. The driver's side of the Hummer had come to rest against the unmoving trunk of a sturdy scrub oak. She was squinting in the darkness, and it looked to her as though the man's left arm really was caught between the tree and the side of the truck.

"It hurts so bad." He moaned. "Please help me."

Joanna moved closer, but she stopped when a voice she recognized as Adam York's called to her from higher up the ridge. "Joanna! Where are you?" he called. "Are you okay?"

"Please," the man insisted again. "If you don't help me, I'll lose my arm."

Joanna Lathrop Brady had always regarded herself as the softhearted type—as the kind of person who was a sucker for a sob story, who unerringly fell for stray dogs and injured cats. In the past, she might have helped the injured man first and thought about it later. This time she realized she was dealing with someone who resembled an

injured rattlesnake rather than an injured dog.
And she knew that anyone foolish enough to go
to the aid of an injured rattler had a more than
even chance of being bitten herself.

"Be still," she said, keeping her distance. "Help's
on the way."

"It'll be too late. My arm. What's going to happen to it?"

"Hold on, Sheriff Brady," Ernie Carpenter called
from somewhere above them. "We hear you.
We'll be right there."

Beams of light danced around her as at least
two people, carrying flashlights, clambered down
the steep hillside. Then the helicopter resumed
its previous position, hovering directly over the
wrecked cars and bathing the whole area in a
wide halo of brilliant light.

Staying safely out of reach, Joanna circled
around to the front of the Hummer until she was
high enough that she could peer in the front
windshield. From that vantage point, she saw the
man's pale face. She would have recognized Alf
Hastings on sight, so this had to be the other
one—Aaron Meadows. Not only did she see his
face and the crushed arm, she saw something else
as well. In his other hand, almost invisible between his tightly clenched thighs, was the handle
of a knife.

Joanna felt a wave of momentary weakness. If
she had given in to her life-long need to help
others—if she hadn't stifled her natural inclination to step forward and administer first aid—he

would have had her. What was it that had held her back?

"Thank you, God," she whispered, aiming her heartfelt prayer at the sky far above her. Then she turned both her eyes and her Colt back on the man in the Hummer.

"All right, Meadows," she ordered. "Throw the knife out the rider's window. Do it now! I want to see your right hand behind your head."

"But my arm . . ."

"First the knife," she said. "We'll worry about your arm later."

After ten seconds or so, he finally gave in and threw the knife outside. Joanna, watching to see where it landed, caught sight of something that looked like a dollar bill fluttering on the ground between her feet and the fallen knife. She hurried over, reached down, and picked up a piece of currency. Expecting to see George Washington's portrait, Joanna was surprised to find herself staring at Ben Franklin's bloated picture. This was no dollar bill. It was a brand-new hundred-dollar bill.

Ernie Carpenter reached her right then. "Joanna," he panted. "Are you okay? Is anybody hurt?"

"He is," Joanna said, pointing at the Hummer. "I've got this guy covered, but I need you to go over to the Blazer and check on Dick Voland."

"He's okay. Maybe not completely okay. It looks to me like he's got a mild concussion, but I'm sure he'll be fine."

"How do you know that?"

"Because we found him up there on top of the ridge, running around like a chicken with his head cut off, looking for you and asking what the hell happened. By the way, what *did* happen?"

Joanna's knees really did go weak then—weak with relief rather than fear. Dick Voland was okay. So was Dennis Hacker.

And so, amazingly, was she.

TWENTY-SIX

ONCE ERNIE Carpenter had applied a tourniquet to Aaron Meadows's mangled left arm, they handcuffed his other wrist to Adam York's left one. While the DEA helicopter ferried the pair off to University Hospital in Tucson, Ernie used the still-working radio in the wrecked Blazer to summon assistance.

"Where's Hastings, then?" Ernie asked Joanna.

"Beats me. The bad guy I saw was Meadows, and I'm stumped as to motive for Brianna's death."

Fortunately, despite having suffered a multiple rollover, the sturdy Hummer still seemed to be drive-able. With a bloody bandage wrapped around his head, Dennis Hacker was busy changing the bullet-flattened tire when Ernie put almost the same question to him. "Where's the other guy?"

"What other guy? I only saw one."

Ernie shook his head. "I guess we'll find him eventually."

"Look at this," Hacker said, shoving the damaged tire in Ernie's direction before the detective walked away. "That blown sidewall is enough to make me a believer in exit wounds."

With the tire changed, Hacker climbed into the battered vehicle, started it up, and drove it right back up the bank, which probably was one of those commercially touted 60 percent grades. When the Hummer was back topside, Joanna loaded the walking wounded into it, ordering both Dennis Hacker and Dick Voland to belt themselves into the backseat. Assured of their grudging compliance, Joanna took it upon herself to drive them out of the war zone.

In the darkness, retracing the path they had followed earlier took longer than she expected. For one thing, because Joanna was taking casualties into consideration, she perhaps drove slower than necessary. She eased the Hummer over dips and bumps both vehicles had taken far too fast earlier when they had been racing in the opposite direction. Joanna found that driving the cavernous growl-and-go Hummer was different from driving either the low-slung Crown Victoria or her old Blazer. In fact, the experience made Joanna miss her Blazer that much more. Months earlier an insurance adjuster had declared it totaled. She wondered if there was any way to get it back.

Here and there along the way the sketchy road became virtually invisible in the dark. Joanna was relieved when the moldering ruins of the ranch house materialized in the wavering glow of her headlights. From then on, the dim path turned into a more well-defined road.

As they traveled, Dennis Hacker related his version of the events of the afternoon—telling how, while he had been on the telephone with Angie, a gun-and-knife-wielding, half-naked, and blood-spattered madman had burst into his camper. He told how they had struggled briefly before Hacker had knuckled under to Aaron's superior firepower. He told how, while being held at gunpoint, he had struggled to free a wrecked Suburban from the flood-swollen stream while on the bank his captor had fumed and raged. And he told how, once the Suburban was on dry land, he had been ordered to open up the secret storage compartments and to remove a hoard of hidden cash and documents.

"He kept telling me to hurry because somebody was after him."

Dick Voland, making notes despite the inconvenience of the bouncing truck, stopped writing then. "Did he give a name?"

"Marco," Hacker said. "I'm sure that's the name he mentioned, but I couldn't tell if that was a Christian name or a family name."

"Neither," said Joanna. "The man's name is Marcovich. Stephan Marcovich. He's an air-conditioning contractor up in Phoenix. Unless I'm sadly mistaken, he's also Adam York's big-fish Freon smuggler."

"That's all, then?" Voland asked Dennis Hacker.

"As far as I'm concerned."

Voland closed his notebook and flipped off the reading lamp. "All I can say is, you'd better thank your lucky stars for a young woman named Angie Kellogg. She's the one who came busting into Sheriff Brady's office yelling that something was up. If it hadn't been for her, there's no telling what would have happened."

Out of sight of both her passengers, Joanna smiled to herself. She found it amusing that her chief deputy had neglected to make any mention of his initial reluctance to believe Angie's story.

"I know what would have happened," Dennis Hacker said grimly. "As soon as that Meadows guy no longer needed me, I would have been history." He paused. "Where is she, by the way? Angie, I mean. Is she still in Bisbee? We should call and let her know I'm okay."

Guiltily, Joanna stole a look at her watch. Almost four hours had passed since she and Dick Voland had left Angie alone at the Cottonwood Creek Cemetery with orders to stay there, out of sight, and wait for them. At the time, the sun had still been shining. The idea of Angie's waiting all that time alone in a dark, deserted cemetery seemed like a cruel joke.

When they came into view of Dennis Hacker's lighted trailer, however, Joanna knew at once that whatever orders had been issued, the free-spirited Angie had disregarded them. As soon as the diesel-driven Hummer rumbled into hearing distance, the trailer's door flew open and Angie bounded outside.

Joanna was in the process of stopping the Hummer, but she hadn't quite finished braking when Dennis Hacker pushed open his door. He leaped out and hit the ground running. By the time Joanna had the vehicle stopped and the emergency brake located, Hacker had Angie wrapped in an all-enveloping bear hug. In order to give them a moment of privacy, Joanna waited a second or two before she climbed down.

"I was so worried," she heard Angie saying. "There was blood all over the place in there and broken glass and the telephone smashed to bits. I was scared to death you were hurt. And you are, too," she added breathlessly, catching sight of the bandage on Dennis Hacker's head.

"Don't worry," he told her. "It's nothing. If it hadn't been for you, I'd probably be dead by now. Right, Sheriff Brady?"

Angie, her face awash in tears, turned from Dennis to Joanna. "You saved him," she said. "Thank you."

"We were lucky," Joanna said. "But he's right. If we hadn't come right when we did, things might have been a whole lot different." She walked over to the trailer, intending to close the door. "Come on now," she added. "As soon as I put up some crime scene tape—"

Glancing in the door, she stopped cold. "What happened in here?" she demanded, turning back to Angie.

"The place was such a mess that I couldn't stand it," Angie said with a shrug. "I know Dennis likes to keep things neat. I didn't want him to come back and find it like that."

"But it was a crime scene, Angie," Joanna responded. "It should have been left exactly as it was. Cleaning it like that destroyed important evidence."

Angie was immediately contrite. "I'm sorry," she said tearfully. "I didn't mean to do anything wrong. I got scared, sitting in the cemetery all by myself. I kept hearing things. Finally, I decided to come here and wait inside. But the place was so dirty. I thought I'd be helping by cleaning it up. Besides, I couldn't stand just sitting here doing nothing."

Shaking her head in exasperation, Joanna looked around at the spick-and-span interior of the trailer. "Never mind," she said finally. "With or without the evidence from here, we should be able to nail Aaron Meadows on kidnapping charges. After all, Chief Deputy Voland and I both saw him in the act. Come on now. Let's get these guys into town to a doctor."

❦ **IT WAS** midnight by the time Joanna finally made it back home to the High Lonesome. Getting ready for bed, she stood in front of the full-length mirror and examined the tattered remains of her three-piece pantsuit. There was a jagged hole in one knee. Two buttons were missing— one from the front of the blouse and one from the sleeve of the blazer. Not only that, underneath it all, Joanna Brady was still braless.

Mother always told me I was terribly hard on clothes, she reminded her reflection with a wry grin. *Fortunately, I didn't have time to go shopping on Saturday. Otherwise, I'd have been out there crawling around in a brand-new outfit.*

Joanna fell into bed and was asleep almost before her head hit the pillow. At eight the next morning, she hitched a ride with a deputy out to the crime scene, where five other deputies were busy combing the rugged rock-strewn terrain, gathering up wads of wind-scattered hundred-dollar bills. Joanna arrived just in time to see Frank Montoya wave away the tow truck that had hauled the wrecked remains of Dick Voland's Blazer up the mountainside.

Looking at the smashed hulk, the chief deputy for administration shook his head. "I can already hear what the insurance guy is going to say," Frank grumbled mournfully as Joanna walked up beside him. "It isn't going to be pretty."

"No, I don't suppose it will be," she agreed. "Speaking about insurance. What's happening on my Blazer?"

"I already told you. It's totaled," Frank said. "Once we knew what it was going to cost to replace that damaged head liner and all the upholstery, he said it wasn't worth fixing. We're lucky we have all those Crown Victorias."

"I don't want a Crown Victoria," Joanna insisted. "I want my Blazer back. I need a vehicle that can get *over* running washes and doesn't have to be parked for twelve hours or so on the nearest bank."

"But we can't afford to fix—"

"Don't fix it then," Joanna said. "Take the head liner out and leave it out. All I want is a vehicle that runs. It doesn't have to be pretty." With that Joanna wandered over to see her lead homicide detective. "How are things going, Ernie?" she asked.

"Not so hot," he answered. "I sent Jaime Carbajal down to Montgomery Ranch to pick up the body."

"Body?" Joanna returned. "What body?"

"The one that washed up on the banks of Sycamore Creek overnight," Ernie answered. "Old man Montgomery himself came all the way up here to tell us about it. Found the guy in one of his cow pastures earlier this morning."

"Montgomery?" Joanna asked, trying to place the name.

Ernie nodded. "Marshall Montgomery from Montgomery Ranch, a few miles north and west of here. Jaime just now radioed me to say that ID on the body identifies the dead man as one Alf Hastings."

"Did he drown?" Joanna asked.

"Sure did," Ernie replied glumly. "But not before somebody poked him full of holes. Jaime says he's got at least half a dozen stab wounds to the heart and lower chest. I'll bet money that his blood will match up with the mess we found on the rider's seat of Meadows's Suburban."

"You think Aaron Meadows did it, then?" Joanna asked.

Ernie nodded. "Most likely," he said. Joanna started to walk away, but Ernie stopped her. "Hold on," he said. "I think I may have found something that belongs to you."

Reaching into the glove box of his van, he pulled out a glassine bag and handed it over to Joanna. Inside was her bra—or what was left of it anyway. The material of both cups had been shot full of holes by pellets from Aaron Meadows's final shotgun blast.

"It's a good thing you weren't wearing this at the time," Ernie said with a grin.

Joanna looked at the shredded remains of what had been one of her favorite bras. "Not much left of it, is there?" she said ruefully. "I filled this with rocks and threw it up in the air in an effort to decoy the guy away from Dick Voland."

"I'd say it worked like a charm," Ernie told her. "Maybe Dick will buy you a replacement."

The last thing Joanna Brady wanted from Chief Deputy Richard Voland was a new bra. "Please," she said, "don't even mention it. I was about to retire this one anyway." Then, in an attempt to change the subject, she motioned toward the deputies still combing the rocky hillside.

"How much money have they recovered so far?" she asked.

"Two hundred thou, give or take," Ernie answered.

"And where does somebody like Aaron Meadows—somebody with no job, no bank account, and no visible means of support—come up with that kind of cash?"

"Nothing legal," Ernie told her. "You can count on that. My best guess is that Meadows was opting out of the smuggling business and making a run for it. Whatever the case, I expect Adam York will get to the bottom of it. Have you heard from him, by the way?"

"From Adam?" Joanna nodded. "Just a message that said Meadows underwent surgery late last night to amputate his left arm. He's still under sedation, or at least he was earlier. He's also under a twenty-four-hour guard. In the meantime, the guys from the U.S. Customs Service have put Stephan Marcovich under arrest."

"Great," Ernie said. "It couldn't happen to a nicer guy."

Frank Montoya had joined them just in time to hear the last few exchanges. "If they're keeping Meadows under guard, I hope no one is expecting us to pay."

Joanna turned to her chief deputy for administration. "You know, Frank," she teased. "You used to be a lot more fun before you started worrying about the budget all the time."

He rubbed his balding head. "Somebody's got to do it, you know."

"Right," Joanna agreed. "Better you than me."

🌵 JOANNA STAYED at the crime scene only long enough to see how things were going, then she hitched a ride back to her Crown Victoria with Frank, who was on his way to give a press briefing. Other than a few traces of sand still left in the dip, there was no sign that the day before the wash had been a dangerous, raging flood.

Once in her car, Joanna drove herself back to Bisbee. It was early afternoon when she pulled into the justice complex and parked in her reserved parking spot just outside her office door.

Inside, she sat down at her desk, kicked off her shoes, and closed her eyes for a moment before punching the intercom button. "I'm here, Kristin," she said. "You might as well bring in today's mail."

When Kristin brought in the stack of mail, Joanna found that the topmost item was a homemade postcard with a Polaroid picture of Jenny glued to the front. Soaked to the skin and grinning from ear to ear, she stood in a downpour outside the door to an eight-person tent. The hand-painted sign over her head said, BADGER. The message on the other side of the card was cheery and brief:

Dear Mom,

It rained today, but we had fun anyway. Wish you were here. Hello to the G's.

Love,
Jenny

Joanna reread the note several times, struck by what it *didn't* say more than by what it did.

There was no remark to indicate that Jenny was lonely or homesick or that she missed her mother or the dogs. It also didn't say that Joanna should come right back up to Tucson to bring her daughter home. Joanna turned the card over and was still studying the picture when her private line rang. The caller turned out to be Eleanor Lathrop.

"Hello, Mother," Joanna said. "What's up?"

"I just had the strangest call from that little friend of yours. You know who I mean. That blonde girl—Angie Kellogg."

"What kind of call?"

"She wanted to know where in Bisbee she could buy Wedgwood. I told her I didn't know of anyplace at all anymore, but why did she want to know? She says her boyfriend broke a piece of his Kutani Crane china. The set was a gift from the young man's grandmother. Angie is trying to find a way to replace it. Do you believe that?"

"That Angie would want to replace something that's broken? That doesn't surprise me at all. She's a very kindhearted—"

"I know Angie's kindhearted," Eleanor Lathrop agreed irritably. "What I want to know is where in the world would she find somebody who has a set of Wedgwood china. Not only that, she says he uses it for everyday!"

"She found him up in the mountains," Joanna said. "She and Dennis Hacker went hummingbird-watching together."

"Wedgwood for everyday," Eleanor repeated morosely. "Now, why couldn't *you* find someone like that?"

Smiling, Joanna thought of the serviceable and often-chipped Fiesta Ware that was used on the Formica tables in Butch Dixon's Roundhouse Bar and Grill up in Peoria, Arizona. It was a long way from Wedgwood, but it suited the rough-hewn Butch.

"I guess," Joanna said, "Wedgwood users just aren't my type."

"I suppose some bald-headed, twice-divorced motorcycle rider is?"

Over the past several months, Frederick "Butch" Dixon had made several trips to Bisbee on his Goldwing. Each time, Eleanor had been quick to voice her disapproval, which, Joanna realized, probably only served to make the man that much more appealing.

"He isn't bald," she said now. "He shaves his head."

"If you ask me"—Eleanor sniffed—"it's the same thing."

Fortunately, the intercom buzzed again just then, saving the conversation from deteriorating any further. "Adam York is on line one," Kristin announced.

"Sorry, Mother," Joanna said. "There's another call. I've got to go." She picked up the other receiver. "Hello, Adam. What's up?"

"What kind of trading mood are you in?" he asked.

"Trading? What do you mean?"

"I just got off the phone with Arlee Jones . . ." Adam began.

"The Cochise County Attorney?" Joanna demanded. "What are you doing talking to him? You two didn't make some kind of deal on Aaron Meadows, did you?"

"Settle down, Joanna," Adam soothed. "Arlee told me I couldn't do any kind of horse trading unless you agreed up front."

"Are you talking plea bargain here? If you are—"

"All the man wants is a guarantee that Jones won't seek an aggravated first-degree murder conviction, that we most likely wouldn't be able to win anyway. If you'll agree to that, I'm pretty sure I can get Meadows to give us a signed confession. In addition, he'll turn state's evidence. From what he's said so far, I'm betting that, with his help, I'll be able to put Marco Marcovich away for a long time. We'll both come up winners, Joanna. Your two homicide cases will be cleared. So will my Freon problem."

Sitting there, staring out the window at the sunny parking lot, Joanna thought again about what she had said to Dick Voland the night before—about how, in the course of being sheriff, she had been forced to become a pragmatist. How she was in favor of whatever worked.

"That's the only thing we'll be conceding here—we won't ask for the death penalty?"

"The only thing."

"And what does Arlee Jones say?"

"That whatever you say goes."

"Get the confession," Joanna said, wearily. "Fax me a copy as soon as you have one. I'll need to go talk to the girl's parents and let them know what's happened."

TWENTY-SEVEN

ABOUT FOUR o'clock in the afternoon, still watching the clock and waiting for the fax to come in, Joanna finished her paperwork and made her way down the hall to the evidence room.

"I believe Ernie Carpenter or Jaime brought in another journal either last night or this morning," she told Buddy Richards. "It'll be one similar to the one I looked at yesterday. It's part of the Aaron Meadows investigation."

"What about it?" Buddy asked.

"I'd like to take a look at it."

Shaking his head in disapproval and mumbling objections under his breath, Buddy found the journal. He handed it over only after making doubly sure the paperwork was properly signed and documented.

Back in her office, Joanna opened the book to the last page:

*I'm sorry Nacio isn't here tonight with me, but
that's one of the things I love about him—he's
dependable. With his aunt in the hospital, his
family needs . . .*

The journal ended in mid-sentence, leaving
Joanna with the bittersweet knowledge that Brianna O'Brien had been interrupted then and had
died in the act of declaring once again her unre-
pentant love for the young man her family had
deemed entirely unsuitable.

Fighting back tears and swallowing the lump
in her throat, Joanna went on to read the entire
book, scanning from back to front. She expected
to stumble upon some reference to Brianna
O'Brien's discovery that her parents were involved in Marco Marcovich's smuggling game,
but she found nothing at all like that. What Joanna found instead was Brianna O'Brien's shock
and outrage that her father had slapped her
face—for wearing the forbidden earrings.

As she worked her way backward through the
journal, though, Joanna found more and more
references to something bad—something Bree
had discovered. Over and over she had wrestled
in her journal with whether or not she should tell
"Nacio what was really going on," but there was
hardly any information at all to say what that awful secret was. Finally, at the very beginning of
the book, Joanna found what she was looking
for. In an investigation that almost paralleled
Joanna's, Brianna O'Brien had come to the same
damning conclusion Joanna had—that Katherine

O'Brien had murdered Ricardo Montaño Diaz—the man responsible for the deaths of David O'Brien's family—his previous wife and his first-born children.

Closing the book, Joanna stared off into space. What was her responsibility here? Katherine and David O'Brien had already suffered an incredible loss. Of course, there was no statute of limitations on murder, but would justice be served by reopening that ancient wound?

By then the confession arrived. In it, Aaron Meadows admitted to not one but two separate murders. He claimed that Bree's death had been little more than an accident. The camping place she and Ignacio had frequented happened to be the same spot where Aaron was supposed to meet Luis, his mule, bringing Marco's next load of Freon north from Juarez. Afraid she would be able to identify him, he had simply run her to ground and killed her. End of story.

On the other hand, he claimed that Alf Hastings's murder had been self-defense. Afraid of being caught in connection with the girl's murder, he had given Marco his notice. What he didn't know was that one of the reasons Stephan Marcovich ran such a successful smuggling business was that he never left any loose ends. His runners weren't allowed to quit. One way or another, they disappeared. Aaron Meadows claimed it was only sheer luck that, in the process of fighting back, he had managed to kill his would-be dispatcher. Reading that, Joanna wondered how long Alf Hastings had been his cousin's Mr. Fixit

Man and how many times, before his attempted hit on Aaron Meadows, Alf had been only too happy to do Marco's dirty work. With no one around to tell the tale, they would probably never find out.

At nine o'clock on Tuesday night, burdened by all she had learned, Sheriff Joanna Brady once again headed for Green Brush Ranch. On the way to deliver the news that Brianna O'Brien's killer had signed a confession, Joanna had yet to reach a decision on that other case—on something that, for more than twenty years, had been officially labeled a wrongful death even though Joanna wondered now if it hadn't actually been a homicide. By the time she pulled up to the locked, electronically controlled gate, she was still uncertain about what to do.

The gate opened without her having to reach out and push the button. At the house, Olga Vorevkin, her eyes red with weeping, opened the door.

"I've come to see Mr. O'Brien," Joanna said. "I believe he's expecting me."

Nodding, Mrs. Vorevkin led Joanna as far as the entrance to the darkened living room. It surprised Joanna to see that there were no votive candles burning on the rosewood prie-dieu at the end of the passageway. The open Bible and the onyx rosary were also missing, as was the marble statue of the Madonna and Child from the artfully lit but empty alcove in the wall.

Turning from there to the darkened living room, Joanna's first impression was that the place was empty. "I'm over here, Sheriff Brady," David

O'Brien said from the far corner. "By the window. I hope you don't mind sitting in the dark. I was studying the stars. It's easier to see them when all the lights are off."

Joanna bumped into a single chair on her way across the room, but by the time she arrived in the far corner, her eyes were beginning to adjust to the dim light. She peered out the window, too. For a space of time, she didn't speak and neither did David O'Brien.

A match flared as he lit a cigarette. "That's one of the few good things I still remember from when I was a child here," he said at last, blowing a cloud of smoke. "The stars in Bisbee always seemed to burn with a peculiar intensity." He paused then and took another thoughtful drag before changing the subject. "I take it from your call that you have news?"

Joanna looked around and hesitated. "If you don't mind, Mr. O'Brien, I'd prefer to share this information with both you and your wife at the same time. . . ."

"Katherine's gone," David O'Brien said.

"You mean she's not here."

"No, I mean she's gone. Left me. She won't be back."

Joanna was stunned. "But where did she go?"

"Where she always goes," David O'Brien returned. "To a Benedictine convent outside Socorro, New Mexico. Only this time, it's for good. It's a sequestered order, you see. Once she takes her vows, she'll never return. It's what she's always wanted."

"A convent!" Joanna exclaimed. "Your wife is going to become a nun? How can she?"

"Because we're married, you mean? That won't be a problem. It'll take time and effort on her part, but I'm sure she'll be able to get an annulment."

"An annulment." It dismayed Joanna to hear her voice echoing back David O'Brien's words. She sounded stupid. "After this many years?" she asked.

"The number of years doesn't make any difference," he replied wearily. "Our daughter was a test-tube baby, Sheriff Brady. One of the early ones. If you'll pardon my being blunt, after the accident I was never able to perform in that department. Since Katherine's and my marriage was never officially consummated, then, it shouldn't be terribly difficult for her to obtain a church-sanctioned annulment. That way she'll be able to do what she's always wanted to do— what she's always done anyway. The only difference is, now she'll be able to do it openly and without any interference." He paused.

"And what would that be?" Joanna asked.

"Why, she'll be able to pray, of course," David O'Brien answered at last. "She'll pray without ceasing, for the sake of both of our immortal souls."

The room fell totally silent. "She did do it, then?" Joanna breathed at last.

"Do what?"

"She killed Mr. Diaz?"

David O'Brien sighed. "Oh," he said. "So you know about it, then. I should have realized. It was only a matter of time before someone here figured it out and brought it up again. I don't believe Katherine killed Mr. Diaz on purpose, Sheriff Brady," he added. "It was an accident. I believe the mixup with the medication really was a legitimate mistake on her part. She was devastated by the man's death. The problem was, the hospital administrator didn't approve of the fact that Katherine and I had become friends. The woman was a witch. She was out to get Katherine—to crucify her if need be. I simply couldn't let that happen. She was a nice young woman—a nurse who someday hoped to join a convent. I turned my attorney loose on the mess. He was able to handle it—well enough, at least, that she didn't go to prison."

"You're saying she was innocent, then?"

"I'm saying she may have been responsible, but that she wasn't guilty. There's a difference, you know. And after it was all over, we had grown close enough that I asked her if she'd be willing to help me try to start another family. She did. Not out of love, mind you. More out of misplaced gratitude. We were partners. We were together all this time, but it never quite worked. The family part. I see now that a lot of it was my fault. Bree and I were always at loggerheads—from the time she was tiny. She must have sensed my disappointment—must have known she could never be exactly what I wanted."

"But she was a smart, bright, pretty girl," Joanna found herself saying. "What more could you have wanted?"

"I wanted my son back," David O'Brien said sadly. "No matter how hard Bree tried, that was something she could never be. How stupid of me, Sheriff Brady. Why did my daughter have to die for me to figure it out?"

As the grieving father choked back a sob, Joanna closed her eyes. She remembered Katherine O'Brien's anguish the first time she had seen her; how anxious she had been that Joanna or Ernie would give away the secret that Brianna was taking birth control pills. Joanna had seen how tightly strung Katherine O'Brien had been and had attributed it to a possible case of domestic violence. And maybe that wasn't far from wrong. For almost twenty years, Katherine O'Brien had been the sole peacemaker, caught in the middle between her family's two forever-warring factions—an angry, controlling father and his lovely, head-strong daughter.

After a long moment of silence, David O'Brien spoke again. "If you're aware of the incident, you know that as a result of a negotiated deal, Katherine lost her license to practice nursing. I always thought of that as a victory, but now I tend to wonder if we wouldn't all have been better off if Katherine had gone to prison instead. If she had, maybe she would have felt as though she had finally atoned for her sin and been able to let go of it. As it is," he added sadly, "I doubt she ever will."

TWENTY-EIGHT

As usual, Marliss Shackleford couldn't keep from gushing. "It was such a beautiful wedding," she said to Joanna. "And it was so touching the way you and your brother both were part of it. What a wonderful gift for you to give the bride and groom. I can hardly wait to write it up for my column."

Joanna managed a tight smile. When she had offered High Lonesome Ranch as the site for Eleanor Lathrop's and George Winfield's second wedding ceremony and reception, she hadn't anticipated that she and her brother, Bob Brundage, would be cast in the supporting roles of best man and matron of honor. So, after spending the morning serving as grand marshal of—and riding Jenny's quarter horse, Kiddo, in—Bisbee's Fourth of July parade, Joanna had spent the afternoon doing her daughterly duty.

And it had been fine. With Marianne Maculyea in charge and with the guests assembled in the afternoon shade of Jim Bob Brady's hand-nurtured apple tree, it had been a nice ceremony. A meaningful ceremony. Reverend Maculyea had a knack for always taking familiar words and Scriptures and then somehow infusing and personalizing them in such a way and with such little extra fillips of sentiment that what might have been commonplace was transformed into something memorable and special.

Now, as dusk settled into evening, the party was winding down. The champagne toast had been drunk. Wedding cake had been cut and served. The bride and groom had gone home to what had once been Eleanor and D. H. Lathrop's cozy little house on Campbell Avenue. There was still plenty of Jim Bob's mouth-watering barbecue beef left despite the fact that everyone had eaten more than their fill. Some of the guests were in the process of taking their leave. They were driving back into town early in hopes of locating the perfect parking place from which to view the evening's coming fireworks.

Just as Joanna was wondering how she would ever manage to escape Marliss Shackleford's clutches, Jenny came to her rescue. "Can't we go now, Mom?" Jenny insisted. "It's almost dark. I don't want to miss the fireworks."

Joanna glanced at her watch and then back at Marliss. "Please excuse us," Joanna said. "I'm due at the ballpark in an hour. On a night like this, parking will be a mess."

"I'm sure that's true," Marliss said. "You go

ahead. I'll be right behind you, but I do want to say a few words to that charming brother of yours before I go."

Gratefully, Joanna reached down and took Jenny's hand. "Where's Butch?" she asked, as they started across the yard.

"He's out back," Jenny answered. "Throwing the Frisbee for Tigger."

Walking through the remaining guests took time. Joanna had to stop here and there long enough to chat and say hello.

"Mom," Jenny said, when they finally cut through the last of the crowd. "Did Marianne call Grandma an awful wife?"

"Awful," Joanna repeated, as if in a daze.

Suddenly she burst out laughing. "Oh, honey, that's not what Marianne said. She said lawful, not awful," she corrected a moment later, just as they came around the corner of the house.

Butch Dixon paused in the act of tossing the Frisbee. "All right, you two," he said. "I heard you laughing. What's so funny?"

"Jenny's way of hearing what's said isn't always on the money. She spent years of her life thinking the Lord's Prayer had something to do with leading a snot into temptation. Now she's worried that Mother is George's awful wedded wife."

Butch laughed, too. Jenny was offended. "You guys are making fun of me," she objected, sticking out her lower lip.

"No, we're not," Butch told her. "Not really. We're enjoying you. Now, what's up?"

Joanna checked her watch again. Surprisingly,

it was far later than she expected. "We're going to have to leave pretty soon," she said. "The fireworks are due to start at eight-thirty. I have to be on tap a little earlier than that. The dedication service is due to start about eight-fifteen."

To her surprise, Butch turned his attention away from her and back to the panting and one-track-minded Tigger, who was watching his hand with unwavering interest, waiting to see if the Frisbee would once again fly through the air. Butch wound up and gave the Frisbee an expert toss, sending it into a complicated spin. The throw came with an extra bounce that faked the dog out twice before he finally managed to catch it on the fly.

"Why don't you two go ahead," Butch said as Tigger came sprinting back for yet another throw. "I'll hang around here and help Jim Bob and Eva Lou clean up."

"You mean you don't want to see the fireworks?" Jenny demanded, her voice stiff with disbelief. "I thought everybody liked fireworks."

"I do like fireworks," Butch insisted. "It's just that someone ought to stay here to help."

Joanna turned to Jenny. "Go on into the house and get my purse and keys," she said. "I'll meet you at the car in a few minutes."

Jenny hurried away while Joanna looked back to Butch. "Is something the matter?" she asked. "Did my mother say something to hurt your feelings?"

"Your mother?" Butch asked. "Nothing of the sort. Eleanor is fine. I just want to stay here, that's all."

Joanna's own disappointment was clearly audible in her objection. "But I thought we'd go into town together," she said. After spending the whole day in what had seemed like a three-ring circus, she had looked forward to having some time alone with Butch—some quiet time for the two of them to talk and decompress—before taking him back uptown to his hotel.

"Jenny's been asked to spend the night with a girlfriend," she said. "After the fireworks, I thought maybe we'd hang out for a while, just you and me."

To Tigger's dismay, Butch dropped the Frisbee, letting it fall without bothering to throw it. "Are you sure?" he asked.

"Of course, I'm sure. Why wouldn't I be?"

Butch looked uneasy. "Didn't you tell me that this was your and Andy's first date years ago—Bisbee's Fourth of July fireworks? I thought you and Jenny would want to go by yourselves."

Inexplicably, Joanna's eyes filled with tears. Butch was right. Years before, the fireworks had been the occasion for her first date with Andrew Roy Brady, but in the busy rush of the day's events, she had forgotten all about it. It touched her deeply to realize that not only had Butch remembered, he had also made allowances.

"That's sweet of you," she said, smiling mistily up at him. "But it's not necessary. I really want you to go with me tonight. There are people in town I'd like to introduce you to. I want to show you off."

"In that case," Butch said with an affable grin, "your wish is my command."

As he followed her toward the car, she gave him a sidelong glance over one shoulder. "You know," she told him, "for a non-Wedgwood kind of guy, you're not bad."

"Non-Wedgwood?" he asked with a puzzled frown. "What's that supposed to mean?"

"Never mind," Joanna said. "It's an 'in' joke."

Minutes later the three of them headed into town in Joanna's Eagle. She had decided that if she and Butch were going out on the town later that evening, she didn't want to be seen driving around in a county-owned car. Besides, if an emergency did arise, Dispatch could always reach her through the brand-new cell phone safely stowed in her blazer pocket.

"Did you know Mom had to have the air-conditioning fixed before she could come get me at camp?" Jenny asked from the backseat.

"I know," Butch replied. "She told me all about it on the phone."

Jenny shook her head. "You guys must talk all the time."

"I guess we do," Joanna said.

At the ballpark, Jenny took charge of Butch and disappeared into the grandstand while Joanna was led to the flag-draped platform that had been erected in the middle of the baseball diamond. It was close enough to starting time that the platform was already crowded with VIPs. Agnes Pratt, Bisbee's mayor, might not have been sufficiently recovered from her appendectomy to ride a horse, but that didn't keep her away from the platform, where she stood chatting with several members of the city council.

On the far side of the platform, near the top of a ramp that had been built to accommodate a wheelchair, sat David O'Brien. He was involved in a conversation with Alvin Bernard, Bisbee's chief of police.

It was the first time Joanna had seen David O'Brien since Brianna's funeral, a week and a half earlier. During and after the service Joanna had heard a few mumbled questions concerning the surprising absence of Katherine O'Brien, who had chosen not to attend her own daughter's funeral. However, since David O'Brien had refused to give any explanation concerning his wife's whereabouts, neither had Joanna.

Two days after Brianna's funeral, Bisbee's Fourth of July celebration had been dealt an almost fatal blow when the fireworks budget had come up $10,000 short of the money necessary to release the fireworks package from the supplier. With the evening's celebration on the brink of cancellation, David O'Brien had stepped into the fray. Saying that his daughter had always loved fireworks, he had coughed up the missing financial shortfall. Not only that, he had agreed to provide a sizable ongoing endowment in Brianna O'Brien's name that would guarantee the continuation of Bisbee's fireworks display for many years into the future. This, then, would be the occasion of the First Annual Brianna O'Brien Memorial Fireworks Display.

Observing the man from the sidelines, Joanna could see that the strain of the last few weeks had aged him severely. He looked old and haggard and beaten. Still, she had to give him credit for being strong enough to show up at all. Joanna respected him for it. She knew what kind of effort it took to carry that off. She had done much the same thing herself.

The intervening days had brought some surprises in terms of the Aaron Meadows / Alf Hastings investigation. Meadows's plea-bargained confession was making life difficult for Marco Marcovich. In terms of bringing down a friend of the governor, Aaron's word alone might not have carried that much weight, but Maggie Hastings, threatened with coconspirator status, had also joined the plea-bargain parade. She had come forward and had named names of some of the other people Alf Hastings had dealt with in Marco's behalf. In addition, she had contributed one more important piece of the puzzle.

One of the reasons Marco had helped his cousin Alf get the job at Green Brush Ranch had been the expectation that eventually Aaron Meadows's smuggling route through the Peloncillos would end one way or the other. When that happened, Marco had expected Alf to have an alternate route already in place—one that would have continued to ferry Freon into the country from Mexico directly across David O'Brien's well-fortified property and without any member of the O'Brien family knowing a thing about it.

Poor guy, Joanna thought, still looking at David O'Brien. *No wonder he looks old. He's outlived his three children, all of whom died for no reason other than being in the wrong place at the wrong time. He's lost one wife to death and the other has abandoned him in favor of a convent. And one of his supposedly good friends has played him for a fool.*

Composing herself, Joanna walked up the ramp and went directly to where David O'Brien and Alvin Bernard were still visiting.

"Hello there," she said, shaking hands with them both. "From the looks of all the cars circling around in search of parking, it should be a great crowd."

"Chief," somebody called from across the platform. "Chief Bernard. Could I talk to you a minute?"

Alvin excused himself, leaving Joanna and David O'Brien on the platform together. "How soon do we start?" she asked.

"Five minutes." O'Brien answered without bothering to glance at his watch. "Although I don't suppose we need to worry about being late. The display won't get under way until I give the official signal to turn off the ballpark lights."

"I see," Joanna said.

It pleased her to hear a hint of the old imperiousness back in David O'Brien's voice, even though he no longer had Katherine to cater to his every whim. "If you'll excuse me, I guess I'll go find my chair," she added.

"No, wait," O'Brien said. "I'm glad the two of us have a moment to talk. I wanted to ask a favor of you."

"A favor? What kind?"

David O'Brien reached into his pocket and pulled out a small velvet-covered jewelry box. "Here," he said. "I found this box in Brianna's room. When the coroner's office returned Bree's personal effects to me, I realized where the box must have come from."

Popping the lid open, he held out the tiny black box, cradling it in the palm of his hand, offering it to Joanna. She looked down at the box. There, nestled in a velvet bed, sat two pearl earrings. One had been found on Brianna's body. The other had been located later outside the gate to Green Brush Ranch.

"I believe you know the young man who gave my daughter these, don't you?" David O'Brien asked.

Joanna nodded. "His name's Ignacio," she said. "Ignacio Ybarra."

"I've read Bree's journal," O'Brien continued huskily. "In it she usually referred to him as Nacio. I was wondering, would you mind seeing to it that these are returned to him? Now that I've had them repaired, I thought he'd probably like to have them back. I certainly have no use for them."

Carefully, Joanna took the tiny box from David O'Brien's hand, closed it, and then dropped it into her pocket. "I'll be glad to," she said.

"I understand this Nacio wants to be a doctor someday," O'Brien went on. "He expected to go to school on a football scholarship, but that's impossible now. The opportunity evaporated when he was injured in that football game last November."

"Yes," Joanna said. She knew all about that, too. She had learned it the same way David O'Brien had—from reading Brianna's journal.

"Would you mind giving him a message from me?" David asked.

Joanna nodded. "Certainly," she replied. "What kind of message?"

"Tell him I have some college monies set aside that I don't want to see go to waste. Tell him my banker, Sandra Henning, will call him next week to set up an appointment. It's a scholarship now," O'Brien added. "Not a loan. And it's not really from me, it's from . . ." Choked with emotion he broke off without finishing.

Looking at the man's ravaged face, it was easy for Joanna to see what was going on. Faced with his own culpability, David O'Brien was trying to make amends—to Bree and to Nacio both.

"It's from Bree," Joanna finished for him. "A scholarship from Bree."

"Come on," Agnes Pratt interrupted, tapping Joanna on the shoulder. "It's time to take our seats."

As soon as Joanna sat down, she was able to see Jenny and Butch sitting in the front row of the grandstand. They weren't difficult to pick out since Jenny was standing on her feet, waving frantically. Joanna waved back at them—a tiny, discreet wave—letting them know she had seen them, too.

A few minutes later, the crowd was asked to stand for the playing of "The Star-Spangled Banner." As the organist from Bible Baptist Church struck up the first notes of the national anthem, Joanna glanced at David O'Brien's face. He was sitting at attention with tears glistening on both haggard cheeks while his lips mouthed the familiar words:

"Oh, say can you see, by the dawn's early light . . ."

As the music swelled and washed over the crowd, Joanna felt tears in her own eyes as well—tears in her eyes and gooseflesh on her arms and legs. That always happened to her when she heard those wonderfully stirring notes of music. On this occasion, though, it was different somehow. It was more than just the music. It was David O'Brien, too.

Here was a man who had lost everything that mattered to him—lost it not once, but twice. And yet he had somehow found the courage to go on. He had figured out a way to turn his personal tragedy and culpability into something else—into something good for other people, for a townful of children who otherwise would have been disappointed by missing the magic of a Fourth of July fireworks celebration. Not only that, David O'Brien was also finding a way to break free of a lifelong history of prejudice in order to reach out to someone else.

Watching him sing, Joanna had no doubt that David O'Brien's unexpected generosity in the face of his own loss would help a brokenhearted boy from Douglas fulfill his dream of becoming a doctor.

Halfway through the song, Joanna reached into her pocket and let her fingers close tightly around the sturdy little velvet-covered box. Somehow, holding on to it helped her hold her own tears in check. For a while anyway. But by the time they reached "land of the free and the home of the brave" Joanna Brady just gave up and let herself cry.

Because she needed to. And because, for a change, crying felt good.

Here's a sneak preview of
J. A. Jance's next novel

BETRAYAL OF TRUST

Available now
wherever books are sold

I WAS sitting on the window seat of our penthouse unit in Belltown Terrace when Mel came back from her run. Dripping with sweat, she nodded briefly on her way to the shower and left me in peace with my coffee cup and the on-line version of the *NYTimes* Crossword. Since it was Monday, I finished it within minutes and turned my attention to the spectacular Olympic Mountains view to the west.

It was June. After months of mostly gray days, summer had come early to Western Washington. Often the hot weather holds off until after drowning out the Fourth of July fireworks. Not this year. It was only mid-June, and the on-line weather report said it might get all the way to the mid-eighties by late afternoon.

People in other parts of the country might laugh at the idea of mid-eighties temperatures clocking in as a heat wave, but in Seattle where the humidity is high and AC units are few, a long June afternoon of sun can be sweltering, especially since the sun doesn't disappear from the sky until close to ten PM.

I remember those long miserable hot summer nights when I was a kid, when my mother—a single mother—and I lived in a second story, one bedroom apartment in a blue-collar Seattle neighborhood called Ballard. We didn't have AC and there was a bakery on the floor below us. Having a bakery and all those ovens running was great in the winter, but in the summer not so much. I would lie there on the couch in the living room, sleepless and miserable, hoping for a tiny breath of breeze to waft in through our lace curtains. It wasn't until I was in high school and earning my own money by working as an usher in a local theater that I managed to give my mom a pair of fans for Mother's Day—one for her and one for me. (At least I didn't give her a baseball glove.)

I refilled my coffee cup and poured one for Mel. She grew up as an army brat. Evidently the base housing hot water heaters were often less than optimal. As a result she takes some of the fastest showers known to man. She collected her coffee from the kitchen and was back in the living room before the coffee came close to reaching drinking temperature. Wearing a silky robe that left nothing to the imagination and with a towel wrapped around her wet hair, she curled up at the opposite end of the window seat and joined me in examining the busy shipping traffic criss-crossing Elliott Bay.

A grain ship was slowly pulling away from the massive terminal at the bottom of Queen Anne Hill. Two ferries, one going and one coming, made their lumbering way to and from Bremerton or Bainbridge Island. They were large ships, but from our perch twenty-two stories up, they seemed like tiny toy boats. Over near West Seattle a collection of barges was being assembled in advance of heading off to Alaska. Nearer at hand, a many-decked cruise ship had docked overnight spilling a myriad of shopping intent cruise enthusiasts into our Denny Regrade neighborhood.

"How was your run?" I asked.

"Hot and crowded," Mel said. "Myrtle Edwards Park was teeming with runners off the cruise ships. I don't like running in crowds. That's why I don't do marathons."

I had another reason for not doing marathons—two of them, actually—my knees. Mel runs. I walk or, as she says, I "saunter." Really, it's more limping than anything else. I finally broke down and had surgery to remove my heel spurs, but then my knees went south. It's hell getting old. I talked to Doctor Bliss, my GP, about the situation with my knees.

"Yes," he said, "you'll need knee replacement surgery eventually, but we're not there yet."

Obviously he was using the royal "we," because if it was his knee situation instead of mine, I'm sure "we'd" have had it done by now.

I glanced at my watch. "We need to leave in about twenty, if we're going to make it across the water before traffic stops up."

Since we were sitting looking out at an expanse of water, it would be easy to think that's "the water" I meant when I spoke to Mel, but it wasn't. In Seattle, however, that refers to several different bodies of water, depending on where you are and where you're going. In this case we were looking at Elliott Bay, which happens to be our "water view," but we worked on the other side of Lake Washington, in this instance, the "traffic" water in question. People who live on Lake Washington or on Lake Sammamish would have an entirely different take on the matter when they used the same two words. Context is everything.

"Okie dokie," Mel said, hopping off the window seat. "Another refill?" she asked.

I gave her my coffee mug. She took it, went to the kitchen, filled it, and came back. She handed me the cup and gave me a quick kiss in the process. "I started a new pot for our travelers," she said then added, "Back in flash."

I had showered and dressed while she was out, not that I needed to. There are two full baths as well as a powder room in our unit. When I married Mel, rather than share mine, she took over the guest bath and made it her own, complete with all the mysterious vials of makeup and moisturizers she deems necessary to keep herself presentable. I happen to think Mel is more than presentable without any of that stuff, but I've gathered enough wisdom over the years to realize that my opinion on some subjects is neither requested nor appreciated.

So we split the bathrooms. As long as we share the bed in my room, I don't have a problem with that. Occasionally I find myself wondering about my first marriage to Karen who is now deceased. Most of the time we were married, we had two bathrooms—one for us and one for the kids. Would our lives have been smoother if Karen and I had been able to have separate bathrooms as well?

No, wait. Denial is a wonderful thing, and I'm going to call myself on it. Despite my pretense to the contrary, the warfare that occurred in Karen's and my bathroom usually had nothing to do with the bathroom. Karen was a drama queen and I was a jerk, for starters. Yes, we did battle over changing the toilet paper rolls and leaving the toilet seat up and hanging panty hose on the shower curtain rod and leaving clots of toothpaste in the single sink, but those were merely symptoms of what was really wrong with our marriage—namely my drinking and my working too much. All the squabbling in our bathroom—the only real private place in the house—was generally about those underlying issues rather than the ones we claimed we were fighting about.

For years, Karen and I never showed up at the kitchen table for breakfast without have spent the better part of an hour railing at one another first. I'm sure those constant verbal battles were very hard on our kids, and I regret them to this day. But I have to tell you that the pleasant calmness that prevails in my life with Mel Soames is nothing short of a dream come true.

And we are married, by the way. Mel is my third wife. She didn't take my name, and I didn't take hers. As for the single day Anne Corley's and my marriage lasted? She didn't take my name, either, so I'm two for one in the wives-keeping-their-own-names department. Karen evidently didn't mind changing names at all—she took mine, and later, when she married Dave Livingston, her second husband, she took his name as well. So much for the high and low points of J. P. Beaumont's checkered romantic past.

When the coffee pot—an engineering marvel straight out of Starbucks—beeped quietly to let me know it was done, I went out to the kitchen and poured most of the pot into our two hefty stainless traveling mugs. This is Seattle. We don't go anywhere or do anything without sufficient amounts of coffee plugged into the system.

I was just tightening the lid on the second one, when Mel appeared in the doorway looking blonde and wonderful. Maybe the makeup did make a tiny bit of difference, but I can tell you she's a whole lot better looking than any other homicide cop I ever met.

On our commute, she drives. Fast. It's best for all concerned if I settle back in the passenger seat of my Mercedes S-550, drink my coffee, and do my best to refrain from back seat driving. One of these days Mel is going to get a hefty speeding ticket that she won't be able to talk her way out of. When that happens, I expect it will finally slow her down. Until that time, however, I'm staying out of it.

And don't let all this talk about making coffee fool you. Mel is no wizard in the kitchen, and neither am I. We mostly survive on take-out or by going out to eat. We have several preferred restaurants on our list of morning dining establishments once we get through the potential bottleneck that is the I-90 Bridge.

The people who planned the bridges in Seattle—both the 520 and the I-90—were betting that the traffic patterns of the fifties and sixties would prevail—that people would drive into the city from the suburbs in the mornings and back home at night. So the lanes that were built into the I-90 bridges, have express lanes that are westbound in the morning and eastbound in the afternoon. Except there are almost as many people working in the 'burbs now as there are in the city, and "wrong-way" commuters like Mel and me, on our way to the east side of Lake Washington to the offices of the Attorney General's Special Homicide Investigation Team, pay the commuting price for those decisions every day.

If we make it through in good order, we can go to the Pancake Corral in Bellevue or to Li'l Jon's in Eastgate for a decent sit down breakfast. Otherwise we're stuck with Egg McMuffins at our desks. You don't have to guess which of those options I prefer. So we head out a good hour and fifteen minutes earlier than we would need to without stopping for breakfast. Getting across the lake early usually makes for lighter traffic—unless there's an accident. Then all bets are off. A successful outcome is also impacted by weather—too much rain or wind or even too much sun—can all prove hazardous to the morning commute.

That Monday morning we were golden—no accidents; no stop and go traffic. By the time the sun came peeking up over the Cascades in the distance, we were tucked into a cozy booth in Li'l Jon's ordering breakfast. And more coffee. Because our office is across the freeway and only about six blocks away from the restaurant, we were able to take our time. Mel had pancakes. She's a runner. She can afford the carbs. I had a single egg over easy with one slice of whole-wheat toast.

We arrived at the Special Homicide Investigation Team's east side office at five minutes to nine. We don't have to punch a time clock. When we're on a case, we sometimes work extraordinarily long hours. When we're not on a case, we work on the honor system.

For the record, I do know that the unfortunate acronym for Special Homicide Investigation Team is S.H.I.T., an oversight some bumbling bureaucrat didn't understand until it was too late to do anything about it. In the world of state government—and probably in the federal government as well—once the stationery is printed, no departmental name is going to get changed because the resulting acronym turns out to be bad news. S.L.U.T. (the South Lake Union Transit) is another local case in point.

But for all of us who actually work for Special Homicide, the jokes about S.H.I.T. are almost as tired as any little kid knock-knock joke that comes to mind, and they're equally unwelcome. Yes, we laugh courteously when people think they're really clever by mentioning that we "work for S.H.I.T.," but I can assure you, what we do here at Special Homicide is not a joke. And neither is our boss, Harry Ignatius Ball—Harry I. Ball as those of us who know and love him like to call him.

Special Homicide is actually divided into three units. Squad A works out of the state capitol down in Olympia. They handle everything from Olympia south to the Oregon border. Squad B, our unit, is in Bellevue, but we work everything from Tacoma north to the Canadian border while Squad C, based in Spokane, covers most things on the far side of the mountains. These divisions aren't chiseled in granite. We work for Ross Connors. As the Washington State Attorney General, he is the state's chief law enforcement officer. We work at his pleasure and direction. We work where Ross Connors says and when Ross Connors says. He's a tough boss but a good one. When things go haywire as they sometimes do, he isn't the kind of guy who leaves his people blowing in the wind. That sort of loyalty inspires loyalty, and Ross gives as good as he gets.

That morning Mel and I both managed to survive the terminal boredom of the weekly staff meeting ritual. After that, we returned to our separate cubicle-sized offices where we were continuing work on cross referencing the state's many missing persons reports with unidentified homicides in all other jurisdictions. It was cold case work, long on frustration, short on triumphs and even more boring most of the time than the staff meetings.

When Squad B's secretary/office manager, Barbara Galvin, poked her head into our tiny offices and announced that Mel and I had been summoned to Harry's office, it was a real footrace to see who got there first.

Harry is a Luddite. He has a computer on his desk. He does not use it. Ross Connors has made sure that all his people have the latest and greatest in electronic communications gear, but he doesn't use that, either. It's only in the last few months that he's finally accepted the necessity of carrying a cell phone and actually turning it on. He and Ross Connors are really birds of a feather in that regard—they're both anti-geeks at heart. Occasionally we'll receive e-mail with Harry's name on it, but that's because he has dictated his message to Barbara who dutifully types it at the approximate speed of sound and then presses the send button. The same goes for electronic messages that come our way from Ross Connor's e-mail account. His secretary, Katie Dunn, sends out those missives.

In our unit, Barbara Galvin and Harry I. Ball are the ultimate odd couple in terms of working together. Harry is now, and always has been, an exceptional cop who was kicked out of the Bellingham police department due to a terminal lack of political correctness that survived several employer-mandated courses in sensitivity training. He would have been stranded without a job if Ross Connors, no P.C. guy himself, hadn't taken pity on him and hired him as Squad B's supervisor.

Barbara Galvin is easily young enough to be Harry's daughter. Her body shows evidence of plenty of piercings, but she comes to work with a single diamond stud in her left nostril. I suspect that her clothing conceals any number of tattoos, but none of those show at work. She's a blazingly fast typist who keeps only a single photo of her now ten-year-old son on an otherwise fastidiously clean desk. She manages the office with a cheerful efficiency that is nothing short of astonishing. She prods at Harry when he needs prodding and laughs both with him and at him. When I've had occasion to visit other S.H.I.T. offices, I've also seen how Squads A and C live. With Harry and Barbara in charge, those of us in Squad B have a way better deal.

When Mel and I walked into Harry's office he was studying an e-mail that Barbara had no doubt retrieved from his account, printed, and brought to him.

"Have a chair," he said, stripping off a pair of drugstore reading glasses.

Since there was only one visitor's chair in the room, I let Mel have that one. When Harry looked up and saw I was still standing, he bellowed, "Hey, Barbara. Can you round up another chair? Who the hell keeps stealing mine?"

Without a word, Barbara brought another office chair to the doorway and then rolled it expertly across the room so it came to a stop directly in front of me.

"Sit," Harry ordered, glaring at me.

I sat.

Harry picked up the piece of paper again and returned the reading glasses to the bridge of his nose.

"I don't like this much, you know," he said.

Mel and I exchanged looks. Her single raised eyebrow spoke volumes, as in "What's he talking about?"

"I'm not sure why it is that you're always Ross's go-to-guy, but you are," Harry grumbled, sending another glower in my direction. "This time the Attorney General wants both of you in Olympia for the next while. It's all very hush-hush. He didn't say what he wants you to do while you're there, or how long he wants you to stay. He says you should 'pack to stay for several days,' and you should 'each bring a vehicle' which leads me to believe that you won't necessarily be working together. You're booked into the Red Lion there in Olympia."

"I'm assuming from that we probably won't be staying in the honeymoon suite?" I asked.

"I would assume not," Harry agreed glumly. "Now get the hell out of here. Time's a wastin'."